Tiger Hills

Tiger Hills

SARITA MANDANNA

Weidenfeld & Nicolson

· LONDON

First published in Great Britain in 2010 by Weidenfeld & Nicolson
An imprint of the Orion Publishing Group Ltd
Orion House, 5 Upper St Martin's Lane
London WC2H 9EA

An Hachette UK Company

© Sarita Mandanna 2010

1 3 5 7 9 8 6 4 2

A CIP catalogue record of this book is available from the British Library

ISBN 978 0 297 85981 9 (cased)
ISBN 978 0 297 85983 3 (trade paperback)

Typeset by Input Data Services Ltd, Bridgwater, Somerset

Printed in Great Britain by Clays Ltd, St Ives plc

The Orion Publishing Group's policy is to use papers that are natural,
renewable and recyclable products and made from wood grown in sustainable forests.
The logging and manufacturing processes are expected to conform to the
environmental regulations of the country of origin.

www.orionbooks.co.uk

For my grandparents

Kambeyanda Dechi & Muddayya and Charimanda Seetha & Biddappa

Through all of time, it's rise and it's fall;
the heart stays blind, yet sees truest of all

COORG PROVERB

Devanna

Chapter 1

≫ 1878 ≪

Muthavva knew her seventh child was special, had known from the very day of her birth, the day of the herons. It was a clear day in July. With almost two months to go before the baby was due, and the sowing season upon them, Muthavva had put off leaving for her mother's home. She made her laborious way to the fields instead, and was standing ankle deep in the flooded flats when she heard a rustling. She looked up, shading her eyes against the sun and rubbing the small of her back. A flock of herons wheeled overhead. In itself, this was not unusual. There were herons to be seen in every field in Coorg, the flash of their wings startling against bright green paddy. But in all her years, Muthavva had never seen as many as were now slowly descending upon the flats. A hundred birds, maybe more, flying wingtip to wingtip, casting the sun-drenched fields into shadow. The fluttering of their feathers drowned out the croaking of frogs, the cawing of crows, even the incessant racket of crickets.

Muthavva could no longer hear her brother-in-law's voice carried on the wind as he called out instructions to the labourers hired to help with the sowing, his words muffled by the steady beat of wings. The birds circled slowly, lower and lower, executing a final sharp turn to land by her feet. Muthavva stood surrounded, still absently massaging her back amongst a sea of silent white. And then, without warning, the herons took wing again. Up they soared on some secret cue, all around her,

3

showering her with the glittering droplets of water that rolled off their wings and the tips of their feet. At that instant, not one moment sooner or later, Muthavva felt a gush of warm liquid on her thighs. Her daughter was here.

The mountains. That is what the dead must notice first, Muthavva had always believed. That very first time, when they rose from the funeral pyres, slipping through ash, borne by the wind high into the clouds. And from there, that first, dizzying, glorious sight of Coorg.

It was a tiny principality, shaped not unlike the knitted bootie of an infant, and tucked into the highest reaches of the Sahaydri mountains that girded the country's coastline to the South. The far side of the mountains was bounded by the ocean, dropping abruptly into the glittering blue of the Arabian Sea. The way down the cliffs was so slippery, so fraught with loose rocks and sharp-edged shingle, that only the most money-hungry traders were foolhardy enough to attempt it. They assembled twice a year at the edge of the bluffs, in time to meet the Arabian ships docked below, with baskets of captured monkeys whose feet they had painted red with betel juice and lime. They would release the monkeys over the cliffs, driving them down towards the sea with a great banging and bashing of drums; as the monkeys jumped terrified from rock to rock, they left behind a map of tiny red footprints for the traders to follow. Even so, each year there were those who fell, men screaming as they spun through the air, finally smashing onto the rocks far below.

Turning inland, the silver flash of the Kaveri river, ribboning the olivine mountains and parcelling Coorg neatly in two like the halves of a coconut. To the North, the undulating hills of bamboo country, softly rounded, dotted with towering arches of bamboo and slender knots of trees. Blackwood and ironwood, dindul and sandalwood, eucalyptus, benteak and rosewood, interspersed with breezy glades where grasses shimmered in the sun. The Scotland of India. That is what the many white folk in Coorg called it, this part of the land that reminded them so much of Europe. They had set about civilising the central town of Mercara, re-christening its streets Tenth Mile, Queens Way and Mincing Lane. They clustered their estates about the town – coffee plantations sprung from Ceylonese beans that had rapidly taken root in this virgin soil. Their planter bungalows lay in a series of rough circles around the town. Low slung, red roofed and diamond paned, replete with verandahs, croquet lawns and racquet courts.

In stark contrast, the Shola forests of the South. Wild, untrammelled tracts of pipal, cinchona, ebony, toon and poon, crowding in on themselves, adorned with club moss and lush, unscented orchids. Tangles of thorned underbrush erupted between their trunks, vast, laboriously spun cobwebs bridging the exposed corrugation of their roots.

Here and there, scattered almost evenly between the North and the South, the local villages. A velvet patchwork of jungle soil, moist, fertile and dark as the night sky where the forest had been hacked away. Peridot swathes of paddy flats lining the wetlands by the streams. The sprawling, golden-thatched homes of the Coorgs, each with its designated wetlands and grazing pastures and the telltale wisps of smoke that rose from their hearths into the trees.

Finally the forest, at the base of the mountains. The thickly knitted toe of the bootie, forming a protective cover over the tip of Coorg that jutted out towards Mysore. This was dense jungle, simmering with a dangerous, compelling beauty, marked only by the faintest of trails. Only the Coorgs knew the jungle trails well, them and the charcoal skinned Poleya tribals who served them.

The trails had always been jealously guarded, especially in the old days when Coorg lay under siege. The sultans of Mysore had tried for generations to bring this stubbornly independent principality under their dominion. The internecine warfare, the abductions, the forced circumcisions and mass executions had only served to unite the Nayaks, patriarchs of the eight most prominent families in Coorg. They had banded together, bidding the clans under their jurisdiction to stand shoulder to shoulder against Mysore. The Coorgs resisted the sultans, digging in their heels and clinging to their land like the copper-coloured crabs that burrowed in their fields.

When the British and their John Company had finally overthrown Mysore, the Coorgs had rejoiced as one. In the peace treaty that followed, Coorg was ceded to the British. They had taken the measure of this little province, looked appraisingly at its mist-laden hills and salubrious climes so well suited to the planting of coffee. They took note of the Coorgs; tall, fierce hotheads who thought nothing of looking them in the eye and speaking as one man to another. Wisely they had been patient, pushing their agenda with polite, manicured resolve. Eventually, fifty years after they had taken Mysore, the British were formally welcomed into Coorg.

Still, despite these days of peace and the syenite roads that the British had carved, skirting the edges of the forest to connect Coorg with the neighbouring provinces, collective memory ran deep. There was a band of armed and able-bodied Coorgs always stationed at the bend over-looking the entrance to the forest where the road from Mysore met the mouth of the trail. The Nayaks shared responsibility for manning this post, each staffing it with men from the clans under his dominion for five weeks at a stretch except for the three months of the monsoons when the trails were rendered impassable by mudslides and trees felled by lightning.

Today, the lookout post was quiet. Men lay snoring in the rough bamboo and burlap machan while Nachimanda Thimmaya kept watch. The afternoon wind picked up, gusting through the branches overhead and scattering dried leaves through the machan. Thimmaya shivered, drawing his tunic closer about him. If only he had picked the white cowrie shell this year, curse his luck. When Pallada Nayak, the village headman, had announced the date of the cowrie picking, Thimmaya had gone especially to the Iguthappa temple, offering its all powerful deity, Iguthappa Swami, a whole two rupees, money he could scarcely afford. He had sacrificed a fowl to the ancestors and yet another to the veera, the ghosts of the valiant. Leaving nothing to chance, Thimmaya had even propitiated the wood spirits with a hefty bundle of pork and rice left in the forest. The day of the picking, when the priest had extended his closed fists towards him, Thimmaya had sent up yet another fervent prayer to Iguthappa Swami. But no, he had pointed at a fist and the priest had opened his palm only to reveal a black cowrie; Thimmaya had been selected once more, three years running, to man the post.

This year was especially hard. It was sowing season and every avail-able pair of hands would be needed in the fields. Muthavva should be in

6

her mother's home, not bending over the paddy, not when her belly swelled round and full with another child. It had been a difficult pregnancy, the dribbles of blood in the early weeks, the pain in her back as her stomach grew. His brother Bopu had offered to take his place at the lookout post, but Thimmaya had refused. Bopu had his own family to feed, and besides Pallada Nayak would not have approved. He sighed. If the price for cardamom fell again this year in Malabar, the family would have to tighten their belts.

He was sitting there, lost in his thoughts, when he started. Someone was running through the jungle calling for him. 'Ayy. Who is it?' he shouted, grabbing his matchlock and peering through the branches.

The runner came into view and Thimmaya recognised him with a pang of alarm. It was one of Pallada Nayak's cattle hands. 'What happened?' he asked tersely, jumping down from the machan.

'The child . . .' gasped the Poleya, wiping the sweat from his face. 'The child is coming.'

Thimmaya's face tightened. The baby was not due for many weeks, wasn't that what Muthavva had said? Why had the pains started so early?

The men crowded round him as he laced his sandals and tucked his dagger into his cummerbund, slapping his shoulder and telling him not to worry. He barely heard them, all his energy focused on reaching his wife as soon as he could. He loped off along the trail towards the Pallada village, the Poleya struggling to match his pace. 'Please Iguthappa Swami,' he prayed, over and over. 'Please.'

He reached the village just before nightfall, and went first to the Pallada house to pay his respects. The evening lanterns were being lit, casting the Nayak in silhouette as he strode up and down the verandah. 'Ah, Thimmaya, have you come?' he said, pleased, as Thimmaya bent to touch his feet. 'It is good, it is good,' he said, 'now go to your wife.' Thimmaya nodded, unable to speak. 'There is no cause for worry,' the Nayak reassured him. 'All is well.'

Thimmaya nodded again, his chest still tight with foreboding. He touched the Nayak's feet, then hurried towards his own home, yet a good six furlongs away. It was dark by the time he got there, the lamps had been lit, the dogs fed and let loose for the night. They rushed barking towards him as he stopped at the aimada, the ancestor temple in the courtyard. 'Ancestors of the Nachimanda clan,' he prayed, passing his palms back and forth over the flickering lamps. 'I will sacrifice a fowl to you, please let my woman be well.'

And then his nephews and his son were running out to meet him, and his mother, laughing, her arms extended. 'Uyyi! You have come monae.'

'Muthavva?'

'She is fine, they are both fine monae. Come in and see your pearl of a daughter.'

They brought hot water from the fireplace for him to wash his hands and feet and then he headed for the bedroom where Muthavva lay flushed and spent upon their cot. His mother put the baby in his arms. He gazed down at his wriggling daughter and the knot in his chest came finally undone, dissolving into an emotion so strong he had to blink to stop the tears.

Muthavva never told him about the herons that had heralded the baby's birth. The labour had started so quickly, the pains had been so insistent that her brother-in-law had hoisted her onto his back and run all the way home from the fields. The baby in such a hurry to be born that the midwife had barely been summoned before she thrust her way into the world. As the women bustled about, looking for the brass gong to announce the birth of a girl child, and the servants were sent to distribute puffed rice and bananas in the village, Muthavva made up her mind. She had birthed six babies before this child. Six healthy, squalling boys, of which only the oldest, Chengappa, had survived infancy. She touched her finger to the tip of the baby's pert, perfectly formed nose. This daughter, she knew in her heart, was special. Why cloud her birth with talk of omens or portents? No, she decided, she would tell nobody about the birds.

She did, however, once. After the ritual forty days of cleansing were over, when Muthavva untied the cloths bound tight about her abdomen, arose from the birthing bed, and was deemed able to perform her household duties once more, the family took the baby to the village temple to have her horoscope drawn. The old priest reached for his manuscript of tattered pipal leaves, wrapped in orange silk and passed down through generations from father to son. The child would have marriage, he predicted, and progeny. Money was in her fate too. But . . . and here he fell silent. Muthavva and Thimmaya looked anxiously at one another. 'What is it, ayya? What do you see?' Thimmaya's mother asked, anxiously clutching the baby closer until she squirmed in protest.

'Nothing . . . it is nothing . . . and yet . . .' The priest fell silent once again and consulted his leaves. He looked up at the worried faces around him, as if debating what to say. 'It is nothing,' he said finally, even as he fished about in a dilapidated wooden box. 'Here.' He pulled out an amulet. 'This will protect her.' The amulet had a powerful mantra inscribed upon it, he advised, it would protect her from the evil eye. Best she wear it at all times. Shushing their concerns, he smeared vermilion on their foreheads and tied the amulet around the baby's arm with black thread.

They touched the feet of the priest and prostrated in front of the idol. They had made their way outside, blinking in the sudden sunlight when, exclaiming that her earring was missing and that it must have fallen off during the reading, Muthavva hurried back inside.

'Ayya?' she called softly, her eyes taking a minute to adjust to the cool darkness of the sanctum sanctorum. The priest was clearing away the debris from their pooja, and he looked up, mildly irritated.

'Yes child, what is it now?'

She told him about the birds she had seen that day, the unnerving precision of their manoeuvres, as if they had come to herald the baby's birth. What did it mean? What had he seen in the leaves? Was there something he had not told them, some awful fate that awaited her daughter?

The old man sighed. Who could say what they meant, the birds? It was said that when a king cobra happened upon a sleeping man and, instead of sinking its fangs into his flesh, fanned its hood instead, to shelter him from the sun, then that man would someday be king. The herons . . . maybe they foretold something, maybe they did not. Who could read the mind of God?

When Thimmaya went to see Pallada Nayak the next day on his

way back to the outpost, the Nayak generously excused him from the remainder of his lookout duty. It was only fair to Muthavva, he said, and besides, it was sowing season, and Thimmaya had another mouth to feed. The Nayak would send his youngest son in Thimmaya's place.

The paddy that year was so bountiful that Thimmaya was able to buy two milch cows with the gold it fetched him; the cardamom prices were the highest they had been in six years. The family sacrificed a cockerel to the ancestors for blessing them with a daughter who brought with her such good fortune. They named her Devamma, after Thimmaya's great-grandmother, but called her Devi, their very own Goddess.

Muthavva never entirely forgot the herons. She kept the amulet firmly tied around her daughter's arm, surreptitiously scanning the skies each time she took the baby outdoors. As the months passed, however, and nothing untoward happened, she relaxed her vigil. The birds had been a figment of her imagination, she told herself, the phantasms of a pregnant woman. She was entirely too preoccupied to notice them the night of Gauramma's wedding.

The village had been abuzz for weeks. It was an excellent match; Pallada Nayak's daughter was marrying the third son of Kambeymada Nayak, from the village that lay two hundred furlongs to the South. The latter was one of the wealthiest men in Coorg, with fifteen hundred acres of wetlands, several hundred more of cardamom country and multiple coffee estates. Even his tobacco spittoon, it was rumoured, was made of solid gold. Nobody had actually seen the spittoon you understand, but then which Coorg in his right mind would openly display such treasures for the Poleya servants to covet? Besides hadn't the old man commissioned a fabulous walking stick just this past month in Mercara, carved from the finest rosewood and inlaid with ivory? Ah, the village concurred, it was a lucky girl who entered the Kambeymada family, and who better than their own gentle Gauru?

Pallada Nayak spared no expense for the wedding. The moon rose high over the village green as liquor flowed freely and cauldrons of wild boar, chicken, mutton, vegetable and egg curries were hauled from the open air kitchens. The two shifts of musicians played without a break,

Thimmaya and the other men dipping and swaying to the wail of their trumpets. The groom had arrived and he and his family were being feted and fed. Women bustled about in shimmering silks, their faces rendered even more alluring by moonlight. Jewels glowed against their satiny skins. Wide adigé collars of uncut rubies banded their necks, and ropes of golden-beaded jomalé, and coral pathaks with hooded cobra pendants, their ruby eyes flashing fire. Half-moon kokkéthathis of seed pearls and gold swung at their breasts. Bangles, elephant headed, gemstone studded, plain and filigreed, were slung about their wrists, diamonds sparkling in seven starred clusters from their ears.

Muthavva sat with the other nursing and pregnant women, exempt from hostessing chores. Children were running about, her own boy no doubt getting up to mischief somewhere in the melee. Thimmaya's mother would keep an eye on him and see that he was fed. She was content to sit here and listen to the chatter, the relaxed weight of her sleeping daughter in her arms.

What a pretty bride Gauru made, the women sighed, a trifle large, it was true, but who could deny the sweetness of her face? He was a lucky man, her husband, and . . . 'Uyyi!' they exclaimed as a pack of laughing boys came hurtling through the crowd and collided with Muthavva.

'Is this any way to behave?' the women scolded, as the boys sheepishly untangled themselves. 'Do you have pebbles for eyes, can you not see where you are going? See now, you have woken the baby and made her cry.'

'Sorry, we are sorry,' they apologised, backing away.

One of them though, barely ten or eleven years old, stood his ground, gazing at the bawling Devi. 'By all the Gods, she is loud!' he observed, his golden-brown eyes dancing with amusement. 'It is a wonder my ears can still hear.' Before Muthavva could object, he reached with a grubby finger to touch Devi's cheek and, flashing an engaging, dimpled grin, disappeared into the crowd.

Shushing Devi back to sleep, irritated that she hadn't scolded the boy more thoroughly, Muthavva never saw the flock of herons that rose silently from the trees, silhouetted against the moon as they passed over the green.

Chapter 2

As the first girl to be born into the Nachimanda family in over sixty years, Devi was the obliging object of adoration of the entire household. Chengappa and her cousins waited on her every whim, hoisting her onto their shoulders as they paraded about the village green, climbing the wild mango trees in the courtyard to pick her the ripest, most sun-kissed fruit and stuffing their pockets with little gifts for her – the velvety plumes of jungle fowl, wild honeycomb wrapped dripping in pipal leaves, and the purple stones to be found occasionally half buried in the forest floor.

Devi had only to frown and her grandmother Tayi would come running, bribing her with salted gooseberries and cubes of jaggery until she deigned to smile again. Tayi rolled out dozens upon dozens of flaky, multilayered chiroti, frying them golden and dredging them in powdered sugar as treats for her darling. When the family realised that Devi was fond of fish, come rain or shine, Tayi would be at the weekly shanty, so early that the vendors would still be setting out their wares. She would exchange weighty baskets of plantains from the grove behind the house for still-slithering sardines, stuffing them with coriander and tamarind and crisping them in sizzling pork lard for her angel.

Tayi would seat herself on a reed mat, her legs extended out in front of her. Placing Devi upon her soft, comfortable shins, she would massage Devi's hair with shoe-flowers steeped in coconut oil. Her gnarled fingers worked rhythmically upon Devi's scalp as she recounted endless stories about Devi's grandfather, the war against the sultans, and the veera in the lane who made the dogs bark and the trees shiver with no seeming explanation. 'You are my precious flower bud,' she would tell Devi, 'my sun, and my moon, along with all the stars in the sky.'

No one, however, was more smitten than Thimmaya. He doted on his daughter, insisting that hers must be the last face he saw before heading out for the fields, otherwise nothing would go quite right. When the Kandahari gypsies came down from the Frontier mountains to Coorg to sell their horses and shawls they heard about the new girl child and came sashaying up to the Nachimanda house. It was customary for every Coorg girl or woman to sport a tiny tattoo on her forehead, a pretty, blue-green dot. The gypsies offered to tattoo Devi's forehead. 'Ah, I have been looking out for you,' Muthavva began, but Thimmaya winced. Unable to bear even the thought of the brief discomfort his daughter would have to endure and ignoring the agitated counsel of the women of the house, Thimmaya bucked tradition and sent the gypsies on their way.

'Why are you after my princess?' he would chide Muthavva as she berated a mud-streaked Devi for being as dirty as a Poleya. 'Let her be, she will leave us soon enough for her husband's home,' he would admonish as she shouted at Devi to be still as she braided her hair.

'You are spoiling this girl,' Muthavva would warn, but even she would smile as Devi tucked her head in her mother's lap, grinning up at her. 'Donkey child,' she would scold, bending down to kiss the top of her daughter's head, fragrant with sunshine and the wind in the paddy.

When Devi was five, a scandal gripped the village, setting tongues wagging for weeks. Pallada Nayak's daughter Gauramma returned to her grandfather's home. She arrived one afternoon with neither warning nor escort, her young son on her hip. She offered no explanation, saying only that if there was no place for her here, then she would go elsewhere, she did not know where, but *never* would she return to her husband's home.

Her mother wept; her aunts cajoled and castigated. Pallada Nayak hurried with Gauru's father to the Kambeymada home, bearing with them five sacks of fragrant red kesari rice, a cartload of plantains, two haunches of salted venison and a gold-threaded cummerbund that one of Gauru's aunts had been saving for her own son's wedding. Kambeymada Nayak was polite but firm. The girl had left of her own accord, he pointed out, stroking his moustache. She would have to return on her own as well.

'What do we do?' her aunts lamented to Tayi, Muthavva and the other village women who had come to commiserate. 'She simply refuses to listen. And look at the child, it's affecting him as well. Four years old but he hardly says a word, just clings to his mother's pleats all day with his thumb in his mouth.'

Gauru gave no sign that she had heard, tranquilly rocking her son back and forth in her lap as she sat on the kitchen stoop. Devi, bored and fidgeting, pulled a face at the little boy. He turned away, burying his face in his mother's neck. Devi composed her features before Muthavva saw her and boxed her ears, but she continued to watch the boy out of the corner of her eye. When he peeped at her again, she pulled the most horrid face she knew, the one Chengappa had made her practise: nostrils flared, tongue protruding and eyelids turned inside out. The boy looked at her gravely and then turned away again. Fascinated by his steadfast refusal to engage with her, Devi sidled over to Gauru.

'Is he your baby?' she asked finally.

Gauru nodded.

'What's your name?' Devi asked, but the boy pretended he hadn't heard and sucked his thumb noisily.

'Devanna,' his mother answered for him, pulling his thumb gently from his mouth.

'Why doesn't he talk?'

'He will, when he has something to say.'

'They are saying you shouldn't have come back.'

'This is my home,' Gauru said simply.

This, Devi understood. She too loved her home, Tayi who made her hot ottis with the faint imprints of her fingertips still embedded in their edges, the roan cow, the bitch mongrel with her warm bellied puppies, her brother and cousins and Appaiah and Avvaiah and Tukra the Poleya

14

servant boy and the frogs that sang in the fields and the mango tree in the courtyard and ...

'I will never leave my home,' she said stoutly. Gauru smiled and ruffled Devi's hair.

The weeks passed and the family slowly gave up hope that Gauru would return. Pallada Nayak decreed that she and her son should be given a room in the Pallada house for as long as she wanted, but otherwise he completely ignored his daughter. Her uncles spat disgustedly into the mud as she passed and her cousins slapped their foreheads. They were doomed, they moaned, for who would want a bride from a family in which the women left their husbands so shamelessly?

Tayi visited the Pallada house as often as she could; the Palladas were related to her after all, through a cousin twice removed, and she felt the pain of her kin deeply. 'Which parents would be happy,' she brooded aloud, 'to see a grown daughter ruin the family name in this fashion, abandoning her husband's hearth and refusing to return?'

'But Tayi,' piped up Devi, 'Gauru akka missed her own home.'

'Be quiet donkey girl,' Muthavva said automatically. Devi rolled her eyes elaborately behind Muthavva's back. What was all the fuss about? She liked visiting Gauru akka, she gave her all those saris to play with. And Devanna was her friend, was he not? For, not one to be put off by an initial rebuff, Devi had set out to bedazzle him with a vengeance. The child had stood little chance; it was not long before he, like everyone else, had succumbed to her charms.

Tayi tried talking to Gauru. 'The boy seems to be doing well,' she said one day, as they watched Devi and Devanna playing. Gauru smiled.

'Have you considered reconciling with the boy's father?' Tayi probed. 'He is your *husband*, Gauru. And Devanna, his only son ...'

'Leave it be Tayi, there's no point.'

'But kunyi,' pressed Tayi, 'as a wife, you have a duty to your husband. And think of your child. You must never come between father and son. Whatever disagreements exist between the husband and wife, why should the child suffer?'

Gauru did not reply, her eyes filling with tears. Soft-hearted Tayi searched hastily for a change of subject.

'Uyyi!' she exclaimed. 'Will you look at this granddaughter of mine, she has got into your saris.'

Gauru looked over to where a silk-swathed Devi was parading in front of Devanna. She smiled tremulously. 'She likes to wear my saris and jewels, the only things she doesn't like are my bangles.' On cue, Devi picked up a double kokkéthathi and put it about her, the necklace reaching to her waist. Devanna clapped delightedly. They watched as Devi draped a veil over her head, tripping over its sequined ends. 'I like having her visit, it does Devanna good.'

Tayi affectionately patted Gauru's arm. There was plenty of time, she thought to herself, she would pick another moment to talk sense into the girl.

Two days later, Gauru jumped into the family well. The servants found her when they went to draw the morning water, floating face down, her waist-length hair fanning about her like the tendrils of a water lily.

The Nachimandas went to the Pallada house along with the rest of the village to offer their condolences. 'Not that she deserves it, the hussy,' huffed the village, 'but we owe it to Pallada Nayak.' The body was laid on a reed mat in the courtyard and people paid their perfunctory respects. When it was time for the cremation, there was a to-do. Where was Devanna? It was the son's duty to light his mother's pyre. Where had that child hidden himself now? They hunted throughout the house and courtyard, the servants dispatched even as far as the fields to look for him. Pallada Nayak bellowed angrily for his grandson but of Devanna, there was not a sign.

Devi slipped her hand out of Muthavva's grasp and went to find her friend. She knew the secret places where adults would not think to look. She searched in Gauru's closet, already bare of saris, behind the copper water-vessel in the kitchen and in between the lantana bushes, and finally found him lying on his back under the chicken coop.

She squeezed in beside him. Devanna ignored her, but Devi knew instinctively there was no need for words. She scrabbled in the dirt until she found his fingers. She took his hand firmly in hers and there they hid, complicit in their silence as the adults shouted themselves hoarse. They had to cremate Gauru without Devanna, a cousin lighting the pyre instead. And still they lay there, the two children, arms intertwined, amidst the mud and chicken droppings, as the afternoon lengthened and the funeral drums fell finally silent.

Pallada Nayak had the servants fill in the well and plant a banana seedling on top of it. There was no mistaking his tone as he addressed his daughters-in-law. 'What's done is done. Manage the house with the water from the stream for now; I have summoned the water diviner who will find us an alternative source of water until such time as the well is purified. There will be no more ill talk of Gauramma or her boy.'

The Kambeymadas came to take Devanna home, but plagued by a vague but persistent guilt, Pallada Nayak suggested that it might be better for all concerned if the boy were raised where he was, under the care of his maternal grandmother. He would return to the Kambeymada home when he was older. It was a convenient arrangement. Devanna's father readily agreed, with the caveat that he would send a monthly stipend of fifteen rupees for the upkeep of his son. He married again shortly thereafter, a plump, pretty girl from his own village who promptly set about bearing him a brood of children. His visits to Devanna grew infrequent, although it was made clear that the Kambeymada house awaited its son with open arms; Devanna could return whenever he chose.

Devanna took his mother's death as might be expected. He started to wet his bed, waking in the middle of the night whimpering for her. The women of the house would stroke his arm, sadly telling him that Gauru had done the best thing she could; her death mitigated the shame she had brought on the family. 'Our raja kunyi, our king child,' they crooned as they tried to get the boy to sleep again, but the only thing that quieted Devanna was the promise of a visit to Devi in the morning. It happened so frequently, and he was brought to the Nachimanda house so often, that it wasn't long before Tayi suggested that it might be easier if he simply stayed there. A mattress was laid down for him, alongside the other boys in the house, and here he slept peacefully through the nights. Gradually, Devanna stopped asking for his mother altogether.

They became a staple sight in the village, the pale-skinned firebrand and her scrawny worshipper; if Devi had fascinated him before,

Devanna now clung to her like a bedraggled puppy. Devi, in turn, was his guardian and protector. No child dared look askance at Devanna or poke fun at him if Devi was around. 'You good for nothing louts,' she would howl, launching herself on the offenders, kicking, scratching and boxing until they begged for mercy. The Nachimanda household also accepted this latest plaything of Devi's, absorbing the boy into its fold.

Still too young for the village school, both children frolicked all day long, roaming the fields and the adjoining woods with Tukra and the other servant children as they took the cattle to pasture. The Poleyas taught them to craft slingshots from the fibrous bark of the bairi tree and darts from porcupine quills; they led them to the secret places where the juiciest mulberries and thickest mushrooms grew. They showed them the sticky honeycombs in the hollows of the kabba trees and the sun-swept rocks where fantastic jewel-hooded king cobras mated at night, or so it was said. They taught them to find the grassy burrows where wild hares lived and to catch crabs using loops of chicken gut for bait.

The crab stream lay at the foot of the fields, a body of rippling water that looked sometimes blue and sometimes the palest green, depending on the light. Devi and Devanna would wade into its shallow end as tiny red, green and yellow frogs, each no larger than a coin, hopped, alarmed, out of their way. The water lapped warmly at the children's shins as they lowered a rope of intestine into the water, a pink end held firmly in each of their hands. They would wait, grinning in anticipation, as the stream shone around them, the gleam of its surface broken now and again by a movement from some underlying fish. The crabs would scuttle towards the intestine, digging their pincers into its length. Then Devi and Devanna would lift it from the water, together, in one fluid movement, the crabs clinging unawares, like gems along some strange, pendulous necklace.

The rains came. Tayi simmered mutton bones seasoned with onions and peppercorns for hours over the fire to make warming bowls of broth. Mushrooms sprouted around the trunks of trees and the trail that led to the Nachimanda house turned into mud. Devanna was content to stay indoors, warming his feet by the fire and playing games of cowrie shells and marbles, but Devi fidgeted non-stop, going time and again to the windows to stare out at the water pelting down, slipping out to the verandah to thrust a hand into the rain despite Muthavva's exhortations not to get herself wet.

Finally, the clouds dispersed. The transplanting season with its long days and backbreaking work drew to a close and the hunting season began. Devanna sat on the verandah of the Nachimanda house, hunched over a pile of bark from the kanni tree. Thimmaya was taking Devi and him on the hunt the following day, but first he had set them the task of making wicks for the ancient matchlocks. Devi had soon run off but Devanna had continued to work steadily. He rubbed the strips between his palms, twisting them into wicks, taking pleasure in the feel of their knobby woodiness and the faint smell of smoke from the kitchen hearth where they were hung to dry.

He sat back on his haunches and contemplated the growing pile. This part of the hunt, he enjoyed. He could sit absorbed like this for hours on end, making sure that the wicks were rolled to exactly the same length and thickness. The cat sunning herself on the verandah stretched against his legs and he reached forward to gently scratch her head. It was the hunt itself he hated. The noises the dying animals made, the frantic pleading in their eyes, the smell of blood and the crunch of cartilage as the men skinned and quartered the kill. Suddenly restless, Devanna looked out towards the fields, wondering where Devi had gone.

They set off early the next morning. Thimmaya strapped Devi to his back with an old sari of Muthavva's and one of the older boys hoisted Devanna onto his shoulders. They proceeded silently through the jungle that surrounded the village, keeping a watch out for snakes and the inch long, rust-coloured scorpions that inflicted such mind-numbing agony that even grown men had been known to pass out from the pain. Devi's brother, Chengappa, suddenly raised his hand and the party came to a halt. 'There,' he whispered, pointing.

Devanna's heart began to pound. Turning his head away quickly, he fixed his gaze upon Devi. She was very still, nostrils flared with excitement, neck craned forward the better to see. He stared at her, forcing his mind to think of nothing else, not the musket that was being raised, nor its sights locking on to the target. There was a sudden, shocking crack, an orange flash of gunpowder. The jungle came alive, monkeys screaming in the branches overhead, birds taking frightened wing, cawing and calling as they fled. Devanna slowly exhaled.

The men usually gave the younger children the privilege of reaching the downed animal first. This day too, Devi won. 'I am the bal battékara,' she panted, exultant as she stroked the warm flesh of a spotted deer. 'I am just as brave as the hunter, I was quickest to reach the kill!'

When the hunting party returned to the village, smug and a little bloodstained, Muthavva cried out in horror like she always did. 'Uyyi, just look at this child. Iguthappa Swami, why can't she behave like a girl instead of a little ruffian?'

Picking up a pair of tongs, Tayi plucked some of the glowing embers from the kitchen hearth and placed them on a bell metal plate, adding a fistful of rice from the cooking pot and a dash of water. Quickly sprinkling the fizzing ash-water over the children's heads to thwart any malevolent spirits that might have accompanied them from the jungle, she thrust the platter at Muthavva. 'Here, quick,' she told her daughter-in-law, 'finish purifying the rest of them and the game before any pisachi take root.' With Muthavva distracted, Tayi whisked Devi and Devanna into the stone paved bathhouse, away from Muthavva's wrath. Pouring pots of steaming water over them as they squatted giggling on the floor, she sang to them in her tuneless voice.

> *The beautiful girl is finally here*
> *Come to visit her near-and-dear,*
> *Rubies glittering about her neck*
> *Anklets shimmering like the sun,*
> *The beautiful one has come,*
> *Drenched in a rainstorm she has come.*

Devi scrunched her eyes closed as the water streamed down over her. To Devanna, she seemed just like the rain-soaked beauty of the song.

Chapter 3

A year went by, and another. The banana plant on the filled-in well sent out whorls of fan-like leaves, then a thick purple tuber that unfurled to reveal row upon row of fragrant white flowers coiled tightly within. These in turn dried and fell to the ground, leaving the plant covered in bunches of tiny green fruit. When the bananas finally yellowed and ripened, the plant was chopped down and the well reopened. Its waters were now deemed to be purified and once more fit for human consumption.

That same week, Pallada Nayak came to see Thimmaya. 'As you know Thimmaya,' he said, peeling one of the loose-jacket oranges that Muthavva had brought out to them, 'I have enrolled Devanna in the missionary school at Mercara. Shouldn't I do at least that much for the boy, give him a good education? But look at the stupidity of this new generation, the fool keeps crying like a girl!'

He thumped his walking stick on the verandah to emphasise his disgust. Really, the boy was testing his patience. Devanna kept pleading to be allowed to attend the village school with Devi, but the Nayak was bent on following through with his plan. It was over four months now since the boy's father had been to visit. Was Devanna not good enough for him? So what if the Kambeymadas were filthy rich? The Palladas were well off too, were they not? The insulted Nayak was determined to fashion Devanna into one of the best educated young men in all of Coorg; he would sculpt the boy into the pride of the Kambeymada clan. Now if only Devanna would show more sense. The Nayak had cajoled and reasoned, even resorted to a good thrashing now and again, but the boy would not stop his whining.

'Cheh ...' he mused absently, spitting out the seeds of the orange into its peel. Thimmaya nodded sympathetically, wondering what all this had to do with him. 'Harrh.' The Nayak sat up and, clearing his throat, decided to come to the point. 'Thimmaya,' he said briskly, 'why don't you enrol Devi kunyi into the school as well? No question of fees of course, I will see to all that. Let the children go together and maybe then Devanna will settle down.'

Thimmaya was pleased. His angel would go to a fancy school, learn to speak English just like the white folk. He quickly gave his consent, but Muthavva was horrified. As it was, the girl was a handful, would he spoil her even more by sending her to that new fangled school? Who knew what devilry they would fill her head with? Would he have his only daughter forget their own ways? 'Why,' she whispered in an agony of embarrassment, 'people say the missionaries don't even wash their bottoms!'

Thimmaya burst out laughing. 'Where do you pick up such nonsense, woman? If you're so worried, send a brass pitcher along with Devi, she can carry it with her to the toilets there.'

It was Tayi who brokered peace. When had education ever harmed anyone, she asked. Devi was fortunate to be given the chance to attend such an expensive school. 'It is the Lord's grace,' she said, 'that our child is getting this opportunity for a modern education. One must move with the times.' And what were they here for, the elders of the household? Was it not their responsibility to ensure that Devi grew up well versed in the Coorg traditions? 'Don't worry,' Tayi reassured Muthavva, 'you and I, we'll see to it that she learns all our customs, and the seven shastras too.'

The two children were enrolled in the first year at the mission school. The novices directed Thimmaya to the piece goods store in Mercara where he bought two yards of Cannanore checked cotton. 'Cheh,' said a scandalised Tayi when Thimmaya brought these to her with specifications for a half-sleeved shirt and pinafore. She cut up an old sari, attaching generous lengths to the shirt until its sleeves flapped over Devi's wrists. She then added a broad swathe of fabric to the pinafore so that its hem swirled modestly about her ankles. The missionaries were so pleased to have the pretty little girl, only the fifth to have enrolled in the entire school, that they overlooked the liberties Tayi had taken with the uniform.

With Devi by his side, Devanna stopped snivelling and discovered a vigorous aptitude for school. He soaked up his lessons, like dried beans in a thunderstorm, immersing himself in his books like a fish dancing through the floods. He mastered the alphabet, learning to read effortlessly, much to Devi's annoyance as she struggled syllable by syllable. He quickly grasped the labyrinthine principles of mathematics while the other children were still muddling through multiplication and division, able to solve sums almost quicker than the teachers could write them on the blackboard.

His teachers were unstinting in their praise, pointing time and again to the quality of his homework and his impeccable cursive handwriting as a benchmark for the rest of their students to aspire to. At first the class bullies whipped around as soon as the teachers' backs were turned, glowering at Devanna and, sotto voce, promising him a thrashing when school was out. Devi, however, soon put an end to that. Eyes flashing, she would mouth silent abuse back at them until, awed by her vituperation, they returned meekly to their books. It wasn't long before they left off taunting Devanna altogether.

Teacher's pet Devanna may have been, but nobody doted on him more than Reverend Gundert, the head of the Mission.

Hermann Gundert had arrived in Coorg over three years earlier. Three years, five months and sixteen days to be exact. When the authorities had suggested he start a mission in Coorg, Gundert had known it would be a waste of time. The Coorgs were stubborn, toddy-loving sybarites, too attached to their pagan ways to change. They called themselves a Hindu race, but just as they had defied the Mohammedan sultans of Mysore and their efforts to convert them, the Coorgs had adroitly sidestepped the reach of the Brahmins. They picked and chose among the traditions of the Hindu faith, refusing to budge from their own primitive beliefs in their ancestors and the spirits of the land. When they had contrived to pass all the major milestones of their lives – to be born, named, married and have their last rites performed with not a Brahmin in sight – what hope had the Christian Church? Nonetheless, Gundert had acquiesced. After more than a quarter of a century in India and having requested to be transferred every third or fourth year, there were few places left for him to go.

He had gone about setting up the mission with his usual efficiency, successfully petitioning for and appropriating the land adjoining the Mercara Church. Then he plunged into learning about the Coorgs and their land. He spent hours picking the brains of local Europeans, sifting through their opinions: charming, but somewhat boorish; militant, best to keep a certain distance; hotheaded, but honest to a fault; a handsome race and winsome women. He visited the local library where he read the accounts of the judges, soldiers, administrators and other upholders of the Empire who had happened upon Coorg. He employed a tutor to teach him the local language and held lengthy discussions with the mission staff and the town residents. Gundert maintained extensive records of these conversations, distilling all that he had heard and observed into a series of notes.

'Note 1: The race is a handsome one of unknown origins. They constitute a highland clan, free from the trammels of caste, with the manly bearing and independent spirit natural in those who have been, from time immemorial, true lords of the soil. They stride about with a confidence that is most becoming. I have often been approached by them, demonstrating a frank, open curiosity in my antecedents and in a refreshing departure from the obsequiousness so readily found else-where, with no hesitation in taking my hand in a grip as firm as any I have experienced.

'The men are far taller than the average Indian male, with an impressive breadth of shoulder and width of chest. They are generally lithe and muscular, with an ease of movement, brought about no doubt by an active life spent cultivating their landholdings and hunting in the forests. The hair is thick and curly, the nose often hooked, the eyes beguilingly well shaped and clear, and many of them possess grey or green-coloured irises. The pigment of their skin varies, with only a few among them displaying the brown tint to be generally seen elsewhere in this country, most being coloured a becoming olive with many so

24

light skinned as to almost pass for European. Their dress is especially attractive, the black tunic, or "kupya", accentuating the well-shaped back and the strength of the arms, the V at the front emphasising the abundant curls springing from the chest in an unbridled proclamation of virility, the wide sash and the ornamented dagger drawing the eye inexorably to the slimness of the waist and hips.

'Indeed, one might wholeheartedly echo Sir Perry in calling them the most alluring and attractive race of men that one's own eyes have happened upon in many years.'

(Refer Sir Eskine Perry: 'A bird's-eye view of India, with extracts from a journal kept in the provinces, Nepal and Ceylon'; circa 1855.)

His comments on the women were markedly more succinct.

'Note 2: The women might be deemed attractive, were it not for the unfortunate habit of chewing betel, especially amongst the older matrons, which renders their teeth and lips a vivid shade of crimson. They appear healthy and robust enough of figure, however most are disadvantageously drawn to the distressingly garish colours of wardrobe that are similarly favoured by their sisters elsewhere in India.

'Note 12: There is a distinct social hierarchy, with great respect accorded those older than oneself. The touching of an elder's feet is a sign of respect and an opportunity to receive the blessings of one who has lived for a longer time. Every older male must necessarily be referred to as "anna" (pronounced un-nah), or elder brother, and every older female as "akka" (uk-kah). The labourers and the servants must address their masters and mistresses, irrespective of age, as anna or akka. All mothers-in-law are called "maavi" (maa-vee) and fathers-in-law, "maava" (maa-vaa). The truly old are considered universal grand-parents, being referred to by all as "tayi" (tah-yee) or grandmother, and "thatha" (thah-thah) or grandfather.

'Note 36: Akin to other highland races, the Coorgs share an unshakable sense of kinship. Each person owes allegiance to his or her family, and each family is bound to every other family and to the land. One is born first a Coorg, and only then an Indian or even a Hindu. Nonetheless, there is a vast pantheon of heathen Gods to whom they pray, the two most powerful being Lord Iguthappa or

Iguthappa Swami, the God of the hills, and Ayappa Swami, the God of the jungle.'

The Coorgs had been hospitable to a fault, Gundert's visits invariably setting off a great fluster and flurry of activity within their homes as the women rushed about, hastily stoking the kitchen fire, donning fresh saris and a slew of ornaments in his honour. He would be received on the verandah with much warmth by the men, where a host of children with suspiciously clean faces and freshly slicked back hair hung on to every word of the ensuing conversation. They plied him with food and drink, but as soon as he broached the topic of conversion, the Coorgs would turn haughty and distant, telling him in no uncertain terms to stay out of their private affairs. When he persisted, they looked at him incredulously, and then, acknowledging perhaps a kindred obstinacy, they reacted with amusement. They placed the crucifixes and rosaries he gave them with great ceremony among the other knickknacks displayed in their homes – giving of course a wide berth to the nooks where their own Gods were installed. They then saw him off with reciprocal gifts of their own – sandalwood statuettes, a handsome pair of deer antlers, jars of hog-plum preserves – cheerfully bidding him to visit again.

After a year of diligent labour, his only converts had been a gaggle of traders from the neighbouring states who had now settled in Coorg. Of the Coorgs proper, there had been only one, a drunken good-for-nothing, attracted by the promise of land and an offer to settle his debts. The Reverend christened him Madappa John, but any hopes of him spearheading more conversions soon dissipated. John had promptly been disowned by his family and his own wife had refused to have anything to do with him. He had gone back to his evenings at the local toddy shop, and soon after, went missing, never to be seen again.

The Reverend decided to change tack, realising that the younger generation was the key to the success of his mission. He gave up all overt preaching, restating his primary objective as the establishment of a school in Mercara. The Coorgs had shown an immediate if cautious response, as the wealthier families began to send in their children in dribs and drabs. The quality of teaching was unquestionably better than anything else in the region, and as the months passed and they realised that their children seemed to be in no imminent danger of contracting Christianity, they had slowly gained confidence in the school. It was only a matter of time, the Reverend knew, before the rosters would be full. It was then that he planned to introduce Bible study classes into the curriculum, possibly even a weekly Mass.

The Reverend paid keen attention to his students. They were the hope of this country, its future, and he took his duty of educating them, of civilising them in the finest traditions of the Western world, to heart. He set high standards, no tougher than the ones he set for himself. Woe betide the child who came unprepared to Hermann Gundert's class. 'No,' he would state flatly. 'Nein, you are incorrect.' The hapless student would make his or her way to the front of the class where the Reverend would make them stand in a corner.

It was strange, the students marvelled among themselves, that despite the fact he never took a cane to them or made them squat holding their ears until their muscles screamed like some of the other teachers did, it was the Reverend's punishments that seemed the most unbearable. 'It's the way he looks at us,' they shuddered, 'with those blue eyes, the colour of the afternoon sky.' It was the way he spoke to them, the controlled, almost too low pitch of his voice, the refined precision of his disappointment, that reduced even the most callous bully to tears.

Gundert could never quite put his finger on what it was that first drew him to Devanna. Had it been a snippet he had heard, something the teachers had said about the boy's mother, God rest her soul, having taken her own life? But no, it couldn't have been that. Committing suicide was almost a way of life here, if one might pardon the pun. Gundert had discovered to his dismay, soon after he had arrived, that the Coorgs seemed to view taking their own lives as an honourable solution to a wide range of issues. Not a month passed without the news of someone or other having held a gun to their heads, swallowed their diamond rings or taken a fatal leap into a swollen river.

It had been something else. There were other children more personable than Devanna, but there had been something about his pale face and apprehensive eyes that had made Gundert linger as he read out the roll call that day. He had contrived to sit in on some of the classes,

27

noting with pleased surprise the boy's obvious intellectual prowess. When the mathematics teacher set the class an especially complicated set of sums that Devanna proceeded to solve in his head, without even needing to put chalk to slate, it had sealed the matter for good. Gundert took the child under his wing.

When Pallada Nayak summoned him, Devanna stood before his grandfather, trying not to tremble and wondering what he had done wrong. To his astonishment, the Nayak thumped him on his back, guffawing that things were obviously going well at school since the Reverend had sought the Nayak's permission to give Devanna extra lessons twice a week. It was clear that Devanna had been blessed with the Nayak's brains, quite unlike the rest of his dull-head brood.

Devanna could scarcely believe his ears. The Reverend had asked for him. Him!

They sat across from one another, the greying Reverend and his protégé, in the rosewood-panelled study, poring over texts from his personal collection. Devanna loved the feel of those books, the creaminess of the paper, their grainy, gilt edges and the naphthalene smell that rose from their pages, tickling his nose. He enjoyed the guttural sound of the Reverend's voice as he read aloud. Devanna could not understand all of the words, but the poems conjured up pictures in his head, wonderful images of green meadows and stone paths and flowers the like of which he had never seen, flowers with names like cro-cus-es and i-ris-es and daff-o-dils, that sounded to him as beautiful as one of Tayi's songs.

The Reverend was reading aloud one afternoon when something fell from between the pages of the book. Devanna bent immediately to retrieve it, noting curiously the ridged indigo stamp upon its back, 'William Henderson & Sons, Photographic Studios. *Madras, circa 1861*'. He turned over the calotype. A much younger Reverend was laughing out at him. He stood beside another young man of stockier build, who seemed equally amused, struck a pose with a hand on his hip and the other thrust into the lapels of his jacket. 'Who is he Reverend?' Devanna asked timidly, as he placed the calotype on the table. Gundert continued to read as if he had not heard, then stopped suddenly, midway through the poem.

'Olaf,' he said curtly, picking up the calotype and slipping it back into the book. 'The man you asked after, his name was Olaf.' Glancing out of the window at the fading light, he shut the book with a snap and abruptly called an end to the lesson. Hurt by the Reverend's brusqueness, Devanna silently gathered up his slate and left.

Gundert sat alone in the classroom, the book still clasped in his hands. He ran his thumb slowly across its leather binding. Olaf. How many years had it been since he had said his name out loud? Olaf, beloved Olaf. Olaf and he, the best of friends, soul mates forever, running carefree through the woods. How beautiful Olaf had looked, the wind in his hair, laughing as his kite soared into the blue.

Brothers in all but blood.

It was later, when the first fuzz stippled their cheeks, that their world had begun to shift. Olaf was suddenly no longer as interested in their fishing expeditions, not even when old man Uwe came home with the largest trout anyone had ever seen in those parts. No longer as keen to go rabbit hunting or to romp in the woods with their dogs, Olaf preferred to lounge about the village square, inspecting the women passing by. 'Her,' he would whisper to Gundert, nudging him sharply in the ribs each time a particularly nubile young thing appeared. To his pleasure, Olaf discovered the opposite sex found him equally attractive. He grinned at them, doffing his cap and winking cheekily, and was rewarded with blushing confusion, sidelong glances and, once or twice, even a wink back that turned his bones to soup.

Hermann was disgusted. It infuriated him when the girls simpered coyly back at Olaf, the assessing looks they threw towards the breadth of Olaf's chest filling him with revulsion. He stared them down coldly if they made the mistake of turning in his direction, and they soon left off making any overtures towards him. He had tried talking Olaf out of this new obsession. He put down the girls that Olaf fancied, pointing out the thick ankles of one, the long hairs matting the arms of another. Olaf was not to be deterred. 'Oh, stop your griping,' he said good naturedly. 'Go on, get one of your own, why don't you, and taste their many pleasures.'

'I have no intention,' Hermann archly informed him, 'of doing anything quite so crass.'

Too proud to demand his friend's attention, Hermann masked his hurt each time Olaf brushed him off, raising an eyebrow, or shrugging noncommittally when Olaf said he was too busy for him. 'It will pass,' he assured himself. 'This is only a phase. Olaf will soon tire of these ... these *trollops*.' Soon it would be just the two of them again, Olaf listening drowsily in the afternoon sun as Hermann read aloud, Heine's Rhampsenit perhaps, or even the Gods of Greece. But he knew, deep down, that he was losing his friend. He watched despairingly as Olaf caroused his way through the village, listened with feigned excitement as Olaf recounted each tryst, his own heart twisting with jealousy and dark, incomprehensible longing.

The Church had been his succour. Hermann had always liked attending Mass, he enjoyed the coolness of the alabaster carvings, the angular pews and the contained lilt of the choir. He had always been a little in awe of the brothers, of the pristine whiteness of their robes and the inherent purity of their abstinence. Now he found himself drawn even more to the serene interiors of the local parish. He began to spend hours there, when the ache inside him grew unbearable and shame coated his tongue in a thick, inarticulate fuzz. He sat unnoticed in the shadowy recesses of the church, watching silently as petitioners trickled in with their unknown pleas for grace. In the stoic acceptance of one, the copious tears of another, the muttered recriminations of a third, Hermann seemed to find a temporary solace of his own.

Christus, du Lamm Gottes, der du trägst die Sünde der Welt, erbarm dich unser.
Christ, Lamb of God, you take away the sins of the world, have mercy on us.

When the mission authorities had come to visit the village, seeking new recruits, Hermann had realised with a small frisson of shock that they were calling out especially to him. The Lord had in his infinite mercy shown him the way. He had left almost immediately for Basle to be confirmed, much to the distress of his parents. 'Why?' his mother had wept, 'Why the Church when there is so much here for you? This land, the manor, all of it yours, why must you leave?' Hermann had remained silent, denying the confusion that swirled within him, leaving without even bidding Olaf farewell.

He had returned nearly two years later, collected and remote. He was ordained, trained in English, botany, history and the rudiments of medicine, fully equipped to spread the word of the mission across the seas. It was to be a brief visit home, a succinct farewell to his parents before he left with the mission for India. Word of his visit had spread rapidly through the village, however, as every bit of news did, and Olaf had come to visit. The old, verboten feelings began to stir at once within Hermann, shaking themselves free from the silt, surging through him with a force that had jolted his moorings.

It was a morose and dejected Olaf who sat before him, jilted yet again and nursing a broken heart. Hermann listened distractedly to his outpourings of woe. He knew his friend well, knew he would bounce back soon enough from this latest episode. Hermann sat there, the very picture of composure, while Dante marched through his head keeping time with the ticking cuckoo clock:

> 'You shall leave everything you love most:
> this is the arrow that the bow of exile shoots first.'

Hermann's eyes travelled hungrily over Olaf's face, committing to memory the barely noticeable scar by his temple from when he had tripped in the woods, the amber tips of his eyelashes that turned bright gold in the sun.

And suddenly, inspiration had struck.

He had leaned impulsively forward, urging Olaf to travel with him to India. 'Think about it,' he pressed, 'the mission needs volunteers. Spend a year there with us and when you return, it will be as a hero.' He had suppressed the brief twinge of conscience by telling himself that he only had Olaf's best interests at heart. They *did* need volunteers in India. The travel would give Olaf an opportunity to expand his horizons, pun unintended, to broaden his experience and get over being jilted.

The plan, crazy as it was, appealed to Olaf's fickle heart. India! What adventures they would have, Hermann and he. How Margarethe would weep when she heard that Olaf had left, how she would rue the day she had spurned him.

They were soon on a steamer bound for Madras. Olaf climbed onto the railings enclosing the deck as the hazy shoreline finally hove into view. 'India,' he shouted, 'Magical, ancient India!' Hermann had stood by laughing, the taste of salt-spray on his lips, luxuriating in his friend's excitement. 'Hermann, you and I, we will change this country forever,' Olaf declared, his eyes shining. 'What stories we will tell upon our return. How will Margarethe ever be able to resist me?'

They had the calotype taken not two hours after they had docked, giddy with youth, intoxicated by the smorgasbord of smells and sounds, spurred by Olaf's enthusiasm and the large sign outside the photographer's studio that said they took all manner of European currency.

Tuberculosis, the doctor at the Our Lady of Mercy hospital had said dispassionately, not a month later. He saw it all the time. Hermann had wanted to claw his hands away as the doctor prodded at Olaf's body, but he steeled his voice instead, courteously thanking the man for his time. He barely stirred from Olaf's side all those weeks, cradling his beloved friend in his arms, murmuring words of comfort or contrition, he would never know which, into the sweat-soaked rankness of his hair. He had watched helplessly as Olaf deteriorated: the pfennig-sized clots of blood and mucus, the discharge that turned the golden lashes a sodden, muddy brown, the confusion rampant in his voice as he called out for his mother, for Margarethe.

When Olaf died, Hermann knew, he *knew* without a doubt, that it was he who had killed him. As surely as if he had taken a pistol to his head. Olaf had come to India only at his urging, had died this awful death because of the desires snaking unspoken within Gundert's weak, despicable heart.

'Hermann, you and I, we will change this country forever.'

Gundert had thrown himself into his work, as if determined to fulfil those sunny words singlehandedly. The young missionary was tireless, preaching the gospel, setting up schools, lobbying the local authorities and recruiting converts, working late into the night and rising earlier than anyone around him. No matter, though, how much he gave of himself, no matter how often he denied himself sleep, eventually the dreams would begin again.

The church spire silhouetted against a clear spring day, and look, there were their kites waltzing in the air. 'Hurry up Hermann,' Olaf would cry, racing through the forest, pine needles crunching under his feet. 'Wait Olaf, wait for me,' but Olaf charged on. No matter how fast Hermann ran, no matter how he begged, Olaf was always just ahead, just out of reach, laughing as he disappeared around the bend. Gundert would awake trembling, his hands still reaching towards a ghost long slipped through his fingers. He would stumble to the chapel, and there he would kneel, the name of the Lord on his lips, begging forgiveness over and over, until daylight began to bleed once more from the stained glass of the chapel windows.

That morning, he would ask yet again to be transferred.

Thunder boomed in the skies outside, startling Gundert out of his reverie. How long had he been sitting here? He slowly opened the window and put his hand out into the dark. It had started to rain some time earlier, and was now hammering down into his open palm. A blast of cool air whirled through the windows, tinged with wood smoke and jasmine and the faintest whiff of dung. A jackal howled in the distance, the sound carrying then fading in the wind.

Gundert thought of his mother, of her fingers fluttering in distress upon his face like the wings of a bird, tracing his every feature as she bid him farewell. He thought of Olaf, cemented permanently in a land he had barely known, of the certainty he carried within himself that he too would be buried here one day. *Brothers forever*. He thought of Devanna, of the innocent purity of his face, the innate, inexplicable chord the boy had struck deep within him.

For the first time since Olaf's passing, Gundert felt peace stealing into his heart. The Lord had given him another chance with this boy, a surrogate son to call his own. 'Rest in peace, Olaf,' he whispered, the breeze snatching the words from his lips. 'Mein Schatz, mein Liebling, farewell.' He stood there a long time, until the novices came searching for him, the rain slashing at his face as he stared at the deluge outside, lightning forking and crackling, the skies weeping all the tears he had been unable to shed.

Gundert intensified his mentoring, drawing a list each Saturday of

33

the ground he was to cover with Devanna the following week. History and geography, language and literature – each month he raised the bar a little higher, and each month Devanna eagerly followed, blooming under the Reverend's tutelage. The other Nachimanda children gathered curiously around as Devanna helped Devi with their homework in the evenings, and soon he began to teach them the alphabet too. He showed them the atlas that the Reverend had lent him, pointing out Germany and England and the numerous archipelagos that lay to the East. He taught them the poems he had learnt that week; 'Ahostoff goldun daffadils' they parroted, infusing Devanna with confidence.

Suddenly it didn't matter that he never did win any of the races that were conducted each year in the freshly ploughed, water-logged paddy fields or that he would never be the first up the mango trees or that he had never been the bal battékara at a hunt. Even the village bully sidled up to him one day, asking if he could learn some Inglis? Devanna flinched instinctively before he realised there was to be no box on the ears that day.

No one was more proud than Devi. Things shifted between the two; with Devanna no longer needing her constant guardianship, she began instead to look to him. When three baby cuckoos fell from their nest, squawking pathetically under the mango tree, it was Devanna she sought out, confident he would know what to do. When Muthavva fussed and scolded, he was the one she complained to; he would hear her out patiently, such a quizzical expression on his face that Devi would invariably catch herself mid-tirade and begin to giggle. When they ran barefoot through the fields, it was Devanna who knelt gently by her feet, picking out the thorns that sometimes breached her soles; he was the only one who didn't laugh and tell her she was being silly when she confided just how much she hated bangles of any sort at all.

When Devanna came to look back upon his life, it was these years that would seem to him the most perfect, the most untainted, suffused with the warm glow of memory.

The time when a jackal had got at the chickens. Two of the hens had hatched their eggs and the courtyard was filled with the buttery fluffiness of their chicks. Devi and Devanna were woken one morning, however, not by cheeping but by a stream of abuse coming from the chicken coop.

They ran to see what the commotion was about and peeped curiously from behind Thimmaya's back as he stood cursing at the carnage. The jackal had killed willy-nilly, leaving a mess of half-chewed birds, entrails and bloody feathers in its wake. When Devi spotted what was left of the chicks, she started to cry. Thimmaya swung her into his arms, kissing the top of her head and telling her to be a brave Coorg, but although she swallowed her tears, she remained pale and subdued.

Tayi packed wedges of raw mango dipped in salt with their lunch as a special treat and Muthavva fastened her silver anklets about Devi's ankles for her to wear all that day, but the tears kept welling in Devi's eyes. Devanna tried to cheer her up as they walked to school, 'look Devi, look at those flowers,' he said, pointing out a bunch of orchids spilling from the branches of an athi tree, 'see Devi, there,' a spider's web in the damp grass, dew drops glistening amidst its threads. The brilliant flash of a kingfisher, the bubbles in the paddy tanks that promised a fat fish lurking below, none of these were able to lighten her mood. Tukra, the servant boy accompanying them, even broke into a ridiculous dance, stomping on the ground with arms akimbo, knocking his knees together, leaping into the air and smartly clacking his heels, but Devi did not so much as smile.

Then Devanna had a brainwave. 'Let's give the chicks a funeral.'

She looked at him. 'A funeral? What do you mean?'

'Leave that to me,' he said, improvising, 'it will be a very special funeral, that's all I can tell you.' Devi brightened at last.

Later that afternoon, they gathered the children of the Poleya servants by the banks of the crab stream. Devanna constructed a rough raft from twigs and banana leaves as Tukra watched agog. They dug out the mangled remains of the chicks from the rubbish heap and wrapped the stiff little bodies in the tufts of silk cotton from the pods that lay scattered on the ground. They lowered them gently into the raft, and then, scattering marigold petals over their silk cotton shrouds, her lips moving in silent, fervent prayer, Devi set the raft adrift.

It twirled slowly in the eddies by the bank for a few moments. Devi bit her lip anxiously, watching. Then, as if following the shafts of sunlight piercing through the clouds, the raft, twisting back and forth, began merrily to pull away downstream.

Devi watched raptly as it sailed away, watching until the last bit of silk cotton shroud disappeared over the horizon. It was then that she turned towards Devanna.

He would never the forget the way she smiled at him, her face luminous, seeming to be lit within by one, twenty, a thousand golden suns.

Chapter 4

The miniature raft that the children had set adrift spun down the stream intact, belying its flimsy construction. It sped past the village boundaries, ferrying its fragile cargo through the rolling hills that surrounded it; through groves of timber bamboo and open glades dotted with pink touch-me-nots; into and beyond the next village, neatly avoiding the pigs rooting by the banks. On it floated, past elegant knots of silver oak and rosewood, as the sun set and the stars came out. Through the night and into the dawn it journeyed, by herds of grazing bison and spotted deer, past sweet-scented bushes of wild rose and seven-layered jasmine and down over a waterfall where the stream poured into a fast flowing river. It swirled through the green waters, gathering speed as it turned sharply into the jungle abutting the Kambeymada village. Here a stray eddy caught it and it was swept down one of the tributaries, finally coming to rest against the far side of a watering hole.

The tiger crouched by the edge let out a low growl. It watched for a while as the raft continued to bob and then, sniffing the air suspiciously, the tiger slowly approached. It hooked the boat with one massive paw and nosed the stiff chicks. Losing interest, it sneezed, and splashing across the stream, made its way into the silent, gently steaming jungle. Its stomach distended from the hunt of the previous night, the tiger padded towards a patch of ferns sprouting under a shady pipal tree. It rubbed its face against the tree trunk, raising a muscular leg to further mark its territory with a jet of urine. Satisfied, it settled itself upon the ferns, and soon fell asleep.

Some distance away, in the neighbouring village, the hunting party was preparing to set off. The trackers had returned earlier that morning, bearing good tidings. The ground was covered with hoof marks, the jungle flush with game. They were gathered now in the village green, along with the marksmen, the dog bearers and the Poleya drummers, squatting on their haunches as they mapped in the mud the routes they would take. The party would approach the selected area in a rough circle, the marksmen fanning out at one end with the best shots among them given the choicest spots. The drummers and the dog bearers would circle around to the other end, using the dogs and the drums to flush out the game.

Each man checked once more the knives slung in his cummerbund – the short, sharp peechekathi at the waist and the heavier, broad-bladed odikathi at the back. The marksmen gathered up their guns as the village priest raised his hands to indicate the auspicious hour was upon them and with a great cheering and banging of drums, the party set off.

Kambeymada Machaiah was near the head of the now silent column, maintaining a steady pace as he hacked through the underbrush with easy strokes of his odikathi. The site of the hunt was still some furlongs away, but they were making good time. How he had waited for the hunting season to begin. All through the transplanting season and the monsoon he had bided his time, itching to try out the percussion cap rifle he had bought in Mercara earlier that year. It hadn't taken the trader long to convince him. The gun had belonged to an English soldier, he claimed, who, having finished his commission, was returning to England. Machu had picked up the rifle, gauged its heft in his hands, held it to his shoulder and lined up the sight. It was unquestionably a fine weapon, but no, it was entirely too expensive. Come, come, said the trader, this little thing? And what was money for the Kambeymadas anyway? This was a mighty weapon, meant for a mighty marksman. Who more worthy than Kambeymada Machaiah, winner of no fewer than five shooting contests in his village although he was no more than – twenty? Twenty-one? Ah, this gun was destined for him, it was almost as if it had been made for him and him alone. Hold it close to your ear and you could almost hear the barrel thrumming his name.

Machu had laughed out loud at such blatant oiliness, but pleased by the flattery and carried away by the gleam of its barrel, he had bought the gun, quite forgetting even to bargain. It had lived up to its promise at the coconut-shooting contest earlier that week, just as he had known it would — a single shot, the coconut had exploded, and Machu had fortified his standing as one of the most redoubtable shots in the village.

It would be a good hunt today, he could feel it in his bones.

The party split up at a gently sloping hillock, the drummers and the dog bearers pushing on to skirt the base and a section of the forest beyond. The marksmen, meanwhile, spread out in a line around the summit, each man within sight of his neighbour to avoid being caught in the crossfire. They crouched silently in the damp grass waiting for the drums to start, chewing on the jaggery ottis that the women of the village had made especially for the hunt. Machu was stationed under a nandi tree, amidst a cluster of wild cardamom.

The trackers had chosen well, he thought, picking at a cardamom pod, crushing its seeds between his fingers and releasing their warm scent into the air. There was a natural clearing in the tree cover just beneath where he sat, offering him a prime view of any game that might head his way. He squinted up at the sun. Another fifteen minutes or so, he calculated, for the drummers to reach their positions. The morning drizzle had ended, revealing a clear, beautiful sky. He shifted restlessly in the grass, feeling the warmth of the sun drifting across his shoulders.

He glanced at the tree above him, scanning its branches for pythons. 'Nothing, thank Ayappa,' not that he had really expected any, but . . . and then he froze. He shut his eyes and slowly opened them again, but no, it was no mistake. He stood up and motioning to the tracker behind him, pointed silently at the tree. On its trunk, several feet above, were ten gouge marks.

A tiger had stood exactly here, not long ago, rearing up on its hind legs to sharpen its claws on the bark.

The tracker shook his head in wonder at the height of the marks, the span of the claws. The beast must be huge. He dropped on all fours, peering at the underbrush. 'It must have moved later this morning,' he whispered to Machu, 'we didn't see its spoor during our scout.' Machu's heart began to pound. A tiger. It had been years since a tiger was last hunted in Coorg. Ayappa Swami, let it come his way. A tiger, felled by his bullet, he would be a hero forever.

The drums started up, shattering the quiet, joined a moment later by the frenzied barking of the dogs. The jungle stirred. There was a rustling in the underbrush and the marksmen took aim. A wild dog shot out and then another, yelping in fright. The hunters lowered their guns and waited. There was a distant thundering of hooves, getting closer and closer, so loud now it almost drowned out the drums. The marksmen lifted their guns in anticipation, but just as suddenly the sound swerved off into the distance. The herd had wisely turned aside. The men cursed and spat into the grass, but Machu remained silent. He wasn't even watching the clearing, his eyes glued to the trees instead. A wild boar hurtled into sight. Machu saw his cousin take aim, out of the corner of his eye he saw the flash of gunpowder and heard the squeal of the boar as it fell. He noted with a strange detachment the men racing towards the animal to claim first privilege. The drums grew steadily louder but he stayed still. And then there it was.

A bone-jarring, spine-crushing roar, shocking the marksmen, silencing even the drums for a terrifying instant.

The jungle erupted. Animals scurried through the underbrush, monkeys gibbering in fright as they bounced up and down the vines. The drums started again, tentatively, as masses of parrots and mynahs burst from the trees, shrieking their warnings. Machu's pulse quickened. This was what he had been waiting for. *The tiger was on the move.* The birds were flying frantically away from the slope, which could only mean one thing: the tiger was headed directly towards the hunters. Let the beast be caught in his sights, 'Bless me Ayappa Swami, let it be my bullet alone that downs it.'

He raised the gun to his shoulder, staring into the jungle. The drums grew louder still. Another deafening roar, making the hairs stand up on Machu's neck, raising gooseflesh all along his forearms. And there it was, a liquid pour of orange and black, moving swiftly, gaining ground in vast leaps and bounds as it charged into the clearing.

'Praise be to you Ayappa,' was Machu's first thought. 'What a magnificent creature.' He dropped to one knee, the tiger firmly in his sights. 'Hold, hold, stay steady, NOW.' The gun coughed ineffectually, thudding against his shoulder. 'Son of a whore! Not now, don't fail me now.' He slammed back the breech and fired again. The bullet flew out of the gun this time, but the stuck breech had shifted the focus of the weapon. The bullet sped, off by a fraction of a millimetre, sailing left past the tiger's ear to slam into its shoulder instead. The beast stumbled, righted itself, then raced on. Machu knelt, frozen in horror. *He had missed.* Kambeymada Machaiah, ace shot of the village, had missed. They would whip his legs with thorned branches as penalty for missing his target, whip him like a rank amateur.

The drums filled his ears, or was it his heartbeat? He heard guns being reloaded all around him, saw a barrel being raised to his right. Another second and the tiger would pass by, be lost to him forever. 'AYY ...' he shouted, jumping to his feet and pounding after it. His odikathi was in his hand although he had no memory of sliding it from his cummerbund. He dashed down the slope, gravel flying under his feet. 'Son of a whore, where are you running, AYY.' The tiger whirled around to face him, eyes ablaze. 'What perfection,' Machu thought again. Time slowed. The jungle was a green blur, he was vaguely aware of the other hunters trying to take aim, but he was now in their crosshairs. It was only him and the big cat.

The wounded tiger crouched, muscles rippling beneath striped, massive shoulders. For an instant they stared straight at one another, man and beast. Machu was filled with a wild, primeval fury. The sky above, the ground below seeming to meld together as the blood rushed to his head. The past, the future, name, identity, all falling away unimportant, his energies, his very being locked in on one elemental equation: the hunter and the hunted.

The tiger roared again, deafeningly loud, and then, almost before he saw it move, it sprang. Machu moved with an ancient instinct, the blood of his ancestors in his veins, the veera singing in his ears. 'Swami Ayappa!' He leapt too, in that very instant, *towards* the cat, coming up just under its breast.

Massive paws, the size of his head. Long, pointed teeth, Swami Ayappa, he had not known they could be this long. Fetid, foul-smelling breath. Orange, such a vivid orange, the colour of the sun as it rose above the fields, smeared with the soot of the night. Clutching the rifle by its barrel, he smashed its butt upwards against the tiger's jaw. The beast swerved slightly in mid-air. Machu dropped to his knee,

41

unnoticing as it smashed into a rock. The tiger was going to fall on top of him. *Those claws*. His other hand rose, the same graceful motion with which he cored the colocasia creepers that sometimes clotted the fields. The sun, glinting from the blade of the odikathi, the fur, such a bright orange, of the tiger. Past skin, through flesh, his blade sinking deep. 'Mine!' Machu gasped, 'You are mine!' The warm gush of blood, the weight of the animal, pushing down on his blade. The splatter of putrid stomach juices across his face, those paws swinging towards him, and still he dug the odikathi in, deep, deep into the tiger's guts. *You are mine*. They crashed to the ground, the tiger falling across his chest.

The jungle came sharply into focus for an instant and then everything was dark.

The day after the tiger hunt, much to Devanna's consternation, Pallada Nayak paid a visit to the mission. He sailed into the classroom, oblivious to the Reverend's purse-lipped disapproval. 'Ayy Devanna, there you are monae,' the Nayak called cheerfully. 'Why are you sitting like a nervous mouse, at the edge of your chair, on only half your buttocks?'

The Nayak turned to the Reverend. He had come, he boomed, on behalf of Devanna's father to invite the Reverend to a very special celebration in the Kambeymada village. A nari mangala was going to be held there, for the first time in almost three decades. Since Devanna's presence was required, he would not be attending school for the remainder of the week. Offering no further explanation, the Nayak then whisked Devanna away.

When Devi returned home that evening, pouting because Devanna had been allowed to leave his classes in the middle of the day but not her, Thimmaya ruffled her hair, amused. 'How would you like to attend a tiger wedding?' he asked.

'Tigers get married? Where? How?' asked a startled Devi, all petulance forgotten. Thimmaya laughed, telling her she would have to see for herself, they were going to a tiger wedding in Devanna's village the next day.

'Tayi, did you hear, I am going to a tiger wedding!' Devi ran into the kitchen. 'A tiger wedding, a tiger is getting married and he has called me to his wedding.' Devi sang all that evening until an exasperated

42

Muthavva shouted at her to be silent. 'A tiger wedding . . .' Devi sang on sotto voce, 'what does she know, I am going to a tiger wedding . . .'

She was up before sunrise, needing none of the usual cajoling to get her out of bed. She wriggled impatiently as Muthavva braided her hair and lined her eyes with lampblack, leaning from the window to call out to the sleepy Poleyas who were hitching the oxen to the cart in the mist-filled courtyard below. 'Ayy, did you hear I am going to a tiger wedding? Tukra!' she yelled as she spotted the servant boy, 'Are you coming too?' Tukra dolefully shook his head. 'Oh . . . Well, don't you fret,' Devi called again, 'when I come back, I will tell you everything that happened, minute by minute.'

'Will you stop distracting the servants and let them finish their work?' Muthavva scolded. 'Stand straight or your plait will be all crooked.' Finally the cart was loaded, Tayi had finished her morning prayers and Thimmaya, the children and Tayi set off for the Kambeymada village. Devi pestered them with questions all the way. Why hadn't anyone told her about tiger weddings before? Did fish and birds get married too? Did the tigress have to wear a sari?

'You'll just have to wait and see,' her brother Chengappa said grinning, 'and you'd better be nice to the bride or she will eat you alive.'

Thimmaya smiled as he listened to the banter. It was good they had left early, they would be in the Kambeymada village by dusk. Some of these stretches were notorious for wild elephants and he did not want to risk an encounter. He let his fingers drift over his matchlock. They would be fine . . . and elephants or not, he would not have missed the tiger wedding for anything. When was the last time a tiger had been hunted in Coorg? Twenty years ago? Thirty? Even earlier?

They arrived at the Kambeymada village a little past sundown. The sky was a swollen, luscious purple, like an overripe jungle fruit, its skin rent here and there to reveal the first of the stars. The young men of the village stood at the entrance to the green welcoming the guests, and women flitted about like fireflies, filling and refilling the brass urns of water afloat with fragrant rosebuds and tulasi. Devi perfunctorily splashed some of this perfumed water over her face and hands as she searched excitedly for Devanna, but it was too crowded to see very far.

People thronged the green, the din of their voices rising above the lowing of the tethered oxen and the pounding drums. A large tent had been erected at the far side of the open space, auspiciously facing East. Rows of chairs and wooden benches were arranged before it, for those who were too old or too drunk to stand. A bonfire burned fiercely in the middle of the green, staving off the cold and the milky strands of fog floating through the air. The commissioner of police, Dr Jameson, the Reverend and a few prominent planters and their wives threaded through the crowd, their presence further testimony to the reach and influence of the Kambeymada clan.

The white sail of the tent billowed in the wind and Devi tugged impatiently at Thimmaya's hand. Smiling, he hoisted her onto his shoulders.

'There,' he said, 'there is your tiger.'

A log shifted in the fire, sending sparks shooting high into the night. Devi blinked. A colossal tiger glared through the smoke, frozen mid leap towards her. It hung suspended from the roof of the tent, its head held high with ropes, its legs splayed, its lips yanked into a rictus of a snarl. The stripes on its back gleamed in the firelight and the rest of its fur was orange, a fiery, burnished orange, the colour of the sampigé flowers that Muthavva liked to wear in her hair.

The music rose to a crescendo, the musicians beating their hide-covered kettledrums into a thunderclap of sound. Instinctively, the crowd parted. 'Look,' said Thimmaya, pointing. 'There is the bride-groom.'

The musicians were moving forward, making their way through the crowd towards the tent. The kettledrums settled into a steady beat as they began to sing.

> Be blessed and listen O friend, listen to this singer's song
> In the depths of these jungles, in this wild heartland
> A tiger roamed fiercely hungry all day, all night long
>
> Restless was the starving tiger, under a twisted tree it lay
> The fey moon had been and gone; no promises had it chanced upon
> Uneasy dozed the mighty tiger, in the fretful first light of day

44

A cheer went up through the crowd. The bridegroom was tall, taller than most of the men there. He moved with an easy grace behind the musicians, his best man almost on tiptoes as he reached an umbrella up high to shield the bridegroom from the damp.

Mortal men were on the prowl again, thus the tiger dreamt
With skill; with stealth; with guns; with arrows;
Their dogs hot upon its scent

It heard a barking and awoke startled. Looking all around
The tiger pricked its ears, its eyes ablaze
And then gnashed its fangs with a thunderous sound

The bridegroom's kupya was a ceremonial white, pure as milk, his cummerbund crimson worked over with gold. A square of red silk was draped over his gold spotted turban, its ends drifting down over his shoulders. He held a gun casually in one hand and a ceremonial walking stick in the other, festooned with silk tassels and tiny bells of silver and gold. Devi stared at him transfixed. Never, *not ever*, could she remember having seen anyone so beautiful.

He turned, laughing at someone in the crowd, and the gold studs in his ears glinted against skin the colour of teak.

'Today,' it reflected grimly, 'not one good omen have I found
Still, if the hunter should dare my path to cross
I shall rip him to pieces, I will fling him to the ground.'

'Today,' thought the tiger, sparks shooting from its eyes
'His gun shall be decorated or the wails of his bride be heard.
Today,' resolved the fearless tiger, 'today we shall decide.'

'But ... but ... I don't understand,' Devi said, bewildered, 'why is he marrying a tiger?'

Thimmaya tugged affectionately at his daughter's plait. 'It is only a mock wedding, kunyi, an ancient custom to honour someone who has slain a tiger.' The man she saw there was a great warrior, he told her, Kambeymada Machaiah. They were all gathered this evening to celebrate his victory and admire his kill.

The mighty tiger arose and roared, its mouth was open wide
As it came bravely snarling, roaring, bounding forward
To where the hunters stood waiting outside

The hero took aim, his bullet sped, it tore a tiny hole
The tiger stumbled, eyes ablaze; then it leaped towards the sky
It fell to the earth; with fire dimmed and dying breath, it gave up its
  noble soul

Devi slowly nodded, her eyes drinking in the pretend bridegroom.

When they went to the tent to congratulate Machu, for the first time in all her ten years, Devi found herself utterly and uncharacteristically tongue tied. Up close, he was even more fetching. He sat astride a squat, three-legged stool, his gun resting across his lap. A dimple flashed in and out of one cheek and when he glanced briefly at Devi, his eyes were a merry, sparkling brown. Thimmaya sprinkled rice over Machu's head and pressed a rupee into his hands. 'You have done us all proud, monae,' he said simply. 'A true son of Coorg.'

Machu bent to touch Thimmaya's feet. 'It is your blessings, anna,' he said and his voice seemed to Devi like honey gliding down the inside of her arm. She hid behind Thimmaya's back, quite forgetting even to look at the tiger.

'Are you tired kunyi?' Thimmaya asked anxiously later, as she clung to his hand in the crowds. 'Why are you so quiet? Shall we go find Tayi and ask the ladies to get you some dinner?'

Devanna came rushing up to them by the food hall, 'Devi! Here you are, I have been searching all over for you. Did you see the Reverend? He is here too. And the tiger, did you see the tiger? My cousin Machu killed it. My cousin! Did you meet him? Come on, you must meet him!'

'No, no . . .' Devi protested, but Devanna was already dragging her along. She swallowed against the sudden dryness in her throat and stole a shy glance at the bridegroom. The ladies of the village had walked through the gathering a little while before, bearing gongs and small brass pots filled with water; with dinner announced, the crowds around the tent had dispersed. Machu had arisen from his stool and was holding court, a group of giggling young lovelies hanging on his every word.

46

'Oh Machu,' they exclaimed breathily, hands pressed to their pert bosoms, 'tell us again how you brought down this beast?'

'Machu anna,' Devanna called from behind the brocaded bustle of their saris, 'this is my friend Devi.' Machu dimpled affably and waved. Devi felt her stomach slide. She forced a smile, peeling her lips back from her teeth. 'My father says that you …' she began brightly, and then halted mid-sentence. Machu had already turned back to the women.

'Machu anna,' Devanna called hopefully again, but Machu was too engrossed in recounting his tale to pay them any attention. 'Well, never mind,' Devanna said resignedly to Devi, 'at least you got to meet him.' He took Devi's arm and turned to leave. A sudden anger spurted within Devi and she shook herself free of his grasp.

'So you killed this tiger?' she demanded rudely. 'Why is everyone making such a fuss? It doesn't seem that dangerous to me.'

There was a collective squawk of outrage from the women. 'Just listen to the brat!' one of them exclaimed. 'Not dangerous?' exclaimed another. 'No, it isn't dangerous at all, hanging dead from the roof, but what would you do, I wonder, if you saw it coming at you in the jungle? Wet yourself, I should imagine!'

'I would not,' cried Devi indignantly. 'I … I am the bal battékara, I'm just as good as any hunter.' She knew how silly her words sounded even as they came out of her mouth; she could see Devanna gaping at her from the corner of her eye. 'Besides,' she continued in a sudden burst of inspiration, as she triumphantly crossed her arms, 'this tiger doesn't even have any claws.'

The women glanced at one another and then burst out laughing. A particularly tall girl bent down to Devi. 'It doesn't have any claws *kunyi*,' she said, deliberately emphasising the word, 'because it was declawed after Machaiah killed it. The claws have been removed to be fashioned into brooches and earrings for the Kambeymadas. Like this one.' She pointed to the brooch that lay curved upon her bosom, fastening her sari to the velvet blouse below. A crescent of a claw, the palest green tapering into ivory, stripped of all menace by its capping of gold.

Devi's cheeks grew hot with embarrassment. She opened her mouth to retort, but Machu stepped in before she could say anything. 'Leave it

47

be,' he said, dimpling at the women. 'My little friend here doesn't seem terribly impressed, but then we can't please everybody, can we?' He winked at Devi and she found herself grinning foolishly at him. 'Ayy Devanna,' Machu continued, 'is your friend always such a tigress?' The tall girl began to protest and he shook his head. 'Come now. Enough. She is but a child.'

Devi froze in horror, the smile wiped from her face. Had he just called her a *child*? Still chuckling, Machu turned to leave, shepherding his entourage.

The tent was now silent except for the tortured creaking of the bamboo frame as the dead tiger swung slowly above their heads. Devi bit her lip, close to tears. Beside her, Devanna took a deep, deliberate breath. 'Did your head suddenly turn inside out?' he asked. 'Why were you so rude?'

He had called her a *child*. She bent to pick up a jasmine bud that had fallen from the garland about Machu's neck.

'Devi, I am talking to you. What madness got hold of you that you had to be so rude?'

Devi closed her palm about the bud and whirled upon the startled Devanna. 'Just leave me alone! Why don't you go pester him instead, your newfound cousin and his group of clucking hens?' She rushed off, ignoring the hurt in Devanna's eyes. 'Where is my father, I want to go home.'

She slept fitfully that night, Tayi's breath whistling in her ears. She was withdrawn all through the journey the next day as well, unaware of the anxious glances from Tayi and the others. When the bullock cart finally turned into the courtyard of the Nachimanda house, to Muthavva's pleased surprise, Devi flung herself silently into her arms.

'What's this?' Muthavva murmured, kissing her daughter's head. 'Missed me did you?' Devi said nothing, but burrowed her head deeper into Muthavva's neck.

As Muthavva tucked her into bed that night, Devi asked, 'Avvaiah . . . when will I get married?'

Muthavva flicked her daughter's cheek affectionately. 'Why? Are you in such a hurry to leave your mother?'

'Don't make jokes Avvaiah. How long before I have my own wedding?'

'Well, let's see now. First, you have to be a good child and listen to your mother. And then when you come of age and are a graceful, well-mannered young woman, we will find you a boy from a good family and have a grand wedding for you, how is that?'

Devi shook her head impatiently. 'Avvaiah, I am not a little girl. And I will marry only Machu anna.'

'Who?' Muthavva asked, bewildered.

'The tiger killer ... Machu anna, Devanna's cousin. I will marry him.'

Muthavva laughed. 'Cheh. What foolishness is this? Little girls shouldn't talk this way, it doesn't become them. Besides, if you call him anna, that makes him your brother, not your husband.'

'Mark my words, Avvaiah. I will marry Machu.'

Muthavva gazed at her daughter's face in the lamplight and felt a strange chill down her spine. She became brisk. 'Donkey girl. Enough of this nonsense. Go to sleep.'

She tightened the amulet on Devi's arm, trying to stay her sense of disquiet by checking and rechecking the knots. Finally satisfied that the amulet was securely fastened, Muthavva lowered the lamp and, kissing Devi's forehead, left the room.

Behind her, Devi stared through the window into the clear, starlit night. Beneath the blanket, her fists were curled into little balls, her nails pressing into the skin. She thought again of the tiger wedding, and of the bridegroom.

'Only him,' she repeated to herself, 'I will marry only Machu.'

Chapter 5

❧ 1891 ❧

Sunlight streamed through the open doors, pooling over the maroon lacquered floors of the mission. Some time during the night, the skies had finally called a truce and the assault of the rains had abated. Mercara had awoken that morning to the forgotten sound of birdsong. Watery shafts of light spilled from behind dark grey clouds, laminating the town in opalescence. As the morning wore on, the sun had gained in confidence, scattering the clouds and blazing forth in all its splendour. All over the town, windows were flung open, mattresses thumped and aired, and damp clothes gathered from around charcoal braziers to be hung out to dry in the sun instead. Feuding neighbours called to one another like long-lost lovers, as their children skittered stones across the puddles in the road. Light danced from every surface, from within the raindrops suspended on a leaf, glancing off glass windows, diffusing from the hills in a shimmering haze.

Gundert stood on the verandah of his apartments, looking out at the dripping garden. He waved at passersby who called cheerfully to him, revelling in the everyday sounds so long suffocated by the rain. The potter calling out his wares, the trrringing of bicycle bells, the whooping of children, the excited barking of dogs as they shook themselves in the sun. He looked up at the skies and smiled. 'Devanna,' he called. 'Come here a moment.'

'Devanna,' he called again, a little louder this time. Frowning slightly, he went back indoors. Devanna sat by the window of the dining room, engrossed in his painting. The colours had to be just right, the mauve tinged with purple. *Cederela toona*. How beautiful the names sounded in Latin, how much more majestic the trees seemed to become when they were called thus, standing straighter and taller, puffing out their chests with pride. Why even the ordinary athi tree that Pallada Nayak cursed and spat at because of the way it extended its jumble of roots under the paddy fields, even that annoying tree carried poetry in its sap. *Cab-arium Stric-tum*.

When the Reverend had introduced him to botany, he had opened up a whole new world. Devanna liked to recite the names of the books in his head:

Flora Sylvatica, Flora Indica, Spicilegium Nilghirense, Leones Plantarum, Hortus Bengalensis, Hortus Calcuttensis, Prodromis Florae Peninsulae Indicae

The Reverend had shown him coloured plates and lithographs, the minute differences in serration that could mark a plant as an entirely new species. A keen amateur botanist, when he had first arrived in Mercara, Gundert had let it be known that he was looking for exotic plants and that he would pay a fair sum for anything that caught his fancy. At first, people had knocked on the mission doors at all hours with plants they were sure would excite him: fiercely coloured orchids, sweet-smelling sampigé and slender shoots of wild jasmine. Gundert politely had these planted in the mission garden, explaining that such plants were already well documented in the scientific world; what he wanted was something new, some of the indigenous medicinal plants perhaps?

They had brought him holy tulasi, so beloved by the ancestors and the Gods, and the delicately fronded narvisha that was planted in the courtyard of every home. The leaves of the narvisha had a pungent odour that was anathema to snakes, poisonous even to the mighty tiger, it was said. These too, Gundert had regretfully declined as mundane. They had then brought him that most powerful of plants, madh toppu or medicine green which, when cooked along with jaggery and coconut milk at the onset of the monsoons, stained their piss bright red and was known to prevent no fewer than forty-seven maladies. Gundert sighed.

Justicia Wynaadensis, he said, that was its name, and there were two specimens already growing in the Botanical Gardens in Bangalore. That was when most of the townspeople had thrown up their hands, shaking their heads over the obduracy of the Reverend. It was impossible to please him, they cried, it was hopeless. Gundert had finally resorted to field trips of his own, and in Devanna he found a gifted apprentice.

He taught Devanna the importance of discipline, the orderly mapping of an area, the close examination and recording of the tiniest detail. They combed through the hills in and around Mercara, sorting through armfuls of specimens and painstakingly documenting the most interesting. Devanna had a keen eye and a steady hand but more importantly, he had a natural instinct for the work. Gundert had been surprised and then awed by his talent. Devanna dipped and swirled his brushes, his usual diffidence banished by his confident use of colour.

As Gundert watched him replicate the specimens, applying a bold wash of green here, a dab of ochre, a hint of pink there, something had broken free deep within him. Spring, it seemed, had stolen softly into his iron-bound heart.

Here, at last, was the student he had searched for.

Here, his son.

He stood smiling in the doorway now, cupping his coffee and watching Devanna from the shadows. '*Sons are a heritage from the Lord, children a reward from him.*'

Devanna traced the outline of a bud with a firm hand, lost in his thoughts and still unaware of the Reverend's presence. *Cede-rela-toona.* Devi had little appetite for his fancy talk, as she called it. She shrugged her shoulders impatiently when he showed her the spores clinging pregnant with life to the underside of a fern or told her that the fig was not really a fruit but a flower. 'What does it matter!' she had exclaimed. What was in a name, figs tasted the same didn't they, whether you called them a fruit or a flower? Far more interesting, she had proclaimed, to know the histories of the trees instead, in the time before they were rooted to the ground, when they walked and talked with the Gods.

The butter tree so beloved to Krishna Swami who used its spoon-shaped leaves to steal butter from his mother's churn.

The pipal and the wild gooseberry, lovers through the ages. To grow two saplings side by side and throw them a wedding after they had matured brought immense luck.

The handsome Ashoka, the tree of no-sadness that banished all your woes if you sat beneath its branches and flowered only when a beautiful woman placed her henna tipped feet upon its trunk.

The agnichatra tree, of the glossy leaves and beckoning flowers that gave a person fever just by standing in its shade.

The gunflower groves that grew in the jungles of Coorg but withered away in captivity. They bloomed each year during the week of Kail-podh, the festival of arms. Just that one week in the entire year, an orange-yellow blossom to decorate the mouth of every cleaned and polished gun in Coorg and then they faded away as silently as they had appeared.

When Devanna had told her about the massive herbarium at Kew, home to the largest collection of specimens anywhere in the world, she had flicked her plait over her shoulder and told him not to bore her. 'Go away Devanna,' she had yawned. 'Leave me alone and stop chewing my brains.'

A shadow passed over Devanna's face as he worked. She had been increasingly strange with him, snapping for no reason and bursting into tears at the slightest pretext. 'Stop following me around,' she had told him angrily. 'Why can't you go hunting or climb trees or whatever it is that boys are supposed to do instead?'

She preferred to spend her time with the girls of the village instead, the very same girls she had found too sissy just a couple of years ago. Now, all she seemed to want to do was sit about whispering and giggling.

'You are growing up monae, you are both growing up,' Muthavva and Tayi had explained, trying not to smile when he wandered disconsolately into the kitchen. 'And Devi is older than you, nearly fourteen she is. Girls, they mature faster than boys, she has different interests now, that's all.'

He had pretended not to care and when the schools had closed for the monsoons and Gundert had suggested to Pallada Nayak that Devanna stay on at the mission for extra tutoring, Devanna had, much to everyone's surprise, agreed. Devi would realise how much she missed him when he was gone.

He glanced briefly out of the window. Twenty days he had been gone from the village, twenty days of never-ending, torrential rain. He had counted each day and waited patiently for a break in the clouds. And then this morning, Devanna had awoken in the mission dormitory, sleepily trying to put a finger on what was so different today. The silence, he realised abruptly, fully awake now and listening intently. The rattling of the rain on the roof was finally ended. Flinging off the blankets, not even noticing the cold draught nipping at his ankles, he had raced to open the window. Today, he could go home at last.

Cederela toona, he said to himself again now, returning to his painting. Two more washes of colour, he decided, and then he would ask the Reverend if he could leave.

He started in surprise as the Reverend placed an affectionate hand upon his shoulder. 'Did you not hear me calling you? It is good, very good,' said Gundert, peering at his work. 'Although, a little more definition here perhaps?' He pointed at the tip of a leaf. 'No matter,' he continued, 'enough documenting for today. Put away your brushes and come outside. There is such a rainbow, likely the largest the town has ever seen. We can pay a visit to the store as well, see what new surprises Hans has for us.'

The mission trading shop! Devanna hurriedly cleared away the pots of paint and put on his shoes. He headed outside, blinking owlishly in the sunshine. The Reverend was right. A huge rainbow hung in the pellucid air, arcing over the town, truly the largest that Devanna had ever seen. He turned impulsively towards the Reverend, pointing towards the rainbow. 'Tayi says it is Indra Swami taking out his bow.'

Gundert burst out laughing. 'Come Dev!' he exclaimed. 'Surely you do not believe that? It is only an optical illusion, yes? The sun reflecting the moisture in the air. Beautiful beyond any mortal creation, and *there* lies the divinity, the miracle of its creation. No bow though, and certainly no militant Rain God.'

Devanna flushed with embarrassment. Why had he opened his mouth? He often felt there were two parts to himself – Mission-Devanna and Coorg-Devanna. The Mission school half could paint, recite Wordsworth, make a perfect Sign of the Cross and knew all about reflection and refraction. He wore shoes at all times, even inside the Mission, the bows of his laces perfectly equal lengths.

Coorg-Devanna, on the other hand, knew of the other, not-so-obvious things. He knew of the veera, the spirits of ancient valiants who, shocked by their own violent deaths, now shadowed the living. He knew the sweetness of the nectar that pooled inside the lantana blossoms, had felt the heat of germinating paddy slush against his bare feet, the mud oozing from between his toes. He knew *full* well that, when displeased, Indra Swami threw thunderbolts from his palace in the heavens.

Devanna usually managed to keep each of these halves separate, each unquestioningly in its place, but every once in a while one would throw a leg over the stile to encroach into the other's territory. Like now. He nodded sheepishly at the Reverend, feeling foolish.

He soon cheered up at the trading store. 'Reverend!' roared Hans, the beefy proprietor, as they entered, startling the two Englishwomen inside. 'Wie gehts?' He bounded up to them and for a minute, it seemed as if he might actually envelop the Reverend in a bear hug.

Gundert took an involuntary step back and glanced at the women. 'Ah Hans,' he replied in his clipped accent. 'I am well, thank you for asking, and you?'

He raised his hat at the ladies and they smiled.

'Reverend. We haven't seen you at the club in a while, has the mission been keeping you busy?'

'Too busy!' intervened Hans. 'Our Reverend, the only things he is to be good for is the books. No ladies or the wine for him. Doesn't needs them, not like the rest of us who needs them always in this always raining land.' He burst into laughter, oblivious to the scandalised expressions of the women.

'Look,' he continued affably, raising his trousers to expose red, scabby shins. 'I am itching so much in these bloody rains.'

'You should let Doctor Jameson take a look at that Hans,' Gundert said, bending down to examine his sores. 'Or come to the mission and I will have someone mix you something from the dispensary. Here, why don't I examine you at the back.'

'Ladies ...' Gundert bowed courteously and propelled Hans away from the women. 'Oh don't worry Reverend,' Hans was saying

55

cheerfully as they disappeared into the innards of the store. 'Doctor Jameson will be treating me, no problem. I have a case of the Pimms ordered for him.'

The women paid for their goods and exited with a huff. Devanna grinned as their indignant voices floated down the street. Really the things they had to put up with. The man was such an oaf. At least his prices were reasonable, that was the benefit, they supposed, of being licensed by the Mission. Still, they could hardly wait for Spencer's to open a store here in Mercara . . .

He took a deep breath, inhaling the scents of lavender and polish that always seemed to hang about the store. He did love coming here. The pyramid piles of porcelain lamps, the Noah's arks carved from wood, the fishing tackles hung from the rafters, the stacks of leather-bound books with their gold lettering. Devanna wandered idly about the store, trailing his fingertips across the rocking chairs and stout writing bureaus, then stopped abruptly by the cabinet. Hans had a new jar of boiled sweets.

It had been the Reverend who had introduced Devanna to their sugary-tart pleasures, presenting him with a sweet each time he was especially pleased by his pupil's progress. Devanna's mouth watered now as he gazed longingly at the jar. Devi loved them too. Once when the Reverend had seen Devanna tuck a sweet away in his pocket, he had asked Devanna why he did not eat it immediately. 'Is it not to your liking? Would you prefer something else?' He had frowned slightly when Devanna explained he was saving it for Devi. 'Here, I will get your friend another one. But this is for you, yes?'

Since then, Devanna had immediately popped them into his mouth, in order to please the Reverend. He saved the wrappers though, and when the Reverend's back was turned, he would spit the sweets into his palm and carefully rewrap them for Devi. He pressed his nose hopefully against the glass front of the cabinet, examining the metallic coloured wrappers. Sherbet lemons. Pear drops. Rhubarb and custard. And there, at the very back of the box, shiny aniseed twists . . . maybe the Reverend would buy him one today?

The Reverend and Hans returned from the back of the shop and Hans guffawed. 'Dev. Seen the sweets have you?' he boomed. 'Have you watered all over my nice clean glass?' Devanna hastily withdrew his head, wiping at the cabinet.

'Salivated, Hans, not watered,' the Reverend corrected him, smiling. 'Leave Dev be, and here, give us a rupee's worth.'

Devanna's eyes widened. A whole rupee? Why, coupled with the sweets he had been saving all these past days at the Mission, that was sixteen, no *eighteen* sweets. He watched open mouthed as Hans opened the cabinet and poured a rainbow blur of sweets into a bag. 'Go on, take it,' said Gundert, smiling as he pushed the bag towards him. 'You have been a most diligent student.'

'Th ... thank you Reverend,' said Devanna, quite overwhelmed. 'Reverend,' he continued in a rush, 'may I go home today?'

Gundert nodded. 'Yes, it has been quite some weeks since you were at your home. Besides I have a matter for discussion with Pallada Nayak. Leave this afternoon, and take him a letter from me.'

Devanna slipped off his shoes as soon as he was out of sight of the Mission, tying the laces together and slinging them over his shoulder. Hugging the bag of sweets to himself, he raced barefoot down the trail. The look on Devi's face when he showed her the sweets. How she would beam! They would sit together on the verandah and work through the bag. He'd listen as she chattered away, her hands dancing in the air as she told him all that had happened these past weeks ... Devanna hurried along, happily dreaming, and was at the Nachimanda house by late afternoon.

'Devi!' he called out, his stomach rumbling at the thought of the hot rice that Tayi would heap on his plate, the fried mutton that she would insist he polished off. 'Devi, Tayi!' he called again, patting the dogs that whined at him from their ropes, but the house was surprisingly silent.

'Devi!' he yelled, as he placed his shoes under the bench on the verandah. 'For goodness sake, where ... Oh,' Devanna said as Chengappa appeared on the verandah.

'Ayy Devanna, it is you,' he said heavily. 'Come in, but be quiet, the vaidya is here.'

The vaidya! Tayi talked often of the medicine man and his powerful magic tantras. He belonged to a tribe from somewhere beyond the hills. For centuries now he and his kinsmen had roamed freely about Coorg, bestowing their healing magic upon those who needed it most. The vaidya was not someone who would be summoned lightly, Devanna remembered with a pang of misgiving, so why was he here?

Hurriedly washing his feet, Devanna went inside. The family was gathered silently outside the central bedroom, the one where Thimmaya and Muthavva slept. Wriggling his way to the door, Devanna saw Devi. She stood at the foot of the bed, pale as a ghost. The vaidya, wire haired and bare chested, his body covered in markings of grey and white ash, was leaning over someone in the bed. He shifted position for an instant, and Devanna caught a glimpse of the patient. Muthavva, he realised, with alarm, it was she the vaidya was here for.

Muthavva lay twitching under the blankets, muttering incomprehensibly. The family watched anxiously as the vaidya took her wrists in his hands to feel her pulse. He frowned slightly and shook his head. Thimmaya's face fell.

'It is not good,' said the vaidya, lifting Muthavva's eyelids to peer into her eyes. 'Not good. The pisachi who has possessed her is strong and may not leave willingly. Still, I will try.' Pulling a length of white thread from the spools wound about his arm, he cut off a length with his teeth. Chanting mantras, he began to tie knots in the thread, one knot for every verse of prayer. On and on he chanted, his voice drowning out Muthavva's mutterings, not a sound from the watching family as slowly the thread began to fill with knots. Finally, when the last knot was done, the vaidya fastened his thread of prayers about Muthavva's arm. Muttering yet another prayer, he then smeared ash thickly over her forehead.

The crowd outside the door parted as he came out with Thimmaya. 'Sacrifice a black fowl,' he told Thimmaya, 'that might appease the spirit. But I have done all I can. No, no payment,' he snapped as Thimmaya tried to thrust some rupees into his hands, 'the power of the mantras is gone if it is sullied with money.'

He finally agreed, grudgingly, to a parcel of puffed rice. Devanna went up to Tayi as she was tying the bundle together. 'Tayi, what happened?'

Tayi looked grey and worn. 'Oh Devanna, have you come? Does Devi know? Are you well monae?'

'Yes Tayi, but what happened to Muthavva akka?'

'The pisachi . . .' Tayi said tiredly. 'They have possessed her for the past week and refuse to leave. The fever grew worse yesterday. Here, take this bundle to Thimmaya anna.'

Devanna carried the bundle over to where Thimmaya was sitting with the vaidya. 'Should we . . .' he said hesitantly to Thimmaya, glancing nervously at the vaidya, 'should we . . . maybe call for the doctor from Mercara?' The vaidya snapped his neck around and trained red-rimmed eyes upon Devanna.

'Doctor? Is there a doctor alive who can do what I can?' he rasped. 'Can they make the spirits dance, these doctors, can they bind them helplessly into knots? Can they summon demi-Gods from the heavens and demons from the netherworld to do their bidding? Do they teach them to do that in the lands across the seas? You mark my words,' he spat angrily as he turned towards Thimmaya, 'call a doctor if you want but he can do nothing I cannot and not half the things I can.'

'Of course we will not, do not worry O learned one,' said Thimmaya hastily. 'We are not calling anyone else. Please,' he placated, 'please do not take away the protection of your prayers.'

'We tried monae,' he said wearily to Devanna after the vaidya had gone. 'We sent word for Jameson doctor, but he refuses to come. It is too far, he says, the trail too slippery from the rains for his horses. So walk, why cannot that son of a whore walk?'

Devanna's face fell for an instant but then he tugged urgently at Thimmaya's hand. 'What about the Reverend? He knows much medicine. He will come, I am sure of it. He will know what to do.'

Thimmaya lifted his head proudly. 'No,' he said. 'I will not ask one of them again and be refused. We have done all we can. May Iguthappa Swami and our ancestors protect us now.'

'Quiet,' he said, as Devanna opened his mouth again. 'I will hear no more of this.'

The evening wore on and then the night, and the moans from the bedroom grew louder. A black hen was killed with a swift twist to its neck and the carcass thrown on the rubbish heap. Tayi burnt red chillies and mustard seeds over burning coals, fanning the acrid smoke into the far corners of the house to exorcise the evil eye, but Muthavva continued to thrash and weep.

Devi too turned on Devanna when he tried to reason with her. 'Reverend, Reverend, Reverend. Is that all you can say? Did you not hear the vaidya?' she shouted at him. 'Do you want him to remove his protection? Just because your mother is dead and gone, do you want my Avvaiah to be gone too?' Tayi shushed her, clicking her tongue, *cheh*, was this any way to talk? Devi burst into tears. 'Avvaiah,' she sobbed, 'Avvaiah,' crying so hard that even Tayi started to weep. Devanna gave up.

'It is God's will,' he repeated to himself. 'There is nothing more we can do, it is his will.'

The Reverend could help, he *knew* he could.

The next morning, Muthavva was worse. The thread the vaidya had tied kept slipping down her sweaty arms. She had stopped moaning now and was almost in a stupor, her eyes glazed as she muttered softly to herself. Devanna could bear no more. He went to Tayi in the kitchen. Hastily wiping her eyes with the edge of her sari, she tried to smile. 'What do you want monae? Are you hungry?'

'Tayi, please, at least you listen to me. Send someone to the Reverend, he will know what to do. Please Tayi, I know he will come.'

Tayi was silent, and then rising to her feet, she went to find Thimmaya. 'Send someone to the Mission,' she told her son. 'Be quiet,' she said, stalling his remonstrations. 'This is no time for pride. If the head is saved today, the turban might yet be tied tomorrow. Call for the Reverend. As for the vaidya, whatever misfortune may befall this house from his curses, Iguthappa Swami, let it fall upon my head. But send for the Reverend, do it for my sake.'

The Reverend left as soon as he received the summons, and arrived soaked in the drizzle that had started again that afternoon. He fired questions at Thimmaya as he removed his shoes on the verandah. How long? What were the symptoms? Why hadn't they called Dr Jameson? His lips tightened as he heard how Jameson had refused to come. 'You should have called me earlier,' he said, glancing briefly at Devanna who flushed and bent his head.

'This is no work of spirits,' he said, cutting short Thimmaya's explanations as he examined Muthavva. 'We have to act quickly, bring me some sugar water.'

Tayi hastily dissolved a lump of jaggery and brought the treacly syrup to Gundert. He poured a vial of powder into it, and cradling Muthavva's head, tipped the contents slowly down her throat. He held her mouth closed as she gagged and when she had downed the entire contents, he spoke with Thimmaya. 'I have given her a strong medicine,' he said, 'and it should stay the fever for some time at least. She will likely have a ringing sensation in her head and complain of giddiness, but then she will sleep.' He sighed as he held out another vial of the powder. 'Give this to her tomorrow morning. I do not know as yet if she will be cured; the fever is in an advanced stage.'

Thimmaya sent Chengappa armed with matchlocks and a servant with bamboo torches to escort the Reverend back to Mercara. In the Nachimanda house, they settled down to wait.

Devi leaned against Thimmaya, gripping his kupya tightly with her fingers. Devanna watched as Thimmaya stroked her hair, assuring her over and over that all would be well. She raised her tear-streaked face to her father's. She whispered something and he hugged her tightly and he shook his head. 'No *kunyi*, don't talk like that. All will be well . . .'

Devanna rubbed his hands furiously across his face, trying not to cry. If only there was something he could do. Then he remembered the sweets in his pocket from the previous afternoon. Nobody noticed as Devanna slipped quietly out to the verandah. Rain was slashing down again, a malodorous damp hovering over the dogs that clustered about him, tails wagging eagerly as they sniffed at his pocket. Clasping his hands together Devanna bent his head. 'Our Lord in Heaven,' he prayed. 'Let Muthavva akka be well. Be merciful upon Devi, do not . . . do not . . . please let her mother live. Do this one thing for me, and I . . . I promise I will never eat a single sweet again. Promise. Not as long as I live.' Devanna opened the mouth of the bag and his precious hoard of sweets scattered about the verandah, rainbow coloured, glinting in the dim light as the dogs fell upon them.

Inside the house, Muthavva thrashed and moaned, her ears were filled with sound, make it stop, she begged Thimmaya. She shivered and shook, the sweat from her body soaking the sheets until, without warning, she fell into a deep, peaceful sleep. 'It must be working,' Tayi whispered to her son when she came in to check on the patient. 'Iguthappa be praised, the medicine is working.'

Muthavva awoke as the cockerels were calling out the dawn. She turned to Thimmaya, her forehead cool to his touch. 'I am scared,' she said, perfectly lucid.

And then Muthavva died.

Devanna sat miserably through the death rites, unable even to look at Devi. Why hadn't he made them listen to him? If only the Reverend had been called sooner. If only he had known what to do. 'Never again,' he vowed to himself. 'Never again will I be so helpless.'

When he finally went to the Pallada house after the funeral, Devanna gave the Nayak the letter from Gundert. In it, the Reverend had written of his plans to expand the attendance in the school by starting a hostel. It might make sense for Devanna to enrol as a boarder in the coming year, he wrote, he was an exemplary student and living at the mission would eliminate all the time spent walking back and forth from the village.

After mulling it over for some days, the Nayak pronounced it an excellent idea. To everyone's astonishment, Devanna quietly agreed, even when he learnt that Devi would not be going back to school because the housework was too much for Tayi and Chengappa's new wife to manage alone. He did not go to the Nachimanda house for the remainder of that monsoon, not until the day before he was due to go back to school. Tayi came quietly out and hugged him to her. 'Where have you been monae?' she asked. 'Have you forgotten us? Devi, look who has come to see us.'

They went down to the fields, by the stream.

'Did you hear I am not coming back to school?' she asked.

Devanna nodded. Devi dipped her hand into the water. 'Do you remember how many crabs we caught that day?'

'Can I forget? They kept coming and coming, we could do no wrong it seemed. We counted them all. Thirty-three we caught, in that single afternoon . . . and Tayi made so much crab chutney . . .'

'Yes, and you stuffed your face till you vomited in the bushes,' Devi said wanly. They sat silently for a while, dangling their legs in the stream.

'Devi, I am really sorry,' he said in a rush. 'I wish . . . I . . . I should have spoken up sooner. Maybe . . . the Reverend, had he come earlier . . .'

Devi blanched and her eyes filled with tears. She dashed them away with the back of her hand. 'No . . .' she said, shakily, 'it was not your fault.'

Devanna looked at her grief-stricken face, and his guilt, the misery of the past weeks, all came bubbling to the surface. He began to cry. 'I am sorry,' he said, 'Devi, I am so sorry.'

'Silly fellow!' Devi said, wiping furiously at her eyes. 'Always talking nonsense. Avvaiah, she . . . she . . .' Devi swallowed, unable to complete her sentence. She reached for Devanna's hand, clasping it tightly in her own. 'Here,' she said finally, her face drawn, but trying bravely to smile, 'I have an idea. Untie this.' She rolled up her sleeve, and pointed at the amulet that Muthavva had tied and retied on her over the years, extending the faded black thread as Devi grew. The metal plaque was battered and worn, its Sanskrit inscription rendered almost invisible. Devanna untied it, struggling with the knots.

'Avvaiah tied this on me when I was a baby. For good luck, she told me. Here.' Placing it in Devanna's palm, she folded his fingers over the amulet.

'I can't take this. It was meant for you.'

'And I am giving it to you.' Devi smiled tremulously. 'I don't need it any more,' she said, rubbing her arm where the amulet had imprinted itself on her skin over the years, verse inverse. 'Avvaiah is there in the clouds with my other ancestors, watching over me.'

They tilted back their heads, gazing at the clouds as they shifted and chased each other in translucent puffs across the glassy sky. There was a hooked nose, there, the shape of a man's ear. And if you looked hard enough, there, right there, you could almost see the back of a woman's head, weighted down with a bunch of sampigé flowers.

High above them, a solitary heron floated on a thermal, lazily dipping and rising in the breeze.

Chapter 6

'Quinine,' Gundert said in response to Devanna's question. 'It was powdered quinine. An alkaloid extracted from the cinchona tree. *Cinchona Succirubra.*' Pulling out a slim volume from the bookshelf by his desk, he opened it to a page, its margins covered with notes in his small, meticulous handwriting. 'Right here,' Gundert said, gently tapping the yellowed paper. 'How to economically extract quinine from cinchona bark. Public knowledge for the very first time, thanks to the largesse of the Government Quinologist in Bengal. Here, read it aloud.'

'*The Calcutta Gazette.*' Gundert had scattered bits of neem leaf through the periodical, to keep the silver fish at bay; naphthalene would have burned through the thin paper. 'An oil process for the manufacture of . . . sul . . . sulphate of quin . . . quinine, sulphate of quinine, by C.H. Woods, Quin . . . Quino . . . Quino-lo-gist of the Government of Bengal.' Devanna painstakingly began to read the article aloud, stumbling over the unfamiliar words and strings of complicated equations. It was his privilege, Woods wrote, to detail for the first time in known history a practical and commercially viable method for extracting quinine using an oil-based solvent of fusel oil and petroleum. '*The alkaloids are extracted from tile bark in a much greater state of purity, so that the final operations for obtaining pure and finished products are much simplified. The whole process of extraction can be performed at common temperatures and the apparatus and appliances required are of a readily available nature . . .*'

Devanna stopped reading mid-sentence, inexplicably furious. 'I don't understand this,' he cried. 'None of this makes any sense. I . . . I . . .' He paused in frustration, stabbing his finger at the pages.

Gundert said nothing, just crossed his arms and looked at him. Devanna stared back defiantly then, cheeks red, looked away.

'It was not your fault,' Gundert said quietly. Devanna's face twisted, but he remained silent. 'Listen to me Dev,' Gundert continued. 'There is nothing you could have done. Maybe if Dr Jameson had been able to see her, or if I had got there sooner ... but even so, who is to say that the quinine would have taken effect, yes? She was very far gone.'

Devanna swallowed, still not looking at the Reverend. 'They say the vaidya cursed her after you came,' he said in a small voice.

The Reverend sighed and shook his head. 'It was no work of demons or curses. Only a tiny mosquito, minuscule in size but lethal in its poison. Malaria, Dev, it was a disease called malaria.'

He came around the desk and took the paper from Devanna's hands. 'Quinine ... You see here? On this page, a cure for *millions*. All we need is for people to *learn*, to know how to use these drugs, to know all there is to know about modern medicine.'

The silence stretched between them. Gundert leaned against the desk, watching his boy. 'All that is needed,' he repeated, 'is for someone to learn.'

'I want to learn,' Devanna said, his words tumbling over one another. 'Teach me how to make this quinine, teach me all the medicine you know. Please Reverend, I will do whatever you ask, I will study as hard as anyone can, but I *have* to learn.'

'The old order changeth, yielding to new, and God fulfils himself in many ways,' Gundert softly quoted. 'The Lord sent you to me for a reason Devanna. You are the one He has chosen to bring this mission and our cause into the next century. I will teach you all I know, I promise, and when you have surpassed me – as you will – use your knowledge for the betterment of your people.'

Some days later, Gundert called Devanna into his study. 'I wish to share something with you,' he said. 'Something of great value to me, and which I think you might enjoy.' Devanna watched curiously as the Reverend took a key from about his neck and unlocked a drawer in his writing bureau.

'You remember how we talked about the difficulty in classifying the various species of bamboo?'

Devanna nodded again. The problem was that all species of bamboo looked essentially the same until they flowered. And when they did flower, it was with maddening infrequency, being rendered with a pollination cycle that occurred only once every thirty years or so on average, fifty or sixty in some of the more recalcitrant species. There were probably *dozens* of species waiting to be discovered in the jungles of India, Java and Sumatra.

Gundert took from the drawer a compact package of white silk and placed it carefully upon the desk. When he had first arrived in Coorg, he explained, he had held high hopes of discovering one such species, hitherto unclassified, blooming in the wild. The locals had shaken their heads when he asked them – the bamboo groves had seeded two years ago, they told him, flowered en masse and then died soon after, as was their wont. It would be at least another fifty years before the seedlings they had left in their wake matured. Still, Gundert had not given up hope. Surely there must be plants that did not follow this general time cycle, at least one clump of bamboo somewhere in the jungles or in the hills perhaps, that was due to flower shortly. The months had passed however, and when he had neither found nor heard anything that would suggest the existence of such a bamboo, Gundert had reluctantly rec-onciled himself to the fact that perhaps it would indeed be another five or six decades before a new species could be identified and established beyond doubt.

Then early one morning, a man was found collapsed in front of the mission gates, burning with fever. Gundert had rushed to examine him and realised from the hide around the stranger's waist and the necklace of tiny bird bones he wore that he was a Korama tribal. He had heard of the reclusive tribe who lived deep within the jungle, quite unlike the docile Poleyas in their distaste for civilisation.

Devanna nodded intently. He had seen the Koramas too, they sur-faced occasionally in the villages selling hollowed-out gourds filled with tiger blood or peacock fat. The children were warned to keep away from them – unprepossessing though they were in size, the Koramas had an uncertain temper and bore quivers filled with poison-tipped arrows. When the moon was high, sometimes their drums could be heard faintly resounding from deep within the jungles.

Gundert had carefully removed the black tipped arrows from the Korama's quiver and, calling to the mission staff, had had him moved into the infirmary. He had treated the Korama for his fever and it was remarkable how quickly the man's body responded to the most basic medical intervention. Gundert paused and glanced at Devanna. 'I made him sweat out the fever,' he explained. 'I had the staff rub salt on the soles of the feet and then covered him with as many blankets as we could spare. If that had not worked, I planned to phlebotomise him, but as it turned out, we had no need of leeches.'

When Gundert was notified the next morning that the Korama was awake, he had asked his usual question: Did the Korama know of any unusual plants that might be of interest to him?

The man had stared at Gundert with deadened eyes. Yes, he had finally responded, there was such a plant, the most special in all the forests, blooming but once every man life. Groves of it were flowering now, and he would get one of the plants for Gundert. He had left the mission that same afternoon, fully cured.

Gundert had not been especially hopeful of his return. He was uncertain if the Korama had even understood what he had asked for. Indeed, he had all but forgotten about him when one morning, one of the novices came to Gundert, gingerly bearing a package. It was a monkey's hide, she told him, her nose wrinkling in distaste. It had been left that morning on the doorstep of the mission.

The Korama! Gundert unfolded the hide and found a container of roughly woven leaves. Tucked away within it ... Gundert glanced at Devanna's rapt face. 'It was large, the circumference of both my palms held together, with a certain waxiness to its petals. It was a perfect specimen, the dew still glistening from its pistil, and with such a fragrance. Sweeter than a rose, richer than jasmine, with the musky underpinnings of an orchid. It perfumed the corridors of the mission for days.'

'The bamboo flower!' Devanna exclaimed triumphantly.

'Yes, the bamboo flower, just as the Korama had promised.' Gundert sighed and began to unwrap the white silk. 'Unfortunately the Korama himself was nowhere to be seen. Eventually, the flower withered away.

Without the mother plant, there was no type to prepare, no specimen to send to the botanical gardens in Bangalore or perhaps even to England.'

Devanna gazed fascinated at the dried flower that the Reverend had uncovered. It was as large as a book. He imagined he could still smell a trace of the perfume that Gundert had alluded to, a heady fragrance just tickling his nose.

He was still hopeful, Gundert was saying. A flowering bamboo existed, somewhere out there, just waiting to be discovered. 'Maybe you, Devanna,' he said, 'are the one who will help me find it.'

Devanna slowly nodded. 'What will you name it, Reverend?' he asked.

Gundert smiled as he carefully packed the flower away. '*Bambusea Indica Olafsen,*' he said simply.

After his friend in the calotype. Devanna was silent for a while, and then he asked, 'But what if I find it first?'

The Reverend laughed and patted his shoulder. 'Well, you will be a good student of course and bring it to me, won't you?' He folded the silk, still chuckling, and placed it back into the drawer.

'I will find it,' Devanna silently promised himself, his lip jutting out in determination. 'And when I do, it shall be named for her and her alone. *Bambusea Indica Devi.*'

Chapter 7

☙ 1896 ❧

Mopping her face with the edge of her sari, Devi lifted the iron blow pipe and blew into the flames. Heat bounced off the pot of oil bubbling on the fire, reeds of blue smoke spiralling from its surface. Devi passed her hands over the pot and heat hammered against her open palms. Grabbing a twist of rag in one hand and wrapping the end of her sari about the other, she hefted the pot off the fire and through the open doors of the kitchen into the courtyard.

A vat of bitter limes lay waiting outside. She had picked the limes herself, from the two trees that Muthavva had planted years ago by the vegetable patch. The limes had been quartered and tossed with salt, chilli powder, sugar and green peppercorns and then put to cure in the sun a week ago. They had lain there, curling slowly about themselves as the moisture was wrung from their skins, the spices working their way into the rinds. Untying the cheesecloth that covered the wooden mouth of the vat, Devi tipped the smoking oil into its belly. The desiccating limes stretched luxuriously in the hot oil, softening and expanding, a rich braid of smoke and citrus rising from the vat to curl about the courtyard.

As it cooled, she dipped a finger into the pickle and raised it to her mouth. Salty, sweet, lip-puckeringly perfect. Tayi would have to admit that this time Devi had outdone even her.

'Ehhh kunyi. Is this what I have taught you, to stick your inji fingers

70

into the pot? Must we all share the pleasure of your spit?'

Tayi billowed forth from the house. Devi sat back on her haunches and grinned up at her mischievously. 'My sweet-tempered Tayi, I was only tasting it, that's all. First taste, I promise. Would I risk your wrath by going in a second time with my inji, spit-coated fingers?'

'Yes, you would,' said Tayi shortly. 'Don't try to charm me now, I am not your father, dancing to your every tune. Get the pickle indoors, it needs to cool completely before it is stored away.'

'What Tayi, why do you make so much anger? Here, taste this and tell me if it isn't the best pickle you have ever had.' Devi dipped the ladle into the pickle and pulling on Tayi's hand, dropped a piece of lime on to her palm. Tayi tasted it, still annoyed.

'It's all right . . . not bad,' she admitted grudgingly.

'Not bad!' Rising to her feet in one fluid, graceful movement, Devi flung her arms about the old lady. 'Come on Tayi, you know your flower bud has outdone herself this time. Come on, say it, say it or I will tickle you! Your flower bud has made the best pickle in the whole world, say it, your sun and moon is the best, *your* sun and moon . . .'

Tayi tried to hide her smile. 'Cheh. What mad behaviour is this? Fully eighteen years old, a grown woman now and still you behave like a silly little girl.' She tugged at Devi's arms. 'Come now, I have a lot of work to do. Stop hugging me like a bear and bring in the pickle. And go see to Tukra – make sure he trusses the chickens properly.'

Devi shook her head fondly as Tayi bustled back to the kitchen. Poor Tayi. Didn't she know better than to take what the village gossips said to heart? Yet another marriage proposal had come for Devi last week. Thimmaya, as was his wont, had asked his daughter her opinion. 'No,' she had said at once, and he had politely turned it down.

News had got round the village, and the women had tut-tutted. Poor girl, they said piously, yet another suitor spurned. Why wouldn't her father allow her to get married? Was he so short of help that he should keep his daughter chained to his hearth? Although really, what did anyone expect? A child without a mother was left bereft at the mercy of the father, they sighed. A girl without a mother, like a crop with no rain.

Devi had grown used to their tongues, they didn't slice into her like

71

they once did, but then she had had over four years since her mother's passing in which to grow a thicker skin. She stirred the pickle angrily, splattering some of it into the mud. Good for nothing gossips. She had told them off at first, telling them to mind their own business, that they knew nothing of her private affairs. 'Cheh,' the women clucked, 'see how this chit of a girl talks back to us. Then again, what can we expect when there is no mother to teach her any better.'

Over time, she had learnt it was better to ignore them, or at least to hold her head high and shrug her shoulders, pretend that what they said was of no import to her. Their barbs slid off her now, like rainwater slip-sliding from the leaves of the colocasia plant. Still, their comments wounded Tayi deeply. They shielded Thimmaya from the worst of it, Tayi and she, but nevertheless, poor Tayi still bristled and wept. Were they dead too, she lamented to Thimmaya, did they not have Devi's best interests at heart?

'Leave it be Avvaiah,' Thimmaya would say tiredly, 'let barking dogs bark, why do you let them get to you?'

They had advised Thimmaya to get married again, these self-proclaimed well-wishers, there was a widow in the neighbouring village who would suit him well they suggested. Thimmaya had refused. He was too old he told them, all he wanted now was to see his children settled. Ah, they had exclaimed, at least there Iguthappa had favoured him. Devi was growing up to be an undoubted beauty, any man would be lucky to call her his wife. They had helpfully inundated the Nachimanda house with proposals, offering up their sons and brothers, their nephews, cousins and cousins' cousins. Each time, Thimmaya had turned first to Devi and sought her opinion on the proposed match. Each time, Devi had tossed her head and turned the proposals down.

This past week, Tayi had, spurred on by the women, hit upon a new scheme. 'Take her with you to Tala Kaveri,' she urged Thimmaya. 'Take Devi to the festival.'

Yet again it was time for the Goddess Kaveri to visit Coorg. Every year, when the rains had ended and the fields were tinged with gold, when fireflies flickered in darkening courtyards and the air was like velvet, when the stars hung so low that the constellation of the seven sages was clearly visible, glittering in the night sky, Kaveri, Mother

Goddess, life-giver, river most sacred to the Coorgs, visited the temple tank at the top of the Bhagamandala mountain. In exactly the second week of October, at a time precisely calculated by the priests from the movement of the planets and the angle of the sun, she burst forth like clockwork into the temple tank.

It was customary for the Coorgs to send at least two members of every household to welcome the Goddess. They trekked to Tala Kaveri from every corner of the land, alongside scores of devotees from as far as Mysore, Canara and Kerala. Young and old, the healthy and the infirm, rich men being carted fatly along by bullocks and horses, beggars hunched over their bowls, bald priests and shaven-headed Brahmin widows, all united briefly in their quest to witness the miracle of Kaveri's rebirth and to seek her blessings.

Being a practical minded race, the Coorgs had long realised the other potential of the festival – that of a vast and convenient meeting ground for the marriageable to see and be seen. The festival was full of anxious mothers chaperoning their nubile young daughters. Knots of flower plaited girls glanced from under lowered eyelashes at the scores of young bachelors cockily strutting through the temple grounds. Many a marriage had been speedily arranged from a meeting at the festival and Devi had realised full well just why Tayi wanted her to go. If her knotty, arthritic legs had permitted, Tayi might have dragged Devi there herself.

'Will you come, kunyi?' Thimmaya had asked last week.

'No,' Devi had replied simply.

Tayi looked daggers at her son. 'Maybe you should,' he pressed Devi. 'I have to find you a good husband soon, so many boys come to the festival . . .'

Devi pouted prettily. 'Are you in such a hurry to see me leave then, Appaiah?'

'No, of course not, it's OK, it's OK,' Thimmaya said, glancing helplessly at his exasperated mother.

Devi turned pensive as she hauled the pickle onto the ledge of the verandah. Even her father was growing impatient with her, she could tell. How long would she be permitted to turn down the proposals? Calling out to Tukra, she made her way around the side of the house to the hen coop.

She sighed as she bent over the squawking chickens. 'Cheh Tukra. This string is nowhere near tight enough, do you want the chickens to flap free half-way through the forest? Are you in such a hurry to get to the shanty today?'

The Poleya blushed under his dark skin in spite of himself, sheepishly rubbing one foot against the other. 'Why?' Devi narrowed her eyes as she expertly retied the strings. '*Ayy* Tukra. So I was correct wasn't I, you are up to something! What are you rushing to the shanty for? Is someone waiting for you there, eyes upon the road?'

The hapless Tukra blushed even more violently. 'That ... I ... she ... nobody Devi akka,' he stammered.

'So!' Devi exclaimed triumphantly. 'Who is she? Come on, you had better tell me before I tell everyone.'

'Aiyo! Devi akka, please! That ... she ... I ... we ... the sardine seller,' he confessed. 'We ... we have arranged to meet there today.'

'Romance, and right under my brother's nose! Shall I let him know what you will be up to at the shanty while his back is turned?'

'Aiyo!' squeaked the alarmed Tukra and Devi relented.

'Don't be such a mouse, I will say nothing,' she said laughing. 'Here, the chickens are trussed tightly, now hold them still.' Smiling, she plucked a single feather from each of the birds. 'All done. And there – I can hear him calling for you.' Indeed Chengappa was shouting from the verandah. Tukra. Ayy, accursed Tukra! Where was he, did he plan on reaching the shanty after the shops were shut? Were the chickens going to take themselves to be sold? And who was going to carry the basket of bananas? Tukra scampered around to the front of the house, chickens slung from both arms, their wings flapping in alarm until it seemed like Tukra had sprouted feathers and might rise into the air himself, fluttering and squawking all the way to the market.

Devi broke into peals of laughter as she watched him fly. And then she stopped abruptly. Even the Poleya had found love, it seemed, in a place as mundane as the local shanty. Meanwhile she had waited and waited but Machaiah remained stubbornly absent.

She had spotted him at a wedding once in the distance. 'Look, isn't that Kambeymada Machaiah, the tiger killer?' she had whispered excitedly to her friend.

74

'Who? Where? Hmm . . . you might be right.'

'Of course I'm right – look, can't you see his galla meesa? Only a tiger killer is allowed to sport a handlebar moustache and those sideburns.'

'Yes . . .' her friend said dubiously, 'but . . .'

'But nothing. Why are we just sitting here? Come, let's walk around and see just who is here,' Devi had suggested brightly, ignoring the suspicious expression on her friend's face. She had dragged her across the gathering but by the time they got to the other end of the crowd, Machaiah was gone.

'Devi . . . leave him be,' her friend had said. 'No, don't look at me with those big-big eyes; I know what you are up to. Machaiah is out of your reach. Haven't you heard he is a devotee of Ayappa Swami, God of the hunt?'

Devi nodded, still anxiously scanning the crowd. 'What of it? They say Ayappa Swami himself came down from the heavens the day of the tiger hunt, to reward his devotee. They say it must have been Him by Machaiah's side, that it was He who guided Machaiah's odikathi, that there is no other way a man could fell a tiger with only a sword. I have heard all of it. So what?'

'So,' her friend admonished, pinching Devi's arm, 'you know that they say more than that. Do you know how many marriage proposals he has turned down? They say that like his celibate God, Machaiah is simply not interested in getting married.'

'Huh,' scoffed Devi, 'maybe it is only because he has yet to see a beauty like me.' She crossed her eyes into a squint and gawped at her friend until they both collapsed giggling.

That had been such a long time ago, Devi brooded now. To her bad luck, she had not seen him since. She let the feathers she had plucked drift slowly from her fingers onto the rickety wooden floor of the coop. 'Swami, kapad,' she prayed absently as they floated down, 'Lord, bless us.' A feather from every bird that left the coop, each feather a surety to the Gods, Tayi had taught her, so that no matter how many hens were sold, still more would come to take their place . . .

Her friend from that wedding had got married herself, almost two years ago now. Her groom had in fact first asked for Devi's hand. After she had spurned him, his marriage proposal rebounded to her friend who had accepted at once. Devi had felt awkward when she had gone to help fill the trousseau boxes. 'Oh don't be,' her friend had assured her. 'Of course he would have asked for you first, who wouldn't?' She smiled. 'I should thank you I suppose for turning him down.' Devi bit her lip and said nothing as they stacked piles of brass pots inside the muslin-lined trunk. 'You are getting yourself quite a reputation you know,' her friend continued sweetly. 'Keep turning everyone down like this, and soon very few will come forward to ask for your hand. No man likes to be rejected Devi, and if you keep saying No even to the best of them . . .' She shook her head.

'Oh don't worry about me,' Devi had retorted, equally sweetly. 'I am not going to agree to the first man who asks for my hand.' The tiniest of pauses. 'I don't need to, for me, there will always be more.'

She expected too much, her friends told her. What was she holding out for? Devi would spread her hands and laugh, 'I will know when I see him,' hugging the memory she held of Machu close to her heart. What could she say to them anyway? That in her heart, she was already bound to someone, had been, from the first sight of him? That she was waiting for the tiger killer? How could she even begin to explain to Tayi, to her friends, what this felt like, this certainty that stemmed from the very core of her, the knowledge that she was born to be Machaiah's alone?

So many years ago it had been, the tiger wedding. She could no longer remember his face clearly. All that remained were impressions. The rich, river-stone timbre of his voice, the height of him, his eyes crinkled in laughter. *So* many years. And yet, the conviction of her feelings had remained, steady as a rock.

It would happen, Devi knew, as surely as she knew that the next breath would come. Machu would happen.

He was still not married. All these years, and the tiger killer had remained a bachelor. It secretly gladdened her heart when she heard of the proposals he had spurned. She paid no heed to the rumour that he had undertaken a vow of celibacy, that he simply did not wish to be wed. How could someone so beautiful remain a monk? It was not possible. He was simply waiting for her, she knew. Surely he must have heard of her, the most beautiful girl in the Pallada village? Soon, very soon, he would come, drawn by curiosity. He would spot her and in an instant he would know. 'Wait, weren't you at the tiger wedding,' he would ask, 'but how you have grown . . .'

Oh, it was useless. Devi scraped the broom over the henhouse floor with unwarranted violence, sending the birds skittering in alarm. Him and his accursed hunting! If he continued to traipse about the jungles, like some, some . . . *junglee* . . . and never attend any of the weddings and funerals and naming ceremonies and whatnots and wherenots, then how would they ever meet? 'And this Devanna,' she thought angrily to herself, shifting the focus of her ire. 'He has done nothing to help.' At first she had pestered him with questions about his older kinsman. 'Tell me about your cousin Machu,' she had said to him with her most winning smile after the tiger wedding. What did Devanna know about him? When was Devanna going back to visit? Would Machu come here to the Pallada village?

Flattered by this sudden interest in his family, Devanna had readily shared with her all he knew. At Devi's instigation, when the servant had come from the Kambeymada home with the monthly stipend from Devanna's father, he had even sent back a lavishly composed letter for Machu, extolling the virtues of the Pallada village and inviting him to visit.

Both children had waited eagerly for a reply. When month after month there was nothing and it became painfully obvious that there would be no response, they had consoled themselves with the thought that maybe Machu was simply too busy to reply. He was probably out there, deep in the jungle, hunting down yet more tigers; maybe if they listened hard enough, they might even hear the death cry of the unfortunate tiger echoing through the hills.

Refusing to give up, Devi had tried another tack. 'Why don't you go back to your father's home?' she had suggested one day in the middle of a cowrie game. Devanna's hand had stopped in mid swing and he looked at her surprised.

'What do you mean? Do you want me to leave the village?'

'Oh no, no, silly fellow,' she had laughed, 'why would I want you to leave? What I meant was, it would do you good to visit your father for a while. Maybe you could go back and get to know all your cousins, and then maybe I could come visit . . .'

Devanna had mutinously stuck out his lip and shaken his head, and Devi had lost her patience. 'Oh, it's useless,' she had burst out, throwing subtlety to the wind. 'Why ever did Gauru akka and you have to leave the Kambeymada house? You could have been there right now and . . . and . . .'

She had known even then that she had gone too far. Devanna had swung to his feet, his face shuttered. 'If my mother had still been there Devi, then you and I might never have been friends.' Setting the cowries down upon the grass, he had walked away.

'Devanna. Devanna! I didn't mean it. Devanna! Don't be silly now, come back, let's at least finish the game . . .'

She had called after him a long while before he had finally turned around. Devi shook her head as she remembered. The things she said to Devanna. And yet he returned, time and again, to be by her side. She shifted the broody hens, feeling their eggs for cracks. How was he doing, she wondered with a rush of fondness, counting the eggs in each of the straw-lined nests. It had been months since she had seen him. Maybe she would ask Tayi if they could send Tukra to the mission tomorrow with some of the lime pickle. Devanna had always loved pickle with his rice, just like a Brahmin, Chengappa used to joke. Cheering up, she gathered the eggs in the folds of her sari and made her way back to the house.

The next afternoon, Tukra returned with some news from the Mission. Yes, Devanna anna was looking well. Yes, Tukra had handed over the pickle and had told him that Devi akka had made it herself. No, there was no letter for her, but Devanna anna had sent her a message. He would not be coming to the village for the October holidays, because he was going to the Kaveri festival this year. His grandfather, Kambeymada Nayak, had decided to donate a copper door to the temple. All of the Kambeymada men were required to accompany the patriarch to Bhagamandala.

'All?' Devi asked Tukra, her eyes enormous. 'Are you sure he said *all* the Kambeymada men?' Her heart leapt. Dear, dear Devanna. She ran inside to the kitchen. The cow had recently calved and Tayi was steaming the rich first-milk into creamy, jaggery laced ginn. Slipping behind her, Devi laced her arms about her grandmother's waist and rested her chin on her shoulder. 'Tayi, do you really want me to go to the festival?'

Tayi snorted and kept ladling.

'Tell me Tayi, because if it is important to you, then I will go.'

Tayi set down the ladle and twisted around to look at her grand-daughter. 'Do you mean it kunyi?' she asked hopefully. 'You will go?'

Devi gazed guilelessly at her grandmother. 'Yes Tayi ... if this is what you want, then this is what I must do.'

Tayi's eyes welled with tears and she dabbed at them with the edge of her sari. 'My darling kunyi. Such a sweet-natured child, is it your fault if only braying asses have come asking for your hand? My flower bud, must you say yes to the first proposal that comes your way? Let it be so kunyi, let it be so, you go to Tala Kaveri, I know Iguthappa Swami will send someone worthy of you. Here, look after the ginn, let me find your father and tell him.'

Calling out to Thimmaya, Tayi set forth from the kitchen. Devi bit her lip and looked guiltily at her grandmother's back. No matter, she consoled herself, Tayi's prayers would soon be answered. For there was someone waiting for her at the Kaveri festival. Someone whose path would finally cross hers, someone entirely innocent of the upheaval that was soon to befall him.

Chapter 8

Devi peered out into the moonless night. The Bhagamandala mountain lay directly ahead, a bulge of deepest black stamped indelibly upon the dark. They had travelled for the past two days, Thimmaya and she, proffering gifts of smoked boar and pickled wild mushrooms in exchange for the hospitality of relatives whose homes lay along the way. Finally, they had arrived at the foothills of the Bhagamandala mountain. She drew the window of her room shut and, willing the slow sludge of minutes to pass, tried yet again to get some sleep. *Tomorrow*. She turned restlessly on her side. After all these years, he was *here*, the tiger killer, somewhere upon this very road. If she pressed her ear hard to the ground, she might even hear his heartbeat she imagined, rising above the thud and carry of the day as it gave up its ghosts, feel his breath intermingled with the scuffle and scurry of the night.

She fell at last into a dazed, disturbed sleep; only minutes later, it seemed, Thimmaya was gently shaking her awake. It was early when they left, still well before sunrise, but despite the little sleep she had had, Devi had never been wider awake. She shifted fretfully in the bullock cart, tracing the crazed patterns that the lantern threw in their wake as it bobbed and swayed from the yoke. She pressed her hands to her cheeks. *A few hours more*. Glancing at Thimmaya, asleep despite the rocking of the cart, she leaned forward to where Tukra sat as he drove the oxen with encouraging 'Hara, har-ra' sounds.

'Ayy Tukra,' she whispered, 'cannot you make these feeble bulls of yours go any faster? I swear even Tayi could outrun them.'

'What Devi akka,' Tukra chortled. 'Always making fun of me. They are making very good time and you know it.'

Devi leaned back against the wall of the cart and sighed.

Eventually they stopped in a large meadow at the base of the mountain, adjacent to the temple grounds. It was already quite full of oxen carts, a coruscation of lanterns winking across its expanse. Thimmaya clambered down from the cart, extending a hand to Devi. 'Come kunyi,' he urged. 'The river.'

He wouldn't be here, Devi knew. Machu and the rest of the Kambeymada family would have arrived a lot earlier at the temple for the installation of the doors. Even so, she looked anxiously about her, patting her hair into place as she tried to make out the passersby in the gloom.

Thimmaya left Devi by the riverbank with the other women devotees and went further upstream to where the men were wading in by the light of their lanterns lined up on the bank. 'Kaveri amma,' Devi whispered. She gathered her hair into a loose knot and hitching her sari above her knees, stepped into water still dyed black by the night. She gasped at its iciness. Mountain water. *Sacred* water, she corrected herself, the confluence of the river Kaveri with her two less venerated siblings, the bubbly, effervescent Kannika and the reticent Sujothi who preferred to flow shyly underground. It was mandatory for every pilgrim to take a dip and salute the three sisters before proceeding any further up the mountain.

She waded cautiously in, hands extended in front of her as she felt with her toes for the firmest footholds. Mist hung over the river in great rolling banks, swaying gently from side to side as it was buffeted by the morning breeze. She waded in further, her breath still harsh and shallow from the cold. The mist draped itself over her, brushing wet, welcoming fingers over her cheeks and arms as it enveloped her in its gauzy cocoon. She waded further in, getting accustomed to the cold. A slow calm began to unfurl within Devi, spreading gently through her benumbed limbs. She turned dreamily to look at the bank, but it was gone, along with the other bathers, hidden by the swirling mist. She was alone in a silent, magical world. Treading water between the past and what lay ahead, balanced delicately on the cusp of all that had ever been, everything that was yet to come. She extended an arm and watched entranced as it disappeared into the grey.

Somewhere in the distance, a cockerel crowed.

On cue, the darkness began to unravel. The night peeled slowly away as the sky flushed scarlet and shapes began to detach themselves from the mist. Tree trunks, a sprawling bush of wild roses, a rock in the centre of the stream like the misshapen hump of a crone. Devi took a deep breath and then, holding her nose, sank underwater. One. The sun began to push redly across the horizon. She emerged for another breath, opening her eyes briefly, and went underwater again. Two. The mist began to thin, the sky now pulsating with colour. Devi came up for air once more and went under for a final time. Three. She emerged from the water and paused, enthralled. The river was luminescent. Its waters rippling, reflecting the molten roil of the skies overhead, until she was bathing in fiery, liquid ore. The mist too alchemised, varnished by this new sun, sparkling, shimmering all around her. Devi stood still, dazed by the beauty. Details began to reveal themselves from the glow, branches, leaves, a scarlet rose slowly unfurling, and look, there upon the humpbacked rock, a pair of herons. They gazed directly at her, the tracing of light over their breasts and wings like the finest gold filigree. And then before she could so much as blink, they lifted into the air and were gone, slicing through the glow.

The moment passed as quickly as it had begun. The light faded as the sun receded into a dull glimmer far behind the clouds. The mist rolled back in, leaden and grey.

She splashed hurriedly to the bank, goose bumps pimpling her skin. *Today*. Her hands shook as she wound the sari about her, the pleats slipping from her fingers. 'Stop it,' she chastised herself. 'Is this how you want to meet him, like a graceless monkey?' Snapping off a couple of roses, she worked them into her plait. She looked at her reflection in the enamelled hand mirror Thimmaya had brought her from the cattle fair in Mysore. Dark, kohl rimmed eyes glittered back at her.

'The Goddess has shrouded herself in secrecy this year,' Thimmaya commented wryly. The Bhagamandala temple was blanketed in fog, only the spire of its double tiered roof poking valiantly through the grey. He shook his head as he took in the crowds. 'Probably avoiding all these people.'

Despite the early hour, the temple courtyard was packed. Devi and Thimmaya had been pushed and shoved as they had made their way inside the stifling shrine, people pressed against one another like so many layers of soggy dough that the new copper doors were all but obscured. Devi had felt faint as they had fought their way outside again. Devotees spilled over the temple stairs, jostling against one other as they reached to ring the brass bells that swung from the eaves, elbowing their way to the temple shop to buy offerings for the Goddess, *'mine is bigger, fresher, longer than yours'* – coconuts smeared with turmeric and vermilion, lumps of rock sugar and garlands of mango leaves and marigolds. The temple elephant was shackled to a tree at one end of the courtyard, bedecked with flowers and a caparison of yellow and red silk. Devotees swarmed before it too, 'Ganesha! O Ganapati Swami!', bananas in their hands, falling to their knees before this supposed avatar of the Elephant God as the beast in question nonchalantly chewed on a bale of hay and waved its trunk over their heads. A priest was shouting at people not to come too close to the animal, sweat dribbling from his shaven head in spite of the chill as he tried to manage the crowds.

Devi laid a hand upon Thimmaya's arm. 'Appaiah,' she shouted above the din, 'Devanna will be here somewhere; we should look for him.'

Thimmaya nodded, distracted as he spotted a friend. The man strode over and they greeted each other heartily, slapping each other's shoulders. 'Ayy Thimmaya,' the man said delightedly, 'have you come to seek penitence from the Goddess for your sins yet again?'

Thimmaya laughed. 'I leave that to you,' he said. 'Me, I am only here to seek blessings for my daughter.'

The man glanced appreciatively at Devi as she bent to touch his feet. 'Well, she is a blessed child, that much is evident ... Have you seen the doors?' he asked, turning back to Thimmaya. 'Magnificent. Pure copper, did you know? Must have cost the old man a fortune.'

'Have you seen them anna, the family, I mean?' Devi asked.

'Who, the Kambeymadas? No, kunyi, not as yet, but then they must already be at the tank, I should imagine. The doors were installed quite some hours ago.'

Devi's eyes went involuntarily to the trail leading uphill from the temple. Her heart began to race. Machu was there, barely hours away, at the temple tank where Kaveri would make her appearance.

She felt oddly lightheaded as they headed up the mountain. Fog lay thick upon the trail, teasing wisps of Devi's hair into soft curls about her face. Disembodied voices carried through the mist, invoking the Goddess, 'Kaveri amma, Kaveri amma,' calling to others in their party, 'stay close now, stay close'. Vendors hawking idlis, dosas and jackfruit puttus steamed in banana leaves had positioned themselves at strategic points along the trail, people drawn like moths to the glow of their fires.

Thimmaya paused by one particularly crowded stall. 'Let's eat here kunyi,' he said. 'All these smells are making me ravenous.' Devi smiled in agreement although her stomach churned at the thought of food. Thimmaya signalled to the vendor who poured a ladle of batter onto his sizzling griddle. The dosa was lacy and crisp but it scraped against her throat like sand.

A group of young men came loping up the trail, bare-chested, bearing tridents in their hands. 'Kaveri amma kapad!' they whooped, and carried away by their youth and enthusiasm, pilgrims all along the trail took up the chant. 'Hail Kaveri amma,' they cried in response, their voices echoing through the hills. 'Kaveri amma, our Mother!' A beggar woman came up to Devi and thrust out a bony hand. 'Amma . . .' Devi did not even notice as the dosa vendor shooed the woman away with a volley of curses. 'Kaveri amma. Kaveri amma.' The chants seemed to vibrate through her blood. Devi shut her eyes. 'Kaveri amma, give me your blessings,' she prayed. 'Let us meet.'

They climbed higher, past fathers carrying children nuzzled sleepily on their shoulders, past mist-dampened saris and transparent white mundus that clung wetly to waists and buttocks. There was a man crawling up the trail on all fours and two others somersaulting their way up the mountain, heedless of the stones that cut their faces, their hearts set upon pleasing the Goddess. What did they seek, Devi wondered, and then forgot the question almost immediately as she scanned the fog.

Where was he? A thought suddenly struck her. What if she did not recognise him? It had been eight years since the tiger wedding. No, she thought, that was silly, *surely* she would know him at once?

Every time she heard a male voice come up behind them, her heart beat faster. 'Don't be foolish,' she told herself, 'he will not be alone, the entire family will be together, all the Kambeymada men.' Nevertheless her breath quickened at each footfall, every pair of broad shoulders hulking through the mist.

They climbed higher and higher, then turned a corner, and there it was, the temple tank where Kaveri would make her appearance. It was even more crowded than the temple had been, a thick haze of bodies obscuring the steps that led down to the tank. Devi's heart began to race. *Machaiah.*

'Appaiah, where should we ...' she started, then fell silent. Where was her father? She bit her lip. Somewhere, at the mouth of the trail that led to the tank, Thimmaya and she had become separated.

Someone jostled her from behind and Devi moved hastily aside. She looked at the streams of people flooding the tank. It was hardly appropriate for a woman to be alone in such a crowd. She should really wait here, by the mouth of the trail, until Thimmaya found her. She turned towards the tank again. Machu was there, she knew he was. She looked about her again for Thimmaya. The chanting grew louder, it would not be long now before Kaveri appeared. Devi looked towards the tank again. And then, mind made up, she plunged determinedly into the crowd. 'Kaveri amma,' the pilgrims roared, as they gazed into the empty tank, willing the Goddess to appear, 'Kaveri amma!'

She had to make her way to the front of the crowd; that's where the Kambeymadas would be, in the best vantage points. She took a deep breath to steady herself and then fought her way down the slippery stone steps. The roses slipped from her hair, and were trampled into mush. People were pressed up tight against her, wedging her hips and breasts squarely into the burly male back before her. The man looked at her and shrugged apologetically but Devi did not notice. She was searching the front rows of the crowd, twisting and turning her head as far she could. '*Where are you?*' The priests raised their hands and a hush fell upon the crowd. '*Machu, where are you? Please Kaveri amma ...*'

The auspicious hour was upon them. And there . . . the faintest gurgle of water. Kaveri burst through the earth, surging and frothing into the tank. The crowd erupted. They pushed even harder against her, crowding as close as possible to witness the miracle.

'KAVERIAMMA . . .'

The water level rose rapidly. The priests tumbled pot after pot of milk into the tank, flinging strings of jasmine and great gobs of vermilion until the waters flowed red. The crowd surged forward and the world spun about Devi for an instant. She shut her eyes. '*I cannot breathe.*' Her feet felt so light, as if they were floating in the air, or had the pilgrims behind her literally lifted her off her feet? '*I cannot breathe.*' Faces seemed to tilt and run into one another all about her, she looked down at the water to right her vision but it too was a whirlpool, spinning faster and faster in on itself. The crowd behind her shifted. The man in front of her slipped and stumbled and Devi swayed precariously over the ledge. '*Kaveri amma kapad.*' Her eyes closed and she felt herself tilt towards the water, so red, red as blood. Devi fainted.

A pair of hands encircled her waist just as she fell, lifting her up and carrying her away from the mob.

The first person she saw when she opened her eyes was Devanna, his face pale and anxious. He had the downy beginnings of a moustache, Devi noted vaguely. So many faces, looking down at her . . . and one in particular coming slowly into focus. A pair of brown eyes, the colour of amber. Fine lines radiating from their corners, laughter lines she hadn't noticed before, but then she hadn't looked at him from this close for so many years. The galla meesa, the mark of the tiger killer, contouring his jaw. She lay propped up against his arm, her head resting against his shoulder. Why had she ever doubted she would be able to recognise him? Her lips parted into a slow, lovely smile. *Machu.*

'Devi. Devi!' Why was Devanna shaking her arm? 'Devi, are you OK?'

Devi sat up flustered, pulling away from Machu's grasp. 'What . . . how . . . I'm fine,' she said. 'The crowds, I . . . I must have got dizzy.' She glanced at Machu, embarrassed. 'Really,' she repeated, 'I am fine.'

'Do you feel well enough to stand?' Machu asked, and she nodded, biting her lip. He rose fluidly to his feet. 'All right everyone, thank you for your concern, but all is well. Go on, go on,' he urged, 'nothing more to be seen, everybody is fine.'

The crowd reluctantly dispersed, feeling vaguely cheated. 'It is nothing,' they said disappointedly to one another, 'just some young girl who fainted. Probably hadn't eaten all day . . .'

Devi looked anxiously about her. 'Appaiah. Devanna have you seen my father?'

Devanna shook his head. 'You gave us quite a scare. We'll find Thimmaya anna, don't worry.' He reached out his hand as if to stroke her hair, dropping it to his side as she moved away. 'You really are silly,' he said, his voice cracking as it rose. 'What were you doing by the tank all by yourself? Didn't you see how crowded it was? If Machu anna had not happened to be behind you . . .'

'Silly yourself,' Devi retorted indignantly. 'So I became a little short of breath, why create such a fuss? The tank isn't that deep.'

Machu laughed; a low, easy sound that glided over her skin like sun-warmed glass. 'Well, I am glad to have made your acquaintance too,' he said. 'Now that we know you are OK, if you two will stop bickering like a pair of crotchety chickens, perhaps we can try to find your father.'

Devi coloured. 'I didn't mean to be rude,' she said, scrambling to her feet. 'I . . . I am grateful of course, thank you. If it weren't for your presence of mind . . .'

'You would be wading in three feet of water,' he finished. 'Come on,' he ordered, already striding away, 'there are too many people here. The mouth of the trail, that's our best bet for finding your father.'

They hurried after him, Devi hastily tucking strands of hair back into her plait and smoothing the creases in her sari as she tried to regain her composure.

'Wait,' she called after Machu as she remembered. 'The nectar. I haven't got any yet.' She held out the bamboo bottle that Tayi had entrusted to her. It was customary for every pilgrim to bring back some of Kaveri's waters from the temple tank, to be sprinkled over the ancestor temple, over the paddy fields and the cattle shed, by the hen house and the piggery. Drops of the sacred water would be touched to the waiting mouths of every person in the family and to each of the Poleya servants to allow them, too, to partake of the Goddess's blessings. The remainder would be stored beside the other deities in the prayer corner, to be used through the coming year, during festivals, at births, deaths and marriages until the next year when the Goddess visited Coorg again.

Machu shook his head, striding on. 'Not now,' he said. 'Your father, we should find him first.'

Why did he make her feel like a recalcitrant child? Stubbornly stopping in her tracks, Devi laid her hand on Devanna's arm. 'Please Devanna,' she wheedled. 'Will you go? Tayi will be so disappointed . . .'

'All right,' Devanna said exasperatedly as he took the bamboo from her hand. His voice rose again. 'Please, this time, just stay here. Machu anna, please don't let her disappear again, I'll be back before you know it,' and with that he plunged back into the crowd.

'So do you always get your way?' Machu asked interestedly.

'Do you?' she immediately countered.

They stood there in silence, as people streamed back and forth from the trail. The wheels were churning furiously in Devi's head. This was not how it was supposed to be. He was supposed to have reacted like all the others did when they saw her for the first time, turn weak kneed and slack jawed. Instead here he was standing nonchalantly by her side, a look almost of boredom on his face. An irresistible urge rose in her to reach up and slap his face. This was replaced almost immediately by an irrational fear. *He would disappear once more and she would never see him again.* Her heart began to pound. More time with him, she decided, that's what she needed. He had not had enough time to take her in.

Think, Devi, think.

She looked at the steps leading up to the peak. Did she dare?

She did.

Without so much as a backward glance, Devi started towards the steps. 'Ayy. You. Girl. Devi!' a startled Machu called behind her. 'Where do you think you're going?'

Devi threw him a dazzling smile over her shoulder. 'They say the views from the peak are spectacular.'

'You cannot be serious. What if your father comes in the meantime?'

Devi sighed. 'Well,' she elaborated slowly, as if to a rank simpleton. 'Let's see now, Appaiah will never leave without me. And you have seen how crowded it is around the tank, I will be back before Devanna returns. Don't worry,' she added brightly, 'you needn't come. And oh, it was nice to meet you.'

Machu shook his head in amazement. 'You really are a handful. What rice does your mother feed you that you are so wilful?'

Devi tossed her plait at him and started up the stairs.

'Fine,' he said, 'as you wish.'

Was he really going to let her go alone? Devi turned around in alarm but he was bounding up the steps behind her. 'If you want to go, well, then I suppose we will have to.' He gripped her forearm in one large hand. 'However,' he promised grimly, 'it will be the quickest journey up and back that anyone has ever made.'

He drove them at a punishing pace, Devi's toes barely touching one step before she was leaping towards the next. She was soon gasping for air, the muscles in her calves throbbing with pain, but she gritted her teeth and stayed silent.

He let go of her when they reached the top and she turned on him. 'You, you …' she gasped, trying to catch her breath. 'You purposely …' she panted furiously as she rubbed her arm. Machu stared down at her red, indignant face and then his mouth began to twitch. A dimple appeared in one cheek and then he burst out laughing.

'What is there to laugh about?' Devi spluttered. 'You, you …' and then she, too, started to laugh.

Thimmaya turned to look at his sleeping daughter. What a fright she had given him this morning. He should have known she would be fine, he supposed, after all she was hardly a child any more. The setting sun filtered through the bamboo weave of the bullock cart, gilding the high ridge of a cheekbone, glossing the dark wing of hair that tumbled about her shoulders. He sighed. Where had the years flown? It seemed like only yesterday that he had held her in his arms for the first time. A mere scrap of a baby she had been, light as a whisker.

He knew they talked behind his back in the village; he loved his daughter too much, they said, adored her so much he was loath to see her leave for her husband's home. Did they not see how anxious he was to see his daughter happily wed before he too followed Muthavva? He would find her someone truly worthy, a veritable prince. Was there another daughter as lovely, as dutiful and accomplished as his golden child? Nobody would do for her but the strongest, bravest lad in all of Coorg. From a family as sturdy as a jungle tree, rooted for generations in the history of this land.

Devi stirred in her sleep. 'Go a little carefully Tukra,' Thimmaya chided. 'Must you aim for every pothole along the way?' He pulled the blanket higher around Devi and then, setting himself to the matter at hand, turned to Devanna who had decided to travel back with them to the Pallada village.

'Tell me monae,' he asked softly, so as not to wake Devi, 'this cousin of yours, Machaiah, he seems like a well brought up lad. No parents, that's what he told me. Do you know if he owns any land?'

He quizzed Devanna until satisfied with Machaiah's antecedents, then settled himself against the wall of the cart. 'You are a good child monae,' he said affectionately, patting Devanna on his shoulder. 'Truly like a son to me. My second son.'

He yawned sleepily as he looked out of the cart. Kambeymada Machaiah. 'Muthavva, you would approve,' he thought, smiling to himself. 'A tiger killer for our child. I believe he is interested too, why wouldn't he be? He has said he will visit us soon.' Thimmaya yawned again and shut his eyes.

The light faded and the first stars appeared. There was silence in the cart, broken only by the thunking of the wooden bells about the necks of the bulls and the soft 'Har-ra ... Har-ra ...' from Tukra as he urged the oxen forward.

Devanna stared unhappily at the gathering dusk. 'My son,' Thimmaya anna had called him. His second son. All the while asking him questions about Machu anna. Did Devanna think Machu would make a good match for Devi? Would he make a good husband?

Devanna had been too taken aback to do anything but nod. He would be the one to marry Devi, no one else, he had wanted to protest to

Thimmaya. Hadn't the whole village said, right from the time that Devi and he were little, that the two of them were inseparable? Like the skin of an orange and its pith, they used to say, that was how close they were, like a grain of rice and its husk. Why should it change now that they were older?

They had not talked about it of course, Devi and he . . . some things did not need to be said aloud. At least that was what Devanna had always believed. When Tayi complained to him about Devi turning down yet another proposal, 'talk some sense into her head Devanna,' inwardly Devanna would smile. Crotchety she may be towards him – and thoughtless and irresponsible, he thought, frowning slightly at the memory of her shenanigans at the temple tank – but he knew Devi was waiting for him.

At least nothing would come of an alliance with Machu anna, he thought, still troubled. He had seen with his own eyes how pert she had been with the poor man today on the mountain. It had been the same at the tiger wedding all those years ago. So inexplicably rude she had been then, and again today . . . It would never happen, Machu anna and she. That tongue of hers, it could cut deep.

All he needed was some time. He would finish his studies, be able to stand on his own feet. 'Harr-ra . . . Harr-ra . . .' Tukra murmured, urging the bulls faster, the wooden bells about their necks clacking in the dusk. Devanna's shoulders gradually relaxed. A little more time, that was all . . . Absently, silently, he began to recite the names of his beloved books in his head, in time to the bells. *Flo-ra Sylvatica. Flo-ra Indica. Spi-cile-gium Nilghirense. Leo-nes Plantarum. Hor-tus Bengalensis. Hortus Cal-cut-tensis. Pro-dro-mis Flo-rae Pe-nin-sulae Indicae.*

The memory of Thimmaya's words cut abruptly through his reverie, 'You are truly like a son to me, monae,' he had said. 'My son.'

All rational thought, all reasoning, was pushed suddenly from Devanna's mind, a strange foreboding raising the hair on his arms. He turned towards the sleeping Devi. 'You are mine,' he mouthed emphatically. 'Mine. I am *not* your *brother.*'

Chapter 9

'Your lemon soda sir,' the bearer repeated patiently. Gundert looked up with a start. 'Yes, thank you Chimma,' he said, lifting the glass from the tray. The bearer smiled, revealing a row of startling white teeth, before melting back into the shadows of the club. Gundert pressed the cool glass to his forehead and sighed inwardly as he looked around once more at the gathering.

The day had not gone as anticipated. The response to his letter had come that afternoon, along with the usual piles of mission correspondence and last month's issue of the *Deutsche Morgenlandische Gesellschaft*. Gundert had immediately spotted the college crest on the envelope, the lion rearing upon the shield, bearing in its paws the sceptre of knowledge. '*Lucet et Ardet*', he read under his breath. It Shines and It Burns. He had balanced the letter in his palm, gauging its heft, trying to judge from its weight the nature of the words within. And then, despite his anxiety, he had laid it aside. He had ploughed systematically through the rest of his correspondence and it was only after every dispatch had been opened and read, each carefully considered response penned, that he had finally turned to it again. He sliced open the envelope, and smoothed the folds of the letter on his lap. Two whole pages of foolscap, he noted, surely that was a good sign.

Gundert had written to the dean of the Bangalore Medical College a month earlier. He had introduced himself, citing common acquaintances within the Church. They had crossed paths many times, he wrote, without Gundert having had the pleasure of actually meeting Father Dunleavy. He hoped the Father did not mind the imposition of this letter upon his time, but trusted that once he had read through the following paragraphs, he would recognise the merit of its purpose.

He was writing, he explained, on behalf of his star pupil, Kambeymada Devanna. The boy was gifted with uncommon intelligence and a diligence of spirit that routinely evaded men twice his age. He came from impeccable lineage, a landed family that traced back through many illustrious generations, and although he was neither born nor yet baptised a Christian, Gundert would personally vouch for his character and the strength of his moral fibre. The boy had sailed through the mission school with an exemplary academic record. It was clearly evident that he was ordained for larger things than a mere apprenticeship with the local government. 'Devanna is well suited to the medical profession,' wrote Gundert, 'indeed, in all my years in this country, never have I happened across anyone as suited as he to enter the portals of your esteemed institution.' He had ended the letter with a modest postscript. He was enclosing, he wrote, a paper authored by him on the commonalities of the Sanskrit language with Latin; he had heard that the Father was an enthusiastic polyglot and he hoped that the enclosed paper would be of some interest to him.

Gundert had carried the letter with him to the chapel for morning mass before he sent it in the post, going over the carefully worded paragraphs a dozen times in his head even after the letter had gone. It had been the perfect pitch; he had built a strong case, he knew, the only thing he could do now was wait.

Smoothing Father Dunleavy's long-awaited response on his lap, he began to read. Of course he had heard about the Reverend, Dunleavy had responded. It was a pleasure finally to make his acquaintance, if yet only through correspondence, and he had read with great interest the paper that Gundert had so kindly enclosed with his letter. It was hard, of course, to comment without further insight on whether there truly were commonalities between Latin and Sanskrit, but Gundert had certainly made some illuminating points. If Devanna came recommended from someone as erudite as he, the Bangalore Medical College would be fortunate to have him enrolled as one of its students.

However, Dunleavy continued, he believed he had an even better idea. The boy's academic prowess seemed remarkable. Had Gundert

93

considered England? Why not apply to Oxford? Dunleavy was sure he would pass the examinations with some coaching. Additionally, wrote Dunleavy, the Vice Chancellor was a personal friend and he would be happy to write him a letter of recommendation on Devanna's behalf. 'Intellects of the calibre you say he possesses are few and far between,' he wrote, 'and are the beacons of our efforts on behalf of the Church here in India. While I would be privileged to have Devanna study here in our college, I believe we would be doing him far more justice by sending him to the hallowed grounds of Oxford itself.'

Gundert's face remained impassive as he read through the letter, only a small tic jumping in his cheek. He reread the letter twice and then carefully folded it and slipped it into its envelope. The mission cat jumped into his lap and Gundert absently stroked her fur as he sat lost in thought.

England. He had never even considered the possibility. There had always been, in his mind, a clear path for Devanna to tread. After graduating at the top of his class from the mission school, he would go on to study at the finest medical college in the South. Returning as a doctor to the Mission, he would then be baptised. Here he would stay, by Gundert's side, using his profession and the respect it would accord him amongst the Coorgs to convince them also to convert to the Christian calling.

It had all worked well, too well almost, it would seem. Dunleavy's response had been far better than he had hoped. England. Gundert knew what a tremendous opportunity it represented. And yet, a little voice reasoned in his head, was it truly required? Where was the necessity for Devanna to be gone all those years, across all that distance, when he could be a mere carriage ride away in Bangalore? Besides, even if he were to go to England, it was not as if he was headed for one of the large cities, Madras or Bombay or Calcutta even, upon his return. No, Devanna would return here to the Mission, back to tiny Coorg after he completed his studies. And realistically speaking, how much medical pedigree was truly needed here?

You know it would be an honour beyond reckoning for the boy's family, another voice pointed out. *A doctor, educated in England.* You have to let them make the final decision.

But to send him so far. What if something were to befall him? A change of heart, a dire illness, what if something were to tear Devanna away from him? Olaf . . . No, thought Gundert, the long-buried stench of the Madras hospital oozing clammily from his pores, he would not, *could not* withstand it again.

He had gone about his day with his usual efficiency, but by the time evening had come around, a headache tugged dully at his temples. The letter lay in his pocket, weighing him down as he had made his way to the Mercara Planters Club for the fortnightly game of billiards.

He was in no mood to attend, but Gundert knew the import of social visibility. How else would the funding be arranged for the Canarese newspaper press the Mission had established in Mysore or the permits for the land in South Coorg? He was well aware of the role that social connections played in the work of the Church. So, donning his whitest cassock and turning on his charm, Gundert attended the do's at the Club, accepted the invitations for at-homes and lawn tennis parties, and made a point of dancing at least one graceful waltz with the Resident's daughter at the annual ball held in the Mercara Fort.

Nice chap, the Reverend, the planters said to one another. A tad reticent perhaps, but cultured and all that, quite unlike that boorish countryman of his in the trading shop. They deemed it their duty to invite him to their at-homes and evenings of Parcheesi and billiards at the Club; it was only proper, dash it.

Gundert had to admit he rather enjoyed himself on occasion. There were some fine sorts tucked away in these recesses of the South – John Gammie, the commissioner of police for instance, or Marcus Updike, a planter with several acres of coffee south of here. There was Charles Anderson, the Conservator of Forests, a quiet, solidly built man with exquisitely tapered fingers and, like Gundert, an enthusiastic botanist. Gundert had been deeply touched when, after the Government had made copies of the 'Bamboos of British India' available to the Forest Department at the reduced price of seven rupees, Anderson, aware of Gundert's hobby, had contrived to obtain a copy for him as well. However, all three were missing this evening. Tuskers had been sighted in south Coorg, trampling through the plantations, and Anderson had rushed there to assess the damage. Gammie was in Mysore and nobody was quite sure where Updike was.

Gundert had hoped to speak privately with Gammie about an apprenticeship for two of his students; with Gammie in Mysore, this visit to the Club had been a waste of time. He was in the midst of making a polite exit when Mrs Hutton, the wife of one of the planters, poked her head around from the women's section. 'Reverend,' she trilled. 'Yoo hoo, Reverend. Come, sit here with us and talk with us for a while.' Gundert had no choice but to go over. 'Here,' Mrs Hutton commanded, coyly patting the velveteen sofa where she sat, 'sit here, right by my side.'

She proceeded to describe to him in tedious detail the Huttons' recent visit to Bombay, as Gundert held the glass of lemon soda to his temples again and suppressed a sigh. When she began to chatter about the Lumiere cinematographe show they had seen, he perked up somewhat. He had seen the advertisements, of course, in *The Times*; it was the first time the cinematographe had visited Indian shores. His irritation mounted rapidly however as it became evident that it was the social nature of the event, rather than the merits of the films themselves, that had captivated the lady.

'Hmm? Yes, five films,' she said vaguely, in response to his question. 'It was six Mama,' her gangling daughter corrected, glancing shyly at Gundert. '*Arrival of a Train*, *The Sea Bath*, *Ladies* and *Soldiers on Wheels* . . .' Her voice trailed off uncertainly as Gundert stared impassively at her, his blue gaze pinning her like a butterfly to a board.

'Really,' he thought, 'what a stupendously unattractive female.' He usually made a point of sitting and talking with Miss Hutton a while, noting with a certain mild satisfaction the colour mounting in her cheeks at the unaccustomed attention. Tonight however, his headache was too painful for him to care for such niceties.

Mrs Hutton rattled on, oblivious. 'The people, Reverend, you should have seen them, the crème de la crème of society.' She pronounced it cream, and her daughter started to correct her, shutting her mouth with a loud pop when her mother shot her a venomous glare. 'Everyone was so intrigued by our life here in this little part of the country,' Mrs Hutton went on. 'Oh, plantation life is just like back home, I said, just like

England . . . except for the leeches and the elephants!'

Gundert set down his glass and smiled politely. 'So you went to the premiere at Watsons, yes?' he confirmed silkily. 'The one strictly for Europeans, none of the local riff-raff?'

'I . . . well, no, we tried but those tickets were hard to come by. We went to one of the following shows, at the Novelty, balcony seats of course . . .' The lady faltered. Murmuring sympathetically, Gundert excused himself and left.

Slowly he walked back to the Mission. The gatekeeper rushed to open the gates and Gundert nodded at him. The lights were turned out in the hostel, with only a couple of lamps, their wicks turned low, kept burning in the hallways and in Gundert's apartments. Moving softly through the darkened building, Gundert headed for his study. He shut the door behind him and, seating himself at his desk, turned up the wick of the lamp. He took the letter from his pocket, balancing it once more in his palm. *Devanna should be given the opportunity, he should go.*

Rising to his feet, Gundert began to pace the length of his study. What should he do? England . . . But was it truly required? Wouldn't it be better for Dev if he remained closer to home? Back and forth he went, and then removing the key from around his neck, he unlocked once more the drawer in the bureau. He took out the parcel of silk, the fabric more cream than white with the passing years, and adjusting the wick of the lantern so that the light shone more fully upon the cloth, examined its desiccated contents. 'Such purity of form, such clarity of delineation.' Gundert stroked the delicate pistil, running his thumb along the striated surface of a petal. '*Bambusea Indica Olafsen.*'

He stared at the bamboo flower for a long time, the panic within him slowly dissipating. And then, mind made up, Gundert rewrapped the flower and placed it carefully back in its drawer. He reached for his ink well, took out a sheet of foolscap, and began to write.

'Dear Father Dunleavy,' he began. 'Thank you for your kind response, received this afternoon, December 9, 1896.' Wealthy though they undoubtedly were, the boy's family was unfortunately conservative, he wrote. Although they were keen to foster Devanna's education, under no circumstances would they agree to send him out of the country. Indeed, all things considered, Bangalore appeared to be the optimal solution. If the Father would be so kind as to have his office send Gundert the relevant forms for the entrance examination, Gundert would get Devanna to fill them out.

He finished the letter, read and re-read it until he was satisfied, and then, innocent of the wheels he had set in motion, of the catastrophic consequences his actions would bring, Gundert turned out the lamp and went finally to bed.

Chapter 10

'Devi! Where are you? Devi!' Devanna shouted, pounding up the path that led to the Nachimanda house. Tayi came out to greet him, fumbling with her glasses. 'Devanna? Is everything all right monae?'

Devanna touched her feet, gasping for breath. 'Yes Tayi,' he grinned. 'Devi, where is Devi?'

'She is there by the cattle shed, but wait monae, what is the matter?'

But Devanna was already gone, sending the hens scattering and squawking in alarm from under his feet as he raced around the house. Devi was kneeling, her back to him as she fertilised the pumpkin pit. Devanna grinned. He crept forward stealthily, stepping soundlessly past the tomato beds and through the trailing vines of butter beans. Devi continued to work, completely unaware of his presence as she mixed cowdung and wood ash together, reaching deep into the pit to slap handfuls of the manure against its sides. He stole up behind her and then pounced with a wild whoop. 'Uyyi!!' Devi screamed in fright, the vessel of ash tipping from her hands.

She glared at Devanna as he stood laughing. 'What's the matter with you? Are you still five years old that you must play these silly tricks?'

'Huh. Just because you are growing old and your hearing is failing . . .'

'Devanna, I don't have the patience for your foolish games. Look!' she cried, 'all the ash has fallen in. Do you think I have nothing better to do than go back and forth from the fireplace all day?'

'De-vi! It was only a joke. Don't be upset. Here,' Devanna offered, 'give me the pot, I'll get you some more ash.'

'No. I . . . it's all right,' Devi said grudgingly. 'Silly fellow . . .' She stared moodily into the pit.

'Ayy Devi . . .' he said gently as he squatted beside her. 'With this temper that you are in, I can almost see thunderstorms around your head.' She looked daggers at him and he pretended to cower. 'Oh now *that* was a flash of lightning!'

She struggled to keep a straight face, but despite herself, she giggled. 'There!' he cried. 'Finally, a hint of sun!'

'*Silly* fellow!' she exclaimed, shaking her head. 'So tell me, to what do we owe the honour of your visit on a school day?'

He took a deep breath. 'You are never going to believe this. I was accepted into medical college!'

She looked uncomprehendingly at him. 'What do you mean?'

'What do you mean, what do I mean? I'm going to become a doctor!'

'A doctor? Like Dr Jameson?'

Devanna nodded. 'Yes, yes,' he said grinning. 'Just like Dr Jameson. Dr Kambeymada Devanna.'

'Uyyi!' Devi screamed again, this time in excitement. 'A doctor!' She thumped him on the arm. 'Whatever will you do next? Do you have brains of gold or what? A *doctor*?! Does Tayi know? Come *on*,' she said, jumping to her feet, 'we have to tell everyone!'

Devanna filled them in on the details as Tayi hurried to light the lamp in the prayer room. The Reverend had had him take the entrance examinations a month ago. He'd said nothing of it to anybody, preferring to wait for the results to come in, which they finally had this morning. He glanced at Devi. He'd run straight here as soon as he'd heard, to give them all the good news.

'Monae,' Thimmaya interrupted, concerned, 'have you not been to see Pallada Nayak yet? He should have been the first person to know.'

'It was just . . . I wanted to . . .' Devanna's eyes strayed towards Devi. 'I am going there now,' he finished lamely.

'College begins in June,' he told Devi later on the verandah as he laced his shoes. 'I will leave for Bangalore in a month or so.'

'Bangalore?' asked Devi, taken aback. 'I didn't know you were going so far, I thought you would be closer, in Mysore perhaps. Are there no medical schools there?'

Devanna grinned. 'Medical *college*,' he corrected. 'The Bangalore Medical College is the best medical college there is. Why,' he asked, 'will you miss me?'

Devi slapped her forehead. 'Look at this boy,' she said archly, 'about to become a doctor and still he says the most foolish things. Of course I'll miss you, you're one of my dearest friends aren't you?'

A shadow passed over Devanna's face. 'Yes. A friend.' He hesitated. 'Listen, there's something I've been meaning to . . .'

'Look!' Devi exclaimed. 'How lucky, a chembuka bird! There, by the jasmine bushes, can't you see the rust of its wings? Quick, make a wish before it flies away.' She leaned excitedly from the verandah, plait swinging forward as she pointed. She stared at the bird, her lips moving silently, then turned to Devanna with shining eyes.

'I made a wish for you,' she said simply. 'That you become the best, the biggest doctor in all of Coorg.'

They were still talking about Devanna's news in the Nachimanda kitchen that night. 'How proud his mother would have been,' Tayi said wistfully. 'Foolish girl, to leave her husband and ruin her life like that.'

'Leave it be Avvaiah,' said Thimmaya, 'why rake up unpleasant memories? Today is a happy day for our Devanna.' He shook his head in wonderment. 'That quiet little boy. Who would have thought it? A doctor!'

Devi's brother Chengappa looked up briefly from his plate. 'Yes, and now watch as his father comes running to reclaim his son.'

Thimmaya laughed. 'Just his father? His grandfather, his cousins, the entire Kambeymada clan, see how they will clasp Devanna to their bosom after this bit of news . . . Enough Avvaiah, enough,' he protested as Tayi served him another helping of rice. 'That family,' he continued, reaching for the ghee, 'must have been conceived under the most auspicious of stars. First old man Kambeymada and his pots of gold. Then Machaiah and his tiger. And now they will have the first doctor in Coorg.' He sighed. 'That Machaiah fellow. I had hoped . . .' Glancing at Devi, Thimmaya changed the topic.

Devi pretended not to notice and continued to feed one of her little nephews. 'Aaaah, say aaah, won't you open your mouth wide for your aunt?'

She had hoped too, she thought bitterly. In the weeks that followed Tala Kaveri, her feet had not once seemed to touch the ground. She replayed every detail of their meeting time and again in her head. The views from the Bhagamandala peak; standing beside one another, not so close that it would seem improper to the few other pilgrims who had braved the peak, but close enough that she could feel the heat of his skin searing her side.

'Look,' he had said simply.

Devi had brushed the hair from her eyes and taken a slow, deep breath. The sun had finally come out from behind the clouds, burning away the last shreds of mist. The air was so fresh it almost hurt to breathe, the breeze steeped in cardamom and roses. All about them the undulating hills, a tapestry of every shade of blue, green and in between, shot through with the brilliant silver of waterfalls. There was the horse-shaped Kudremukh, ancient landmark for mariners homebound. There the Chamundi hill of Mysore, named after the deity whose temple adorned its face like a gold-studded nose pin. And look, there, the indigo ribbon of the Arabian Sea, snaking into the distance. A stillness crept into Devi's heart.

'My roots,' Machu had stated quietly beside her. 'I come here, every year. Just to look at all of Coorg laid out before my eyes.' Softly, he began to recite the words of the prayer. 'O Kaveri amma, O blessed maiden, what need have you for garlands of flowers? What need of gold, of necklaces, jewel laden? Adorn yourself with this land, Mother. This land of golden fields, of pearl-like showers. Our precious land. These shining hills, its moonlit bowers.'

'This,' he said, gesturing towards the sweep of the hills, 'this is where I belong.'

Devi felt a calmness, a rightness she had never experienced before, a sense of belonging, natural as breath. Like the wooden planks of a ship hearkening to the harbour, like a bird, folding its wings, come home to roost at last.

She slowly nodded. 'This is who I am too,' she said softly, 'who I will ever be.' She took a deep breath, the cool mountain air catching at the back of her throat. Turning to Machu, she looked steadily into his eyes. 'Right here,' she said. 'Right here is where I belong.'

He had looked down at her, an unreadable expression on his face. He started to say something, then checked himself. 'I will not keep your father waiting any longer,' was all he finally said as he turned back down the hill.

They returned in silence. Devi struggled to keep up with him, a welter of confusion within her. Had she said too much, been too forward? Should she say something? What? They seemed to descend in even less time than it had taken them to climb. Devanna had returned from the tank, she saw, and Thimmaya was with him. Devi looked guiltily at the worry etched on her father's face.

'Cheh, Devi!' he began, but Machu intervened.

'I am Machaiah, of the Kambeymada family,' he had said, bending to touch Thimmaya's feet. 'Your daughter wished to see the views from the peak. Please do not worry, I escorted her all the way there and back.'

They had walked down the mountain, the four of them, Machaiah deep in conversation with Thimmaya as Devi and Devanna followed closely behind. Devanna put Devi's silence down to one of her moods, blissfully oblivious to the way she kept staring at Machu's back the whole way.

When they had reached the paddock where the oxen were tethered, Machu had taken his leave. 'I shall see you soon,' he said politely to Thimmaya, but his eyes flickered towards Devi. Just a brief glance, but Devi had immediately understood. The message was meant for her, she realised, casting her eyes modestly down even as her heart soared.

He had visited soon after, ostensibly to see Devanna before the school holidays were over. Devi had been in the fields, squelching in the mud as she transplanted the paddy seedlings, when Tukra came galloping from the house. 'Coo! Devi akka! Coo, Devi akka, where are you? They're calling you inside, come quickly.'

She straightened her back, squinting against the sun. 'Ayy Tukra! Over here. What's the matter, why all the excitement? Has your sardine seller sweetheart left you and run away with the crab monger instead?'

'Aiyo!! What Devi akka, why do you trouble me all the time?' Tukra asked in a whisper, glancing worriedly about to see who might have overheard her. 'Someone has come to see you,' he said sulkily.

'Who?' asked Devi, puzzled.

'Devanna anna. And there is some man with him; Tayi says you are to come immediately.'

He had come, just as he had promised! Devi raced back to the house, washing her feet hurriedly by the kitchen door and plucking a red shoe-flower for her plait. Chengappa's wife thrust a platter of hot banana fritters into her hands. 'Where have you been!' she said. 'Here, go serve these.'

He was seated on the verandah with Thimmaya and Chengappa. He had looked up as she appeared, his eyes locking with hers in an intent, searching gaze. Her lips parted at once, as if by their own volition. His eyes dropped to her mouth, a brief caress that left her insides molten, and then he had turned away. She served the fritters, and setting the plate down on the ledge, she had sat demurely next to Thimmaya. To her shock and to all their confusion however, Machu had almost immediately got up to leave. It would be dark soon, he had insisted, shouldering his gun. It was a long way to the Kambeymada village. He did not even look at her as he left.

After that, there had been nothing, not for the past five months. Had she imagined it all, Devi sometimes wondered despairingly. The way they had stood laughing together on the peak, the fleeting vulnerability she had caught in his face before it had turned unreadable again. All these years she had been so sure. She had waited, steadfast in her conviction that all they had to do was meet. One look at her, and he would know. He would *know*, just as she had known, from the time of the tiger wedding all those years ago.

How foolish, how vain, how *stupid* she had been that not once had it occurred to her that it might be otherwise. She grew listless and dull, withdrawing into herself as Tayi and her friends glanced anxiously at her. A good proposal had come, the boy was apprenticed at the commissioner's office in Mercara and this time Devi had thought for a while before turning it down.

'It was good to see Devanna today,' Devi thought to herself now as she fed her nephew. In the weeks following the Kaveri festival, it had seemed as if she could take barely a step without tripping over him. He had clung to her side like he had done when they were little, following her everywhere. 'Devanna!' she had shouted exasperated, 'I don't want to hear about your plants any more, I don't! Just leave me alone, why can't you?' She had been relieved, and immediately felt guilty about her relief when the school term had recommenced. Of course she had then perversely missed him as soon as he was gone . . .

She smiled to herself as she wiped the baby's chin. A doctor! He had always been brilliant, but this – Pallada Nayak would be thrilled beyond measure.

He was, and so was Kambeymada Nayak, each old man vying energetically with the other to claim the honour that this prodigal grandson had brought the family. Finally, a compromise was reached. It would be from the Kambeymada home that Devanna would leave for Bangalore. However, Pallada Nayak would throw a grand feast to felicitate Devanna, with all of the Kambeymadas in attendance.

Excitement built steadily in the village over the celebrations, until at last, after weeks of waiting, the afternoon of the feast was upon them. Devi feigned indifference, but she dressed with special care that afternoon. Her sari was emerald silk, setting off the paleness of her skin. There were faint smudges under her eyes and beneath her cheekbones, but the weight she had lost only drew attention to the delicacy of her bones, the narrowness of her shoulders and wrists. She pressed the top of a finger into the little tin box of vermilion and painted a perfectly round dot on her forehead. He would be there along with the rest of the Kambeymada clan, she supposed, the great tiger killer. She lifted her head high. Well, she would give him something to look at. Unwrapping the plantain leaf bundle that Chengappa had brought that morning from the shanty, she wound the long strings of jasmine it contained around her plait, all the way down to her hips.

Thimmaya paused mid conversation as she emerged from her room, and even Chengappa was at a loss for words. Devi looked ethereal, like the last wisp of a dream. Tayi dabbed a smear of lampblack behind Devi's ear. 'To ward off the evil eye,' she muttered, 'people will be jealous.'

All that afternoon, people stared openly. Devi seemed aglow, her doe eyes aflame. Women sniffed as she went past – there she was, that Nachimanda girl who thought no end of herself, while their sons and brothers tugged at their saris like little boys, beseeching them to approach Thimmaya on their behalf. Devanna seemed dazed when he saw her, as if someone had planted a fist in the pit of his stomach. 'You look ... very nice,' he managed, and Devi swung her jasmine laden plait and laughed.

She felt Machu's presence even before she saw him. He came over to touch Thimmaya's feet; he said nothing to her, however, barely even glancing at her as he exchanged a few pleasantries with the deliberately offhand Thimmaya. Through the afternoon, he ignored her. Devi grew angrier and angrier as the hours wore on, the intensity of her allure increasing until she seemed to be scorching, dazzling, blinding her way through the gathering. Still, while all the other men could scarcely do more than gawk at her, Machu remained blithely unaware of her charms. Time and again, she thought she sensed his eyes upon her but when she turned towards him, he was always deep in conversation with someone or other, completely at ease and unheeding of her.

Lunch was announced and Devi served him a scant spoonful of the cardamom, clove and cashew studded rice while she heaped the banana leaves of the men seated on either side of him. He accepted the insult without so much as looking at her. Course after course of vegetables and meats followed, and when even the most redoubtable belly was sated, out came vats of jaggery sweetened milk payasam clotted thick with raisins, orange jaangirs dripping syrup and coconut barfis ordered especially from Mysore, coloured a blushing pink and sheathed in hammered silver. Betel leaves and areca nuts were shown around, and finally, pots of steaming coffee. Shadows lengthened into late afternoon and the guests began to depart. The fire slowly dulled within Devi. There was nothing here. The Bhagamandala mountain, the hidden messages in the way he had looked at her and the things he had said.

She had imagined it all.

She watched with a sinking heart as Machu too took his leave of Pallada Nayak. Clapping Devanna on his back, 'Do the family proud, you hear?' he walked briskly from the courtyard and without so much as a backward glance, headed down the lane.

She watched him leave, the tall bulk of his frame silhouetted against the trees. *He was leaving.* She stood on the verandah, oblivious to the crowd of guests, the breath snagging in her chest. She sank against the carved rosewood pillar, staring wretchedly after him. *Once again, he would be lost to her.* A wave of despair rose within her, so bleak, so abject, that for an instant, her vision seemed to blur.

And then, possessed of a conviction she would never truly understand, her feet moving even before the thought was fully formed in her head, she raced inside the house. The rooms were empty, the kitchen deserted, the hustle and bustle of the afternoon ending at last. There was no one to stay her, nobody to call, 'Here, Devi, where are you going?' as she slipped out of the kitchen and headed determinedly down the path that lay to the side of the house. It skirted the kitchen, cutting unseen through the adjoining banana groves to finally intersect the lane that Machu was even now headed down.

Picking up the ends of her sari, Devi flew down the trail like a flash of emerald fire. The jasmines in her hair loosened, their petals spiralling to the earth as she bolted forward, oblivious to the mud splattering her anklets and the blossom-studded wake of her passage.

'Machu!' she called, as at last he came in sight. 'Machaiah!!'

He turned, the flare of surprise in his eyes quickly extinguished, his lips tightening.

She drew abreast of him, trying to catch her breath. He looked at her, his expression shuttered, and when he spoke his voice was cold.

'What do you think you're doing? Have you no thought of your reputation? If someone were to see you, don't you realise how they would talk?'

She tossed her head, the movement letting loose a fresh shower of jasmines. She pressed a hand to the stitch in her side. 'I don't care.'

'*You don't care?* Have you no shame whatsoever? Or do all the women of your household behave in this wanton manner?'

'And what of the women in your family?' she retorted, taken aback. 'Are they of the lowest breeding then, to have brought forth such boorish sons?'

He advanced upon her, his face, to her consternation, taut with rage. 'The women I know do not make cow-eyes at every man they meet, do not giggle for hours on end with them, like common sluts.'

Devi blanched. '*What* did you say?'

'You heard me.'

'How dare you?' she cried, equally furious. 'What gives you the right to speak to me like this?'

He bent his face so close to hers, she could see the dark rings around his irises, smell the toddy on his breath. 'I will talk with you any way I want,' he snarled. 'Any way I please.'

Devi slapped him across the face with all her strength.

For a second she thought he was going to hit her. She glared defiantly at him, and then inexplicably his shoulders began to heave with laughter. The dimple cut a deep groove in his cheek as he ruefully stroked his chin. 'Tigress.'

'Village imbecile,' she spat, her eyes blazing.

'If I am an imbecile, then why did you bore holes in my back with your eyes all afternoon?' Devi opened her mouth to protest but suddenly she couldn't think of a word to say.

They stood staring at one another as the sun slipped further and cuckoos called from the trees. The anger left her with a rush, leaving her limp.

'Why didn't you come?' she asked then, helplessly. 'Why didn't you come back all these months?'

'I ... Devi ...' he began wearily. Abruptly he turned his head, listening. People were approaching. 'You must go back.'

'No. Not until you tell me why you never returned.'

'There is nothing to tell. Stop behaving like a child,' he said, and began walking away.

'That's the second time you've called me that.'

He paused, puzzled.

'The tiger wedding.' Her voice trembled. 'Nine years ago. I was there. You ... you called me a child. I told myself then that one day you would see that I was anything but.'

He stared at her, then shook his head. The voices were coming closer, a gaggle of guests departing the feast. 'Leave. If they see you here, alone ...'

'Not until you tell me.'

'Fine,' he said, almost angrily, 'we need to speak. Meet me tonight at nine, in the lane that leads to your home. Now go!'

'At night? How, wait . . . Machu . . .' But he was gone.

The evening passed in a muddle of excitement; Devi complained alternately about it being too cold, '*look* at the gooseflesh on my arms', or too hot, 'has someone shut all the windows, I can hardly breathe . . .' She nearly dropped a platter of ottis on Tayi's foot, and had to be told thrice to stir the curry before she heard. Tayi became quite worried and placed a hand on her granddaughter's flushed forehead. 'It doesn't seem like you have a fever,' she said puzzled.

It was quite late by the time dinner was over and the house finally dark and resting, nearly a full hour past the time Machu had asked her to meet him. Devi slipped down the lane, her pulse racing. Such a familiar route, one she had taken a thousand times before, and yet everything about it was changed. The moon, sheathing every twig, branch and leaf in silver, drawing pools of liquid shadow from under the stones. She hurried down the shimmering road as if in a dream. A bat looped noiselessly through the air, then another.

And there he was, waiting.

She lifted her chin truculently, but instead of chiding her for being late, he looked at her, an expression almost of pain on his face. 'I didn't know if you would come.'

All the pithy responses Devi had prepared flew out of her head. 'How could I not?' They stared hungrily at one another. *Five* months it had been, five long, empty months. When Devi spoke, her voice was husky. 'So why did you ask me to meet you here?'

The dimple flashed briefly in his cheek, his eyes still locked with hers. 'You look far more presentable in the moonlight.'

She flushed. 'Do you have something to say to me or not?' she asked tremulously.

He looked down then and taking a deep breath, ran his hands thickly through his hair. 'Yes. We . . . Devi, there can be nothing between us.'

Pain knifed through her. 'Am I . . . am I not to your liking?'

He laughed; a low bitter sound. 'Are you not to my liking. Are you not to my liking,' he repeated, his eyes lingering on her mouth, the fullness of her lips. 'I haven't been able to sleep since the Kaveri festival. Not a single night's rest have I had, not since I saw you.' His voice, like lush, full-bodied moss. 'Why should it be so, I do not know. All I know is that I can neither hunt nor eat nor drink in peace, all I can think about is you. So to answer your question, yes. Yes, I find you to my liking. Nonetheless, there can be nothing between us. I am spoken for.'

She stared at him, stricken. 'Who ...? How? Who is she?'

'It's no woman.' He told her then about the vow he had taken. In an impulsive bout of gratitude over the tiger that Ayappa Swami had allowed him to fell, Machu had vowed not to take a wife for twelve years. Celibate he would remain, just like his God, for twelve years, two years for every lobe on the killed tiger's liver. Nine had passed, with less than three to follow. It had never mattered, his vow, not until he had met Devi.

'A vow?' Devi asked, such a wave of relief washing over her that she felt almost lightheaded. 'So it was true, the rumours ... a *vow*. So? We can still be betrothed.'

'What difference between a betrothal and an actual wedding?' No, he said, he could not, would not extend a formal commitment to any woman until the twelve years were over. He swore Devi to secrecy. To reveal a vow diluted its potency; she, he had needed to tell, but nobody else could know.

She was silent for a while, then smiled. 'I'll wait for you.'

Hope blazed across Machu's face for an instant but then he shook his head. 'How are you to wait for me without a formal betrothal? On what grounds will you refuse the other proposals that will come your way? When you continue to refuse, if you can, they will start to say things about you. List imaginary defects where there are none, claim you are unsound of mind or worse, sullied of character.'

'So?' she asked softly. 'I'll wait for you nonetheless. And when you finally come to claim me, they will be silenced.' She stepped closer to him, so close she could feel the heat from his body. His shoulders tensed, his breathing ragged as he stood his ground. 'You're the one for me,' Devi said quietly. 'The only one.'

'You are placing your reputation at stake.'

'I have never cared very much for what people say,' she said smiling.

'We will not be able to see one another,' he said, proudly lifting his head. 'I'll not meet you like this, in secret, slinking about behind everyone's back.'

'I waited years without knowing if I would even see you again.' Devi raised a hand to his face, amazed at her boldness. She rested her palm against his cheek, registered the sharp intake of his breath as she traced a finger along his jaw. 'Come to me when you can, when you will. Once a month, or a year, it doesn't matter. I will wait.'

'No,' he said stubbornly, his breathing hoarse as he removed her hand. He gripped her fingers tightly in his own. 'You don't know what you are saying.' How would she stay potential suitors, he asked, how long could she keep turning them away? The pressure would build at home for her to be wed; her father seemed a good man, but even he would run out of patience. Devi was already older than a lot of brides in Coorg; three years was a long time. What if something befell him, what would happen to her then?

'Make sure nothing does,' she replied calmly.

Her head was buzzing, her heart beating as if it might explode, and yet, she was filled with stillness. Here. This was where she belonged. So natural, so right . . . so unthinkingly right for her to be by the side of this man. Doubt, despair, conviction, anticipation all laid momentarily to rest, a sea of glass with all tides soothed. Raising her other hand, she laid it gently against his cheek. Her eyes filled with sudden tears, surprising even herself.

'Mine. You are mine. I will wait for you forever.'

Chapter 11

☙ 1897 ☙

We're all a bunch of faggots
Our arses stuffed with maggots
We bugger one another,
Brother to brother
Faggotty, maggotty, bleedin' arse FAGGOTS

Devanna dully belted out the lyrics of the verse. It was late, the windows of the darkened hostel firmly shut to prevent the sound of voices carrying over to the masters' quarters. Once again the first years were aligned naked in rows, like the tracks of some perverse railroad.

Martin Thomas and his cronies stood leering at the head of the column. 'Louder,' they commanded. 'Louder fags, we can't hear you.'

Why hadn't the Reverend warned him, Devanna wondered bitterly again. He had painstakingly prepared Devanna for his first term at college, pre-ordering his textbooks from Higginbotham's so they could review the course material together. He had accompanied Devanna to Bangalore, meeting with Father Dunleavy in order to introduce Devanna personally to him, much to Devanna's embarrassment. He had even settled Devanna into the hostel and, while leaving, clasped him in a brief hug, the unaccustomed show of emotion taking Devanna by surprise. He had promised to visit as often as work would permit, slipping Devanna ten rupees, 'pocket money', he had murmured over the latter's protests, something small to tide him over until the holidays. When he had done so much, why then had the Reverend omitted to prepare him for ragging?

It had started that very first night. Martin and his gang had waited for the warden to finish his rounds and then they had swooped upon the new students like vultures spotting carrion, rousting the first years from their beds and gathering them in the hall. 'Strip,' they had commanded. Devanna had gingerly got out of his pyjamas, like the rest of them, but it hadn't ended there. The seniors had handed out wooden rulers, and ordered the first years to measure one another and tabulate the results. They had looked at each other, the freshers, and someone had giggled nervously. It was a joke, it had to be? For a few seconds, nobody moved. A hockey stick flashed through the air and a fresher slumped groaning to the floor. 'Well, what are you waiting for? Get to it fags, unless you want some more of that.'

Devanna had squatted disbelievingly in front of a classmate's groin, trying to distance himself from the spongy squiggle of flesh brushing against his fingers. They each had to announce the inches they had claim to, to the strident mockery of the raggers. Then bunched together, they were marched through the hostel corridors. 'We're all a bunch of faggots . . .'

It had become a recurring ordeal – barely a night went by when the first years were not booted from their beds on some pretext or another. Those few who dared to protest were roundly thrashed; Devanna had immediately realised it was best to keep his mouth shut and walk fast. Even so, Martin had spotted him with the unerring instinct of all bullies for the more vulnerable of the herd.

A burly senior with green-brown eyes the colour of ditch water, Martin Thomas was the offspring of a quixotic lieutenant posted with the Second Sappers and the daughter of his head clerk. Ginny had the brown hair of her English father and the voluptuous hips of her Indian mother and Lt Thomas had been enthralled from the moment she swayed past him. He was shocked when three quick, sweaty trysts later she had announced she was pregnant, but ever a gentleman, he had pledged his troth. They had been married in the cantonment chapel, and at the party he had thrown for his fellow officers, Ginny and he had danced all night to the brass band. It hadn't taken long however, for disillusionment to set in; when the Sappers were posted to Malaya, it was a stroke of luck as far as Thomas was concerned.

Martin learnt early on not to ask after his father for fear it would trigger one of Ginny's rages or hysterical bouts of crying. Country born, they called him in the colony where they lived, podgy Chee Chee Thomas. 'Faster Chee Chee,' they shouted as he fielded to their cricket elevens, 'catch that ball, quick, or next time, you can go play with your chokra brethren instead.'

So loudly did Martin laugh, always the loudest of them all, at the tasteless barbs, the stupid jokes they directed at him, that one morning, when six pet dogs were found lying stiff and poisoned in front gardens throughout the colony, nobody thought to connect it with him. Nobody made anything of the fact that each family had a boy about Martin's age, who played in the elevens; nobody thought to have a word with Ginny either, about the rat poison she had bought just a few days ago to set beneath the sink of their home.

His grandfather used his position with the forces to get Martin into the Army Reserve; Ginny lit three candles at the church of St Thomas in gratitude. Military life suited Martin. Here, nobody cared about his Anglo-Indian parentage. He performed the training exercises with gusto, imagining his black boots landing with a satisfying crunch on his father's neck. A year of army life, and things began to happen to his body. The puppy fat melted from his frame and in one summer alone, he shot up four and a quarter inches. Veins popped from newly muscled arms, his shoulders widening and thighs thickening into a palpable physical presence that, to his astonishment, drew a wake of less endowed cadets like a magnet to his side.

Somebody suggested medical college and he took the entrance examination as a lark. Nobody was more surprised than he when he was accepted; this time, his mother ran a small advertisement in the *Madras Herald* to thank the Infant Jesus. Despite his bulk and the sycophants it immediately fetched him, Martin never publicly protested his own ragging. When a senior called him a coolie, asking if Martin had a thing for black velvet – native women – like his father before him, Martin had convulsed with laughter along with the rest of them.

At the Freshers Ball, the event that officially marked the end of the ragging season, that same senior had come up to Martin and shaken his hand. 'A good sport,' he had cried, slapping Martin on the back, and the second years had taken up the toast. 'To Martin Thomas, a good sport,' they roared appreciatively. Martin and his gang had accosted the senior alone by the lavatories later that evening. One of them twisted the senior's hands behind his back as Martin slammed the boy's face repeatedly into the wall. 'Tell a soul,' Martin said to him genially, 'and the next time, it will be worse. You hear me? I'll rip you apart, starting with your goolies.'

The following year, Martin set a whole new standard for ragging at the College. 'This is for your own good,' he assured the freshers as he bullied them into submission. 'Survive me and there is nothing in the world that you will not be able to face like men.' It had been wildly addictive, the power he wielded, and the following year, despite becoming a third-year student, Martin had broken with tradition and continued to spearhead the ragging.

He could not have explained his loathing for Devanna even if he tried, except that it had been immediate and absolute. The few other chokras in the batch were replicas of those who had gone before them; brown-arsed runts who shivered at the very sight of him. Devanna's skin was lighter, almost exactly the same pale olive tint as Martin's; nearly pale enough to be white, *nearly*, but not quite, the olive undertones betraying the native blood pulsing beneath. He asked casually after Devanna's background. Rich family, he was told. Landholding, hunter buggers from the hills.

Martin would never admit it, not even to himself, but there had been something about the tilt of Devanna's head, the quietness of his movements, that reminded Martin of himself. A privileged, refined, *could-have-been* version of himself.

At first Martin had merely watched Devanna, out of the corner of his eye every evening, as he orchestrated the ragging. Devanna had not fought back like the more hotheaded of the freshers, but neither had he cracked. No matter how exigent the task, Devanna had undertaken it impassively.

Inevitably, one day he accosted Devanna himself. Had he dared look Martin in the eye? The blank surprise on Devanna's face had only made him angrier. 'Don't try to deny it,' Martin barked. 'Don't you know the freshman protocol? Do I have to teach it to you myself?' Solomon's Chair, he had declared, making Devanna bend his knees and extend his arms forward, just like a chair. He had placed his tennis racquet across Devanna's arms. 'Hold steady now, you hear?'

Devanna had crouched stoically, as the pain in his knees grew unbearable. When they gave out eventually, Martin slapped him across the face, calling him a sissy. 'What are you, chokra?'

Devanna's voice had remained even, although anger spurted in his eyes. 'A sissy.'

The first years were too ashamed to discuss the ragging. They would return to their dorms from yet another nocturnal parade, shoulders thrown back in a belated show of bravado, careful not to look one another in the eye. It was only ragging, they exclaimed, a coming of age ritual. It happened to everyone. That was just what happened; one had to take it like a man.

Devanna, too, took it like a man. He blearily got out of bed, belted out the fresher anthem, performed all the inanities asked of him. He tried his utmost to stay out of Martin's way, succeeding for barely a day or two before, invariably, he would hear the familiar words. 'Chokra!' Devanna would turn, heart sinking as he braced himself for whatever new humiliation would follow.

His resoluteness, the resignation with which he executed Martin's every command, only served to fuel Martin's anger. His directives became ever more punitive, directly targeted at Devanna until all the hostel knew that, for some reason, Thomas had it in for the chokra freshman.

Devanna had not risen promptly enough from the dining table to offer Martin his seat.

'No Martin,' Devanna agreed evenly.

'Two hundred sit-ups.'

'Yes.'

He hadn't been able to complete them, of course, and Martin had drawn back his leg and kicked him with such force that Devanna had buried his teeth in his lips to keep from crying out loud. He was bleeding, Devanna realised then with a frisson of shock; there was the salty, mineral taste of blood in his mouth. A bruise was slowly blossoming on his skin where Martin's boot had landed. Beneath it, a septic bitterness, beginning slowly to pool.

The thrill of pleasure as his boot connected with Devanna's skin remained sharply etched in Martin's mind and the next morning, he confronted Devanna again. Devanna had not wished Martin a good morning. Anger flared inside Devanna at the unfairness of this accusation, but he struggled to keep it from his voice. 'You've only just entered the mess, Martin,' he pointed out reasonably, 'and my back was to the door.'

That bit of snotty backchat earned him a box on the ears. He would have to polish all of Martin's boots, right now, pronto.

'Yes.'

His boots were not polished to an adequate shine, Martin shouted, as he laid into Devanna with his fists. Chokra bastard! Devanna would now have to lick them clean. Had Devanna heard him?

'Y . . . yes . . .' Devanna had barely been able to speak from the pain.

'Yes sir, yes sir, three bags full. Can't you say anything else faggot? Are you a sheep or a man?'

'I—'

'You know what I think fag? I think you need to be taught how to be a man.' Martin's face creased into an oily grin. 'Grab him,' he shouted to his sidekicks, and they hoisted Devanna off his feet. They lifted him to the hostel windows and, 'careful, now, the bugger's sweaty as hell', they held Devanna upside down over the ledge. He swung there, the blood rushing heavy to his head, fingers scrabbling in the air as the seniors held him by his ankles, hooting and jeering. 'Are you a man yet faggot? Are you?'

Finally they pulled him up. 'No hard feelings, hey chokra?' Martin smirked. 'It's only ragging, just toughening you up, that's all.'

Devanna barely made it to the bathrooms before vomiting up his dinner, continuing to retch into the sink long after his stomach was empty. 'It's ragging,' he told himself that night. He lay stiff, waiting under the blankets, ears pricked for the door to slam open once more, bloody maggots, out of bed with you, you heard us, *now*. 'It's only ragging, take it like a man.'

Martin began to heap ever more punishments on him, willing him to crack, to crumble into pieces. He didn't like the way Devanna had combed his hair that morning. 'Choose,' he told Devanna, swinging the hockey stick and the cricket bat in front of him.

Devanna pointed to the cricket bat.

'Bend over, bend over then, chokra. So,' Martin continued affably, 'which shot do you prefer? Hook shot or defensive?'

The instinctive squeezing together of his knees, trying to keep from trembling. 'Defensive.' It was the gentler shot.

Martin nodded. 'Good choice. Defensive it is.'

Eyes shut, waiting tensely for the shot to fall across his thighs and buttocks. And then the bat came crashing down upon him with such force that he was propelled forward onto his face. 'Would you look at that, fresher, I changed my mind. Had to go with the hook shot after all, felt like stretching my arms.'

The days began to lump together in a haze. Devanna withdrew into himself, a silent figure standing resolutely in front of his tormentor no matter what the latter put him through. Chanting the names of the old, beloved books in his head to take his mind away from what was being done to him:

Flora Sylvatica. Flora Indica. Spicilegium Nilghirense. Leones Plantarum. Hortus Bengalensis. Hortus Calcuttensis. Prodromis. Florae. Peninsulae. Indicae. Flora Sylvatica. Flora Indica . . .

He started suffering from nightmares, bolting awake in the middle of the night; to his shame, sometimes with his cheeks damp from tears he had no recollection of having shed. It's only ragging, he told himself, it means nothing, but every beating he suffered at Martin's hands, each naked debasement, began to stoke within him a poisonous, bewildered rage.

A few of the first years reached out in overt sympathy, nudging him awake when he dozed off in class because he had been kept up all night, slipping anonymous sheaves of notes into his desk after yet another class missed because he was in the infirmary having tincture applied to his bruises. For the most part, however, they gave him a wide berth, terrified of Martin's wrath. Keep your chin up, they muttered to him in the dormitories, there are only three months left until the Freshers Ball.

The nurse in the infirmary shook her head each time Devanna limped in, pursing her lips when he mumbled that he had walked into a door again. Finally, she went to the doctor with her suspicions. Father Dunleavy called Devanna into his office, noting the contusions on his arms. What was going on? He heard rumours of course, of ragging, but surely that was all in good spirit? He had his suspicions, there was that boy who had broken his nose two years ago, how in God's name does anyone walk into a wall? But how was he to mete out a suitable punishment when nobody stood accused? Walking into walls and doors indeed. Had his students suddenly gone soft in the head?

He steepled his fingers and looked at Devanna, his kindly eyes clouded with concern. Was there something else he should be aware of, something to do with Martin Thomas and his friends perhaps?

'No,' Devanna said, 'nobody is to blame.'

'Please Father,' he added, 'say nothing of this to the Reverend, he will only worry. I . . . I've been clumsy of late, that's all.'

Devanna also remained silent on his ordeal in his long letters home. What could he say, after all, how could he even begin to describe the things that were being done to him? It was only ragging, and he had to take it like a man. He wrote pages and pages to Gundert, describing his classes in meticulous detail. When could the Reverend visit? He penned long, meandering letters to Devi, telling her about Bangalore and the fortnightly outings they were taken on.

Two weeks earlier it had been the theatre. 'How you would have laughed to see the man who played the role of the heroine,' he wrote. 'He had an especially large Adam's apple and every time he sang falsetto, it seemed to grow even larger.' This week, they had gone to the Botanical Gardens. 'The gardens belonged to Tipu Sultan, yes that same Tipu of Mysore who so infamously tried to slash his way through Coorg. How he managed to produce something so beautiful . . . You should see the gardens Devi. They are managed by experts brought in especially from Kew Gardens no less. The new herbarium is the spitting image, they say, of the Crystal Palace in Hyde Park.' He described the masters and the dour librarian, and the decorous English breakfasts of soft-boiled eggs, toast and (watery) tea.

'Will you write to me?' he asked wistfully. 'Once in a while, just a few lines?'

Devi laboriously read his letters, word by word, translating them for Pallada Nayak, Tayi and Thimmaya. She saved every one of them, storing them in the felt-lined box where Muthavva's jewels were kept.

She read them aloud to Machu too, when he came secretly to visit, unable to withstand the separation, drawn against every ounce of his will to her side. They met that first time, in the hollows by the paddy fields. It was late in the afternoon and the fields were deserted. He stood before her, a hunted, angry look upon his face. Devi reached up, standing on tip-toes to lay a palm against his cheek. He looked away, refusing to meet her eyes. 'I had to come,' he said stiffly. 'I could not stay away.'

'If you hadn't, I might have gone mad,' she replied softly.

He said nothing, then ruefully glanced at her. 'Huntress.'

They began to meet, as often as they could, most often in the fields that abutted the Nachimanda property, and once, in the late evening, in the lane that led to the house. Devi quoted bits and pieces of Devanna's letters to him. 'So intelligent he is. Always was, from the time we were children. All the teachers used to fawn over him, and rightly so – look at him, he is going to become a doctor. Did you know they work with actual dead bodies? He says so, right here. And did you know ...' Machu would nod, eyes closed, and then he would pull her onto his chest.

'How much do you love me?' she asked him once, impetuously. They were lying side by side in the fields, the paddy waving bright green all around them. Buffaloes wallowed in the stream and now and again there was a gentle splash as a fish jumped, breached the waters, then fell back in. Butterflies, tiny, pastel winged, flitted here and there and herons skimmed the afternoon currents.

'Who says I do?'

'Oh, come now. Say it. Tell me how much you love me.'

He shook his head in amusement.

'Tell me, tell me, tell me.'

'Why don't you tell me instead? How much do *you* love me, huntress?'

She was silent so long that he opened his eyes to look at her. She had sat up and was staring at the sky, her eyes dreamy. 'Loving you is like having wings. Like a great, massive pair of wings have been attached to my back, so that my feet no longer touch the ground.'

She turned to him, her face aglow. 'You?'

He shut his eyes again. 'You're going to get an answer out of me, aren't you?'

'Yes,' she said simply.

He shook his head and sighed. 'Like running.'

'Running?'

'Yes. Through a forest.'

She waited, and when there was nothing more forthcoming, she began to bristle. 'Like *running*? You love me the way you like a sport? Like *running*?'

He raised a quizzical eyebrow. 'Devi . . .'

She was storming to her feet. 'Like running?'

He reached over and caught her in his arms. 'Ayy tigress,' he said gently. 'Yes, like running. Like running through a forest, faster than anyone else can, than anyone ever has. When I run so fast that the trees begin to blur together, when I can almost see the shapes of the veera in their shadows. When my feet move so fast that time, distance, every-thing else falls away, when all that is left is the magic of the moment, that one moment when I'm carried by the wind.' He looked steadily at her. 'This is like that. Time, distance, it all seems to fade, all that matters is this one moment, this time spent with you.'

In Bangalore, time passed slowly as the first years counted down to the Freshers Ball. Martin grew increasingly obsessed with Devanna. He had become, for Martin, the itch that had to be scratched, sometimes three or four times a day.

Martin had fumbled with an answer in class that morning. 'Chokra. Get over here.'

His cow of a mother had sent him another of her letters, asking why he didn't write more frequently, had he forgotten all she had sacrificed, her marriage, her looks, everything just so he could be where he was today? Guilt creeping over his skin like an army of black ants; where, WHERE was that chokra fucking fresher?

'Fucking maggot bugger,' he would mutter later, massaging his tender knuckles.

Still, the more he thrashed Devanna, the less pleasure he felt. It gave him a fierce, spine-tingling thrill, the hatred stamped in Devanna's eyes, the impotent anger. But it wasn't enough. He wanted the chokra to . . . to . . . *fall* at his feet perhaps, to plead to be left alone, please Martin, I *beg* you, please.

He halted Devanna in the corridor one morning. Devanna's heart sank. 'Good morning Martin.' Martin said nothing, just cracked his knuckles and stared broodingly at him.

'Martin,' Devanna tried again, trying to keep his voice even. 'I need to get to class, may I . . .' He gestured past Martin at the first years hurrying along, eyes fixed firmly to the ground. 'I need to get to class,' he repeated. Martin said nothing. 'Excuse me,' Devanna said and, not sure what else to do, started to walk away.

Martin shot out his arm, blocking his way. 'Such little respect,' he murmured. 'I was talking to you and you just walk away. And here I am, a senior.'

He turned. 'No classes for you today, chokra. I will see you in my room. Now.'

Devanna stood in the middle of the room as Martin's chums lounged against the walls and watched curiously. What would their leader think up next?

Martin walked slowly up and down, not even looking at Devanna. 'So little respect,' he said quietly, picking up the ulna bone that lay on his study table. The second years were in the midst of anatomy lessons and there was a plethora of bones to be found in each of their rooms. Martin caressed the bone, running his fingers over its calcified surface, from proximal to distal end, gently probing the extremities and then slowly back again. The hairs rose on Devanna's neck.

Martin shook his head and then, suddenly becoming brisk, he turned. 'You leave me no choice. Drop your pants chokra. Drop your pants and bend over.'

Devanna sat huddled on the library floor in the musty anthropology nook. This part of the library was always quiet and deserted. Besides, the rest of the first years were still in class. He sat on the cold floor, hugging his knees to his chest, trying not to shake. 'Nothing happened,' he said to himself, over and over. 'NOTHING happened.'

'*Flora Sylvatica. Flora Indica.*'

The bile rose in his throat and he swallowed hard. 'Stop it. STOP IT.' Cold, he was so cold ... He began to rock back and forth, his arms wrapped tightly about himself, and the back of his head connected with the library wall. The dull pain of impact, the solidity of the bricks behind him, was strangely comforting. He mechanically hit his head against the wall once more, then again. Thud. Thud.

He shut his eyes, willing himself away from the nightmare of the past hours, far from here. The paddy flats of the Nachimanda village. Coorg-Devanna.

Thud.

Thud.

Pain blossomed forth from the centre of his forehead, like an orange-petalled flower. Coorg-Devanna, back at the Mission. The Pallada village. Look, the grass. Springing beneath his toes. The smell of her hair, a fresh, hibiscus smell.

Devi.

Close they had been, ever since he could remember, like two eggs in a nest.

At last, the first term drew to a close and it was time for the Freshers Ball. Father Dunleavy kicked off the festivities with his address. 'No more,' he warned from the podium. 'Ragging season is done, boys.' He looked pointedly at a bland-faced Martin. 'I expect all of you to treat each other cordially, as professionals and as gentlemen.'

Later, he summoned Martin into his office. 'I have my eye on you

Thomas,' he told him. Any more untoward incidents and proof or not, Martin would have him to answer to. If Devanna in particular were to walk into one more door, he would have no choice but to suspend Martin. Martin had blustered angrily at the unfairness of it all, but had been unable to meet the Father's eyes.

'Tattle tale!' he later raged at Devanna, spittle flecking the latter's face. 'Bloody snitch, I'll get you for this.' Not daring to lay another hand on Devanna, Martin let it be known through the hostel that from now on, nobody was to acknowledge Devanna's presence, let alone speak to him. If he saw anyone so much as glance as Devanna, there would be hell to pay.

So thankful was Devanna to be done at last with ragging, or so he believed, that at first he didn't even realise that he was still being singled out. The Freshers Ball was over, was it not? Ragging season was finally over. He had taken it like a man, paid his dues. He revelled in the stillness about him, at being able to walk the corridors without having to peer anxiously over his shoulders. At being able to have a full night's sleep without dreading what new torture the day ahead held twisted in its palm.

He turned away from the ordeal of the previous months, willing himself to compact the awful memories, the flailing rage, the bitter hatred he felt for Martin, into a hard, dark pellet buried deep inside.

It was finally over.

Slowly though, he began to notice it, the hush that descended as he entered a room. The hubbub would begin self-consciously again but as soon as Devanna attempted to join a group, it melted away. When he sat at a table in the mess, it emptied; when he tried to speak with someone, it was as if his words had fallen on deaf ears. Finally he turned to one of the Indians in his batch, a slight, hardworking student with a prominent overbite. The boy attempted to brush past Devanna, ignoring his questions, but the naked bewilderment in the latter's expression stopped him. He told him then, hugging his books to his chest as he glanced nervously around him, about Martin's decree.

Devanna stood shocked as he watched the boy scuttle away, the hatred that he had tried to bury fermenting into a slow, dull fury. What had he ever done to Martin? He would go and demand that he treat him fairly, he would beat Martin's head in with the heaviest rock he could find, he would . . .

No. This was beneath him. He took a deep, slow breath, willing himself to calm down. Mission-Devanna knew what he had to do. Let his actions speak for him. He would do nothing, say nothing in retaliation, except for making sure that he was the finest student this college had ever seen.

Yes. He would earn, he would *command* the respect of the college.

Devanna pushed himself as hard as he could, but he grossly miscalculated the results. For the more attention the professors lavished on him, the more annoyed his classmates became. The sympathy they had harboured towards him in the previous term was rapidly eroded by the sight of Devanna's hand in class, perennially in the air. They started to jostle past him in the corridors and openly jibed at him in the dorms. Teacher's pet they called him, insufferable brown-noser. Once there was a dead frog in his bed, another time someone poured sulphuric acid over his book of practicals. And still, nobody would speak to him.

Confused, Devanna soldiered on, too proud to do any differently, carrying all the while an acid taste in his mouth. He sailed through the final exams and then finally, it was the last day of the school year.

Devanna set out immediately for Coorg, thinner and taller than when he had left, a scar over his ribs and a permanent discoloration on his lower back from an especially vicious thrashing. Gundert rushed beaming from his study where he had been standing by the window for the past half hour, ostensibly going through his correspondence but truly waiting for the first glimpse of Devanna at the gates. The novices gathered around Devanna, making much of him, marvelling at how tall he had become, but Gundert had immediately noticed the gauntness of his face. There was a tautness about the child, like a spring coiled too tight.

'Everything is in order Dev, yes?' he probed later when they were alone in his study. He had placed a special order at the trading shop for the fruit cake that he knew Devanna enjoyed but the boy had barely touched it.

'I wish I could have come to visit you. Believe me, I very much wanted to, but it has been impossible to get away.'

Devanna nodded.

'Dev . . .' Gundert tried again. 'Is all well? Is there anything you wish to share with me, my child?'

For a split second, it was on the tip of Devanna's tongue. The brutality of the past year, the wash of black rage he felt whenever he thought of Martin. 'Why me,' he wanted to ask, 'what have I ever done to that lout?' The words locked in his throat and he looked down at the floor instead. An ant had happened upon the crumbs from the cake and was unsteadily carting its booty across the floor. A slight shift of his foot was all it would take to mash it into oblivion. He glanced briefly at Gundert. 'I am well, Reverend,' he said flatly and returned to his contemplation of the ant's progress.

'You know you can come to me with anything child.' Gundert paused, troubled by the brittleness in Devanna's voice and searching for the right words. 'I have known you since you were in half pants and about this high.' He smiled and held his hand a couple of feet from the floor but Devanna did not notice. He nudged at the ant with his shoe, watching as the creature wobbled and then, righting itself, began to scurry across the floor. Gundert slowly let his hand drop. 'Dev . . .' he said yet again, 'if there is anything I can do, my son, any way that I might be of help, remember all you have to do is ask.' Devanna was silent, then he looked up at the Reverend and nodded. The ant hurried away, disappearing safely into a crack in the floorboards.

'Come,' said Gundert, trying to ignore his sense of disquiet, 'a little poetry, that is what this evening has been lacking.' Selecting a volume from the bookshelf, he began to read aloud.

> *On a poet's lips I slept*
> *Dreaming like a love-adept*
> *In the sound his breathing kept*

At first Devanna merely listened, the familiar cadence of the Reverend's voice soothing him, sanding down the jagged, exposed snarl of his thoughts. Gradually, his own lips began rustily to move, keeping time with the beloved words.

He will watch from dawn to gloom,
The lake-reflected sun illume
The yellow bees in the ivy-bloom

He slept through that night, for the first time in a long while, lulled into an exhausted, dreamless sleep.

Still, it was only the next day, when he finally saw Devi and heard her wild whoop of joy, that the shadows webbing his eyes began at last to lift. The sweep of the fields. Tayi's smoke-filled kitchen. The tiny mole by the side of Devi's mouth, a canopy of forest trees against a cerulean sky. These things seeped into his consciousness like rain into parched earth, bringing to life the words that had lain dormant within him all this past year. Devanna began to speak again. He talked almost without taking a breath, the sentences pouring from him in an unending, sometimes disjointed stream, as if they might bury the unhappiness of the past year in their stead.

At first Devi was all ears, alternating between amusement and fascination as he described endless, imaginary vignettes of college life. 'So many friends I have there,' he boasted, 'and I told you, didn't I, how I topped the last exams? You should see the way they all clamour after me. "Dev, come to dinner with us." "Dev, interested in a spot of tennis, join us at the Cubbon?"'

Devi laughed fondly.

Egged on by her interest, he began to spin ever larger yarns, the sophistry of Bangalore growing by leaps and bounds in his accounts. 'Really Devi,' he said to her time and again, 'if only you could *see* the city.'

'Hmmm,' she said at last, 'I am sure it is very fancy there in the city, but surely our Mercara is not so bad?'

He stared incredulously at her. '*Mercara*? My dear girl, you know nothing. Once you have seen Bangalore – why, Mercara is nothing more than a sleepy, provincial little town!'

Devi jumped to her feet, stung by his pomposity. 'Maybe I *like* sleepy little towns,' she retorted, 'because I've no desire to see your precious Bangalore.'

He called, stricken, after her. 'No, Devi, wait, that is not what

I meant.' A lump rose in his throat as he scrambled behind her. 'You don't know how much I wanted to ... how I waited to ... Devi, *wait* ...'

Much as she had been looking forward to seeing her old friend again, Devi gradually grew irritated. His never-ending stories. From daybreak to sunset, all he did, it seemed, was seek her out and babble on. She began to avoid him, slipping away when she spotted him come whistling up the path to the Nachimanda house. 'Iguthappa Swami, but he is here yet *again*. Tayi, tell him ... just tell him I have gone to visit a friend,' she would whisper, ducking out the back door.

'Cheh,' Tayi clucked, 'is this any way to treat that poor boy? Making me lie to him ...' She would herd Devanna into her kitchen, baking him hot ottis, stuffing him with crab chutney and fried bamboo shoots until the blandness of hostel food was burned from his tongue, but it was poor consolation. The more he wanted to see her, the less time Devi seemed to have for him.

She was going to the shanty and no, he could not come, there was simply too much work to be done there.

She had to visit a friend.

She had a headache and needed to rest.

Once, despite her recriminations, he had stubbornly followed her. 'Why can't I come with you?' he argued. 'Anyway, the fields are deserted, can't you see? What is so urgent, what work so pressing that you must go there now, in the heat of the afternoon?'

Unless, he added, only half jokingly as a thought suddenly struck him, unless she had arranged a secret tryst with someone?

Devi burst into frustrated tears as he tried awkwardly to apologise. 'Why can't you let me be?' she cried. 'There, I won't go to the fields, are you happy now?'

'Sorry, I'm sorry, I shouldn't have said that ...'

'Stop following me around! Everywhere I look, there you are, like a shadow. Leave me alone, I beg of you, let me be.'

He left for the Kambeymada house soon after, much to Devi's relief. They slaughtered two pigs there, for a feast in his honour, and Devanna was allowed to drink for the first time in his life. The rice liquor burned a fiery path down his gullet, making his head swim until he seemed to see Devi everywhere, smiling at him from the rosewood-framed mirrors, reflected in the silver tumblers, dancing on the wooden-beamed ceiling.

When Machu said casually that he was going to Mercara later that week to look for some guns, Devanna asked to accompany him. 'You must love Pallada Nayak very much,' Machu probed along the way, 'for you to want to return so soon.' Devanna flushed and mumbled something unintelligible.

That afternoon, when Machu told her that Devanna had returned, Devi smiled. She had missed the silly fellow after he was gone.

'The boy is in love with you,' Machu said. 'You're the reason he's here.'

Devi looked startled and then she burst out laughing. 'Nothing like that,' she spluttered. 'We've been the best of friends since we were little, that's all.'

'There's no such thing as friendship between a grown man and a woman,' Machu said flatly. 'Do you see it in the jungle, two elephants walking trunks entwined, just being friends? Or in the cattle shed perhaps, between a bullock and a cow? It's simply not a thing of nature, for an adult male and female to be only friends.'

'Huh,' said Devi mischievously, throwing a handful of grass at him. 'If you are right, then perhaps I should take his suit seriously. Better a doctor than this rough-hewn hunter of mine . . .'

Machu was not amused. Devi too, banter notwithstanding, was pensive that evening, thinking about what he had said. When Devanna came to visit, she was guarded and awkward, hating the hurt her stilted responses brought to Devanna's face, but unable to help herself.

Devanna slowly withdrew into himself as the holidays came to a close. The initial torrent of words that had burst from him, the animation that had marked his return, replaced by a silent, simmering intent. He spent most of his time at the Nachimanda house, waiting doggedly for Devi to return from wherever she had disappeared to. The Reverend sent repeated messages, asking him to visit until, doctor-to-be or not, Pallada Nayak lost his patience and shouted at Devanna, 'Ayy donkey boy, how many times must the Reverend send word for you, eh dull-head?' Devanna went to the Mission, but by late afternoon he was back at the Nachimanda house, swinging his legs slowly back and forth as he sat on the verandah with Tayi. Devi grew ever more short with him, but Devanna was beyond caring, drinking her in with his eyes until again she burst into tears and Tayi had to tell him gently that perhaps it was best if he did not visit for some time.

The days ticked by and fear dead weighted into Devanna's heart as the hostel loomed large once more. Wild plans swam through his head. Devi and he would be engaged and then next year, they could be married. They could live together, in the married students' quarters – he would not have to go to the hostel any longer. But then he would recall the look on Devi's face, the expression of disgust as she had turned suddenly and caught him staring at her. Such disgust, or worse, had it been pity? The intensity began to seep from his demeanour and Devanna grew drawn and unhappy again.

The day he was to leave for Bangalore, Devi came to visit at the Pallada house. 'What?' she demanded, 'were you going to leave just like that, without saying 'bye?'

'I was going to . . .'

'Yes, yes, I'm sure you were. Here,' she said, 'these are for you.'

There were two jars of mango pickle, three of salted bitter limes, five more of pickled boar and six parcels bursting with the coconut laddoos that Devanna loved. He stared astonished at the mountain of food. 'How am I ever supposed to eat all of this?'

'Huh,' she said, tossing her plait. 'Your Bangalore might be fancy, but tell me, can you find pickle as wonderful as mine there?'

He grinned.

'Wait,' she said. 'There is something more.' She placed a small squirming bundle into his arms. 'Tukra found her in our fields. I thought . . . I thought you should have her to remind you of all of us.'

Devanna looked down at the baby squirrel snuffling in his palm. 'Pets are not allowed in the hostel,' he began but stopped when he saw Devi's disappointed expression. 'No matter, I'll keep her a secret.' He stroked the squirrel's red fur gently with his thumb and she looked up at him with bright, inquisitive eyes.

'Devi,' he said in a rush, 'I have to ask you . . .'

The squirrel began to butt her tiny nose against his thumb. 'Oh would you look at her,' Devi exclaimed. 'The poor thing is obviously hungry!'

Devanna hugged the squirrel close all through the journey back to Bangalore, unwilling to set her down for an instant, not even when she urinated all over his top coat. He smiled to himself as he thought back to that morning. Devi and he had fed the squirrel together, squeezing twists of silk cotton soaked in diluted milk down her throat. The tension of the past weeks had magically evaporated as they laughed over the baby's antics, trading silly jokes until things were just as they had always been between them.

Next year, he promised himself. One more year and then when he was back in Coorg for the holidays, he would propose.

Chapter 12

Devanna was determined to keep the squirrel. He did not yet know *how* he was going to hide her away from the rest of the hostel, but of this much he was certain: nothing would make him part with her.

Things went smoothly at first. The other students paid him so little attention that he was able to smuggle the little thing in and keep her presence in his shoe box completely hidden for two whole days. On the third afternoon, however, they walked in on him as he was feeding her. 'If you so much as . . .' Devanna began tensely but they stared fascinated at the squirrel. 'What is it?'

He cradled the baby protectively to his chest. 'A Malabar squirrel.'

'A squirrel? Do they get this big?'

'She's still only a baby,' he said warily. He stroked the squirrel's head and she rubbed her cheek ruminatively against his fingers.

'How large will she get?' 'Johnson, come in here, you have to see this.' 'Its fur is so red.' 'Does it bite?' 'Here, can I hold it?' 'What does she eat?' 'Shut the door, ass, you don't want the warden seeing her now, do you?'

They crowded about him. The squirrel yawned, revealing tiny pink gums, and then, to whoops of appreciation from her audience, ambled up Devanna's arm and wrapped herself about his neck. Devanna smiled.

She became a mascot of sorts for his batch, their collective secret. They bribed the sweeper two rupees so he wouldn't report her presence to the warden and took turns to smuggle in milk from the mess. They consulted the library for what to feed her and brought her little treats, monkey nuts, chopped-up fruit, bits of boiled egg. They christened her

Nancy, after the proctor's wife – 'same flaming red hair,' they pointed out – and Nancy, in turn, did her utmost to charm the class off their feet. She roosted up on the curtain rods and as soon as the door to the dorm opened, would drop chittering gently onto the entrant's head. She ate from their palms, brushing her tail coquettishly over their arms, and when the morning bell rang, she raced about the dorm, leaping from bed to bed until they were awake.

Although she distributed her affections with impartiality, her love was reserved for Devanna alone. Scoffing at the cotton-lined shoe box he had prepared for her, she insisted on sleeping beside him instead, curled atop his pillow. Devanna eventually gave the pillow over to her altogether, sleeping flat on his back for fear he might turn over during the night and inadvertently crush her. She woke him each morning by nipping gently at his fingers, climbing into his shirt and padding back and forth over his stomach as he sat at his study desk. She would especially fawn over him when he returned from class, draping herself about his shoulders and nuzzling his neck with scolding *chik chik* sounds, 'where have you been, *how* could you leave me alone?'

Devanna had always been surrounded by animals in Coorg. The cats that wound themselves around everyone's legs, the dogs in the verandahs, the cow in the Nachimanda yard, a gentle, affectionate soul whose greatest pleasure lay in having her horns rubbed, the pigs who hoisted their hoofs onto the wall of their sty to watch the various comings and goings in the yard. Never before though, had Devanna owned a pet of his very own. He was soon entirely besotted.

Still too wary of Martin to disregard completely his decree, the class gave Devanna a wide berth in the public spaces of the hostel – the mess, the library, the study rooms. Nonetheless, there was a change in their demeanour, and Martin watched, puzzled, as they – almost apologetically? guiltily? – walked past Devanna's table. He shifted his gaze to Devanna who was quietly eating his porridge. There was a change, too, in the chokra. He couldn't put his finger on it, but there was something different.

When they were back in the dorm at night, his classmates would empty their pockets of treats for Nancy, handing them to Devanna as if trying to assuage their guilt. 'Hey man, here . . . and this too. Did she eat today?' Devanna accepted their tokens without comment, watching proudly as she performed her little vaudeville routines, keeping his classmates in thrall.

'Hey Dev, tell her to come to me ...' and he would gently nudge Nancy from his shoulders.

'You doing OK, man? Here, I got these for her ...'

'Would you look at her? Where on earth did she learn to do that – almost a back flip, wasn't it?'

'Nancy, here, Nancy, there's a good girl. What's this?' someone exclaimed, looking at the papers in Devanna's hands. 'Have you already finished the assignment?'

'Oh, it isn't that difficult, once you ... I can walk you through it, if you would like,' Devanna offered shyly, and his classmates began to take him up on it.

Nancy's presence made this term infinitely easier than the previous ones. He was still unable to look at Martin without revulsion, but at least he no longer had to endure the prickling hostility from his class. He was resigned to the fact that they would never stand up for him against Martin, but truth be told, he no longer cared. Whether they liked him or not, whether or not they respected him – it just wasn't important any longer.

And it was all Devi's doing. He wrote her lengthy accounts of Nancy's every escapade, thanking her repeatedly. 'You cannot know what she means to me Devi. Thank you, thank you a thousand times over for what must be the best gift anyone has ever received.'

She never did respond. He had asked her once during the holidays why it was that she never wrote to him. He had tried to sound nonchalant, as though her response did not matter. 'Oh I kept meaning to,' she replied blithely, 'and then something or other would happen. You know me, I was never one for writing and such.'

His retort had come out sharper than he intended. 'A letter isn't that difficult, you know Devi. You don't have to be a ... a ... *quinologist* to write one.'

Her brow had furrowed over the word, as he had known it would, but stubbornly she did not ask him what it meant. 'Well, you send me so many, one after the other and then another and then still more,' she countered tartly, 'that where is the time to even read them, let alone reply?'

'*If* you even knew how to read them ...' he began, but then he had shaken his head. 'Never mind.'

'What's this?' Tayi had asked, when he walked stiff legged into the kitchen, 'why is your face as small as a mouse's?'

'Nothing ... this Devi,' he had muttered, fiddling with the spoons. 'She said I write her too many letters.'

Tayi smiled. Later, after the dishes had been cleared, she brought out a box from inside the house and deposited it in his lap. It was a rosewood box, tooled with brass. He had opened it, puzzled, and there, among a jumble of bangles and such were his letters, opened, every single one of them.

'Look monae,' Tayi said gently. 'She saved them all.'

So he continued to write to her, diligently. He knew better now than to expect a reply, but every day when the post was delivered Devanna couldn't help but wait anxiously for his name to be called. And when it was, it was hard to contain the surge of excitement, followed by the inevitable disappointment, no matter how unfair, when he would look at the envelope and recognise the Reverend's precise copperplate. 'She didn't write,' he would tell Nancy unhappily as he picked her up in his arms. 'Nothing in the post Nance, not today at least.'

Nancy, as if sensing his distress, would begin her ambulatory sojourns over his shirt, nuzzling his ear and neck, curling up on his shoulder until at last Devanna would smile. 'I know, I know, I'm being silly. She misses us, I know she does. Next year, just wait and see, just a few more months Nance.' The squirrel would wrap herself about his neck in commiseration and Devanna's heart would lighten.

The freshman class came in. Father Dunleavy expressly forbade Martin and his lot from having any, *any* hand in the ragging at all. His warning was redundant. For Devanna's batch mates pounced upon the first years with glee, determined to extract revenge for all that they had endured the previous year. 'This is for your own good,' they assured the first years, 'you should be thankful to us, we are toughening you up for the real world.'

Devanna stayed away from the ragging, but one evening, as he was returning from the library, a pile of books in his arms, his classmates called to him in the corridor. There was no danger of incurring Martin's wrath. He was away with the rest of his classmates, travelling to a village deep in the interior of the state as part of the field training prescribed in the curriculum. 'Come on Dev,' his classmates cried, 'join in.'

Devanna hesitated. And then, loath to disregard their olive branch, he reluctantly joined the crowd around the apprehensive first years. 'Off with your pants,' the second years cried, handing out wooden rulers. Devanna's eyes fell upon one oversized boy, so obviously distressed by the exercise that even his jowly buttocks were flushed a vivid red. He bent trembling in front of a classmate, wiping the sweat from his eyes. 'What's the matter, fatty?' someone demanded. 'Hurry up.'

'I . . . I . . .' His hands were trembling. And then he set the ruler down on the floor. 'I . . . I cannot. This is wrong, it is a sin . . .'

They pounced on him then, twisting his ear, hooting and jeering as they kicked that flabby bum. 'You a saint or what, fatty? Get him, get him good.' 'Fat crybaby!'

Devanna stood silently by, a faint taste of bile on his tongue, watching as the fresher collapsed in a vast, blubbering pile. 'Stop it,' he wanted to shout at the raggers. 'Be a man,' he wanted to tell the boy, wanted to tell him to pick himself off the floor, but the words remained stuck in his throat.

Nobody noticed when Devanna left. Heading straight for the deserted dormitories, he sat down heavily on his bed. The faint sound of laughter, travelling up through the floors. Devanna swallowed. The image of the boy, crying in a heap on the floor. 'Be a man.' Again the sound of laughter. His heart started to race, sweat beading his forehead as memories of the past year came suddenly alive once more.

Flora Sylvatica. Flora Indica. Spicilegium Nilghirense. Leones Plantarum.

With a small, choking sound, Devanna rose to his feet. Yanking open the drawer on his desk, he began scrabbling about for an inkpot and his fountain pen. Barely noticing Nancy as she raced into his lap, he tore out a sheet of foolscap and, breathing harshly through his mouth, began to write. 'Devi.' No more, enough of his reticence, this waiting. He would tell her everything. The tangle of emotions within him. The revulsion he had felt at the freshman's tears, the ghosts it had dredged up as he watched them crowd about the boy. He had stood by, watching. Despite all he had gone through himself, his own silence, his inability, his *unwillingness* to say anything, to stop the ragging. All he had done until now was to stay silent. With them. With her. No more.

'Devi,' he wrote, the jeering from downstairs ringing in his ears. The nib of his pen scratching at the paper. 'Devi. I miss you, *how* I MISS you. I am turned to shadow by your absence. Coorg-Devanna, lost without you. Mission-Devanna, an empty, posturing shell. Devi-DeviDevi.' He wrote with such vehemence that the nib ripped through the paper, depositing a copious blot of ink that began to spread through his words.

Crumpling the ruined sheet into a ball, he flung it from him with a force that made Nancy leap from his knee. She bounded up the curtains in alarm, scolding and nagging at him from her perch until at last he sighed and turned to look at her. 'I am sorry Milady,' he said, holding out a placatory arm. 'You are right, I should not be so impatient.' Nancy cautiously descended, still making reproachful noises. Devanna capped his pen and drew her into his lap. He stroked the squirrel's fur, the anxiety that had gripped him receding.

The laughter from the ground floor had ceased; a halt, presumably, had been called to the ragging. There was the faint clatter of footsteps on the stairs. He hugged Nancy close to him, unsettled by the evening and loath to give up this brief pocket of solitude. He looked unhappily outside. Somewhere to the West, dusk must be claiming the hills. She would be lighting the lamp atop the courtyard pillar. Unconsciously biting her lip as she stood on tip toes, carefully now, carefully, so as not to spill the oil. Lamplight flickering across her face, a stray tendril of hair curling across her cheek.

The squirrel, as if sensing his mood, curled herself about his neck, not even so much as looking up when the rest of the dorm trooped triumphantly in.

Martin was sullen and irritable all through the field trip, pondering the faggot chokra. Maggot chokra faggot. Something seemed to have changed over the holidays, Martin knew it had. But what?

By the time they returned to the college some weeks later, even his cronies gave him a wide berth, sensing the blackness of his mood. He sat at the very back of the coach, occupying the entire seat and broodingly cracking his knuckles. It was mid afternoon when they arrived. The hostel was silent, all the students in class. On a sudden whim, Martin strode to the second year dorms. He flung open the door to Devanna's room and then yelled in fright, as Nancy flew through the air to land on his head. 'Gerroff. Gerroff me!' he shouted, and the squirrel scampered up the curtains and perched there, angrily chiding him.

'What the . . .?' Martin peered upwards. He shook the curtains and whistled softly. Whatever *was* that thing? 'Heeere . . . Come here.' He held out his hand. Nancy descended slowly, pausing every couple of seconds to scold him. 'Come heeere.' Barely had she put her nose in his palm, when he clamped down hard with his other hand, trapping her in his grasp. Struggling in panic, Nancy opened her mouth and dug her tiny, needle-sharp teeth into his thumb.

He threw her off with a howl of pain and she bounded up the curtains again, chittering in fright. Martin shook them so hard that she fell off. She righted herself in mid air and landed on the sill. Flying across the room, she made straight for Devanna's bed and dived trembling beneath her pillow.

Nursing his sore hand, Martin began to laugh. *Chokra.*

Devanna knew immediately, as soon as he returned to the dormitory, without even entering the room, that something was terribly wrong. The huddle of boys around his bed, the horrified pitch of their voices. He stood in the doorway, turned to stone. 'Dev. Dev, old chap . . . I am so sorry.' Someone took his books from his arms, the crowd parting as he approached his bed with leaden feet.

Nancy lay splayed upon his – her – pillow. Someone had performed a vivisection on her, pinning her to a dissection board and cutting her open from chin to tail. Devanna could not but help notice the precision of the cut even through the fog swirling in his brain. Impeccable. Absolutely impeccable. A clean slicing, right through the epidermis, the specimen presented in perfect dorsal perspective. The neatness of the labels affixed to the innards.

Oesophagus.
Kidney.
Heart.

Nancy twitched feebly on the board. 'She's still alive,' someone to his right said, sickened. 'The bastard didn't even use chloroform.'

Devanna unpinned Nancy's paws and lifted her into his arms. 'Nancy?' he whispered, his face pallid. 'Nance?' The squirrel tried to turn towards him, failed, opened her mouth in a yowl of agony. 'Hush. Shhh . . . No Nance, hush.'

He carried her to the hostel garden, whispering to her all the while. That lush, vibrant red tail spilling over his arms, a crowd of sombre boys following in his wake. He set her down in the grass by the rockery. Nancy twitched again, trying feebly to rub her head against his thumb. 'My good girl, my best girl. Nancy, my good Nancy . . .' His voice faltered and he stroked her fur. Then, lifting a large rock, Devanna raised his arm high above his head and brought it smashing down upon Nancy's skull. The squirrel's paws jerked once and then she was still.

'Why?' he asked raggedly. 'Why her, why in God's name, why my squirrel?'

'What squirrel?' Martin asked innocently. 'Did you have a pet in the hostel? I am sure not, chokra, it is against the rules.'

'I *know* it was you.'

A sheen of pleasure passed across Martin's face. '*Finally.*' He stepped closer to Devanna, flexing his massive arms. 'So? What are you going to do about it fag?'

Hatred, compacted so determinedly inside him, flaring alive. The room around them was very still. Devanna's heart was hammering so loud, he was certain everyone must hear it. 'Come on faggot,' Martin whispered. 'Give me a reason, just give me a reason.' Devanna's fingers bunched into a fist and with a wild, inarticulate cry, he launched himself at Martin.

Martin swatted at him as he might a bug, laughing as he effortlessly fended off Devanna's blows. 'My turn chokra.' Devanna never even saw him move, but he found himself suddenly sprawled on the ground, the sweet-salty taste of blood in his mouth. Martin bent over him, grinning. 'Chokra faggot.' Devanna tried to rise but Martin punched the side of Devanna's head with all his strength. Devanna gagged. 'Say it out loud,' Martin coaxed, raising his fist and hitting his head again. '*Say* it fag. Pets Are Not Allowed.'

'Stop it Martin,' someone said. 'Let him go.' Martin swung about to tell the person to bloody mind his own business but something about the crowd, the hostility in their faces, made him hesitate. 'Stop it,' someone said again, and fear prickled along Martin's spine.

'Not worth my time anyway,' he blustered, his voice unusually high, and calling to his cronies, he pushed his way out of the room.

Behind him, the crowd slowly started to dissipate. 'Come on man, get up,' they urged Devanna.

Devanna lay unmoving, his head buzzing unbearably, grief and humiliation grainy upon his tongue.

He left for Coorg that same afternoon. It was the only thing that made sense to him any more. Devi ... He wove unsteadily out of the hostel gates, heedless of the classmates who tried to stop him. He needed to go the infirmary, they said. 'You're *concussed* man, you need to rest. Come on, get back inside before the warden does his rounds.' When they saw it was futile, they shoved a few rupees in his pocket and gave him whatever grub they could lay their hands on, a small tin of biscuits, plum cake, even a precious quarter litre bottle of gin.

He caught the coach to Mercara, a delicate crusting of blood in his hair. It kept playing over and over in his head, the image of Nancy, splayed open. The sound her skull had made as the rock came crashing down, a crunchy, brittle sound like an eggshell coming apart. He began to shake. A brisk breeze wafted through the open windows, cold upon his face; he lifted a hand to his cheek and found to his surprise that he was crying.

The coach broke down midway; they managed eventually to repair it, but by the time the lights of Mercara came into view, it was well after two the next morning. Devanna's scalp ached as if someone had taken an axe to it, the buzzing in his ears was even louder than before. He stumbled off the bus into a blanket of mist, so thick it was impossible to see more than a few feet ahead. Mercara was deserted, even the beggar who ordinarily trawled the coach stop was missing, curled up somewhere asleep. Devanna glanced once, shivering, towards the Mission, and then, turning westward, he set off at a blundering run towards the Pallada village, despite the wild elephants and the ghost who frequented the trail.

Chengappa anna used to scare Devi and him with tales of the ghost when they were little. 'Very tall, she is, and beautiful, ah, so beautiful that a man can burn with fever just by laying eyes on her. But if you look down, beyond her ankles to her feet, that is when you know she is a pisachi. Her feet, you see, are turned *backwards*.' Devi would slip her hand into his and he would resolutely clutch her fingers, frightened too, but trying not to show it.

He raised an arm now, pushing through the mist. If he saw the ghost tonight, he would push right through her. Right *through* her. He giggled. He touched his fingers to the side of his head. The swelling was worse, he noted detachedly, but at least the bleeding had stopped. The buzzing in his ears, though, was even louder, like a hive of jungle bees swarming over his scalp. '*Flora Sylvatica, Flora Indica*,' he muttered to himself, his teeth chattering. '*Spicilegium Nilghirense, Leones Plantarum*.'

So pink, so unbearably tiny, that pink, pulsing heart. She had waited for him, he knew, held on to life until he found her. '*Hortus Bengalensis, Hortus Calcuttensis, Prodromis Florae Peninsulae*.' He started to shiver uncontrollably. Butchered wide open, and yet again, he had been unable to do a thing. There was such a thirst in his throat . . . Remembering the bottle in his pocket, he took a long swig, coughing as the gin hit his mouth. She had been his. She had been HIS. Devi . . . He started to run even faster, lurching from side to side along the trail.

Dawn was breaking, gunmetal grey, as he approached the Nachimanda house. The mist began to thin, but nonetheless, it would be a subdued sunrise this morning, a throng of clouds advancing grimly in the sky. A chorus of bullfrogs started up, serenading the clouds and thrilling to the smell of rain in the air. He stumbled on.

The dogs, after a few sharp barks, rushed towards him, gambolling in delight as they recognised him. 'Yes, yes,' he mumbled as he abstractedly patted their heads. He would sit a while he decided, wait on the verandah perhaps, until this ache in his head subsided. Before he spoke with Devi and proposed. Silver flickered in the East, a cockerel crowing from somewhere behind the house.

'*Flora Sylvatica, Flora Indica* . . .'

Devanna wove forward, then stopped abruptly, his blood turned to ice. There, down below, near the fields. Was that a woman? *The ghost* . . . He stood frozen, his breath escaping in little puffs into the leaden air. The buzzing in his ears grew louder as the figure slipped from sight.

And then he started. 'Devi,' he said thickly. 'Devi,' he called, louder this time, 'Devi!'

She had always liked mornings such as these, even as a child. Devanna would still be half asleep, extracting every extra minute of warmth from the blankets, when she would run into his room and fling open the windows. 'Oh stop your grumbling,' she would say. 'Here, breathe this in. The fragrance Devanna, the perfume of rain. There is *nothing* like it.'

'Devi,' he called again, the mist muffling his voice as he stumbled after her.

She had gone surprisingly far, almost to the paddy tanks, by the time he caught up with her. 'Devi!' he called and this time she heard.

'Who?' She turned startled, the shawl slipping from her shoulders. 'Devanna? *Devanna*? Whatever are you doing here at this hour?'

It rose within him like a tumult then, the memory of the previous afternoon. Nancy . . . Martin, standing over him and laughing, *laughing* . . .

'Devanna?' she said incredulously again and then, shaking her head, she began to smile. 'Silly fellow, I cannot believe my eyes. What are you doing here, is the semester over already?'

'Devi, I . . .' He began to tremble. He shut his eyes to calm himself, then opened them once more.

'What is it?' She stepped closer, worried, and then blanched as she smelled the gin on his breath. 'Have you been drinking?'

Where to begin? What could he even begin to say to her, were there even words to describe . . . Wrapping his arms about himself, Devanna moaned softly and began to rock back and forth on his heels. '*Spicilegium Nilghirense. Leones Plantarum.*' This time, he would not simply stand by. This time . . .

'Mm . . . marry me.'

'What? What? Come now Devanna, what is all this – who has put you up to this joke?'

'Joke? This is no . . .' He ground his teeth together to stop the shivering. 'Marry me,' he said again.

The smile vanished from her face. 'Stop this nonsense. I am going back to the house. Are you coming?'

She turned to go but he caught hold of her wrist.

'Let go of my hand.'

He let go at once, starting at the sharpness of her tone. This was not going at all the way he had imagined it. This sawing in his head, as if it were being cleaved in two. He shook his head slowly, to clear it. Martin, laughing down at him.

He reached clumsily for her hand again.

'LET. GO. Whatever is the matter with you?'

'What is the matter with me?' He stared tormented at her. 'Nothing, except that I am completely, irrevocably in love with you.'

Devi went very still. 'Stop it,' she said, then, tremulously, 'just . . . stop this.'

Jungle bees swarming over his scalp, buzzing in his ears. Sliced open like a laboratory specimen, her tiny heart, still beating, *Oesopha-gusKidneyHeart.*

'You are mine Devi. Mine, do you hear. Only mine.' Unexpectedly, he giggled. 'How do I love thee? Let me count the ways,' he recited, his eyes aglitter and then, bending his head, he awkwardly kissed her.

She struggled to free herself from his grasp, but he held her so tightly that his fingers raised angry red welts along her arm. She began to shout, her free hand flailing at him, the sounds in his head so loud that he could not make out her words. The shawl fell from her shoulders, he grabbed reflexively for it, connected with a breast instead. She gasped in shock.

It sent a thrill through his body, that sound, as if a fire had suddenly been lit in his blood. He began to kiss her in earnest, her face, her throat, her shoulders, pulling her closer. 'You are mine.' She fought him, hard, biting and scratching and kicking, but in his muddled state, it only served to inflame him.

He couldn't think any more. Nothing mattered except this, being with her, the fire raging inside him, this insistent pressure in his groin. His breath was coming very fast, he was almost panting despite the chill. Her nails raked his cheek and he pushed her backwards into the grass, falling on top of her as he fumbled urgently with his clothes. She cried out, bit his shoulder; he grimaced and held her even more tightly.

'Bend over chokra,' Martin had said to him that afternoon last year, stroking the ulna bone. 'You leave me no choice.'

'You leave me no choice Devi, you leave me no . . .'

He had dropped his trousers and slowly bent over. Martin had waited, deliberately prolonging the tension as Devanna's knees began to tremble and his hair flopped forward onto his forehead. And then, in one quick, savage movement, Martin had jammed the bone in hard, high into his anus. A pain so intense that Devanna had screamed out loud. 'To teach you respect,' Martin had gasped from behind him, the sweat pouring into his eyes as he had pushed and thrust, harder and harder, his pelvis moving unconsciously, keeping rhythm as he tore into the chokra.

Bitterness, blossoming beneath his skin. Petal by petal, unfurling, spreading, black as tar.

Devanna pushed his hand up her thigh, fumbling, searching. Beneath him, Devi froze, her pupils dilated in shock.

This was to teach her respect, it was for her own good. Thunder boomed and a few drops of rain began to fall, splattering fatly into the earth. A fragrance, such a fragrance all around, 'the *scent* of rain, there is *nothing* like it.' He shuddered. Shifted over her, thrust, missed. Thrust again. Soft skin tearing under unyielding pressure, offering up warm passage, silk cotton soft. Devanna shut his eyes and moaned. He began to thrust, faster and faster. This was who he was made for, this was the one he had waited for.

Close as two spores on a fern they had been, ever since he could remember.

Rain pattered down upon Devanna. He grunted softly and rolled onto his back. His head felt cleaved in two, the gin crooning love songs in his ears.

I love thee. To the depth and breadth and height my soul can reach.

He opened his eyes, squinting against the rain. What ... where ... The previous night came back to him in flashes. The bus ride to Mercara. Gin, the sear of it down his throat. Devi ...

Devanna convulsed. He tried to get up, shaking so hard that he kept slipping forward onto his hands and knees. She had begged, he remembered, fought, pleaded and then she had grown very still. He began to retch, throwing up into the grass until there was nothing left to bring up. He had ... what had he ... *Devi.* Chengappa anna would kill him, he would take his gun and blow out his brains. Tayi, Pallada Nayak ... *What had he done?*

He staggered upright. The rain grew heavier, plastering his hair to his skull. The house loomed far above, silent. He took an unsteady step towards it. Devi. He must ... The front door was opening, someone was coming out. *They would kill him*. Devanna ran. He crashed through the fields in a wild panic, weeping hysterically as he fled towards the Mission.

Gundert took one horrified look at him and dragged him into his study. 'Sit,' he ordered, his heart pounding. 'Here, water. *Drink* this. Steady yourself son. What happened? Why are not at college? Dev, look at me. *LOOK* at me. What happened? Who did this to you?'

Devanna shook his head, struggling to get the words out. 'For ... forgive me Reverend. Forgive me Father for I have sinned,' he sobbed.

A cold fear began to unfurl inside Gundert. 'What happened?' he asked tersely again. He grabbed Devanna's shoulders. 'Calm down Dev. What happened? Tell me.'

Devanna clutched his head in his hands and began to rock wildly back and forth. 'She ... I ... Devi ... last night ... She is *mine*, Reverend, I only took what is mine.'

Gundert froze. His hands slid from Devanna's shoulders. Devanna slumped from the chair onto the floor and clasped Gundert's legs. 'Help me Reverend, you said you would. Please Reverend, do something. Devi . . . Reverend, do something.'

My Dev.

Gundert kicked out hard, with all the strength in his spare, sinewy legs. He caught Devanna a glancing blow just beneath his chin and he went skidding across the waxed floors. 'Pagan,' Gundert hissed, his face white and twisted. 'Filthy, common native. Olaf . . . you are nothing, *nothing* like him. I thought, I hoped . . . How could you betray me?

'Get out,' he said, and his voice trembled. 'Get out and never let me see your foul, whoring self again.'

Devanna rose shuddering to his feet. He limped to the chapel, and knelt by the altar. 'Our Father who art in heaven,' he wept, 'Hallowed be thy name.'

Chapter 13

✤ 1899 ✤

The wedding was a rushed affair, nothing like the elaborate send-off Thimmaya had always imagined for his daughter. Five days earlier, when he sent Chengappa in search of Devanna, Thimmaya had cautioned his hotheaded son to be circumspect. 'The family's reputation is at stake,' he said, 'or what is left of it.'

Devanna had approached Chengappa like a goat might a butcher. 'Anna,' he began, but a stony faced Chengappa cut him off.

'Not a word,' he said. 'Do not open your mouth, do not so much as look in my direction or by Iguthappa Swami I shall cleave you to the ground.'

Pallada Nayak had shown no such restraint, launching himself upon Devanna with a bellow of fury and laying into him with his walking stick. Gauru's mother and the other women of the household came running out in alarm, shouting at the servants to hurry to the fields, to race, quickly, 'why are you standing there like donkeys, G O,' and summon their husbands before the Nayak tore Devanna apart. 'What happened? In God's name, what has the boy done?' they cried in fright, trying to pull the Nayak away from Devanna.

'What has he done?' roared the Nayak. 'What has he left undone, that's what you should be asking me. A taint! A taint on this house, that's what he is. No thought for her, that innocent child, he . . .' The Nayak stopped short then, at the mute appeal in Thimmaya's face. He flung his stick down in disgust and sank trembling against the ledge of the verandah. His hand shook as he mopped at his forehead. 'He . . . the boy has refused to go back to Bangalore,' the Nayak improvised. He looked at the ashen Devanna and a fresh spasm of disgust crossed his face. 'Yes. He will never go back to finish his studies.'

It was testimony to the Nayak's standing in the village, perhaps, that nobody thought to question the hurried wedding or the bloodied scratches along the bridegroom's cheeks. 'We knew it,' said the gossips. 'Inseparable, that's what those two have always been, close as the holes in a coconut shell from the time they were little. A canny one, that Devi, kept turning down everyone, and now look at her, married into such a wealthy family, to a *doctor* no less.' When they heard that Devanna had dropped out of medical college, they were only momentarily stumped. It was all Devi's doing, they said. It was she who had asked Devanna not to return to Bangalore and so smitten was he that he had readily acquiesced. Slender as a moonbeam she might be, but even she knew that she was no match for the painted, leg-baring molls of the cities. Smart girl, to know how to keep her husband tied firmly to the pleats of her sari.

Devi sat motionless amidst the hubbub of the wedding, an exquisite alabaster doll draped in the brocade sari that Tayi had worn as a bride. It was good luck to wear the bridal sari of one who had enjoyed a long married life. Blood-red talisman this, the promise of wedded bliss in its weft, its drape butter soft from the years.

Women were bustling all about her and she faithfully followed their instructions. 'Sit,' they said, and she perched on the three-legged bridal stool; 'Bend,' they said when her veil of silk tissue snagged on the crescents ornamenting her plait, and she bowed her head so that they might untangle its ends. Not a word did she speak all through the ceremonies, going through the motions as if in a dream. They scattered handfuls of raw rice on her head and forced black glass bangles on her wrists, and if they noticed the deep ridges her nails had scored across her palms, they put it down to the nerves of a bride.

How she had screamed that night, stop, *stop*, fought him, cajoled, begged. She had scratched at his face with her nails, tried to pry his hands off her body, calling frantically to the sleeping house, to someone, anyone, please, Iguthappa Swami, *please*, her cries drowned out by the brewing storm.

He had finally fallen into a stupor, lying slack across her, and she had broken free. The water in the bathhouse had been freezing but it hadn't mattered. Her stomach hurt, the very pit of it, plagued by a deep cramping as she picked up the pumice stone and began to scrub. She had scrubbed every inch of her body, thoroughly, dazed, her skin turning a raw pink, sloughing the memory of him from her pores.

Tayi had known immediately, as soon as she laid eyes on her. She had come knocking on the door of the bathhouse. Had common sense deserted her, Tayi clucked, that she was bathing in cold water? Did she want to fall ill? Wait a while, Tayi called, she would heat water in the fireplace and bring it to her. Devi opened the door, and a shocked Tayi fell silent, taking in the sari lying in a stained heap on the floor and the bits of twigs and grass and other debris of the previous night that lay scattered about her grandchild.

Devi had started to weep then, a thin, high-pitched keening like a bird trapped in a bramble thicket. 'Tayi,' she sobbed, 'Tayi', her cries piercing her grandmother's heart. 'De . . . Devanna . . .'

Tayi wrapped her shawl around Devi with hands that shook. 'Shhh kunyi, hush child. My darling child, my sun and moon, please be quiet before the servants hear. All will be well, Tayi will make it so. Come kunyi . . .' She hurried Devi back to the house as rapidly as her arthritic legs would allow. She bundled Devi into bed, tucking the blankets high about her and then woke Thimmaya.

'Devi . . .' she said to her son. 'Our Devi, my flower bud . . .' Tayi began to cry.

He had stared uncomprehendingly at her, hearing the words, but unwilling to take them in, no, it could not be, not his angel daughter. And then Thimmaya cried out, a sound so anguished, so filled with fury, so at odds with his ordinary gentleness that it seemed nearly inhuman. He stormed from his room, Tayi hobbling after him in a panic.

'Monae, wait, where are you going? Thimmaya, listen to me, wait a moment, what are you doing?'

Chengappa came rushing into the hall, rubbing the sleep from his eyes. 'Who ... what ... Appaiah? What is it Appaiah, what's happened?' he said alarmed. Thimmaya was loading his matchlock, wild with rage.

'I will blow his brains out. Is this how he repays our hospitality after all these years? Did it mean nothing to him, that we considered him a son? He ... my own daughter. *My own blood.*' Thimmaya was shaking so much the wick kept slipping from his hand. Tayi gently took the gun from him and placed it behind her, out of his or Chengappa's reach.

Thimmaya sat down abruptly, as if his legs would no longer bear his weight. 'How Avvaiah?' he asked, and Tayi's heart ached at the bewilderment in his eyes. 'Why? What will Muthavva say to me when I see her, how am I to face her?'

'What's done is done, we have to look now to the future. Find that boy,' she counselled her son, 'find Devanna. I don't know how ... what he did ... I do not understand it. But this much I do know. I know he loves Devi deeply. Go to Pallada Nayak. He will do the right thing by us. We must ... we have to get them married.'

Chengappa was dispatched to find Devanna while Tayi returned to Devi's side, a tumbler of hot milk in her hand. 'Shh kunyi,' she said, 'hush. Tayi will make it all right. Quiet now.' She stroked Devi's hair, crooning lullabies and whispering reassurances until at last Devi fell into a deep, exhausted sleep.

It was well into the afternoon when at last she awoke. She lay unmoving on her bed.

'Devi? Are you up? Will you eat something?'

It came back again, in a flood. His hands upon her, under her, inside. Devi began to retch.

She slept again, and did not awaken until the stars were out.

'Devi? Kunyi, you must eat.'

She lay as if in a stupor, staring blankly at the wall. Tears sprang anew into Tayi's eyes. She leaned forward, surreptitiously wiping them away as she fussed with the wick of the oil lamp. The flame flared high with a hiss, casting a golden light against the lime-washed walls.

'Kunyi,' Tayi said, trying to inject a cheeriness into her voice. 'I have some special news for you. Do you know what is going to happen two days from now?'

Devi remained silent.

'Two days from now ... in two days ...' Tayi's voice faltered. 'In just a few days, my precious flower bud is going to be married.'

Devi turned to look uncomprehendingly at her grandmother.

Tayi nodded and tried to smile. 'My little sun and moon is to be a bride.'

'Married? Who to?'

'Devanna.'

Devi recoiled. 'After what happened? I will not. Never, not if ...'

'This is the only way. If word gets out ... your reputation ... no man will ever consider you after this. What is done is done. Devanna has always loved you, he ...' Tayi choked up again. 'It is for the best,' she said after a moment. 'It is the only way.'

'Machu.

'*Machu*,' Devi said again, her voice hoarse. Trembling, barely even audible at times, she broke the promise she had made to Machu and told Tayi about him, about the two of them. His vow, the necessity for secrecy. He was leaving for Kerala soon, he had told her the last time they met, with a caravan of rice from the Kambeymada fields to barter. He would be gone for nearly a month. 'Send word to him. Tayi, you have to. Send Tukra. Machu will come, I know he will.'

'Enough!' Tayi rose to her feet. 'Not another word. Not to me, not to anybody and never, *ever* to your father. *What* have you been up to beneath our noses?'

'Tayi, no, you don't understand.'

'ENOUGH, Devi. Stop. *Send for Machaiah*? Send for him, and what will you tell him then? That you have been violated by another? Even if his intentions towards you have been honourable, do you think he would follow through after what has happened? *He is a Coorg*. Did you forget that? He would never accept you, even if he wanted to, his pride would *never* allow it.'

*

She was married. She repeated the words silently to herself, but they were empty, devoid of meaning. Devi looked down at her hennaed palms, noting the silver glinting upon the arches of her feet, the gold chains threaded over her fingers and the backs of her hands. The wedding party had travelled through the night to the Kambeymada village. They took her to the well, where she broke a coconut and drew the first, ritualistic water.

What had Tayi said to her? 'He will want you as he might a rotten tooth, picked over by many toothpicks.'

She was seized by an absurd urge to laugh. She had often told him not to pick at his teeth, it would make them fall one day from his gums. He had smacked his lips at her. 'So will you still love me then? When I am an old, toothless Thatha, will you still make eyes at me?'

Devi extended her right foot first, over the threshold of the Kambeymada house. She placed the pot of water on the hearth and then was led to the south-west corner of the house to light the ceremonial lamp. She dotted her forehead with sacred ash and bent to touch the feet of the elders of the household.

The women took her to the flower-bedecked nuptial room, apologising for the slipshod decorations; everything had been organised in *such* a hurry. They seated her upon the enormous rosewood bed, giggling as they offered bawdy advice to the new bride, and then adjusting the veil about her face, they left Devi to await her groom. The bedroom doors were shut, and for the first time since the previous morning, there was silence.

She looked blankly about her, at the breadth of the room, at the massive teakwood rafters. Her eyes travelled over the intricately carved wall pegs, the painted porcelain lamps casting light into all but the most distant corners, the jug of milk and the areca nuts placed upon a silver platter for the newlyweds to share. Jasmine was strung along the bedposts, hung along every wall and strewn across the bedsheets, so much of it that the sweetness of its perfume was almost overpowering. She dug her nails into her hands, fighting the urge to gag. There was an oval mirror by the side of the bed. She stared at her reflection, the pallor of her skin, the dilated pupils. Overcome with weariness, Devi shut her eyes.

There was a hesitant knock on the door, jolting her out of her stupor. She began to tremble, suddenly terrified, huddling against the headboard as there was another shaky knock. Slowly the doorknob turned. Devanna walked in, cowering. He shut the door and leaned against it as if his legs would not hold him. 'Devi,' he said, and the breath caught in her chest. 'Devi, I . . .' and Devanna began to weep.

He loved her, he sobbed, *how* he loved her. 'What I did, if I could take it back . . . I was not myself Devi. Nancy . . . they . . . so *helpless* Devi. For what I did to you, I know I will pay, I will pay a millionfold.' The words tumbled out, making little sense except to repeat how *sorry* he was. He knew he was not worthy, he said, his voice raw with self-loathing, but *please* Devi, he begged her forgiveness, he was at her mercy forever.

Her eyes were huge, fixed upon him. Flashes of that fateful morning, red hot and searing, setting off a tremor in her hands. Fingers furling, unfurling, picking at the gold threads in the sari, clutching and releasing the silk. She stared at Devanna, unable to look away. His face, contorted with grief, so utterly wretched. 'I am sorry Devi, *so sorry* . . .' Slowly, the terror within her began to subside, leaving in its wake a dark, stygian cold, blasting hope, shearing every dream at the root.

'Say something,' he pleaded. He took a step forward, hands outstretched, stopping as she shrank away. 'Say *something*.' Again he tried desperately to explain all that had happened at the hostel. 'I was not myself that day, Martin—'

'Nothing excuses what you did,' she said, cutting him short. She shivered. '*Nothing*. I will never forgive you. Not as long as I live, not for all the lives I will ever live.'

Devanna's mouth opened and shut as he struggled with the words, and then he nodded hopelessly. He pulled a sheet off the bridal bed, jasmines drifting down as he curled upon the floor.

When Machu returned from Kerala with oxen laden with the coconut oil, dried fish and salt that he had bartered in exchange for the paddy, he heard about Devanna's sudden wedding and his disappointing decision to leave his studies midway. 'What have we here?' Machu hollered jovially as he entered the house. 'A new bride and why hasn't she brought me anything to drink?'

Devi emerged mutely from the kitchen. She bent to touch Machu's feet and his face turned white.

'Swami kapad,' he said automatically. 'May you live long, my dear.'

Chapter 14

Devi was catatonic with grief, a biting lament with neither expression nor relief. Machu stayed away from her, taking great pains to ensure their paths hardly crossed. He found every pretext to be gone from the Kambeymada house, often for weeks at a time. When it was time again for the family to send someone to man the post at the entrance to the forest, Machu offered to go. When Kambeymada Nayak wanted to gift the new Commissioner of Mysore a handsome peechekathi dagger in silver, Machu immediately volunteered his services; when the servants brought news of a bison sighting, no matter how improbable the source or distant the location, Machu at once shouldered his gun.

Devanna and she hardly saw one another during the day and shared the nights in silence. Devanna's father was belatedly attempting to connect with his son by trying to interest him in agriculture. Every morning he insisted Devanna accompany him to the paddy fields and the acres given over to coffee, and in the afternoons, the Nayak assigned Devanna the duty of looking over the accounts. There was also the constant trickle of villagers, come to Devanna to seek treatment for their fevers and sores.

When at first an alarmed Devanna had tried to explain to them that he was not a doctor, he had only studied medicine for a couple of years, they had pleaded with the Nayak to convince his grandson to treat them. Kambeymada Nayak had yet to overcome the crushing disappointment he had felt when he learnt from Pallada Nayak that Devanna did not intend to return to medical college. He had tried his utmost to cajole and even threaten the boy, tugging agitatedly on his whiskers all the while, but Devanna had stood silently before him.

The Nayak had found, in the villagers' touching belief in his grandson's capabilities, some partial consolation; it was for his sake that Devanna finally capitulated. He saw his patients every evening, in the shade of the enormous butter fruit tree in the courtyard, performing common sense diagnostics, while the Nayak kept track of the proceedings from the verandah, his moustache puffed with pride.

All in all Devanna was kept so busy, he barely saw his new wife. Every night he paused at the foot of their bed, searching desperately for a sign, however small, that she may have begun to forgive him. Every night she looked away, and he would sleep on the floor again. He would move to the bed the next morning after she had arisen, so that nobody would guess the newlyweds did not sleep together. The sheets would still be warm from her skin, a faint, grassy scent of hibiscus on her pillow.

Devi immersed herself in housework. The Nachimanda household had been far smaller, Thimmaya and his brother Bopu having broken years earlier from the larger joint family to set up an independent home. As Devi's cousins had grown, they too had wandered away one by one, and Bopu and his wife had left too, to live with one of their sons; it was only Chengappa, his wife and his sons who now lived with Tayi and Thimmaya. The Kambeymadas, however, were a traditional joint family. Kambeymada Nayak had sired eleven sons, and they and their families, along with his brothers and their own children and grandchildren, all lived together in the sprawling central house and the adjoining rows of rooms.

With such a large family, over fifty members living together, and an endless stream of visitors, there was always something to be done. Apart from the preparation of the day's food – in itself a gargantuan task – there were children to be cleaned, fed, disciplined and pampered, the retinue of servants to be directed, and sheds of buffaloes to be milked. There were rows of rooms to be swept and cleaned, mounds of laundry to be sorted – 'whose underclothes are these now, they all look the same' – dogs to be cared for, shanks of game to be cured, pigs to be fattened, vegetable plots to be tended, and the pumpkins, cucumbers and brinjals to be carefully stored in layers of banana leaves and hung from the eaves of the wooden-floored attic.

Devi took on the task of sweeping the floors each morning and sterilising them with a paste of fresh dung from the cattle sheds. At this early hour, the house was serene, the clamour of voices, the click-clacking of wooden slippers through the rooms and the crash of pots and pans from the kitchen not yet begun.

She worked without a sound, like something slipped from a dream. Each morning she would pause, momentarily halt her sweeping, outside the room where the bachelors of the family slept in a row of rosewood cots. Had he returned, she wondered, from wherever it was that he had gone the previous evening? She would lay her hand on the door, as if to sense the heat of his breath, to feel the beat of his pulse through the distance that separated them. She would stand there, listening intently until the ache in her heart grew unbearable. Then she would turn away and begin to sweep again, her broom arching noiselessly across the floors.

They had spoken only once. She was returning after replenishing the box of soapnuts in the bathhouse when he accosted her.

'Why?' he asked scathingly.

She stood looking at him, her eyes huge and dark.

'I *know* something must have happened. What?'

'You be silent,' Tayi had said to her. 'Swear to me that you will never breathe a word of what happened to anyone, anyone at all, ever.' She had grabbed Devi's hand and placed it on her own head. 'Swear on my life that you will keep this a secret, or by Iguthappa Swami and all the ancestors, may I be cursed for the next nine lives to follow. May I be born a servant, may my body be ridden with pox, may sorrow dog my every step.'

'No, Tayi,' Devi had wept, 'don't say such things . . .'

'Then swear on me that you will protect your reputation. Promise me you will never, ever speak of what happened last night.'

'*Why*, Devi?' Machu asked now. He stepped closer, his fists balled at his sides. 'Was this nothing but a game to you?'

She stood woodenly before him. *Look into my eyes. You are my breath, my being. The ripples of my passing, the shadows of my soul. Look into my eyes and read the things I cannot say. Know, you must know I could never betray you, not if I tried.*

She opened her mouth, heard her voice as if from a great distance. 'Someone may see us.'

The lines around his mouth turned white. 'Someone may see us? Is that all you can say? That is what worries you most, *what if somebody were to see us*? Why did you tell me you would wait?' He was livid with rage. 'Why did you give me hope? Was I just your passing fancy while you waited for your doctor finally to summon the courage to declare himself?'

'Machu ...'

'You waited until my back was turned, until you knew I would be gone, and then you pounced on him as soon as you could. Does he know about me Devi? Does he know how you slipped out in the middle of the night to meet with me? Do you tell your educated, intelligent husband, do you tell him as he reads to you, do you tell him in your big marital bed how you bloomed to my touch?'

He bent his head close to hers. 'Tell me,' he whispered in her ear, 'does he keep you *satisfied*?'

'What's done,' she said, her voice shaking, 'is done. If you think so little of me ...'

Machu laughed, a harsh, curdled sound. 'It doesn't really matter any more, does it, what I think of you? What's done is indeed done. Well, sister-in-law,' he said, 'I wish you and your husband a lifetime of happiness.'

At the village shooting contest later that month, Machu was so drunk, he could barely raise his gun to his shoulder. His shot went wide, missing the mark by a mile.

A month went by slowly and then part of another. Devi was three weeks late before she realised her monthly blood was yet to arrive. She counted and recounted the days on her fingers, but there was no mistake. She sank upon the edge of the bed, trembling with revulsion.

She began stealing into the kitchen each morning, boiling cinnamon and turmeric, hastily gulping down the water before anyone saw her. When that did not work, she gathered the unripe papayas fallen to the ground in the vegetable plot, hiding them under her sari, in the folds of her chemise, to eat in the privacy of her bedroom. They had given her such cramps that night that her groans woke Devanna. He hurriedly lit the lamps and tried to examine her. 'What is it? Where does it hurt?' he asked anxiously, pressing her abdomen. She slapped his hand away.

'Don't touch me. Don't you *ever* touch me, do you understand?'

The cramps had finally subsided, but there was no bleeding; the pregnancy had survived.

Devanna barely slept that night from worry. The next morning, he secretly followed her into the kitchen and when he saw her retching outside he guessed. 'Are you pregnant?' The light in his face dimmed as he spotted the cinnamon brew boiling on the stove. 'And you want to terminate the pregnancy.' He swallowed. 'Please Devi,' he said quietly, 'I know I deserve every ounce of your hatred. I know I will never be able to forgive myself for the atrocity I committed.' His eyes filled with tears. 'But Devi, I beg you, don't take it out on our child.' He prostrated himself in front of her, not caring who might walk in on them. 'Do as you will with me, but do not harm an innocent life.'

Devi said nothing as she backed away from him, but from that day on she gave up trying to rip out the life that clung like a barnacle within her. She lost even more weight in those initial months, then gradually the nausea ended. Her waist began to thicken, the tautness of her stomach gave way to a little potbelly, and it was not long before the women of the house guessed. When they announced the happy news at dinner, Devanna was at once subjected to much backslapping and ribaldry. Machu said nothing and barely touched his rice.

Devi went home for the confinement, the first time she had visited the Nachimanda house since the wedding. Thimmaya folded his hands in blessing as she touched his feet, at a loss for words. The house had grown quiet after Devi left, a shifting in the quality of light that permeated its windows, a stillness creeping into its bones.

He had held stoic all through the wedding. Not a tear had he shed, even when the wedding party had departed to the Kambeymada home with his precious child. It had only been once, many months later, that he had crumbled. He had not slept all the previous night, his thoughts filled with Devi, as they had been ever since the wedding. To get Devanna and her married had been the only recourse left, he told himself again, the only means with which to protect his daughter's honour. It swam before him again, the memory of her face, so expressionless, as she had sat at the wedding altar. Her eyes vacant, devoid of their customary fire, barely a flicker of recognition as he blessed her with a handful of rice and pressed a gold sovereign into her hands. He shifted restlessly, thinking of Muthavva. 'What would you have me do?' he silently asked his long-dead wife. 'You'd have done the same.'

He had tossed and turned until, giving up on his sleep, he arose, deciding to start the day's ploughing earlier than usual. The fields were deserted and still. Muthavva's breath was in the trees, the scent of sampigé in the air. Up and down he had furrowed, directing the bulls forward, his feet sinking into the rain-washed earth. 'I tried,' he whispered desperately to his dead wife. 'Why did you leave, how was I to be both father and mother?' The breeze lifted, as if in response, tugging at his hair. 'I *tried*,' he said again. He leaned against the plough, the oxen placidly flicking their tails as the sobs burst from his chest, no one to hear him but the softly sighing breeze.

'It does my heart good to see you, kunyi,' he said heavily now, 'it does us all good.'

Tayi never did ask when the child was conceived, whether it had been before or after the wedding. Neither did she comment on the unhappiness dimming her granddaughter's eyes. 'Best to let bygones be bygones,' she thought to herself. 'She is a grown woman now, she will see sense soon enough. Besides, is there any gloom in the world that an infant cannot disperse?'

The village came to visit, bearing with them vast parcels of curd-rice and the nine meat, chicken and vegetable curries that were customarily required to appease the appetite of a pregnant woman. Devi lifted her head then, proudly. Tayi sat by, listening without comment as she laughed a little too loudly and recounted to the visitors the pleasures of married life, the goodness of her husband and the grand Kambeymada house. The sprawl of the fields from the carved windows in every direction, as far as the eye could see, the numerous servants, the enamel washbasins ordered from England. There was no golden spittoon, contrary to the rumours, but the family owned no fewer than three of beaten copper.

The infant slipped out of her with minimal fuss, in the middle of the day, waiting until the midwife had been summoned from the village, as if he were trying to cause his mother as little inconvenience as possible. Tukra's wife brought a bale of hay from the courtyard and Chengappa's wife and Tayi spread it across a cot, smoothing a sheet over it. They slung a rope through the rafters and handing Devi its ends to hold onto for support, they sat her on her haunches upon the sheet. The midwife spread Devi's knees apart and feeling with a gentle finger between her legs, nodded in satisfaction. 'Not long now,' she said. 'Push, kunyi.'

'Push!' they encouraged, and on the fifth try, out he came.

'A boy,' Tayi cried, 'it's a boy!' She bent over Devi, pushing the damp tendrils of hair away from her forehead. 'My flower bud, ah, my precious child, you are a mother now, to a healthy, beautiful baby boy.' Thimmaya fired his gun in the courtyard, a single shot to announce the happy news of his grandson to the village. Chengappa's wife plucked some stalks from the castor plant growing by the cattle shed and fashioned a miniature bow and arrow. She placed these in the crib beside the baby. 'May you be keen of eye, fleet of foot and of faultless judgement,' she said, reciting the ancient blessing as she kissed the top of his downy head.

Tayi looked anxiously at Devi, who lay staring at the rafters. 'Here, hold him kunyi,' she said, placing the baby in her arms. Devi looked at her son, at the red, wrinkled face, at the minuscule fingers and toes, each capped with a perfect half-moon nail. She had produced this human being. She gazed wonderingly at the stub of the umbilical cord still protruding from his abdomen, at the thimble-sized penis. It was from her loins he had sprung, perfectly formed, fully jointed. She looked at the broad, high forehead, the large eyes so unmistakably like his father's. Pain shafted through her then, great, swamping waves of grief, and Devi began to weep.

Devanna came rushing to the Nachimanda house to see his son. He rocked the baby clumsily in his arms, loath to give him to anyone else, until Tayi almost had to pry the child away. He hung over Tayi's shoulder as she burped the infant and swaddled him in layers of muslin, reaching out time and again to stroke his son's head until the baby balled his fists and wailed in protest. 'Cheh. Leave him be Devanna,' Tayi chided.

'*Sons are a heritage from the Lord,*' Devanna quoted, beaming from ear to ear, '*children a reward from him. Like arrows in the hands of a warrior are sons born in one's youth.*'

Tayi asked him then if all was well and Devanna looked at his feet, the smile wiped from his face. 'She needs time Tayi,' he said finally, his voice raw. 'Our son . . . things will get better.'

They named the baby Nanjappa. Three months later, when it was time for Devi to return to her marital home, Tayi hugged her tight. She tucked a dot of lampblack behind Devi's ears and in the middle of the baby's forehead. 'Be well kunyi,' she said, tears in her eyes, 'my sun-and-moon, be happy. Forget the past, it is gone. Look to what you have now, count the many blessings you have been given.'

When they arrived at the Kambeymada house, the family welcomed this newest addition to their folds with a bounty of blessings and gold sovereigns. Machu had contrived to be absent that day, but on his return, he too presented Devanna with a quarter sovereign to celebrate the birth of his son.

She had spoken so little before the baby's birth that nobody noticed how listless Devi had become. If anything, after producing a child, the women seemed to accept her into a secret club she had not previously realised existed. They included her in conversations in which Devi startlingly discovered that there was virtually nothing that was deemed too private to discuss. The most intimate details of their marriages, the most personal of their husbands' foibles, everything was aired in the kitchen. When they prodded Devi for the spicier details of her own marriage, however, she shook her head and smiled.

A strange lassitude began to slide into her days. She couldn't seem to feel anything – neither joy nor sorrow, anger nor laughter. It was an effort even to think or to remember the simplest of things. She looked at her baby every morning and was gripped by a vast indifference. He lay in his crib, cooing and gurgling up at her as she absently stroked his head. The other women told her how lucky she was, he barely cried, her son, what a little angel. Would you look at him, they said, truly like his father, a miniature Devanna, both in looks and in gentle temperament. Devi's milk had barely come forth before it had dried up and here too, the child had been most accommodating, taking to diluted cow's milk without a fuss.

She hardly saw Machu any more, he was gone from the house so very often. She began to use the pretext of the baby to hardly step out from her room. What was the point, Devi began to wonder, of any of this? The child, this life, this dull progression of morning and evening. Devanna thanked her every single night for his son, standing hesitantly at the foot of the bed. Every night, Devi turned away to the wall. She wished he would stop. It meant nothing to her. None of this meant anything to her.

Increasingly dark thoughts began to swim through her head. 'Like a flower,' that's what she had overhead the adults say all those years ago; Gauru akka's hair had floated about her head like a many petalled flower. Why had she chosen to jump in the well, she wondered absently. She thought of the well in the backyard of the Kambeymada house, its yawning mouth, the obsidian glint of water far below. She imagined herself spiralling downwards, the dankness radiating off the moss-covered walls, the patch of sun growing smaller and smaller above her head. Devi shivered.

She took to walking along the river in the afternoons, when the fields lay deserted. It was a direct tributary of the Kaveri, a fast-moving body of water very different from the gentle stream in the Nachimanda fields, and one that the children were warned to stay away from. If someone were to fall in, she realised idly one afternoon, they would be carried a long distance before their body was found. She stood on the bank, turning this over in her mind, vaguely wondering what she ought to do next. She would sit, she decided. Just a while, until her head stopped aching. The child was fed and asleep, the morning chores were done and nobody would be looking for her. She perched absently on the bank. How inviting it looked, the rushing water. Possessed of a strength, a force of will she no longer possessed. *Kaveri amma kapad.*

It was said that when her husband, the great sage Agastya, had wooed

163

her, the Goddess Kaveri had accepted his offer of marriage on two conditions. The first was that he never abandon her, not even for an instant. The second, that he never would try to contain her. Agastya had abided by these conditions, until one day, called away by an urgent summons, he had trapped Kaveri in his pot. There she would remain, he planned, until he returned.

Ah, how he had misjudged his free-spirited spouse. Kaveri had been furious. She burst free from the pot and flowed away, faster and faster, even as the contrite sage chased after her, until finally, she had disappeared underground. Free to go where she pleased, unfettered, unbound.

Devi remembered the old legend as she stared at the river. Maybe her ankles, that's all she would place inside, just to see how the water felt against her skin. She lowered her feet into the water, feeling the impetuous tug of the current willing her to come with it. '*Like the tendrils of a water lily*.' She touched her fingers lightly to her neck, to the tiny black beads of the kartamani, the dark-jewel chain that every married woman wore. The water tugged again, a little more urgently, and Devi reached behind her to unclasp the chain.

'I didn't know you came here too.' Devi jerked upright, nearly losing her balance. 'Uyyi, careful,' cried the woman, 'the current here is especially strong.'

It was one of Devanna's aunts. She made herself comfortable beside Devi without waiting for an invitation. 'I like to come here as well. So peaceful.'

Devi nodded, looking down at the water.

'Is the baby asleep?'

Devi nodded again.

'It is good to have new life in that room again. Happiness. After all that happened . . .'

She looked at Devi's confused expression. 'Surely you knew?' she asked, surprised. 'That room once belonged to Devanna's father and mother.'

'Gauru akka?'

'Yes. Gauru.' The woman looked sadly into the river. 'It has been many years since anyone has spoken of her in this house.'

Devi looked down at her ankles, distorted by the current. Gauru akka. It was strange to think she was sleeping in the same bed that Gauru had once lain in as a bride. She wondered if Devanna knew.

Devi turned to look at his aunt. 'What happened?' she asked simply.

'Between Gauru and Devanna's father you mean? What else. The same old drama. Some of the men of this house, my husband included,' she confided to Devi, 'are blessed with a little too much virility. The mere touch of a woman, that's all it takes for them to start pawing and snorting like a bull.' She sighed. 'And sometimes one wife simply isn't enough for them. They need other women. Different women. Gauru . . . she loved him too much. Couldn't bear to share him. We all heard the shouting that used to come from that room late at nights, sometimes there would be a bruise on her arm or her cheek the next day. Then one day, she just left.'

She snorted. 'A man is like a dog, dipping his snout into every ditch, but he will always come home in the end. If she had only looked away, she would still have him. What did it amount to, this great love she had for her husband? A sodden ending in the well. And he waited not six months before he was married again.'

The woman sighed again. 'One has to live, not run away from one's problems. One has to fight for happiness. It isn't easy for a woman, I am the first to agree with that. But where is the sense in throwing everything away? One must fight.'

She turned and looked back at the house, shading her eyes against the sun with her palms. 'I should go check what is happening with the dinner,' she said, and rose creakily to her feet.

Devi looked up at her briefly and smiled. 'Go ahead,' she said, 'I am right behind you.'

She remembered how softly spoken Gauru had been. It was hard to imagine her raising her voice at anyone. She had been waiting, Devi realised, waiting in vain for Devanna's father to come and take her home. Like a flower, everyone had tut tutted, a many petalled lily, and then they had moved on with their lives.

One has to fight for happiness.

Devi looked at the river for a long time, at the currents urging her to slip forward. *One must fight*. Moving very deliberately, she withdrew her feet from the water. Rising from the bank, she turned and walked back towards the house, her damp footprints flaring briefly upon the grass before vanishing in the sun.

Chapter 15

The sari that Devi chose that evening was of simple cotton, but it was tinted a delicate pink. 'Oh, what a pretty colour!' one of the aunts exclaimed. Devi smiled.

'Someone told me,' she said softly, 'that it reminded them of the roses that grow wild in the hills.'

Machu stiffened, his hand making a small, shocked movement at her words. 'Like a rose,' he had said to her once, 'this colour on you, you look like a mountain rose.' His lips tightened and then, deliberately drawing his plate closer, he continued to eat in silence.

He was away for the next two days. The evening of his return, Devi contrived to spill the gravy from the mutton curry onto his sleeve as she was serving him. 'Just see what I went and did,' she exclaimed, her hands flying to her cheeks in chagrin. 'Here, let me.' She reached for his hand, heart pounding, her fingers closing tight about his as she poured water over the stain.

Machu snatched his hand away. 'You do not need to go to such trouble,' he said, his voice even, despite the muscle jumping in his jaw. 'It will wash off easily enough.'

So it went for the next few weeks, as Devi plied her wiles. The darkness that had so clouded her lifted, leaving in its place a manic, single-minded purpose. *Machu.*

She washed her hair and sat in the courtyard, just beneath the window of the room where Machu slept, to dry it. The sun caught in the unbound silk of it, spinning shine through its length. At dinner, where once she had hardly paused over what to wear, she now agonised over her wardrobe. She began to wear flowers in her hair once more; her slender ankles were adorned with silver. The breath stopped time and again in Devanna's throat as he looked at her, and in the other men of the family too as they glanced shyly towards her. Machu's lips would tighten, the only indication that he had even noticed her presence.

Devi did not know what she would say to him, or how she would convince him, or indeed what it was that she must convince him of. Perhaps the intent, the seed of what was to follow, was already there, buried deep within her. Devi, however, was little inclined to such introspection. All that mattered, with fevered, hammering urgency, was *now*. This moment, every minute they stayed apart, each hour wasted, every day that Machu and she could have, *should have* been together.

Whether Machu was puzzled, or shocked, or even angered by her overtures, she did not know. His only response was to pull back even more, to disappear for ever greater stretches of time from the Kambeymada house. And when he returned, each dawn when Devi swept the floors, she paused outside the room of the bachelors. She pressed her palms against the shut doors, her thoughts, her being, focused entirely on him, reaching through the wood. '*Yours. I am yours.*'

It was some weeks later that Machu's appearance caused much consternation among the women of the house. He had been gone these past few days to Mysore, and when he returned in the middle of the day, the back of his kupya was torn and muddied, the fabric marred with dark stains of what looked like blood.

'Nothing, it's nothing,' he reassured them, 'I slipped down a gully that is all.'

'Took quite a tumble too, from what I can see,' one of the older women said, worried. 'Let's get Devanna, he'll know what to do.'

'No!'

'No,' Machu repeated, his tone more even this time. 'There's no need for anybody. Is there turmeric in the kitchen? That's all I need, it's just a scratch, believe me.'

'Turmeric? No, no, you need something more, here, look, you are still bleeding . . .' One of the women flapped away to Devi's room where she was putting Nanju to sleep. 'Devi! Devi! Where is your husband? Machu anna is here and he is hurt . . .'

Devi rushed to the kitchen, her face white. He was still surrounded, trying valiantly to calm the women. She stared anxiously at him; he glanced at her and immediately looked away. 'Please, all of you, there is no cause for concern . . . no medicine, no doctors, just give me some turmeric and I will be on my way.'

'You need more than turmeric.' Devi was surprised at how calm she sounded. 'I agree, from what I can tell there is no need to call . . .' She hesitated, the pause of a mere split second, but he noticed it at once, her reluctance to name Devanna.

'No need for a doctor,' she continued smoothly, 'but I know the medicines that must be applied; they are stored in my room.'

'Do not trouble yourself,' Machu said curtly when she reappeared with iodine and a roll of cotton. 'Give me the bottle and I will apply the medicine myself.'

'Cheh!' one of his aunts admonished. 'Stop being so mulish. She is your sister-in-law, not some blushing, unmarried maiden. Here, hand me your kupya and stay still while she cleans you up.'

Machu knew when he was defeated. His face set, he slowly began to untie his kupya, wincing as he pulled the fabric away from the skin on his back. Devi stared decorously away as he undressed, ostensibly fiddling with the bottle, heart thudding as he stripped to his waist.

'Sit,' she said simply, and again she marvelled at how composed she sounded. Her heart was beating so fast she almost felt lightheaded. He seated himself on a stool, his back to her, tension visible in each roped muscle. The women gathered around.

'As I thought, the wounds are not deep,' Devi murmured, relieved.

Machu's lips tightened. 'That's what I said in the first place.'

She said nothing in reply, drawing some water from the pot bubbling on the stove instead. She dipped a cloth into it, then wrung it out. Machu was silent, holding himself very straight, his hands balled upon his knees. His senses heightened to fever pitch, painfully aware of the minutest things. The drops of water as they fell, twisting, catching the light from the fireplace; steam rising gently from the cloth as she dipped it in the water again; the tinkle of glass as her bangles moved back and forth along her wrists.

She began to swab his back, felt before she heard the short, swift intakes of breath as gently she grazed the tips of her fingers along his skin. His fists opened, balled, opened again. Slowly she cleaned the gravel and mud from his lacerations, the women around them exclaiming now and again, pointing to a bit of debris she might have missed, 'there, no, *there*, ah, now you have it.' Devi heard them as if from a great distance, like voices floating disembodied through a pool. It was as if her vision had suddenly contracted, perception and consciousness limited to a few narrow feet of space, so that all she was aware of was the man sitting in front of her. The heat of his body as she stood behind him, barely a finger's span away. Each tiny strand of hair along the nape of his neck. She swirled the cloth over Machu's skin, over the back of his neck, across his shoulders and the small of his back, delicately marking his spine with her nails.

'Oh just see, the sweat is pouring from you,' someone said. Machu grimaced, rubbing his arm absently across his forehead.

Devi poured iodine on to a swathe of cotton. 'This will sting,' she murmured, daubing it on his wounds. The sun shot a shaft of light through the double-paned skylight; dust motes leapt shivering into the air. She bent her head close, so close that her plait swung against his arm, so near that she could see the minute pores in his skin. The hairs rose along Machu's arm, a muscle jumping in his jaw. Devi touched his shoulder lightly, as if to steady herself. She leaned closer, and pursing her lips, blew gently on his skin.

'Enough.' Machu shot from the stool. 'That,' he said rawly, 'will do.' His lips pressed together in a thin, taut line, he snatched the ruined kupya from the floor and strode outside.

Behind him the women collapsed into laughter. 'Men!' they exclaimed fondly, mistaking the source of his discomfort. 'What funny creatures they are. Will think nothing of facing down the wildest of beasts, and then will rush away from the tiniest sting!'

Devi said nothing. Her breath was coming fast as she tightened the cap on the bottle.

*

Machu stayed so determinedly out of her way after that that she barely saw him over the next month. And then, just as she was beginning to despair, he volunteered to pick the gun flowers. The festival of arms was upon them, and the bright orange flowers were needed to adorn each and every gun, sword and knife in the household.

He would leave early the next morning, Machu said to Kambeymada Nayak at dinner. The flowers had bloomed in the jungles earlier that week, and he knew just where the most profuse blossoms were. No, it wasn't necessary for anyone to accompany him, how hard was it, after all, to pick a few flowers?

It was very early when he left, a chill mist enveloping the courtyard. The watery moon that had risen the previous night floated in and out of the clouds, stars flickering moodily through the mist. Machu moved briskly, down the stone steps carved to one side of the courtyard, then along the path that led first towards the fields and then on to the jungle. He was well on his way when abruptly he halted midstride.

'Devi?' he said, shocked. '*Devi?*'

She stood half hidden in the mist, having slipped from the house before him. A hard rage built inside him. He moved even faster, was at her side in seconds. Even in the fitful light, there was no mistaking the anger in his face. 'Have you gone mad?'

From somewhere among the paddy pools, a bird, then another, took flight at his voice, their wings brushing palely through the dark.

'Why are you here, at this hour?'

She tossed her head nervously. 'You look better in the moonlight.' It was the same thing he had said to her all that time ago, when he had asked her to meet him in the lane outside the Nachimanda house.

'Go back,' he said harshly. 'At once. The wives of this family, *sister-in-law*, do not stand in wait for unmarried men.'

Devi flinched, and taking a deep breath, stepped towards him.

'Don't,' he warned. She stepped forward again and he shot out his hand, the harness of his rifle jerked off his shoulder by the sudden movement. 'DO NOT. I do not know what game it is you are playing but if you think I will be your pawn, you are sorely mistaken.'

'Machu,' she said shakily. 'What happened . . . All I know is, without you . . .' She spread her hands helplessly in front of her. 'Nothing makes sense Machu. Without you, there is nothing.'

Her eyes fixed upon him, she very deliberately stepped forward again. A pulse began to beat in his neck.

'What do you want?' There was a wildness in his tone, almost desperation. 'Ayyappa Swami, what is it that you *want* from me?'

Her eyes were huge, the pupils dilated. 'You,' she whispered.

He grew very still. Around them, the skies were lightening. Just a hint of dawn, the slightest shift, as layer by diaphanous layer, the night started to come undone. She stepped even closer, so close, he could feel her breath. She reached up, then slowly, deliberately, she pressed her lips to his neck. The scent of her, a clean fragrance, not too sweet, like freshly cut grass. An involuntary tremble as she ran her hands over his chest. She began to kiss his neck. His eyes, clouding over, closing of their own accord; her lips soft, feather soft, Ayappa Swami, why did she have such sway over him . . .

'No.' He pushed her roughly from him, and she swayed drunkenly for a moment, certain she would fall.

He shouldered his gun, looking at her with such hatred that Devi quailed. 'Leave, just leave before I . . . *Leave!*'

Tears welled in her eyes, her previous bravado gone. 'Machu, please . . .'

'Go!' Without another glance at her, his face implacable, Machu strode towards the forest.

He was so angry, he could barely think. He knew that she was still standing there, staring strickenly after him. He would wring her neck if she so much as . . . She began to cry. He faltered for a moment, strode stubbornly on.

Devi stumbled towards the house, tears spilling down her face. What a fool she was, what an utter fool. The despair of the past year and a half came crushing down on her and she began to weep bitterly, so hard, she could barely see. He *hated* her. He would never forgive her for all that had happened.

And then Machu stopped. His face hard, hating the hold she had on him, hating himself even more. He turned back along the path, moving catlike, coming up behind her in just a few strides. He reached for her arm and swung her roughly around.

'I can't,' she wept, 'I can't . . . no more . . .'

His hands dug into her shoulders as he began to shake her, so hard that her hair came undone from its loosely tied bun. His hands tangled tightly in its spill, the silken length of it, and still he shook her, anger, bitterness, raw, festering hurt stamped equally in his eyes. He shook her like a rag doll, back and forth, back and forth, and then twisting her face violently upwards, he crushed his mouth against hers.

They met in a hollow by the stream, inside a secret thicket of laburnum that Machu directed her to. She pushed the overlapping branches aside and crouched through the narrow opening. Inside was a natural arbour, high enough for a man to stand comfortably, bounded by athi trees to its back and a canopy of flowering branches to its front and sides. Petals lay in drifts of brilliant yellow upon the mossy floor; high above, the sun flashed through the tight weave of leaves. They stood facing each other, strangely shy. He had found this place as a boy as he was chasing a hare, he told her. He didn't think anyone else knew it existed.

She laughed; a bright, artificial laugh. 'You mean nobody but your previous conquests.'

He shook his head and without another word, took her into his arms.

It was liquid, it was fire, the hollow at the base of his spine, the animal sound he made as she nipped at his ear. It had always been chaste between them previously, Machu's sense of honour preventing him from doing much more than press his lips achingly against hers before he would pull back again. Now, it was different; this prolonged separation despite living under the same roof, the heartache of watching her disappear into another's room night after night, his overpowering need of her, a kinsman's wife, sweeping over him in a tidal wave of guilt and desire until he was no longer sure if it was her skin that he felt or his own. Her gasping, unbridled response setting him aflame, goading him on, taking them both higher, unbearably higher, the grief lodged in each of their hearts imploding in an indelible act of possession.

Mine. Forever.

They met there as often as they could, in the afternoon quiet. The shine returned to Devi's eyes, there was a spring to her step, rosiness in her cheeks. Machu, on the other hand, swung between a wild, fierce elation and burning shame. 'What am I *doing*,' he would think as he lay awake at night, staring at the ceiling. He would think of her, the tilt of her head as she looked at him, the velvet softness of her skin. 'This is right,' he would say to himself then, 'it has to be; it cannot be wrong when it feels so right.'

Devanna mistook the song on Devi's lips as a sign that she might finally be thawing. He left a bunch of sampigé for her one day on the chest of drawers in their room, wrapped in leaves and string, where he knew she would find it. Devi stared at the flowers, her face inscrutable. The baby, spotting his mother, gurgled happily from his crib. She turned and looked at him, and he waggled his chubby hands in joy. She smiled tremulously at her son, her heart unaccountably heavy. She picked him up, feeling his warm baby weight settling trustingly into her arms, and tears sprang into her eyes.

That evening at dinner, when Devanna saw her wearing his flowers in her plait, his heart leapt. He approached her that night as she lay in bed, reaching out timidly to stroke her hair. Devi, however, blanched.

'Don't you dare,' she said to him, trembling. 'Don't you *ever* lay a finger on me.'

'How much Devi?' he asked, the hurt unmistakable in his voice. 'How much longer will you make me pay?'

'Lower your voice. Please don't make a spectacle of me amongst your family.'

'Don't make a spectacle of you? I know Devi, what I have put you through. I live with it every day, I know I will have to pay for it when my day of reckoning comes. But it's been over a year. *Fourteen* months. We are married, we have a son, how much longer will you punish me?

'Tell me Devi,' he said in anguish. 'Just tell me, what is it that I need to do for you to forgive me.'

Devi turned away from him, her heart pounding.

*

'Come away with me,' Machu said to her once.

'Where?'

'Away. Anywhere.'

'And live in sin? You know you would not be happy with that.' She bit her lip as soon as she uttered the words. She knew how deeply it shamed him, the fact that he had not completed his vow. There had been less than a year before the stipulated twelve years were up, and yet he had chosen to be with her, choosing her over his God.

'Besides,' she added quickly, tilting her head from where it lay on his chest to squint at the sun glinting through the leaves. 'This is your land.'

He was silent a long while. 'Many years ago,' he said, 'when I was a lad, there was a meeting of the council of the elders. A man from the adjoining village was on trial. Thievery, his crime was appropriating nine acres of land that had been entrusted to his brother. Kambeymada Nayak presided over the trial. It was the evening hour, I remember. From all directions, from all the villages under the Nayak's command, people were coming down the hills towards the village green. The cattle were being herded back to their sheds for the night, you could see their heads bobbing over the hills, hear the faint sound of their bells. That was the only sound, for each of us was silent, completely silent, over-whelmed by the gravity of the situation and waiting for the sentence that we knew must befall the accused.'

'The man stood before the elders, his back straight. Stripped of his peechekathi and odikathi; they lay to one side, in the dust. The Nayak rose to his feet and recited the man's crime. Did he agree to the charges? "Yes," the man said simply, scorning to lie, his shame written plainly upon his face. "We have reached a decision," the Nayak continued gravely. "For his crime, the accused must be punished. From the onset of the next dawn, none may offer the accused either wood or water, throughout the length and breadth of our land."'

Machu paused, his eyes distant. 'The man stood for an instant. And then he crumpled, Devi, he simply crumpled to the ground, like a bison whose knees had been hacked off. All his composure gone, he curled up and cried like a child.'

Neither wood nor water. Devi rubbed the gooseflesh prickling her

175

arm. *Neither wood nor water*. She knew what that meant. Able to claim neither food nor shelter anywhere in Coorg, the accused had been banished, excommunicated forever.

'This is your land,' she repeated unhappily. 'Your heart is here, you would wither away anywhere else.'

'With you. My heart is with you.' They turned towards each other again.

They grew more reckless, staying longer and longer in the arbour, holding onto one another, each acutely aware of the minutes ticking by but unwilling to be the first to break the spell. Invariably, it would be Machu. 'We should go,' he would say resignedly. 'They will start to wonder where you are.' They stole deep kisses in the attic and sometimes in the early morning, in the inner courtyard, right under the noses of the sleeping family. They became careless. Once one of the children awoke crying, and swore he had seen a ghost flit through the house; another time Machu left a mark on her neck that was too high for her blouse to hide. She had pulled her plait forward over her shoulder, but it had slipped aside as she was serving the rice. One of the women had noticed and nudged her mischievously. 'Been keeping you awake has he?' she asked, winking towards Devanna. Devi looked at Devanna with a beating heart, but luckily the Nayak had drawn him into a discussion about the accounts and he didn't hear.

Inevitably, a cold, hard discontent began to set in.

'Does he touch you here,' Machu whispered, as he traced a path down her neck. 'Or here? Or here? Can he make you feel this way?'

'Stop it,' Devi said. 'I've told you, don't bring Devanna into this.'

'Oh?' Machu raised a cynical eyebrow. 'So now we are not even allowed to talk about your husband?'

'I am your plaything, aren't I, Devi?' he asked into the silence a while later. 'A lover to be dallied with, alongside your precious husband.'

Devi left the arbour in tears.

'*Why* didn't you wait for me?' he asked despairingly another time. Devi looked down at her hands in silence. She had promised Tayi. Besides, it was too late now. She knew how he would react if she told him, the blind, unthinking rage he would unleash upon Devanna. The scandal that would soon spread through the length and breadth of Coorg. The taint upon Nanjappa. Whose son was he, they would ask snidely as they looked askance at the child. And at her.

A rotten tooth, picked over by many toothpicks.

'Devi,' Machu began again. She reached up, silencing his lips with her own.

The days began to get cooler. Their fights grew more frequent, the endless, exhausting subterfuge eating away at them. Baby Nanju learnt to walk, quick as a sardine, the women said he was, toddling off to goodness-knows-where in the blink of an eye. The ball-flower bushes turned golden with bloom and winter yams grew spongy and fat. Soon, it was time once more in the Kambeymada home for the annual ancestor propitiations.

The mystic invited especially for the occasion all the way from Kerala ponderously donned his gear on the verandah, a gaggle of open-mouthed children following his every move. He painted his face into an exaggerated mask of black, white, red and green, accentuating his eyes with a thick outline of black that stretched all the way to his temples. His headdress was at least a foot high, made of gauzy indigo netting that glinted in the dusk. He wore a long-sleeved tunic of white and over this he fastened a voluminous skirt of hay that reached to his ankles. Finally he tied a girdle of sticks around his waist, overlaying the hay skirt, pushing out and away from his body. A little brass cup was tied to the end of each stick into which Devi and other women of the house placed cotton wicks and spoonfuls of oil.

The sun disappeared in a boil of red and the evening crickets began contemplatively to click their wings. The children were bathed and fed, the prayer room and the ancestor corner decorated with flowers. The scent of jasmine wafted through the room. Faintly nauseous, Devi went outside to the verandah for a breath of fresh air. The courtyard was filling up already with people from the Kambeymada village and those surrounding it who had come to receive blessings from the oracle. She looked about her surreptitiously, but of Machu there was no sign. They had had another row the previous afternoon. She hadn't been able to get away from the kitchen soon enough and when she finally did, he was in a black mood. She had reached towards him with placatory kisses, but he had been bitter. 'The kitchen, or was it your husband who delayed you?'

They had fought then, and it had been particularly bad. Tears pricked behind Devi's eyes even now as she remembered.

'Why?' he had asked her yet again, 'why, when you swore to stand by me, why could you suddenly wait no longer?' Once again, she had nothing to say.

'Let's end it,' he had said, a deep weariness in his voice. 'Let's end this Devi, there is no future to it.'

She bit her lip and anxiously scanned the courtyard again. He had gone missing the previous evening, had been gone all day. Surely he would not miss the propitiations tonight?

Night rolled in to the hills, torches flaring alive from the pillars along the verandah. Bats flitted overhead as the slow, rolling beat of drums began to reverberate through the dark. The mystic stepped weightily into the courtyard to the collective intake of breath by the crowd. He stood there quivering, as the women lit the wicks in his girdle, his mighty frame vibrating in time to the drums. And then, as the beats got faster, he began to spin, slowly at first and then faster and faster, a vast, moving circle of lamps about his middle, the headdress glimmering in the firelight, his eyes flashing in his painted face.

Round the courtyard he went in his ring of fire, once, another time and yet another. He entered the house, spinning from room to room, bowing his head before the ancestor corner and then whirling back into the courtyard. Again and again he spun, people jostling with one another to pour their offerings of oil into his girdle of lamps as the relentless beat of the drums continued. The stones of the courtyard grew slippery from the spilled oil. Sleepy children were lifted into arms or put to bed inside the house, and still the mystic spun, inviting the head ancestor of the Kambeymadas to speak from his body.

Finally, many hours later, it was done. The oracle's eyes rolled backwards in his skull as the spirit of the ancestor descended into his body and began to speak. The guests were invited to ask their questions first and it was while the oracle was answering them that Devi saw Machu. He had materialised silently some time during the proceedings. From where or when she had no idea, but there he was on the verandah not five feet from where she stood, staring steadily at her.

Devi smiled apprehensively at him, '*Please let us leave yesterday behind us,*' the late hour and the strain of an entire day of worrying, of wondering jealously where he was, making her less circumspect than she might otherwise have been. The full force of her feelings displayed beseechingly, eloquently in her eyes for all who cared to see. They stood there, the both of them, in plain view of the entire family, drinking one another in. And then Machu looked away, deliberately flicking his gaze away from hers. Devi flinched as if he had reached across and struck her. She swallowed and looked out into the night, blaming her smarting eyes upon the smoke.

Across the verandah, Devanna stood immobile in the shadows.

When it was time for the Kambeymadas to seek the oracle's blessings, the Nayak went first. He thanked the ancestor for descending from the heavens to grace them with his presence. He thanked him for the bountiful harvest, for the birth of another grandson, for the continued prosperity of the family. Bless us all, he asked, bless us with your provenance. They went forward then, the rest of the Kambeymadas, couple after couple seeking the ancestor's blessings, asking him their questions. Would their child pass the coming examinations? Would a job application in Mercara be accepted? Would there be a proposal for a daughter?

When finally it was Devi and Devanna's turn she did not notice how stiffly he walked at her side. She bowed before the oracle, her heart leaden. 'What is this?' the oracle suddenly roared, shocking the crowd into silence. 'Husband and wife, I said. Husband and wife. Where is your man?' he demanded, training bloodshot eyes on Devi.

'I . . . here, he is right here.'

'No. No!' cried the oracle impatiently. 'Where is your man? You . . .' He swung abruptly towards the rest of the family staring nonplussed at him. 'A tragedy,' he roared, his entire frame quivering. '*I warn you, a tragedy!*'

They stared at him aghast, the courtyard completely still. The Nayak was the first to recover, pulling Devi and Devanna away from the oracle as he urged the next couple forward. The drumbeats started up again. Devi was shaking. 'Don't worry kunyi,' the Nayak comforted her, although his own voice was troubled. 'It happens sometimes, the oracle says things that we cannot understand.' Devanna was very quiet.

Devi fled inside the house to calm herself. Pressing clammy hands to her cheeks, she stood trembling by the crib and her sleeping son. 'Where is your man,' he had asked. How had he known? The scent of jasmine was clogging her nostrils.

Devanna came up behind her and shut the door. Devi whirled around. 'It's Machu isn't it?'

Devi looked down at Nanju. '*Stay silent*,' her brain warned.

'It's Machaiah. How could I have not seen it before? Have you, have you both been . . .' Devanna stopped, unable even to voice the words, but he knew the answer already, knew the secret behind his wife's happiness of the past months.

'Do you love him?'

Stay silent. Devi slowly looked up at Devanna, her eyes swimming with tears. 'I always have. From the time I first saw him. You remember, the tiger wedding . . . it has always been him.'

Devanna's lips twisted into a smile. 'And I have always loved you. Ever since I can remember.'

He stood there, looking at her, an immense sadness in his eyes. 'How did it come to this? This hatred . . . I cannot bear it Devi.'

Devi shook her head and swallowed, trying to compose herself. 'Devanna, please. I . . . it's been a very long day. Can we talk about it tomorrow?'

He started to say something, stopped. That strained smile again and then Devanna nodded. 'If that is what you want.'

Devi wiped her eyes. 'We should go out. People will wonder . . . as it is, the oracle said those things . . .'

'Yes. People will talk.'

He moved away from the door and opened the latch. 'Go on,' he told her, 'I will just be a minute.'

Devanna looked at his son for a long time. He bent and gently kissed the downy head. The scent of jasmine was in the air. He steadily climbed the stairs to the attic and took a gun from the gun rack. The light from the courtyard was reflected in strange, fire-red shapes upon the attic windows. He could hear the muffled beat of the drums. '*It has always been him.*'

'You are free Devi,' he said clearly, and then resting the gun on the floor and aiming its barrel at his chest, Devanna pulled the trigger.

Machu

Chapter 16

≈ 1901 ≈

Machu scraped the edge of the blade a final time against the stone. He held it up to the light and the sun pounced on the newly sharpened edge, bursting from the finely honed surface. He held it there for a second, noting the sparks shooting along its length.

It was time.

Moving with great deliberation, he bent towards the Kaveri and cupping some water in his hands splashed it over his face. He shut his eyes for a moment. His mind was purposefully blank, a black void behind his eyes, an erasure of all that was past. '*Swamiye Ayappa, I give back to you what you bestowed.*' And then raising the blade, trusting his reflection in the rippling water to guide his hand, Machu began steadily to shave off his galla meesa, the badge of honour bestowed on but a chosen few, the sideburns he had sported for the past decade that marked him as a conqueror of tigers.

The fields were bare, shorn bald of their crop, the dark underbelly of soil naked and exposed to the winter sun. The land held the quiet of the afternoon in its palm; not a stray bark nor even a distant clunk of a cowbell to be heard. There was not a person in sight, none to glance wonderingly towards him or attempt to stay his hand.

'*Take it back, take it all back, I am not worthy.*'

A kingfisher dived towards the river, a brilliant blur of blue slicing into the water to emerge triumphant a moment later, a tiny koilé fish slithering desperately in its beak. The hunter and the hunted. This was the natural order of things was it not?

And he had hunted a tiger, the greatest hunter of them all. Yet with what ease he himself had been taken.

It had been the nape of her neck. The first, fatal hook. The smooth-skinned grace of it, all but obscured by the plait that swung to her hips. She had thrust past him at the Kaveri tank, the very picture of determination, and his spurt of irritation was swiftly replaced by amusement. And then, as she had wedged herself before him, he had found himself unable to tear his eyes away. Following every dip of light and shadow, the interplay of muscle beneath the translucent skin as she craned her neck this way and that. He had shut his eyes for only a brief moment in prayer; when they opened, she was tilting slowly towards the water. The compactness of her waist, fitting neatly into the span of his hands.

And the shock, the bone-jarring jolt he had felt when finally he had looked into the perfection of her face.

She had startled him with her forthrightness. 'By your side,' she had said, up on the mountain peak, silhouetted against the clouds. 'Here is where I belong.' Those eyes, staring at him, with not a trace of guile or embarrassment.

He had tried to convince himself of the foolishness of his obsession. Tried to persuade himself after the festival that he had exaggerated the memory of her; that nobody could possibly be as bewitching. She was spoilt, he reminded himself even as his feet made their way to her father's house. A wilful child-woman. And then she had walked out on to the verandah, a flash of red tucked into her plait, and all he could think about was pulling out that flower, petal by petal, letting loose that silken weight of hair till it tumbled freely down her back.

He had left her home abruptly, for the first time in his life, afraid. Of what he might do or say if he was around her too long, shaken by this tongue-melting heat, this untenable tenderness she managed to evoke in him by just one long-lashed glance.

At least his face had betrayed nothing, he was sure of that.

And then Machu had started to laugh, doubled over on the trail at the bitter absurdity of it all. What a fool he was, behaving like a lovelorn yokel. There were three years for the vow to be over. How could he ask her to wait for so long? It was just an absurd obsession, it would pass.

He had stayed stubbornly away through the slow sludge of the next months, blocking her from memory. And then a heron would take sudden wing, its neck held elegantly against the clouds, bringing to mind an unbidden, heartstopping flash of her. Ah, it was foolish, he would insist to himself, turning away. This. Made. No. Sense. Then, the sight of her at the feast, even lovelier than he had remembered.

The sharp flush of pleasure as he had felt her eyes following him, the thrill as he had realised that *she too had been unable to forget*. He had been amused at first at her blatant efforts to make him jealous. Deliberately turning his back on her, enjoying their little game. Then despite himself, he had grown angry.

Why did she insist on taking matters so far, making eyes at every poor fool who crossed her path? 'Fickle-hearted tramp,' he had cursed silently to himself, she knew full well the effect she had on those hapless idiots. And on him. Or did she even care? He had looked worriedly towards her then, but she was busy twirling her plait at some slack-jawed oaf. Machu's fingers had tightened around his drink.

She had looked at him that night in the lane that led to her home, with the same guilelessness he had tried so hard to forget. 'I will wait for you,' she had said. 'I am yours, forever.'

He was the *tiger killer*. And yet, played for a fool.

Machu's hand shook, a mere hint of a tremor, but that was all it took for the freshly sharpened blade to slice into his skin. He paused, shocked by the sudden sting after the epochal darkness of the past months. The fingers he raised to his cheeks came away stippled with blood.

The drums in the courtyard had been so loud that night that nobody had heard the gun go off in the attic. Devanna's blood had soaked into the floorboards by the time they found him, a dark, mushroom-shaped stain that would cling to the wood even weeks later despite the repeated scrubbings with rock salt and linseed oil. A colony of ants had already been foraging in his shattered flesh, raising the hairs on the back of Machu's neck even now as he remembered.

Mercifully, it had been late, long after the crowds come to witness the ancestor propitiations had dispersed. The family had lifted Devanna's body down to the inner courtyard and there they had found, to their shock and horrified pity, that under the mess of blood and tissue, his pulse was still faintly beating.

It had been Machu who had raced to summon Dr Jameson. He remembered little of the ride save the sweating flanks of the horse beneath his thighs and the fitful light of the moon, casting a dim light now and then along the path. He had burst into the Jameson home, not even noticing the squawking watchman. Jameson had emerged purple with fury, his night cap askew and the Remington rifle in his hand. He had swiftly calmed down however, recognising the Nayak's name and prudently choosing the lure of handsome payment over a night's sleep. Gathering up his bag, calling for his horse to be saddled, and throwing a coat over his pyjamas, he had hurried out into the night after Machu.

He had shaken his head as he took Devanna's pulse. 'Yes, he's alive. How, I don't know. It's a miracle. The bullet – one centimetre to the right and it would have gone through his heart.'

Many years later, Jameson, long retired to his village in England, would recite the story over and over to his cronies at The Flying Owl, none of whom even pretended to listen any more. 'Just like that. Bang! One bullet, through the heart, that's the preferred method. Clean and quick, that's what they believe. You see it so often in that pagan country, one might almost think it's taught to them in the cradle. So this lad . . . barely whiskered, early twenties, no more, decides for some obscure reason that he too has had enough and wants to end it all. Sneaks up to the attic while the rest of the family is at yet another ungodly feast. Takes a gun from the rack, only . . .' Jameson would artfully pause to take a long swig of his ale, '*only* the poor sod chooses the one gun in the rack that *listed to the left*!'

'Some sort of ceremonial gun,' Jameson would explain. 'It had once taken down a tiger, and was prized by the family despite its fatal flaw.'

They had transferred Devanna to the Mercara Medical Clinic and through the bumpy ride and the next months he had held on.

Rumours had flown through the family. That girl Devi. The oracle had warned them, had he not, of an impending tragedy? She was at the root of it all, they were sure. Look at her poor husband, caught in a living hell, not even able to end his life honourably. Some wife she had turned out to be . . .

Machu had listened to them silently, unable to come to her defence without betraying her further. The words cold and congealing on his tongue. He had brought this upon them after all, this curse. He had broken a sacred vow, forsaken his dharma. And for what? To be the plaything of a married woman? To betray the trust of a *kinsman*?

He began to shave again, roughly, not caring about the cuts that appeared under the blade.

How old had he been the day of the cobra? Seven? Eight? His uncles had taken him on a hunt. It had not been going well; all they had to show for an entire day was a single gamy jungle fowl. They had pitched camp that night, sharing the few ottis they had carried with them and roasting the fowl on a spit, cursing at the stringiness of its flesh. They had started early the next morning, but nonetheless, it had not been until many hours later that they had spotted the bison herd. Silently, with the utmost care, they had begun to take their positions. Nobody had needed to tell him what to do, he knew instinctively to melt into the brush, watching as his uncles lined their sights. One of the bison glanced in their direction, peering shortsightedly towards them, and then lowered its snout again into the grass. His uncles motioned to one another. *Soon.*

He had taken his eyes off the bison for an instant, squinting at the sun blazing down on them through the jackfruit trees. A sudden hiss, like the exhalation of an irritable crone. A burn in his leg so sharp that Machu had shouted out in agony. The bison had whisked their tails and spun instantly around, thundering away in a flurry of hooves. His uncles lowered their guns and raced towards him. 'Cobra! Watch out, careful!' they had cried as they speared the snake.

Machu had known that he had to compensate. 'No, let me, let me,' he had insisted, gasping through the pain. He had barely been able to see, his hands slippery with sweat, but he knew that he had ruined the hunt. He knew that he needed to pay, that he alone now must kill the snake. He threw his peechekathi, the dagger flying in a single, graceful arc, slicing the reptile in half.

This will hurt, his uncle had warned, kneeling by his side. Machu had nodded, clamping down on his lower lip. Not a sound he had uttered as his leg was sliced open. Not even a murmur, all through the agony of the wound being squeezed until the black, poisoned blood had spilled and clotted down his leg. His uncles had packed gunpowder into the hole, then ignited it with a match to cauterise the wound, and still he had gritted his teeth and remained silent. 'Truly not one word,' they had said admiringly of him that night at the Kambeymada house, thumping him on the back. 'Can you believe this boy, not a sound!'

He had visited only once, nearly two months after Devanna was admitted to the Mercara Clinic. He went, drawn by his guilt and the unbearable absence of her. The November squalls were ended and December was upon them with its fog-filled mornings and clear, crisp nights. In a couple of weeks, it would be 1901. Mercara was gearing up for New Year's Eve – 'Pirates and Wenches', the Club Committee had decided the theme would be, and Hans' trading store was filled with a press of giddy women and their reluctant husbands examining the latest shipment of haberdashery. The harvest festival of Puthari too was around the corner, village greens filled with the sound of laughter and crowded until late as Coorgs across the land began to practise the songs and dances for this all important festival of new-rice.

The clinic had been hushed, its antiseptic air catching at the back of Machu's throat. The initial crowd of relatives had now been reduced to two young cousins stationed in Devanna's room. The child was there too, Nanju, toddling about while his mother sat by the bed, still as a statue. *That neck, the curved elegance of it.* The sound of Devanna's breathing, a snuffled wheezing, like an animal might make as the life drained from its body.

She had looked up sharply. The hope flooding her face, the colour staining her pale cheeks. 'You came.'

He sent the boys out with a couple of coins. 'Get yourself some sweets,' he told them, 'I will stand watch for a while.'

'You came.' Her face was radiant. 'I *knew* you wouldn't leave me, that you would come.' Her eyes filling with tears, she shook her head, not yet noticing he had not said a word.

The slow, accusatory wheezing from the bed, of a man trapped between life and death.

'Take me away,' she said desperately. 'Take me away Machu, just . . . Let's go away, anywhere, we will make it work, just the two of us.'

He had jumped at her touch. 'Your *husband* is lying there.'

'No, you don't understand.' She had reached towards him, trying to cup his face in her hands and he had brushed them away. 'He did this for me, don't you see? I know Devanna, he was trying to right the wrong . . . he did this for *us*.'

A numbness was descending upon him. The sound of Devanna's breathing echoing in his ears, like a trapped animal pleading to be set free. *I am the tiger killer*. The weight of the tiger settling into his bones.

'He knew? He *knew* about us?'

It was he who had killed Devanna, as surely as if he had pulled the trigger himself.

'Machu, you don't understand.' Her eyes were ablaze, the words tripping off her tongue. 'He was trying to set things right.'

Machu shook his head, trying to clear away the cobwebs. 'He *knew* about us. He found out the night of the oracle, did he not?'

'He wanted you and I to . . .'

'Enough. You married him Devi. You chose HIM. And yet, I . . . You . . . we have done enough.' It hurt to breathe. 'No more Devi. We are finished.'

The last few hairs from his sideburns sailed towards the water and were immediately carried away downstream. His jaw itched. Machu slowly ran his fingers over the expanse of nicked, newly shaven skin. It was done. The solution had finally come to him that morning. The payment, the rightful dues, to balance this wrong.

No more the tiger killer, no more the chosen one. He had given away everything he had.

All he had ever been.

He washed his face, the water cool, soothing his skin. '*Do with me as you will, Swami Ayappa. But spare his life.*'

A school of tiny koilé rushed to the surface, gulping at the flecks of his blood swirling in the Kaveri.

The stupefied family clustered about him that evening. 'But why?' the shocked Nayak asked him. 'Why this foolishness? You are *Kambeymada Machaiah*. The tiger killer. Do you not know what an honour this is for the family? How could you spurn this?'

'It was the tiger who was the true hero,' Machu said tiredly to the Nayak. He gestured towards the tiger skin, now a little frayed about the edges, but still hanging proudly along one wall of the inner courtyard. 'I happened to be the one to wield the sword, but Swami Ayappa . . . he had already willed the tiger to be felled. I was but an instrument. A plaything.'

Chapter 17

The rains were early and especially perverse that year, washing away the first racemes of laburnums that had begun shyly to dot the hillsides. Clouds hunched beetle browed over Coorg; nobody, it seemed, could remember when they had last seen the sun. There was hardly a break in the downpour; barely would a bedraggled songbird shake out its plumage and begin to warble, than the deluge would begin again.

The placid rills that had skirted the fields were changed into swollen, roaring monsters, bringing down orange trees and vast tangles of pepper vines, threatening to swallow everything in their engorged paths. The Coorgs checked and rechecked the bits of bear hide that they tied to the horns of their cattle to ward off the evil eye and, cautioning their Poleya cowherds to stay vigilant, fed the Poleyas with copious amounts of ghee and horse gram to stave off fever. Even so, twenty-three cows and six oxen were lost, swept away, lowing frantically, while crossing one of these fjords. Crocodiles began to frequent the streams, one was even found lurking in a paddy tank. Another, fully nine feet long, was shot and killed in the murky waters of the Kaveri; when it was dragged ashore and cut open, a woman's toe rings and silver bracelet were found in its stomach.

Gundert's arthritis acted up, an involuntary groan escaping his lips every morning as he got out of bed. At times the throbbing in his joints was so acute, he could barely kneel in the chapel. The novices watched anxiously as he hobbled across the school, but he refused their offers to relieve his inflamed knees with warmed castor oil or poultices of sandalwood paste. The pain was welcome flagellation.

He had not seen Devanna again, not since that awful morning. Too exquisitely mannered to do otherwise, he had composed letters to both the Nayaks. He regretted his inability to attend the wedding, he wrote, but it was short notice and there was too much to be done at the school. And with that, with the final curlicued flourish of his pen as he signed his name to the letters, Gundert had called on all of his resolve to blank the existence of his protégé from his mind.

The years he had spent mentoring the boy, crafting him into the torch bearer he had believed him to be. The paternal proprietorship so blatantly evident every time he spoke of him, making the novices smile fondly behind their hands.

'*My* Dev.'

The unquestioning expectations placed on, reserved for, none but the most deeply beloved. Devanna's ghastly confession, his blood turning cold as he had listened. 'You are not of me. You *never* were, you could never be.' A heartbeat later, a surge of rage, an all-consuming, blistering fury. 'Get out of my sight,' he had screamed, '*get out.*'

All of these things Gundert swept aside, like the brittle leaves of some discarded type specimen.

Once again, the Reverend buried himself in his work. Unsmiling, untiring. He sent letter after letter to the Mission authorities, asking to be transferred. Until the day when a white-faced novice broke the news to him that Devanna had shot himself. The pain in his chest was so intense that for an instant, he was certain his heart too had stopped.

The mineral stench of the hospital in Madras swirled through the decades to swell around him. The sound once more echoed in his ears, of Olaf, coughing up unending quantities of blood. How Gundert had prayed then, prayed endlessly as he wiped the sputum from Olaf's lips, swabbed the sweat from his ribs. 'Save him, Lord have mercy, save him.' And still Olaf had coughed, chest turned concave from exhaustion, coughing to death in front of Gundert's eyes.

'Reverend, did you hear what I said? Our Dev, he . . .' The novice started to cry.

Gundert blinked. 'Let me . . . Leave me be, Sister,' he said. His voice sounded cracked to his ears, a rusted key turning painfully in its lock. *He too, like Olaf, was gone.* Gundert sat at his desk, looking blankly at the drive. *His* Dev. His fingers rose stiffly, automatically, to the silken cord about his neck. He slipped off the key, opened the drawer in his desk, pulled out the package of silk. He unwrapped the bamboo flower. So fragile, still perfect after all these years, 'such delicacy in the delineation of the stamen and pistil'.

He rose shakily to his feet. The sleeve of his cassock caught his precious flower, spilling it from the desk. Gundert did not notice. He shut the door to his office, his breath coming in short, sharp bursts as he reached for a volume of poetry from the shelf. Slowly, like a struggling student in one of his own classes, he traced the words with his fingers as he read.

> *How stern are the woes of the desolate mourner*
> *As he bends in still grief o'er the hallowed bier*

Dev was gone. He had shot himself. What was it about Gundert that whatever he touched, whatever he cherished, crumbled to nothingness?

> *As enanguished he turns from the laugh of the scorner,*
> *And drops to perfection's remembrance a tear;*

'My *Dev*.'

The last rites. Gundert snapped the book shut as he remembered. 'Sister,' he called urgently. 'Sister Agnes, hurry, I must perform his last rites.'

It had taken the persuasive powers of all of the nuns to dissuade him. 'No Reverend, you must not. He isn't a Christian, his family would take it amiss.'

Later, when the news arrived that Devanna was not dead – indeed, he was barely alive, but alive he miraculously was – Gundert rushed to the chapel and fell upon his knees. 'Have mercy,' he begged, 'spare the boy's life. He has sinned grievously . . . but Lord, not again, do not visit this sorrow upon me another time. Take *my* life instead, I give unto you this service, all I possess.'

He knelt at the altar, blue eyes clouded with pain. 'I . . .' His voice failed him then, in the face of the enormity of what he was about to offer. 'I promise . . .' he started again and faltered once more, the words choking his throat. Then, mustering up all the will he possessed, Gundert struck an exacting bargain with the Lord.

'I shall never speak another word to him,' he vowed, 'not in all the years that lie ahead. I beseech Thee, in return, bestow Your mercy upon him.'

Slowly Devanna began to heal, innocent of the barters made on his behalf, by the tiger killer and the priest. Mission-Devanna and Coorg-Devanna bought back from the Gods, both Christian and pagan. His breathing eased and the fever abated as the open lips of the wound began to pull together.

Dr Jameson shook his head again in wonder. 'A miracle, that's what it is. That and the fact that the patient is young.' It appeared that the boy was going to make a full recovery.

Devanna regained consciousness one damp afternoon. *The rain, pattering down on the roof. When would it end? So many days. . . . He had to go and see Devi, when would the rains stop?*

'Where . . .' he whispered, his tongue like cotton.

'Shhh monae. Don't talk, you need to rest, you've been very ill.'

Tayi's wrinkled hands stroking his brow. His throat felt raw. 'Devi . . .?'

She was standing by the window looking at him. Those large, lovely eyes so dark, so riddled with pain. Devanna blinked as he remembered. '*It has always been him.*' It was more than he could take, the despair in her voice. To know that he was responsible for placing it there. The solid weight of the barrel against his chest. He had had to manoeuvre a while before he had got the gun aligned. The sound of the drums, the chanting from the courtyard.

Even at this, he had failed.

Devanna suffered a major stroke that evening. Jameson diagnosed a clot that had likely travelled to the brain. What a pity, he said, just when he was headed for a complete recovery. 'I am truly sorry,' he told Devi, running up and down her with a practised eye. Not bad for the youngster, to have snared himself such a bonny one. 'I'm sorry, but your husband – one side of his body is paralysed.'

*

196

The rains continued their hold over the land, turning the ploughed fields into mud-flecked foam. Coorg was no longer visible from the peak of the Bhagamandala mountain, only the tips of the mountains rising from the fog, like isolated islands in a boundless, churning sea.

Gundert's transfer order finally arrived, but he quietly turned it down. 'Mercara shall be my final post with the Mission,' he wrote to the authorities, 'I shall stay here as long as you deem it fit for me to do so.'

Fevers began to claim their victims, a life plucked here and there. Pallada Nayak collapsed in the paddy nursery where he had gone to survey the seedlings despite the remonstrations of his daughters-in-law. He had been shouting at the Poleyas, 'Ayy, donkeys, do you have stones for eyes, cannot you see that the seedlings need more manure?' when, overcome by a fit of coughing, he had slipped in the ankle-deep mud and hit his head on the stones that edged the bank. He had never recovered, simply sinking deeper and deeper into unconsciousness. They did not tell Devanna.

Devanna's condition gradually stabilised and he was discharged from the clinic. Nonetheless, it was advisable, Jameson recommended, that he remained in the vicinity. 'Just in case, you understand? Relapses are not uncommon.'

Kambeymada Nayak bought a house for Devi and Devanna in Mercara. It was a low, dark, unfortunately planned structure that had been built by a Muslim trader. The man had thriftily hoarded the coins he had earned, first from selling river fish, then from chickens and great fat-streaked slabs of goat meat. His savings had been translated over the years into no fewer than three houses that he had built in Mercara and a thriving clothing store – *fine wedding silks, cotton lungis, best funeral purpose muslin* – in the heart of town. Although his talents did not, unfortunately, stretch to architecture, the house did have one redeeming feature – a set of large windows in the front room, set with imported embossed glass and boasting a panoramic view of the town. Devi hardly noticed, giving her new surroundings only the most cursory of glances as she admonished the men carrying Devanna into the house. 'Carefully, go gently, *carefully*, he is an invalid.'

Thimmaya gave his daughter the services of Tukra the Poleya servant; the latter and his sardine-seller wife settled into the little shack tacked on at the bottom of the house. Tukra gave Devanna a massage with hot coconut oil every morning, kneading and pulling at the slackened muscles, maintaining a steady flow of chatter as he bathed the invalid and dusted his skin with talc. It was a hodgepodge conversation, a nonsensical, cuckoo's nest of words. The latest gossip from the shanty, lamentations over the paddy fields he had left behind – the town was so crowded, too many people for Tukra, no space to lie flat on one's back and contemplate the sky – and recountings of the decidedly one-sided arguments with his wife. Once a fisherwoman, always a fisherwoman, he grumbled to Devanna; they never did lose the shanty lungs developed from screaming out their wares.

Tukra knew he talked a lot of rubbish, but Devanna anna enjoyed their one-sided conversations, Tukra knew that he did. A man needed to be spoken to, did he not? And Devi akka . . . Tukra would never say anything of course, it was not his place, but she did not spend as much time with her husband as she ought to. So busy she was, all the time doing something or other. She made sure Devanna anna's meals were prepared meticulously, none but she was allowed to mash his bananas or cook his rice gruel, but a wife sometimes needed to place her hands upon her husband's arm, did she not, to sit by his side, to lay her head on his chest?

Whenever these distressing thoughts crossed his mind, Tukra drowned them out with even more babble, mumbling away as he dressed Devanna and lifted him gently into the wide-armed planter's chair that faced the living room windows. Devi did not like to have the windows opened, the rain in Mercara fell almost horizontally, she complained, it took barely a minute for the room to be flooded. Tukra knew though that Devanna enjoyed the rains. He would carefully open the windows, barely a scratch really, to let in the fresh, moisture-rich air. They would sit there, dampness dancing on their skins, Tukra squatting on the floor beside Devanna and reaching mid soliloquy to wipe the saliva that pooled at the corner of Devanna's lips. Until Devi would pass by and slam the windows shut with a sharp cry of impatience.

What was Tukra doing, dawdling by the windows? Was there so little work for him? Who would go buy the milk for that day, she?

Tukra would sheepishly scurry off then while Devanna would give no indication that he had heard. There he would sit, in the wicker-bottomed chair, staring blankly ahead as the wind beat its palms against the shuttered windows and the bells from the Mission church tolled ponderously over the town.

The only times they managed to elicit some reaction from him was when Devi sat Nanju on his father's lap. Nanju would reach up to pat Devanna's cheeks with his fat toddler hands, covering his face with little-child kisses. There was a slow animation about Devanna then, a contortion crossing his stiffened features as he tried to smile at his son. Devi would pause, distracted momentarily from the all-consuming rigour of cleaning, disinfecting and cooking that she had set herself. She would stand in the doorway, watching the two of them, a tender, almost wistful expression on her face. The anger coiled unspoken beneath her tongue, the years stretching meaningless ahead; these things seemed momentarily laid to rest as she watched her son reach for his father. And then propelled by a sudden bitterness, she would stalk over to them and snatch up Nanju. 'It's time for his nap. Tukra, here, ready him for bed.'

Devi began to cultivate pumpkins, bitter greens and tomato plants in the small patch of soil behind the house. Most of the crop was needed for the household, but what was left she began to sell at the weekly shanty to bring in some cash. Unfortunately, she made the mistake of going to the shanty herself; when the Coorgs realised just who the seller was, they demurred.

'Don't want, don't want from her,' they muttered, recalling the debacle at the Kambeymada ancestor propitiations. 'Besides, just look at her,' the women carped to their husbands, 'has she no shame, standing here amongst all these men?'

Eventually she was forced to sell her produce to a middleman for a pittance.

Yet again, the bamboo groves remained barren of bloom. They grew tall in the rains though, great thorned masses of them reaching sixty, eighty, sometimes even as much as a hundred feet into the air. Their fronded tops interlacing, forming colonnades of domes, naves, arcades and archways, like some vast, asymmetrical Gothic cathedral. The Poleyas set about harvesting the new bamboo shoots, tender and yellow skinned, that sprouted within the groves. Devi sent Tukra too, armed with a sickle and sachets of salt tied about his ankles to ward off the leeches. The bamboo shoots brought in some money at the shanty, but once again, not nearly as much as she had hoped.

Devi turned next to the lace making that the nuns at the mission school had taught her as a girl. It was painstaking work, involving complicated patterns that were threaded using multiple layers of cloth. When the design was complete, the pattern and the cloth were pulled slowly away, leaving behind a gossamer length of lace. Devi's knots were never quite as delicate nor as neat as those of the nuns, but nonetheless she managed to sell quite a few of her pieces at Hans' trading shop. Now and again, there were custom orders from the wives of the white-folk planters, for luncheon sets, tea cosies and dressing table doilies edged with lace. This venture too, the Coorgs found fault with. For a woman to go alone to the trading shop! Devi was too weary to pay heed.

Finally, the monsoon ended. The drip-drip-drip of water from the leaves slowed and the sun emerged wetly blinking. There was a hesitant birdcall, followed by another and yet another, until soon, the rain-softened air was filled with melody. Wrens, bulbuls, cuckoos, finches and warblers skipped through the trees and skimmed the lantana hedges, their throats swelled in song. Cats reappeared magically upon stoops and ledges, purring in the sunshine. Even the houses seemed to stand straighter, throwing off their hunched dampness, their tiled roofs glowing a warm red as the water stains evaporated from their walls.

Once more, from all across Coorg and the neighbouring states, a steady stream of the faithful made their way to the Bhagamandala mountain for the Kaveri festival. Machu made it half-way up the mountain before turning abruptly back. At the village hunt later that year, when he was assigned the usual choice position from which to man the forest, he demurred, saying that someone else ought to be given a chance. He removed himself to the outskirts of the circle, a poor position that was usually given to none but the rawest of hunters.

'. . . lost his nerve,' he overheard a couple of the hunters say disdainfully and he pretended not to hear, running his fingers along his clean-shaven jaw.

'Let them say what they will,' he told himself. 'Opinions are like buttock holes, every fool has one.' Nevertheless, Machu began to spend most of his time in the fields. Despite the herons that still brought a dull ache to his heart, it was only there, under the unfettered skies, that he was able to find any peace.

The paddy grew tall but thin. The early onslaught of the monsoons had ensured that the yield would be sparse that year; the granaries would hardly be half filled. This, too, the family blamed on Devi. The oracle had *warned* them, had he not?

The clot in Devanna's brain gradually began to recede, the deadened nerve cells beginning to regenerate. He started to regain sensation, a buzzing pins and needles movement in the tips of his fingers and the pads of his toes. The paddy grew taller still, gradually ripening into gold under the winter sun, and Coorg readied herself for Puthari, the harvest festival, once more. The sizzle of roasting meat filled the court-yard of the Kambeymada home. The three sows that had been fattened these past months had been killed with a neat shot to the head, their meat steeped in garlic, cumin and thick black garcinia vinegar and set to roast over a wood fire. The vast granary at the back of the house was filled with chatter as Poleya women powdered sack upon sack of raw rice. Fine, white rice dust hung thick in the air, making the women cough and delighting the children as it settled indiscriminately on skin, clothing and hair.

'Donkey children, don't bother the servants, there is much they need to do,' the harassed daughters-in-law of the house chided as they rushed back and forth, some carting endless platters of rice powder from the granary to the kitchen, others employed in kneading the powder into dough with cardamom and jaggery syrup. The kitchen verandah was already lined with row upon row of banana leaves laden with balls of this dough, ready for the brass steamers being hauled from the attic. Elsewhere in the house, fresh coats of lime wash were being applied to the outer walls, lampshades washed and the tiger skin taken down from the wall to be aired and for alum to be rubbed on its gigantic underside.

Nonetheless, despite the hubbub of activity, something was lacking.

There was a pall hanging over them all; it had been hard to shake the memory of the oracle's portent and Devanna's attempted suicide.

A grand gesture, Kambeymada Nayak decided, he needed a sweeping statement that would wipe the glumness from the faces of his family and reassure them all of the might of the Kambeymadas. But what? Gold bangles for each of the women? No, too trite. A holiday perhaps, to Mysore? Too dangerous. Hadn't the papers all this past month been filled with news of the plague that had swept the Madras Presidency? Fifteen thousand corpses, the papers had said. Mysore had been spared the brunt of the epidemic but nonetheless, being of a fastidious and cautious bent of mind, the Nayak thought it would hardly be wise to risk exposing his family. Besides, the Nayak proudly maintained that he had never set foot outside Coorg in all his life; he was not about to start in his dotage and ruin what had been a perfect record.

He was still pondering the best course of action when he paid a visit to the Commissioner's office in Mercara. Two peons were engaged in placing, in precisely the centre of a wall and under the tense directions of the aide de camp, a magnificent photograph of Queen Victoria. The Nayak was stroking his moustache and admiring the ample bosom of the matriarch, when, Ah!, it dawned on him. He had the perfect idea – he would summon the finest European photographer from Mysore to capture for eternity the entire family on film.

Machu was in the fields when one of the Kambeymada men came looking for him. Kambeymada Nayak wanted Machu to go to Mysore, he told him, to escort a photographer back to the village.

'All?' Machu asked as the man continued. 'Does he want all of the family present?'

'Yes, everyone is to attend. Well, not *everyone* I suppose. That boy Devanna is still not fully recovered. And surely that Devi girl will not be so brazen as to attend without her husband, not after all she has wrought.' Machu nodded, absentmindedly dehusking an ear of paddy between his fingers.

Devi sent a prompt note back with Tukra. Her husband would be unable to attend, but she and her son thanked the Nayak for the honour. They would be present without fail.

*

Devi dressed with care for the occasion, making Tukra drag the trunk of good saris out from beneath the bed. She rifled through the layers of silk that had lain so long unworn, the neem leaves that Tayi had scattered through the trunk to ward off silverfish dried and crumbling beneath her fingers. She finally settled on a deep pink sari, its gold border wider than the span of her hands. She tied a veil of pale pink silk over her head, its embroidered edges tucked behind her ears and flowing down her back. Two necklaces around her neck – the black-beaded kartamani and the gold-knubbed jomalé. The ruby dotted jodi-kadaga double-bracelet on her right wrist, six gold bangles upon the other. A pair of ruby jhumkis dangling from her ears. A perfect round of vermilion high on her forehead, lamp soot mixed with almond oil accentuating her eyes. And finally, on her bosom, a tiger claw brooch.

He had given it to her in their laburnum hideaway, a peace offering after one of their fights. Her face had been radiant as she looked up at him. 'Is this from your tiger?'

He had laughed. 'Yes, from my tiger. For my tigress.'

Devi ran her fingers over its smoothness now, tentatively probing the sanded down tip. She bit her lip. Would he even notice?

He gave no indication that he had, his studied indifference proclaiming to her his awareness of her presence. They circled each other throughout lunch, each maintaining a formal distance from the other, carefully avoiding the other's gaze. The Kambeymadas were unfailingly gracious, extending to her the polite hospitality one accorded a favoured guest and making her cheeks grow hot with anger. Here, she must have another helping of ghee rice, and oh no, no, not *that* bony piece of chicken, here, she ought to try this piece from its breast instead. The women refused to allow Devi to lift a finger. 'No,' they said firmly when she insisted on helping, 'you have the child to manage.' Devi seethed as she counted at least six women effortlessly balancing their own tots on their hips as they went to and from the kitchen.

'You are not one of us,' it implied, this formality. 'You are not welcome in this family.' She held her head high, and rocked Nanju upon her lap.

At the coconut shooting contest later that afternoon, with great ceremony, the Nayak called upon Machu to fire the first shot. He shook his head.

'What's the matter with you Machaiah?' the Nayak asked sharply, finally losing his patience. 'It isn't a request, it's an order.'

'Leave it be. Not this time.'

'Ayy, it is only a coconut, Machu, not a *pisachi*,' one of his cousins called. The onlookers laughed and Machu stiffened. The Nayak thrust the gun at him. 'Here. Don't be foolish.'

Machu stood unmoving, his hands by his side. Her eyes were upon him, he could feel them in his back. *The tiger killer*. Yet malleable as clay he had been, insubstantial as the summer clouds. 'No,' he repeated quietly.

'By Iguthappa Swami! Here.' Turning on his heel with an oath, the Nayak shoved the gun into someone else's hands. 'Here. Show me that the Kambeymadas have not all lost their manhood.'

The crowd tittered again and Devi turned despairingly away from where she had been watching at the fringes. It was stupid of her to have come. She walked out of the side gate, past the banana and orange groves and the thicket of areca palms, Nanju heavy in her arms. Everything had changed. *One must fight for happiness*. What was left to fight for? Her feet moved of their own volition, past the stream. It was over. Over. With a start, Devi realised she was standing in front of the laburnum arbour. The trees were bare now, long shorn of bloom. A purple honeysucker bird hovered nonetheless, wings beating madly as it searched among the boughs.

Phantom flowers.

Nanju stirred restlessly in her arms and she pointed at the bird. 'Look,' she told him, 'look ...' The trees were bare now. But still carrying within their sap, or so it seemed to her, an imprint of the lovers that had once lain below. The breeze rustling through the grass, whispering their names. *Ma-chu*. Taking Nanju's hand in hers, Devi crawled through the narrow opening of the arbour.

'Ma? Amma?' Nanju asked uncertainly. His face was hot and sweaty, the trace of a brocade rose upon his cheek from where he had pressed it against her blouse. Devi pushed the hair back from his forehead, blowing gently into his face.

She didn't start at all when Machu pushed aside the branches fringing the opening.

'They are looking for you.'

The breeze picked up, whistling through the arbour. He looked older, she saw, a smattering of grey at his temples that had not been there before.

'Did you not hear me? Everyone has been looking for you. The photographer is waiting.'

'Why did you shave it off?'

His hand went instinctively to his jaw and then he impatiently dropped it. 'The photographer . . .'

'Tell them I am not coming.'

Machu made a sharp, irritated sound. 'Don't be foolish. You accepted the invitation did you not, even when you knew you would not be welcome? Well, then, follow through with your actions. Come and get your photograph taken with the rest of the family.'

She said nothing. *Ma-chu.*

'Have you gone deaf?'

Still she stared at him.

'Fine. Have it your way, I'm leaving.'

'They blame me, don't they? For what happened?' Her eyes filled with tears and she looked at the ground.

'By Ayappa Swami, please . . . Devi. *Listen* to me. They are about to take the photograph. Think how poorly it will reflect on you if you are not there.'

'Oh?' She brushed the tears angrily away with the back of her hand. 'And did you think how poorly it would reflect on you before shaving off your galla meesa?'

The same stiffening of his shoulders. 'That is not your concern.'

'No, you are right. It's not my concern, you are not my concern, you've made that amply clear Machaiah. Yet, it pains me when I see the man you have become.'

He said nothing, his hand again rising unconsciously towards his jaw.

'Not even a coconut Machu?' she taunted. 'The tiger killer, afraid of bringing down a simple coconut? How could you let these people poke fun at you?'

'It doesn't matter. People will talk, no matter what.'

'And since when have *you* stopped caring what people said? Come now Machu, why don't you speak the truth?'

She stepped closer to him, holding Nanju so tight that he squirmed in her arms. 'The truth is that you are hiding from yourself. Where is the tiger killer I once knew, what have you done with him?'

'Hiding . . . Please.' His voice was icy. 'Don't be foolish.' He turned to leave.

'Foolish? I can see it in your eyes, Machu. You're living half a life, have shrunk to just the shadow of the man I knew.'

'Enough!' His lips parted in an ugly grimace, the dimple cutting mirthlessly into his cheek. 'Do not presume to know me. You. Do. Not.'

'Really?' Her voice had risen, but she did not care who might chance upon them. 'So tell me then Machaiah, since I don't know you at all, since all is well with you, since our story is over, since you will not deign even to look at me when I *know* that every pore of your body is aware I am near, since all of this is true and more, then why is it *that you still remain unwed*?'

For a second, she thought he was going to strike her. Nanju whimpered, alarmed by the angry exchange. Machu looked at the child, as if noticing him only now. 'It was foolish of you to have come,' he said then, distantly. 'All you have done is create a spectacle of yourself. Still, now that you are here, complete what you set out to do. They are waiting for the photograph.' He strode back towards the house without a second glance.

He was filled with a cold, hard fury. How dare she? How *dare* she? He was so furious all through the photograph session that the flash from the camera caught him unawares, making him blink. The shadow of a man? Who did she think she was?

He was still bitter that night when the Kambeymada family wended their way down to the fields. The moon was full, a slight breeze moulding the paddy into an undulating silver sea. 'Poli, poli Deva!' 'More, ever more, O God!' the family cried, their voices resounding in the night. The first sheaves of paddy were cut to a thunderous round of gunshot and hoisted into a wicker basket for the most senior daughter-in-law to carry into the house. Sprigs of this new crop were tied to the lamp hanging in the prayer corner, and to doors, pillars and bedposts all through the house. *May we never hunger for grain.* Machu barely noticed the crackers bursting in the yard although when the liquor was brought around, he downed two hefty pegs in a swallow.

The next day, when Machu informed the Nayak that he would represent the family in the paaria kali that evening, the Nayak delightedly stroked his moustache. It was good magic, the photograph – already, it was working!

Machu was expressionless as he danced the kolata dance in the village green with the other men, moving in intricate, ever-decreasing circles to the steady beat of the drums. The thin red canes felt light in his hands after the heft of his odikathi. The bells at the ends jingled softly as the canes swooped and fell through the air. His head was empty, devoid of thought, the same jungle weightlessness of old. The drums grew more and more rapid, the canes singing breathlessly to their beat. Slowly most of the dancers stepped back until only the contestants for the paaria kali remained.

The paaria kali was an ancient technique of warfare, an expert series of parries and thrusts handed down through the generations. It had been tamed now into a game contested during Puthari and used occasionally by the village elders as a means of settling disputes: each contestant was armed with a bamboo shield and a pair of canes with which he was allowed to strike his opponent only below the shins. Nonetheless, these mock battles were often heated affairs, with the elders sometimes having to intervene before one or other of the men involved was seriously injured.

The village shouted out encouragement as the contestants squared off against one another. Machu circled his opponent like a jungle cat, taking his measure, his eyes scarcely blinking. The hum of the crowd, the dust rising in puffs around his feet. Her eyes upon him, an unwavering gaze no matter which way he turned. The man thrust at him and Machu gracefully blocked the blow with the shield, his hands sweeping in a blur towards the other's shins. The canes came back bright with blood. No need for thought, just this dance, the eternal dance of the hunter and the hunted. Was there anything more pure? The drums grew faster, but Machu could no longer hear them, his attention fixed upon the canes shrieking in the air. The sting of blood on his legs, the canes dancing in his hands. Faster and faster, elation in his veins.

'*I am the tiger killer.*'

His opponent's shins grew more and more bloody, the crowd increasingly silent. And then the man threw down his shield with a yell of pain. 'Enough,' he cried, 'I have had enough. You are the victor.'

Machu blinked as a great cry arose from the crowd, 'Kambeymada Machaiah! Machu! Machu is the victor!' He looked straight at Devi. Her lips were moving, she was too far for him to hear what she was saying, but she was beaming proudly at him, her eyes bright with tears.

Both men embraced. 'You were invincible,' his opponent exclaimed ruefully. 'But then I should have known better than to go up against the tiger killer.'

'*I am the tiger killer.*' And yet, malleable as the clay at a potter's wheel he had been. Inconsequential as a summer cloud, blown hither and thither by the wind.

'You were a worthy opponent,' Machu said. Still locked in that gaze, unable to tear his eyes from hers. He took a deep, shuddering breath. 'There is nothing I would like more than to cement our friendship on this auspicious occasion of Puthari. You have a sister, don't you? With your parents' permission, I would like to marry her.'

Chapter 18

꠶ 1904 ꠶

The terracotta floor felt smooth and cool, like a pebble from the Kaveri. Nanju lay still, contemplating its texture against his cheek. After a while, he lifted his head and turned it so the other cheek now lay on the floor. 'She does not like flowers,' he repeated to himself. Nanju ought to have known that his mother did not like flowers.

Devanna had beckoned to him early that evening, pointing out the bloom from the living room window. It was the first of the season, perched high on the sampigé tree. Larger than his fist, infused with musk. 'What about this for your mother then?' Devanna asked, and Nanju had clapped his hands in delight. Father and son, complicit in their plan, sent Tukra clambering up the tree. Devanna had shown Nanju how to blow gently on the stamen of the flower, probing the creamy, tapering petals with the fingers of his good hand to rid them of ants. He had sent Nanju to present it to Devi.

'Did your father put you up to this?' she asked. He had nodded vigorously, unable to stop grinning.

Without further comment, Devi had plucked the flower from his palm and placed it in the prayer corner.

'No, Avvaiah,' Nanju had protested, 'this is for your hair, like the other ladies wear.'

'I have no time for such frivolities Nanjappa. Tell your father that.'

Nanju's face had fallen. Avvaiah did not like flowers. He needed to

209

remember from now on that she simply did not like them. He had tiptoed unhappily from the room. Appaiah too had fallen silent. Certain that it was all his fault and not knowing how to make amends, Nanju had once again crawled under the bed.

He did not remember how or when he had started to shelter here. He knew he really shouldn't, he was nearly five after all, a big boy now. Still, it remained his secret burrow, a place to cocoon himself among the tin trunks filled with silks and copper vessels. He would watch, hidden from view, as adult feet moved in and out of the room. Avvaiah's slim, delicate feet, adorned with a pair of silver toe rings; Tukra's cracked and dirt-blackened heels. Appaiah's slow shuffle as he selected a volume from the rainbow stacks of books piled around the room and the rest of the house.

Nanju turned his head again. From where he lay, he could just about make out the legs of Appaiah's chair. It was placed in its customary position before the living room windows. Nanju did not think that Appaiah had moved at all. He had sat there all evening, staring silently out the windows, at the lane that ran in front of the house and the brief patch of lawn with its beggared, sweet-scented sampigé tree.

The house had fallen quiet once more.

It was kept shut for most of the day; too much dust, intolerable noise, Avvaiah said, it was bad for Appaiah. The house was located in the Muslim quarter of the town and Avvaiah neither mixed with any of their neighbours nor encouraged the advances of their children towards Nanju. Nonetheless, he could not remember ever chafing against the quiet. Years later, when people would tell Nanju he was a man of few words, he would never know quite what to say. He had always seemed to prefer the stillness of silence, the room it accorded for thought.

That's what he would remember most about their home in Mercara, the quiet. Tukra's non-stop mumbling did not count. Having listened to it practically from the cradle, Nanju had grown as accustomed to it as another child might the ticking of a clock. It burbled in the background, a mishmash of words soft as Appaiah's gruel.

Avvaiah spoke with him of course. Each morning, Nanju would stand before his mother as she inspected the parting of his hair – straight as an arrow it ought to be, she always said. She would dot his forehead with vibhuti, the sacred ash from the prayer corner, asking him if he had remembered to brush his teeth. She would smile as he nodded, a quick softening of her mouth that made Nanju's heart glow like the sun.

That was on the good days. There were bad days too, when she would be brittle all morning, trying hard not to snap at him, a sharpness creeping nonetheless into her voice no matter how carefully he combed his hair. Or worse, she would become disconcertingly silent, her face drawn, filled with a sadness that made him ache. How he longed then to be able to reach up and remove the unhappiness from her eyes. She would faithfully stand in the window as she saw him off, but on such days, she would barely notice as he turned around to wave. Her eyes so unbearably sad, fixed on something far beyond that Nanju could never see.

He was never any good at predicting Avvaiah's moods, at anticipating the good days or bracing himself for the bad. So it was that when Nanju found Tukra waiting anxiously outside the mission school one afternoon, he was immediately filled with dread. He knew something was wrong from the way Tukra was fussing and fidgeting with the dust cloth that hung always from his shoulder. 'Avvaiah?'

'No, no, Nanju anna, your mother is fine. It's your great grandfather. Kambeymada Nayak died last night. You are to go with your mother to the Kambeymada village.'

Dead! Nanju had never known anyone who was dead. He tried to imagine the Nayak lying on his bier, but all that popped into his mind was an image of his immense moustache. Nanju used to stare at the Nayak, fascinated as the old man stroked and restroked that great silver appendage. And now he was dead . . .

He headed home with leaden feet, dreading the grieving mother he was sure he would find. To his relief, however, Devi had called almost gaily to him. 'Nanju monae? Come, quickly now, we have to leave shortly. The barber is here. And after that, get changed, there's a shirt and a pair of shorts on your bed. Quick, quick. And don't get your clothes dirty, they must remain perfectly white for the funeral.'

Appaiah's planter chair had been carted outside to the lawn where the barber was shaving his head bare with quick, deft strokes. His face looked funny without that covering of hair; Nanju had never before noticed how it seemed pushed to one side. 'Can I touch?' he cried. 'Appaiah, let me touch?' and Devanna smiled wanly, tilting his head. The barber began to work up a fresh lather, and Devanna heavily patted his son's arm to reassure him. Nanju wasn't nervous at all. The male relatives of the deceased had to offer their hair to the Gods so that they would open the gates to heaven, Nanju knew. He sat still as the barber's knife rasped against his scalp, watching the locks fall about him. Struck by a sudden thought, he twisted to look at his father, the barber tut-tutting under his breath.

'Appaiah, will you be coming too?'

'I—' Devanna began.

'No!' Devi emerged from the bedroom, cutting him short. 'No kunyi,' she repeated, her voice gentler this time. 'You know it is too difficult a journey for your father to make. It will be just the two of us as usual, just my sweet boy and me.'

Devanna hesitated. 'I should be there,' he said to her quietly. 'The last rites, the reading of the will . . .'

'Fine. Then come. You *know* you are still not up to the travel, it will only exhaust you.'

'Yes,' Devanna said tiredly, 'you are right. Nanju, you take care of Avvaiah, you hear?'

Nanju nodded, staring agog at his lovely mother. He thought she shone like a pearl, the pristine white of her sari almost blending into the colour of her skin.

She talked throughout the journey to the Kambeymada village, her hands dancing in the air as they kept time with her words. She told Nanju about the Kambeymada house, the massive threshing ploughs with their ends shaped like horse heads that had taken three years to carve and the prayer lamps dipped in twenty-four-carat gold, so ornate that it was said the Commissioner of Mysore himself had coveted them. She described in detail the massive tiger skin that hung inside the central area. 'This brooch, here.' She touched a finger to the brooch at her shoulder. 'Did you know it is made from a tiger's claw? Yes, I swear kunyi, from a real tiger!' She had been to the tiger wedding as a girl, she told him laughing, many years ago, when she was not much taller than he was now.

Nanju knew these stories by heart. Avvaiah recounted them to him each December when they visited the Kambeymada house for the Puthari festival. It never occurred to him to stop her though, it made him so happy just to sit there by his mother's side, listening. He liked to place his head in her lap as she spoke and she'd draw him close, laughing. He beamed now as she pulled him affectionately into the crook of her arm.

So absorbed was Nanju in Devi's chatter, that he forgot the reason for their visit. When they reached the house, the crowds of mourners were a sudden, shocking reminder. Nanju looked overwhelmed at what seemed to him like a river of milk. Lapping against the outer pillars of the house, spilling over the steps and onto the verandah, sitting, standing, talking, weeping; men, women and children all come to pay their last respects in spotless funeral white. He stayed close to his mother as they manoeuvred through the crowd and into the inner courtyard. The Nayak's freshly washed body was decked out in his finest velvet kupya and laid on a mat, his moustache oiled and twirled into a magnificent silver handlebar, his forehead smeared with sandalwood paste and anointed with a single gold sovereign.

'Touch his feet monae.'

The dead Nayak's toes felt waxy, like the translucent plugs of camphor Avvaiah kept in the prayer corner at home. Nanju hurriedly withdrew his hands and followed Devi as she sat with the other women. 'Go outside, why don't you,' she encouraged, 'go talk with your cousins.' He shook his head shyly and leaned against her. After a moment, she sighed and stroked his arm.

People kept streaming in, packed so close he could not even see to the far wall where the tiger skin was hung. A group of children of varying ages sat at one end of the courtyard, trying to be solemn but forgetting every so often, whispering and giggling among themselves until an adult told them sharply to be silent. Nanju peeped at them from behind his mother. They beckoned to him to join them and he at once got flustered, looking away as he shifted even closer to Devi.

They sat for what seemed like hours. Nanju began to fidget. 'Sit straight,' Devi whispered. 'Don't slouch like a Poleya, are you Tukra's child or mine?'

213

'How long must we stay?' he whined. 'I'm hungry Avvaiah.'

'Shhh. Look.' A group of his uncles entered the inner courtyard, each of them freshly shaven-headed like Appaiah and he. 'It must be time for the cremation.' Nanju watched curiously as his uncles lifted the Nayak's corpse into a chair and hoisted it upon their shoulders. The funeral drums started to play and women began to cry as they rose to their feet. Avvaiah was standing ramrod straight, her eyes fixed on the pallbearers. They slowly circled, East to West, once, twice, three times, Nanju counted under his breath. The Nayak's head slumped forward on his chest, the turban slipping askew. The pallbearers started down the steps that led towards the field. Sombrely the men in the gathering filed after them.

Unsettled, Nanju slipped his hand into his mother's. She flinched, startled, as if she had entirely forgotten that he was there too. 'Nanju,' she said, as if reminding herself of his name, 'you must go with your uncles to the cremation.'

'No . . .' Nanju began in alarm but she was already approaching one of his uncles.

'Will you take Nanju with you?'

'Avvaiah, no,' Nanju protested again in fright but his uncle had taken his hand.

'What monae! Stop hiding behind your mother's pleats, we will find her when we return. For now, your place is here, with the other men of your family, yes?'

Tukra had once told Nanju what happened to dead bodies. The Poleyas had originally left their dead in the forests, tipping them into pits and piling leaves and stones over them so wild animals could not get at them. Slowly though, they had begun to mimic the Coorg tradition of cremating their dead. Tukra had attended many, many funerals, he claimed. *Aiyo*, it was dangerous work! The ghost of the deceased had been known to rise up from its sizzling corpse many a time, *fssst*, just like that, and possess one or other of the onlookers.

Nanju had jeered at Tukra's tall stories, but now his words seemed all too real. He tugged experimentally at his uncle's grasp, but it was firm and would brook no nonsense.

He was a man, he told himself, was that not what Appaiah had said to him, that he was growing so fast? He was nearly five, and he would not be afraid. His head started to itch and he rubbed a sweaty palm over it. It was a hot afternoon, the dust rising around him as he descended reluctantly towards the fields. 'My shorts,' he fretted to himself, trying to brush them down with his free hand. Avvaiah had told him that he must not dirty them.

The cremation pyre had been assembled at the far end. The pallbearers lifted the corpse onto the logs. Nanju tried his best not to stare at his great grandfather and attract the ire of his ghost, but try as he might, his eyes returned time and again to the corpse. The logs shifted slightly and the Nayak's hand slipped lifelessly to one side. From where Nanju stood, it seemed as if his great grandfather was pointing an accusing finger straight towards him. He swallowed and looked away.

Cuck-oo, cuck-oo, a cuckoo called sweetly from the branches overhead. Nanju glanced up at it, but his eyes were pulled back to the Nayak. Three of his uncles circled the pyre, the cuckoo called again as they torched the wood. Flames crackled their way towards the corpse, wisps of smoke reaching into the air. The fire probed at the figure of the Nayak, testing the tasselled ends of his sash. Nanju made a small sound in his throat as it coiled slowly about the sleeve of the Nayak's kupya, setting it aflame. The flames crept higher, flickering over the wide expanse of chest. Nanju was transfixed, unable to look away. The fire rose higher still, lapping at the Nayak's chin, scorching that magnificent, gleaming moustache. A slow, sizzling sound, like fish in a pan. Cuck-ooo, the bird trilled, twitching its tail, and with a sudden WHOOF the entire pyre burst into flame. To Nanju's horror, the Nayak's hand seemed to rise through the flames, *pointing straight at him*. Nanju tore free from his uncle's grasp and, pushing through the mourners, fled pell-mell across the fields back towards the house, screaming for his mother.

'Avvaiah! AVVAIAH!'

She whirled around, eyes wide with fear. 'Nanju? What is it, are you hurt? What's the matter, monae, what happened?' He shook his head, that burned-hair smell still in his nostrils, trying hard not to cry. 'Then what ... is the cremation already over? What's this? Did you wet yourself? Nan-ju.'

Nanju looked down at himself, his cheeks hot with shame. 'Avvaiah,' he mumbled, hanging his head.

'Nanju ...' Devi began, aware of the women looking in their direction.

'Here, monae.' One of the grand-aunts bustled towards Nanju, a plate in her hand. 'You look hungry. Will you eat some ottis? The other children have already eaten, you must be hungry too. It's OK kunyi, stay here with us and eat.'

Nanju sat down heavily with the plate, trying to hide the wet stains on his shorts. His legs were still trembling. He began stuffing chunks of otti into his mouth, trying to block the memory of the jerky, puppet-like movements the Nayak's body had appeared to make in the midst of the leaping flames.

'Really Devi,' his grand-aunt said softly. 'What were you thinking, sending the child alone?'

Devi stiffened, masking her guilt with a haughty toss of her head. 'He is a man of this house too, is he not? It is his duty.'

'His *duty*? There is a time and place for everything, you should not have ...' She stopped short as a third woman approached them.

The woman smiled at Nanju and he smiled tremulously back, trying not to stare. She was so fat!

'Devi akka, how are you?'

'Not as well as you evidently.'

Nanju looked up at Avvaiah. Her voice sounded funny. She was smiling, Nanju saw, but it was one of those pretend smiles that did not reach her eyes.

'Yes,' the other woman laughed. 'It took a few years, but my husband has done me in at last, good and proper.' She rubbed her belly contentedly.

'I saw him carry the body down to the fields.' Devi said the first thing that came to her mind. Machu's wife looked quizzically at her and Devi turned hastily towards Nanju to compose herself.

She was pregnant. Machu's smiling, happy wife was full with child. The child that should have been hers. *Theirs*. Filled with a sudden fury, Devi snapped at Nanju.

'What are you doing, staring up at me like that? Stop dawdling and eat your otti, or is even this too much to ask?'

Devi lay awake that night, neither able to sleep, nor rail nor weep for fear of who might hear. She had not attended Machu's wedding. She had vowed to, at first. She would look her best, she promised herself, look so beautiful she would trounce the bride. Ultimately though, she had been unable to, sitting frozen at the edge of her bed, the sari she had so painstakingly selected lying in a crumpled heap on the floor. Tukra had had to repeat his question many times before she had finally responded. No, she had said dully, they would not be travelling to the Kambeymada village after all.

She had steeled herself that following Puthari to be civil to his wife. Fat, she had told herself, the girl would be fat and simple, but even she had to admit that Machu's wife was pretty. It had taken every ounce of Devi's willpower to sound even-keeled as she congratulated the girl. 'May you live long,' she had said, unable to complete the blessing: *May you live long, may you have a happy life, may you die a married woman.*

Once again, Machu had stayed away from her.

Still, as a year went past, and then another, Devi found consolation in the flatness of his wife's stomach. Machu may have told her that it was over between them, but she knew, she *knew* from the way he held himself, from the way he stood when she was near, that it was far from over. It could never be. Every year, she would anxiously scan her rival's midriff; every year, she was rewarded with a sharp sense of triumph at its virgin emptiness. He may be married in name, she told herself, but it was clear he did not desire his wife. And who could blame him? Why, one had only to look at the woman's backside, flat as a washing stone.

Her eyes burned now with the image from that afternoon, of that monstrously pregnant belly. The bellybutton poking so impudently through the folds of the other's sari, drawing attention to the life swimming within. Machu's son. There was not a doubt in her mind that the child would be a boy. The bile rose in her throat. 'What did you expect? That he would be celibate forever? It was you, was it not, who asked him why he remained unwed?'

Nanju moaned softly, caught in some disturbing dream. She was reminded of that afternoon, the look of sheer terror in his face as he had come running up to her. What kind of a mother was she, she asked herself unhappily, staring at her sleeping child.

'How many children should we have?' she had asked Machu once.

'Six.'

'Huh,' she had replied, 'I want *ten*. Five boys and five girls, and then, when the tenth is born, you and the rest of village will throw me the customary feast to commemorate my giving birth to ten healthy children.

'Why do you look so dubious?' she had continued merrily. 'Just think, what a fine household ours will be – you, the tiger killer, and me, the mother of ten children!'

He had grinned. 'I don't care about ten children, or two. However many, let them be healthy and happy, that is all.'

'Hmm . . .' She pondered this point. 'Maybe you are right. Still, our first should be a boy, don't you think?' She had rested her chin upon his chest, smiling at him. 'A boy, just like you.'

Nanju moaned again, burying his face into the pillow. Pressing her teeth into her lip to keep from crying, Devi patted him wearily on his arm. He shifted and then, curling himself into a tight ball, grew still once more. Devi turned towards the wall.

She awoke bleary-eyed and disoriented. It was a grey, leaden morning, an anaemic mist drifting through the inner courtyard. A mass of clouds threatened rain at any moment, setting off a nagging ache in the middle of her forehead. She lay still for a moment, gathering herself. There was one last detail to take care of and then she could leave.

When the Kambeymada men gathered on the verandah, scratching their itchy, stubbled scalps, they looked startled at Devi as she walked out to join them. Did this girl have no sense of propriety? Daughters-in-law had no place in discussions about property. 'My husband cannot be here,' Devi offered by way of explanation. 'I . . . I am here in his stead and for my son, Kambeymada Nanjappa.' She pulled the end of her sari closer about her as if to ward off their disapproval.

'Yes, well. We could have informed you of our decisions later.' She pretended not to hear, casting her eyes downwards as she stationed herself firmly by a pillar. The men glanced at one another, unsure of what to do, and then proceeded as if she were simply not there.

The times were changing, they concurred, the old joint family system no longer worked; the Nayak had managed to keep the family together through sheer force of will. With him gone, who would keep the peace? Better for each male member of the family to take his share of the property or its equivalent in cash. The house along with the surrounding land would go to the Nayak's oldest surviving brother and his family; the rest of the estate would be divided. They began to move through the ranks of the family, apportioning the assets. To the oldest surviving brother, a parcel of five hundred acres. To the second, four hundred and sixteen gold sovereigns. To the third . . . When it was the turn of the Nayak's sons, Devanna's father was given four hundred and thirty acres. He beamed and nodded. It was fair.

'And to Kambeymada Devanna, the house he is currently residing in.'

Devi's head snapped up. 'Is that all? What of my husband's share of the land, or its equivalent value?'

'Land? There is no land. What need does Devanna have of land when he can barely walk? We are giving him the house.'

'The house will not pay us an income. What need does he have of land, you ask? All the more reason when he is an invalid! He has a wife to support, does he not, and our son?'

The elders glanced at one another. The temerity of this woman. 'There is no land that has been assigned to Devanna, nor any other assets,' they told her curtly. 'Still, if you are dissatisfied, you should talk with your father-in-law.'

'It is like this, you see.' Devanna's father would not look her in the eye. 'Not a lot of land has been given to me. And as you know, I have four other sons besides Devanna.'

'Four other sons?' Devi's voice sounded unnaturally high even to her ears. She paused, trying to regain her composure. 'Four other sons, father-in-law? May I remind you that Devanna is your first born?'

'Yes kunyi, I know . . .' Still he would not look at her. 'My hands are tied unfortunately. Things are so expensive these days . . . In any event, you have the house.'

'A house? My son, a scion of the Kambeymadas, and all he is entitled to is an ill-ventilated chattel? Is this fair?'

She looked around pleadingly at the elders. 'Please,' she said, her voice cracking. 'We do not have much. The Nayak sent us money every month, and even with that, I have had to ... each grain, we count each grain that goes into the cooking pot. I do not see the money continuing now that the Nayak is gone. Be fair to my son, how are we to survive without any land?'

'No, kunyi,' Devanna's father hastened to explain. 'I will continue to send you money each month. How much do you need? A hundred rupees? Two hundred?'

'I do not want any more charity,' Devi flared. 'Just give my son his due. Give us the land he is entitled to.'

They shook their heads regretfully at her. This was the best they had to offer, and a generous offer it was too. She should take it.

Finally, desperate, Devi looked towards him. '*Machu. Make them see reason.*' She realised with a shock that he was not even looking at her, gazing out instead at the green smudge of the fields, the small tic in his jaw belying the deliberately bored expression on his face, telling her just how unwilling he was to intervene on her behalf.

Devi nodded, her eyes brimming with tears. 'So be it,' she told them, turning to go back inside. 'Keep your charity, I will make ends meet without you.'

Nanju looked at Devi, alarmed. She was always sad when it was time to leave the Kambeymada home, but he had never seen his mother cry like this before. 'Avvaiah?' he asked, staring crestfallen at the tears running down her face.

She shook her head, trying to smile. 'Nothing, it's nothing. Come, hurry up, gather your things, we must leave for Mercara.'

She made him seek the blessings of every elder in the house, touching all of their feet herself as they stiffly wished her well. Only then did she seat herself in the cart. Nanju looked anxiously at her as they pulled away from the house. He searched for the right words. 'Don't be sad Avvaiah,' he began hesitatingly. 'Appaiah told me that we have to let

Kambeymada thatha go. He told me that thatha had lived a very long life and—'

Devi nodded. 'Yes, yes. I'm tired Nanju that's all.' She touched his cheek to soften her words. 'Avvaiah has a bad headache. Do you think you can be quiet for a while?'

Nanju nodded stoutly. He was glad to leave. He wanted to go back to the calm of Mercara, to Appaiah. He looked at his mother. At least she had stopped crying. He drew his knees up to his chin, gazing out of the cart. It would be better at home.

The clouds shifted wanly across the sky, the Kambeymada house coming into view one last time between the trees before vanishing altogether.

Tukra had just negotiated the third bend in the lane when Nanju raised his head. 'Avvaiah,' he pointed. 'Look.'

Machu rode right up to the cart. 'Devi.

'Devi,' he said again.

She alighted gracefully and they moved to the side of the lane. Nanju craned his head, trying to hear what they were saying, but the breeze snatched away most of their words.

'Congratulations.'

'Yes.'

'Are you happy?' She tried to smile. 'It will be a boy. A boy, just like you.'

'Devi. What happened back there. It was not right.'

'And yet you did nothing to stop it.'

'What good has it ever done to go up against an army? Better to catch them unawares, or take them on one at a time. Anyway,' he shook his hand impatiently, 'I came to tell you this. Do not worry. I will see to it that you get your fair share.'

She laughed, a shrill, mocking sound. 'I'm sure you will, just like you did this morning.'

'Devi . . .'

Tears threatened the back of her eyes and she laughed again to cover them. 'Here.' Nanju saw Avvaiah reach into her blouse and place something in his uncle's palm.

'I gave this to you.'

'A tiger's claw for your tigress? Yes, I know. But you have a wife now, Machu, you will have a child soon. This . . . you should take this back.'

He put the brooch back in her hands, cupping them hard in his own. 'This is yours,' he said roughly. 'Do with it as you will, throw it in the Kaveri if you wish. But it was meant for you alone. None other than you.'

To Nanju's dismay, Avvaiah started crying again when she returned to the cart. 'Hurr . . . Hurr,' Tukra encouraged the oxen, and they steadily moved forward again.

'Avvaiah,' he said helplessly. He was a man, wasn't he? Appaiah had told him that he needed to take care of his mother and Nanju knew he must not fail her again. 'Avvaiah, Kambeymada thatha . . .'

'He is gone Nanju,' she sobbed. 'He is lost to me forever.' She hugged him to her, so tight that his ribs hurt, but Nanju knew it was important, very important not to move at all.

Machu went to see the elders of the family that same evening.

'Have you gone soft in the head?' they asked incredulously when they heard what he had to say. Machu, however, was adamant.

Two days later, when his wife went into labour, it was a boy, just as Devi had predicted. He cradled the baby in his arms, gazing wonderingly at him.

'*Are you happy?*' she had asked.

His son roared lustily and for the first time in a very long while, the shadows shifted momentarily from Machu's heart.

Chapter 19

When the Kambeymada family sent word to Devanna that they had reconsidered the division of the property, Devi knew it was all Machu's doing. '*I will see to it*,' he had said to her, '*that you get your fair share.*'

Devanna stared in wonder at the letter, and then he read it once again to make sure he had not misunderstood. 'My father! He did this, I suppose . . . I hadn't expected, I never thought that . . . *Look* Devi,' he said hoarsely. 'A hundred acres!'

Devi had spared him the details of the denouement at the Kambeymada house, how she had pleaded with the elders and especially his father to treat Devanna equitably. She said nothing now to disabuse him of the notion of his father's largesse, but there was a fierce exultation in her eyes as she stared at the letter. '*I will see to it*,' Machu had promised her.

She sent Tukra to the Nachimanda village with news of this windfall, bidding Thimmaya to come at once, and they set out the very next day to inspect the property. The land that had been bequeathed to Devanna was a coffee estate that lay about half an hour outside Mercara. It had belonged to a Scottish planter and when he had left Coorg – I have had it with these blasted rains, he had shouted, after an especially poor season – Kambeymada Nayak had promptly bought it from him. 'Buy paddy acreage, this is not the time to be investing in coffee,' the Nayak's cronies had urged, but the Nayak had gone ahead regardless. 'Land is land,' he had pointed out. 'It can lie untended for a while until coffee prices improve.'

Devi knew little of this as she looked around her, at the array of coffee bushes, the pond glinting in the distance, the vast, dilapidated bungalow at the head of a winding gravel drive. 'Iguthappa Swami,' she said softly to her father, 'is looking after us once more. We will—' She stopped short at the worried look on his face.

'What?' she asked anxiously. 'What is it?'

Thimmaya shook his head. 'There would at least be some paddy, I hoped. This – the land is all given over to coffee.'

'It is. That's a good thing, isn't it? To own a coffee plantation, like the white folk?'

Thimmaya glanced at Devi, trying to curb the anxiousness in his breast. His poor child, how would she ever be able to . . . nothing she knew of coffee planting, where could he even begin?

'Appaiah?' Devi asked again, her eyes huge. 'Please. Just tell me, what is the matter?'

'The thing is kunyi, coffee yields have not been . . . they have been poor for quite some years now.'

'When the first coffee estates were planted – many years ago, when your Tayi herself was no older than you are now – in those days, they say the coffee crops did very well indeed.'

The yields realised by those pioneer white folk had been so rich, he explained, that multitudes of their brethren had followed, pouring into Coorg. The Seventies and Eighties had seen their estates proliferate around Coorg. Even the Coorgs began to scatter handfuls of coffee berries here and there among their holdings, acquiring such a taste for the beverage that no kitchen was complete without a pot of strong black coffee sweetened with jaggery brewing on the fire. The truly wealthy among them, like Kambeymada Nayak, had acres of underbrush cleared from beneath their holdings of rosewood, and turned over to coffee. The plants had grown robustly, producing profuse clumps of berries season after season.

And then, towards the turn of the century, things had taken an abrupt downturn. Coffee yields had fallen inexplicably low all across Coorg. No matter how the planters weeded or pruned, no matter whether the hands that tended the estates were white or brown, no matter the soil scientists brought in from Mysore nor the cockerels sacrificed to the wood spirits. For nearly seven seasons now, the coffee in Coorg had been reduced to a few measly tons of output.

A breeze stirred through the estate, ruffling the coffee leaves. Devi swallowed. 'How . . .' she asked Thimmaya haltingly, 'just how bad is it?'

'It is a beautiful piece of land, kunyi,' he tried to reassure her. 'Look how it undulates about us, so many orange trees.'

'We can't live on the oranges alone,' Devi interrupted. 'Please Appaiah, just tell me. Can I do anything at all with the property?'

'Yes,' Thimmaya replied, 'sell it. The price per acre will not be good, but there are one hundred of them − your own father tills but twelve. Sell the land, and buy paddy wetlands with the money, or some acres of cardamom.'

She stared around her, crestfallen. 'I will see to it,' he had said to her, 'I will talk to them.' It was Machu who had talked sense into the family; it was he who had got her this land.

She reached towards a coffee bush. Its leaves seemed to glow as they brushed against her fingers. 'Machu got me this land,' Devi thought again. It was all she had of him.

'I will not sell,' she said quietly.

'Kunyi, come now, be practical. From the look of things, this estate has not been tended to for years.' He pointed at the trees arching over their heads. 'The shade trees, look how overgrown they are. Even in good times, they must be pruned each year so that the coffee gets enough sun.' The European planters were known to be fanatical about clipping back the tree cover, and in some estates there had been a mass felling of timber. Should even a single tree trunk be left standing, these planters had warned their workers, it would be grounds for instant dismissal. 'They are completely overgrown kunyi, where will you get the money to have them pruned?'

'I will not sell.'

'Devi, don't be foolish. Even timber prices have been low this year, you will get next to nothing for the trees.'

She turned pleadingly to him. 'Don't ask me to sell this property, Appaiah. There *must* be something else I can do.'

Thimmaya stared helplessly at his daughter. For an instant, she seemed no more than a little girl. Muthavva would be scolding her over something or other and she would race helter-skelter towards him, seeking amnesty from her mother's wrath. Such a look she would have in her face then, as he swung her high into his arms. As if her father could do anything, *anything* at all, to shelter her from all the ills of the world.

He ran his hand over a pepper vine that had been trained about the trunk of a shade tree. The vines had suffered from neglect too, there would hardly be anything from them that year.

'So be it,' he said at last. 'Try turning over the land to paddy instead. Let's start clearing it of coffee, acre by acre.' He injected a confidence he did not feel into his tone, tugging purposefully at a length of rotting vine. 'It won't be easy, but when did hard work ever harm anyone?'

They held a small puja at the estate the next day, breaking a coconut at the entrance and spilling its water into the soil. Tayi had Tukra wring the neck of a black fowl and bury it in a corner of the estate, to ward off the pisachi and their evil eye.

'We need a name Avvaiah, what should we call our estate?' Nanju asked, gazing about him in wonder.

'Nari Malai,' his mother immediately responded, her face aglow. Tiger Hills.

Devi sold the oranges from the estate and with the proceeds, hired three workers with whose help she planned to clear a few acres of coffee. The going was slow and arduous. The woody stems of the coffee bushes had to be hacked through and then their roots wrenched free from the soil. Devi's nails grew ragged and torn as she slogged alongside the workers, blisters erupting on her palms. And yet, after months of labour, from when the sun rose in the East to when the stars began to speckle the evening sky, barely a patch of the estate had been cleared.

Devanna watched from his chair as she sank onto the edge of her bed one evening, so fatigued she could barely think. All these months, he had not said a word even as he chafed at the thought of her toiling there, at being unable to help, and the limitations of his broken body. 'Talk sense into her,' Tayi had urged him. 'This is a fool's errand, to try to turn the estate around. Sell the land while there is still some value in it, buy some paddy fields instead.'

Devanna had hesitated. 'The estate . . . it is this land that she seems to want, Tayi, this and no other.'

And so he had held his counsel, sitting anxiously by the window each evening until she returned. Devi never gave any indication that she noticed, let alone appreciated his vigil. Still he waited, pretending to be absorbed in a book while she made sure Nanju was tucked in tight, had her bath and lit the prayer lamps. Only when she finally sat down to her supper would he, too, begin to eat. They ate in silence, both of them. He picking at his gruel, Devi swallowing desultory mouthfuls of whatever it was that lay on her plate. The house so quiet, they could hear the mice scrabbling in the walls.

Today, she had been too exhausted to do anything but retreat to her room. Devanna waited then rose hesitantly from his chair. He limped towards her door, breathing hard from even this small exertion.

'Devi,' he rasped. 'What is it? Is it the estate? Can I help?'

She glanced wearily at him. 'Help? Really Devanna? How else are you going to *help* me?'

Nonetheless, she told him about the estate. 'Coffee bushes, nothing but coffee,' she said bitterly. 'Even the pepper vines are rotted from the rains. It was too much to undertake, to try to turn the land back to paddy. The money from the oranges has almost gone and we have barely made any progress. I . . . I don't know what else to do.'

'Coax a coffee crop instead. The newspapers say that prices are not bad this year.'

'Coax a . . . ! The estate has lain untended for years. Even the tree cover has grown again. Appaiah says it will cost a great deal to clip it back. Where is the money going to come from? And so much expense for what? A few quintals of yield?'

She looked down at her smarting hands. 'I might have to sell,' she said to him shakily.

Devanna was staring at her. '*The trees have grown in?* But Devi, this could be just what we need.'

Ignoring the pain stabbing his leg, he limped to a stack of books and pulled an atlas from the pile. 'Look,' he said.

Devanna's body had slowly begun to solder together over the past year, but he was still far from recovered. It had been a slow, agonising process. Even shuffling from one room to another exhausted him; he would have to rest in his chair for quite a while afterwards, eyes closed, mouth hanging open. Still too weak to venture outdoors for any significant period of time, and with even Nanju away at school, he had desperately sought a distraction to prevent his mind from meandering too deeply into the past.

He had turned once more towards the familiar refuge of his books. Weighty parcels arrived for him every month, from publishers in Bangalore, Bombay, Madras and London. It was an expensive business, but despite their strained monetary circumstances, Devi hadn't found it in herself to object. When, in fact, realising the burden his purchases must be placing on their budget, he had not ordered any books for nearly three months, she had noticed. 'Why did you stop?' she had demanded. 'Don't be silly now, you go and get your books.' She told herself the only reason she had done this was for Nanju's sake; it would do him good to grow up surrounded by the written word, in an environment of learning.

Devanna read voraciously. History, geography, philosophy, religion, mathematics, the sciences, fiction, biographies, travelogues, and most of all, his first love – botany. Training his attention on coffee planting in Coorg, he had set his mind to understanding the puzzling decrease in yields.

A widespread deficiency in the soil, he had thought at first, but no, that did not make sense. Paddy yields had been consistently high in the same period. There had been no epidemics either, no hosts of pests that could explain the scanty harvest. Even the rain had generally fallen as it usually did, maybe more in some years than others, but nothing that should have so adversely affected the crop.

He had been deep in the middle of a memoir by a planter from Ceylon when it had occurred to him. Could it be? Could it really be so simple an explanation?

'Look,' he said now to Devi, gesturing at the atlas. Devi peered suspiciously at the page, at the latitudes running through India and the neighbouring islands. 'Here,' he pointed, 'look at Ceylon.' The planters in Coorg had made a serious error of judgement, he told her, in following the coffee plantations of Ceylon too closely. 'When they removed as much of the tree cover as they did here, I believe they made one fatal error. They forgot that Coorg is situated at a higher sea level than Ceylon.'

The coffee in Coorg was getting entirely too much sun.

Devi gazed doubtfully at him. 'Are you certain?' she asked.

He nodded excitedly. 'It is only a theory Devi, but yes, I do think this is the answer. Do you remember that story from the mission school – the one about Jack and his giant beanstalk?' The soil in Coorg was so fertile, he told her, that in the initial years it hadn't mattered. Push a coffee bean into the mud and a plant would have practically sprouted overnight, too much sun or not. Yields had been high in those early days. But as the years passed, the initial advantage of virgin soil had been eroded. The bushes had not been able to withstand the excessive sunlight, the buds withering on their stalks before they could mature into fruit.

'So ... you mean that ...' Devi worked through the implications.

'We may not need to trim the tree cover at all. If my hypothesis is right, letting the shade trees grow might in fact be the *best* thing that could have happened to the estate.'

Could it really be? Devi stared at him, weighing her options. Gold in his brains, she remembered, Devanna's head had always been filled with gold. She rose to her feet, suddenly energised. 'So be it. We have so little to lose, we may as well try your way.'

She pawned her wedding jewellery – the bangles Muthavva had left her, the necklaces and the double chain – at the local jeweller at Mercara. With the rupees she got from him, work began in earnest to coax a coffee crop from the estate. Thimmaya was dubious, but nonetheless he visited as often as he could, showing his daughter the right mix of cattle bone and manure with which to fertilise the plants, how to keep the soil around the plants entirely clear of weeds. Devi laboured alongside Tukra, his grumbling wife, and the few workers she had been able to afford. Weeding, hoeing, composting, manuring, hacking, pruning, standing, bending, reaching, plucking until the muscles in her back and her arms cramped in pain.

Still, in some strange way, it was cathartic. There was honesty in the physical labour, with the sun hot upon her face. A bluntness to the blisters the hoe raised across her palm. She didn't know what they would do if, after all this, the crop was a poor one. They always had a home at her father's she knew, but it was hardly right, placing their financial burdens upon his head. Nanju's school, how would she ever afford the fees? No matter how many towels she edged with lace.

And then Devi would yank even more violently at the weeds. All she could do was work. And work she would. She would work till she dropped, she promised herself. Machu had got her this land, and she would make something of it. 'Grow,' she whispered fiercely to the plants as she hoed around their roots, his name bitter-sweet on her tongue. 'Grow now, you hear me?'

She had heard how, when it had come to his share of the property, Machu had elected to receive cash rather than land and had then given all of it to the Ayappa temple. 'What a staunch devotee,' people said of him in awe, but the news had pierced her like a shaft. For him not to have staked a claim to this land. To have chosen, deliberately chosen to stay rootless. The money taken in lieu and donated to the Gods was no mere offering, Devi knew. It was a penance, an unending expiation for their past.

She had heard, too, of the birth. Machu's son, a boy, just as she had known. She had had to fight to keep her face composed, to mask the pain from her voice. 'Oh? So all are well then, the wife and the baby?'

Here in the estate, it was all left behind. Here she could pretend that things were as they once had been. That she remained unmarked, branded by neither fate nor circumstance, her heart wild and unfettered as the wind. That the only thing of consequence was the task at hand, the mulching of the soil with dried leaves to retain as much moisture as possible, the pruning of the bushes and selecting, from the many shoots springing forth from a node, the three most promising that would then be allowed to grow. Sometimes, when she looked up, she imagined she saw Machu's shoulders silhouetted against the jackfruit trees. Sometimes she seemed to hear his voice, carrying distinctly through the hills.

*

It was months later that Devanna's theory was finally proven right. They had been able to tend only a small section of the estate, but nonetheless, those acres burst forth with white, spangled bloom. Devi was astonished by the fragrance of the flowers. Her father had cultivated a small patch of coffee on his land, and she had noticed the delicate beauty of the blossoms, but never before had she realised just how magically scented they were. A honeyed, evocative bouquet perfuming the air for two heady weeks after they bloomed.

The berries that followed were so plentiful that with the money from their sale, Devi was able to pay off her debts at the pawnbroker and have enough left over to afford workers for almost the entire hundred acres the next season.

A year later, Devi stood on the crest of the hill that overlooked the estate, admiring a sea of coffee blossoms. It had rained a few days ago, a strong morning shower that had washed the dust from the trees and at once tempered the heat. Blossom showers, they were called, these warm rains of March; this year, they had arrived with perfect timing. The coffee had budded the previous month; small 'spikes' of green, each the size of a grain of rice, sprouting in profusion. The spikes had slowly matured in the sun until a mild stickiness had appeared on their surfaces, a sign that they were ready to bloom.

That was when the blossom showers had come.

The coffee had bloomed in their wake. Tiny, brilliant white flowers, clustered so thickly that entire branches were covered in ivory, thrusting pristine and spear-like from the green as far as the eye could see. The estate lay before her, heavy with perfume, hugging the swell and curve of the land as it steamed gently in the sun. Its orderly rows of shade trees – orange, jackfruit and silver oak – yielding gracefully to the jungle knotting the borders. Away in the distance, the bluish haze of the mountains, plumed with clouds. Frogs croaked from the damp grass around the estate pond, and insects, shiny winged, skimmed over the coffee blooms.

Devi had dragged Tayi with her to see the blossoms, triumphant testimony to nearly two years of hard labour. 'Cheh kunyi,' the old lady had protested, 'my knees cannot handle so much rough use,' but Devi would hear none of it, getting Tukra to drive the carriage almost to the very crest of the hill. She turned to her wheezing grandmother.

'Look Tayi,' she said, gesturing with a quiet, determined pride. 'Mine. All of this, mine.'

Tayi looked askance at her, trying to catch her breath. 'It is Devanna's property,' she reminded her granddaughter.

The breeze whipped around them, moulding their saris to their legs. Devi took a deep, satisfied breath, inhaling the fragrance of the coffee blossoms, but saying nothing in reply.

Once again, the blooms were an accurate indicator of the crop to come. When it was time for the harvest, the yield was so high that the drying yard was occupied for almost a month. Its cured surface seemed perpetually carpeted with red-brown berries drying in the sun; all along its boundary, hillock after hillock of berries lay mounded as they awaited their turn. Tukra sat beady-eyed over this bounty, cheh-chehing as Nanju dived and rolled through the mounds. 'Oh leave him be Tukra,' an amused Devi intervened. 'He's only a child. Besides, there are plenty more where those came from!'

She went to Mincing Lane herself to negotiate the price of the harvested crop with the European consolidators, conducting the discussions in her limited but serviceable mission school English. Devanna, whose condition had continued to improve, insisted on accompanying her, refusing to let his wife go unescorted. Devi had not objected. He had very nearly fallen as he tried to get into the carriage, righting himself at the last minute and seating himself heavily inside, a stubborn set to his chin, his brogues and walking stick polished to a shine.

Gordon Braithwaite, one of the largest planters in Coorg, was astounded at the yield that Devi had realised. 'Coffee King no more,' he said ruefully later that evening at the club. 'I believe the honour this year goes to a rather winsome local. Coffee *Queen* that is.'

Jealous heads turned all over Coorg in her direction. That girl Devi! Went to Mincing Lane, to talk with the white folk herself. Did she have no sense of propriety? It was no wonder that she had got such a high price, what man could resist a woman shaking her breasts at him?

Tayi tried to make her grandchild see reason. 'Why must you openly defy convention, kunyi?' she asked, distressed. 'You are not a child any more, but a grown woman. Spare a moment to think of us, and what we must feel when we hear you talked about so.'

'Oh Tayi. People will talk, no matter what,' Devi said impatiently.

'You have to live in society, remember that, and so do your near and dear.'

Devi laughed.

'You have become hard, my sun and moon,' Tayi said sadly. 'Do not make yourself so brittle that a single touch should make you shatter.'

'Not hard Tayi. Strong.' Devi thought again of the Kambeymadas, the humiliation of having to beg for Devanna's rightful share. 'In this life, if one is not strong, people will trample you underfoot. One has to fight for happiness. For one's dues.'

Chapter 20

'Another,' Machu called, and the scruffy server promptly placed another pot of arrack in front of him. He tore into the mutton chop garnished with red onions and chillies, and washing it down with a draught of the strong spirit, belched pleasurably. At least the food at the shack remained as good as it had always been.

The English had their velvet-curtained club; the Coorgs frequented the palm-frond-thatched shack that lay at the entrance to Mercara. The old woman owner ran it with a canny hand. She knew to keep a continuous supply of potent, home-brewed arrack coming to her customers, while at the same time keeping their stomachs filled with generous helpings of dosas, masala chops and chicken-liver fry to take the edge off the liquor. Machu took another swallow of the arrack, feeling it burn along his veins. Coming to the arrack shack was the one bright spot in this otherwise misbegotten day.

After weeks of coming home empty-handed, he had downed a brace of rabbits that morning, and a young deer. He had skinned the game and his wife had hung the meat over the hearth to cure in the smoke of the kitchen fire. Machu had brought the skins immediately into Mercara to sell. It had not gone well. 'Ten rupees,' the buyer had said, an air of finality about him, and no matter what Machu said, he would not budge.

Ten measly rupees, what would that buy them? Game had been scarce all this season. These days, without land to call his own or a job with the Government, it was hard for a man to care for his family. Ten rupees. Cursing under his breath, Machu lifted the pot of arrack to his mouth again.

'Machu! Ayy Machu!' He turned towards the acquaintance approaching him. 'What's this? Not four in the afternoon and you've already begun?' The man slapped him on the shoulder, laughing. 'No matter, whether in your joy, or in your sorrow, whichever the case might be, I'll keep you company.'

'Yes. Win or lose, we shall booze,' Machu said wryly, and the man guffawed.

He shook his head when Machu told him about the sale. 'Too difficult, everything is too difficult these days. How is a body to manage? Paddy prices are next to nothing and coffee yields are still low. By the way,' he griped, 'heard about that woman Devi?'

Machu grimaced. He had. Many times.

But not to be deterred, the man launched into yet another account of how Devi had managed to get unheard of prices at Mincing Lane. 'Not today,' Machu thought to himself. Not with the disappointment over the skins compounding the financial worry that seemed to hang constantly over his head. Today, the very mention of her name cut deeply.

He had married well, Machu knew. His wife was virtuous and dutiful, her devotion to him written all over her pretty face. What more could a man possibly want? And yet, it was someone else who haunted him, dancing tantalisingly through his dreams. 'What is it?' his wife would whisper as he jerked awake, night after night. 'Do you want some water?' Machu would say nothing as he lay there, staring blindly into the night, and then he would reach for her, pulling her towards him. He would take her, with a force born of desperation, a passion that rendered him spent.

And yet it lingered, the pungent after-odour of loss.

He tilted the pot of arrack to his mouth and draining it, threw it to the floor. 'Enough,' he said to his companion, cutting him short as went on and on about coffee prices.

'If I hear another word about coffee, or the Nari Malai estate, it will be one word too many. So I don't have any land. You think I regret it? Not for an instant.'

'I never . . .' protested his companion, but Machu wasn't listening.

He rose, steady on his feet despite the arrack sloshing about his insides. 'You think I cannot provide for my family? Watch this. Ayy.'

Summoning the server, Machu dipped his hand into his pocket and drew out the ten coins from that morning. Picking off one, two, three, four, *five* coins, he dropped them with a flourish into the palm of the stunned boy who promptly prostrated himself at the feet of his benefactor.

'Get up, get up,' Machu said irritably, and then, struck by a sudden notion, he raised his head proudly and began to chant.

> *Be blessed and listen O friend, listen to this singer's song*
> *In the depths of these jungles, in this wild heartland*
> *A tiger roamed fiercely hungry all day, all night long*

He chanted the tiger song, his eyes fierce, as if recalling something irrevocably lost. The timbre of his voice lending a wild, untrammelled beauty to the words, rendering the occupants of the shack into silence. And then, struck by the absurdity of it all, Machu started to laugh. He stopped just long enough to nod goodbye to his companion. 'Watch, just you watch,' he called, making his way down the steps of the shack.

About a month before, Machu had been approached by one of the regulars he hunted for. They were looking for good men to join the Army, the Englishman had told him, why didn't Machu consider it? At the time, Machu had brushed the offer aside. Leave Coorg? Never.

But now, it seemed to make sense. Squaring his shoulders and lifting his head to the sky, Machu made his way to the local garrison.

Even when the effects of the arrack wore off, Machu knew he had made the right decision by getting drafted. It had been the sensible thing to do. 'New beginnings,' Machu said to himself, as he fastened the regulation breeches. 'New beginnings.'

Nonetheless, it was difficult to leave, especially to bid his son farewell. Appu looked up at him, brown toddler eyes questioning. 'When will you come back?'

'Soon, monae, I promise.'

He hugged his son to his chest. 'Take care of your mother,' Machu told him. 'You will look after her while I am gone, yes?'

Appu nodded solemnly. 'When you return, I want toys. Lots of toys.'

Machu grinned, the dimple flashing in his cheek. He scooped Appu into his arms, swinging around and around with him until the child squealed with laughter.

He looked fondly down at his wife, stroking her hair as she clung to his chest and wept. 'Come now. What is this foolishness? I will come back soon, will I not? Now tell me – the sari that I shall bring you, what colour would you like?'

That afternoon, Machu was very quiet as he and the other new recruits filed past the Coorg border towards Mysore. He took a deep breath, saturating his lungs with the jungle smells of mulch and game he had loved all his life. The sky was overcast with clouds, his ancestors crowding and tripping over themselves to bid him farewell. A flock of herons took silent wing, launching themselves into the air from some secret, paddy covered fell. Machu watched, a catch in his throat, as the birds swept low and languid over the column.

He was leaving it all behind, everything he held dear.

It was time, however. Time for all of them to move forward.

Machu was assigned to the 20th Lancers in Madras. Not two weeks later, he found himself standing stiffly to attention, staring straight ahead at the wall in front of him. It had been painstakingly whitewashed, all the better to show off the medals that were hung on it. Squares, stars, circles, ovals and rectangles, all mounted proudly upon velvet and displayed in glass cases. The heat of the plains pressed in from the open windows, wrapping itself around him. The tamarind trees outside were perfectly still, mynahs wilting from its branches. There in the distance, the bass note of the sea as it boomed against the shore. Sweat beaded Machu's spine under his khaki shirt, coursing maddeningly down his back.

'So,' Major Climo said to him, 'you are a renowned hunter I hear? Killed a tiger using only a sword?'

Machu's Hindustani was still rusty. 'Yes,' he flatly replied.

'That will be Yes Sir to you soldier.'

'Yes . . . Sir.'

'We are lucky to have you it seems.' The Major took off his glasses and blowing once on each lens began to polish them. 'And you are privileged to be part of the 20th Lancers. We are a proud division, Sepoy Machaiah. One of the finest.' He gestured at the wall behind him. 'Sudan. South Africa. Cambodia. These medals you see? There are more. Our officers and men have earned a Victoria Cross, two OBEs and five

Mentions-In-Despatch. Wherever we have travelled, we have held our heads high and struck terror into the hearts of our foes. *Sabse achha*. The finest, soldier, we strive to be the finest.

'And how do you think we have achieved this exemplary record? Discipline. Through all the tasks that might not be to our liking. Why, you see this very wall, how white it is, despite the sea air? It is whitewashed every Saturday. Each and every Saturday, without fail. Discipline, soldier.'

Machu's eyes flickered briefly over the brilliant whiteness of the wall, but his face remained impassive. Major Climo was continuing. 'It is part of your duties as a soldier with the 20th to care for the officer you are assigned to. You are to draw the water for his bath, turn down his bedclothes at night, lay out his kit in the morning and see to it that his shoes and belt are polished to a shine. And what's more, you will take pride in it soldier.'

A muscle twitched in Machu's jaw. This was not why he had joined the army. A soldier was meant to fight, to wage war, to live and to die with his head held high. Where was the soldierliness, the honour, in scraping the boots of another? 'No,' he had refused that morning, 'I am no servant,' and Major Climo had summoned him to his office.

The Major put his glasses back on and looked at Machu. 'So. Which will it be then? Do I have you thrown in the stockade for insubordination, or are you going to see reason? Come now soldier. You are more of a man than this pettiness would indicate.'

Machu said nothing.

'So. We have decided then.' The Major became brisk. 'I have assigned you to Lieutenant Balmer. You should be proud to be his batman.'

Machu snapped his heels to attention, startling the mynahs on the tamarind tree into a brief, breathless flurry of motion. Saluting the officer, he marched from the tent.

Climo's words impressed themselves on him, but it was not easy. Discipline, he told himself, discipline, but sometimes when he lay awake in his barracks, humiliation arose in him like dank, rotting scum afloat upon a forest sinkhole. His fists would curl in disgust. How far he had fallen. The tiger killer, reduced to doing the work of a menial.

Then Machu would remind himself of the reason he was there. He would think of his wife, the stiff shoulders of his son as they had waved him goodbye.

At least Lt Balmer was a good lad. He treated Machu with a curious mixture of deference and authority, acknowledging the stiff-backed pride of the older man while conducting himself with a dignity that impressed Machu in spite of himself. He had once asked Balmer how old he was, and had shaken his head in amazement. Only twenty-two? Ayappa Swami!

Balmer had smiled. 'Why? I am hardly younger than most of the officers here.'

Machu shook his head. 'You must be very good indeed, to be leading so many men at such a raw age.'

That night, Machu lay awake mulling over the lieutenant. It all came down to education, he decided. Look at Devanna, he had almost become a doctor. A *doctor*. Machu still remembered in what high esteem he had been held by the family. He grimaced in the darkness. Why, even Devi had chosen . . . Devi.

A memory floated unbidden into Machu's mind. They were lying on the floor of the arbour, her eyes limpid and smiling from their love-making. A sudden breeze rustled through the laburnum trees, shaking free vast handfuls of petals that spiralled down towards them. Devi sat up, running her arms in wonder through the swirling yellow. The petals fell thickly upon her hair, layering her upturned forehead and outstretched arms, sliding thickly over her bare breasts, till she seemed to Machu like a wood sprite, something other-worldly, carved from the trees themselves. She had turned to him and said something in English. 'What?' Machu asked startled, and she laughed merrily.

'Poetry,' she said. 'In Inglis. A hostoff goldun daffadils. It is very well known, you should recite it to the white folk you hunt for.'

He had been ashamed of his ignorance, and had masked it with a scoff. 'As if you know Inglis. You babble something or other and expect me to believe . . .'

But she was in too good a mood to be baited. Lifting handfuls of petals from the grass and from her lap she had flung them at him, laughing all the while.

With an effort, Machu brought his thoughts back to the present.

Discipline, he told himself, discipline. He lay still, steadying his breathing. Ayappa Swami, when would this end? He passed a hand over his chest. Over two years since he had seen her, and yet . . .

He forced his mind back to his conversation with Balmer and thought of his pay accruing rupee by rupee. 'If there is one thing I will accomplish in this life,' Machu promised himself, 'it will be to make sure that Appu is well educated. One day,' Machu thought, 'one day, maybe Appu will be an officer himself.'

Slowly, crafting grand plans for his son, for the children to follow, Machu fell asleep. His dreams that night were filled with drifts of laburnum petals, floating softly down.

A warm wind gusted through the trees that bordered the bricked-over drying yard, shaking the laburnum petals free from their branches. They floated over the workers weighing the coffee beans, drifting bright yellow into the gunny sacks. Devi held out a palm to the falling petals as she supervised the weighing. Struck by a sudden notion, she examined the skin on her hands. How she had tanned! She had begun to spend even more time on the estate, the sun basting her once porcelain skin to a light olive tint. Tayi, Appaiah, Chengappa anna – they all said she was working far in excess of what was required, but they did not understand. She needed to be here in the estate, come rain, thunder or shine. Otherwise, these good for nothing workers would take the first chance they got to loll about beneath the trees, smoking their beedis.

She looked with satisfaction at the rows of bags, filled to bursting with coffee. Iguthappa Swami had favoured them once again that year. She would ask the owner of the clothing store in Mercara to send a selection of his wares to the house, she mused. Devanna and Nanju needed new shirts and trousers. She would buy shirts for her father and brother too, and a couple of saris for Tayi. She mustn't forget Tukra and his wife; they had been indispensable this past year. A shirt for Tukra, she thought, and a sari for his wife.

'Ayy,' she shouted at one of the coffee pickers, 'tie the sack properly, or the beans will spill. Must I do everything myself?' Shaking her head, Devi went over to him to show him how it should be done.

Some months later, after the crop was sold, she heard of two more estates on the market. 'I am thinking of buying them,' she told Devanna, more a statement than a question. 'It's a stretch, but I think it is doable.' Devanna nodded. When they went to get the papers registered, Devanna had the estates listed in Devi's name. She gave no indication she had noticed, but clutched the papers tightly in her hands all the way home.

With these new purchases and the improvement in Devi's circumstances, there came a remarkable turnaround in her standing in the community. Invitations to weddings, naming and house warming ceremonies, virtually non-existent for the past few years, now poured in. Devi refused almost all of them. She had not even been to the Kambeymada village, not since the Nayak's funeral. When Puthari came around that December, she quietly told Devanna that he ought to go. 'You are well enough now,' she pointed out, 'Tukra can help you. Take Nanju with you and go.' There was nothing there for her any more.

She could no longer clearly see Machu's face; it floated in and out of her memory like shadows cast by an afternoon sun. Sometimes, when the yearning became acute, she would ask offhandedly after the Kambeymadas. Was all well with them, she would ask; with *so* many acres of coffee to manage, she had no time to go anywhere these days. Sometimes among the many bushels of useless news, there would be a nugget about Machu.

She heard that he had joined the army. That he had been stationed in the garrison at Mercara for a few weeks, and then transferred outside Coorg. Madras, some said, Mysore, said others. Devi hoarded each new piece of information, examining it carefully from all angles as she bent over her coffee bushes. She tried to imagine him in hot, flat Madras. 'How you must miss these hills,' she thought. The sea that lapped at Madras's shores would be poor consolation, Devi knew.

She saw him that summer, in Mercara. It was the child she spotted first, standing alone in the shade of the ammunitions store. Just one glance and she knew immediately. For a moment she could barely breathe. Those same golden-brown eyes, the identical dimple. Machu in miniature. She sank upon her haunches in front of the boy, uncaring of her sari trailing in the dust. 'What is your name monae?'

He looked curiously at her, none of the flinching shyness her own child would have shown. 'Appu.'

She nodded achingly, fighting the urge to tousle his hair. 'So tell me Kambeymada Appu, who are you here with?'

'Appaiah.'

Devi swallowed. 'Your father? Is that so, kunyi? Where, inside the shop?' Machu must be here on his furlough. 'Is . . . is he here long?'

'Yes. No . . . don't know . . . .' Appu replied, losing interest. A thought struck him. 'Do you have toys?' he asked.

Devi smiled tremulously, reaching into her blouse. Pulling out a roll of rupees, she pressed a ten rupee note into his hand. 'I don't. But here, this is for you. Tell your father to buy you lots of toys, you hear?'

She rose hurriedly to her feet so the child wouldn't notice the wetness in her eyes, then crossed the street. She stood in a storefront, apparently entranced by a window display of bonnets. Would he see her? Would he cross the street to speak with her? Her hair, she must . . . She anxiously patted her curls back into their plait, watching in the glass as Machu came out, pocketing a carton of buckshot. He looked puzzled at the money in the boy's fist, and then looked around him, searching for the mysterious benefactor. Devi bolted inside the store, heart pounding.

'Yes?' the proprietor asked, looking perplexed at her sari-clad figure. 'May I interest you in some bonnets madam?'

'No . . . no, I am just . . .' Her eyes glued to the window, Devi watched as Machu strode down the street and disappeared from sight.

Chapter 21

≈ 1908 ≈

Six months later, after a panther carried away Clara Anderson's favourite tabby, Reverend Gundert watched her advance towards him through a most uncharitable haze of annoyance. Really, now, what more could he say to the woman? It must have been a tremendous shock of course. Rudely awoken in the middle of the night by her yowling pet, Mrs Anderson had apparently descended to the verandah, lantern in one hand, hairbrush in the other, determined to extract vengeance. Only to be greeted, to her horror, by the sight of the cat disappearing down the jaws of its decisively larger cousin. The poor lady had stood there frozen, as the panther, taking one look at the lantern, had leapt over the ledge and vanished into the night with its prey.

She had naturally been distraught over the entire episode, and Gundert had made a point of seeking her out at church the following Sunday to offer his sympathies. She had nodded tearfully, twisting and tugging at her handkerchief, her nose turning bright red with the effort of not breaking down, and Gundert had felt quite sorry for her. But it had been nearly a fortnight now, and really, what else could he do?

Still, they were a fine couple, the Andersons. Composing his features into an appropriate gravity, Gundert turned towards them. 'What?' Mrs Anderson said, in response to his query. 'Oh no, no, Reverend, it isn't Socks who weighs on my mind today, although . . .' her nose turned red again, 'although, not a day has passed that I do not grieve him. Still,

243

there are other things that concern me. My brother James has been called to the North West Frontier.' She glanced at her husband who stood stoically at her side. 'One hopes for the best of course, but one can't help but worry . . .' Her voice trailed off.

'The Afghans,' her husband explained succinctly to Gundert. 'All still rather hush hush, but I gather from the garrison that an officer of the Border Force was set upon. Locals at a bazaar. An attempted raid as well last week, on an army ammunitions dump. Foiled of course, but still.' He shook his head. 'We have had peace for over ten years.'

After a period of relative quiet, insurgent activity had indeed begun to rise again along the high reaches of the North West Frontier. Seemingly isolated incidents, sparking here and there along the border, but the British Government had been burned once before, by the frontier wars of 1896. At the time, a fiery cleric had begun to make his presence felt in the region. The Mad Mullah, as the cleric was dubbed by the European press, made rousing, incendiary speeches in the bazaars. He chided the pensioners of the Anglo Indian Army when they marvelled at the reach of the Empire and its intrinsic code of honour which ensured the arrival of their pensions month after month without fail. The Mad Mullah snapped at them not to be so blind.

'Yours is the bloodline of kings and mighty warriors,' he reminded them. He recalled an ancient empire far mightier than this. One that had ruled half the earth, spawning kings from Baghdad to Delhi. He reminded them of the days when Islam hearkened free and proud to the call of the Prophet. When it stalked down the corridors of the richest palaces and occupied the highest echelons of power, when it would have scorned to exist as it did today, forced by that harami Empire they spoke of so highly to skulk about in mountain caves and mud-walled hovels.

The Afghans had gathered around the Mad Mullah, his words mining a deep vein of memory. Why, they had been robbed! Denied the respect that was their due, duped by the British of their rightful place in this world. Hearts ablaze, they prayed to Allah to send the infidels across the sights of the rough Martini Henry rifles they carried, so they might fire a shot in retaliation for the many humiliations that had been heaped upon Islam.

'No,' the mullah said to them, 'why must you risk your necks?' He

244

would take care of it for them. Hadn't the Prophet entrusted to his command hordes of djinns and avenging angels for this very purpose? They were massed already in the shadows of the mountains and by the whispering lakeshores, awaiting a signal from him to fall upon the British forces.

The tribesmen had mulled over this piece of information. How could they lose with the holy forces on their side? They had clamoured to join him in his efforts and the Mad Mullah had given in with a great show of reluctance. Under his command, the insurgents had proceeded to launch a series of bloody attacks on the army camps in the region.

The Empire was caught napping. By the time the wheels of government began to move quickly enough to send adequate reinforcements, nearly thirty officers and two hundred and fifty native troops had been sacrificed.

The government had since adopted a wary stance towards the North West Frontier. It was determined to stamp out the slightest hint of unrest, lest a collective fuse should ignite once more amongst the Afghans, flaring through the region to explode in the face of the Empire. Telegraphs crackled their way to every corner of the administration bearing news of the current unease. Troops, such as could be spared, were corralled across the country to reinforce the border.

When the 20th Lancers received its posting orders to the North West, the battalion at once began the long journey north. Machu was relieved. Finally he could leave soggy, stifling Madras and the incessant clamour of the sea. They rode the railways to Rawalpindi and from there to the cantonment at Nowshera, then began the march by road to the camp at Chikdara.

Mountain air. That was the first thing that struck Machu; the air was crisp and cold, like the air that sometimes graced the Bhagamandala peak after the rains. He drew a sharp breath as he looked about him. These mountains though ... he had not seen anything like them. The fabled Hindu Kush, the throne of the ancient Kushan empire. Ring upon ring of them, dusty brown and faded green, forbiddingly high and bounded in the distance by glittering ice-capped peaks. Even his beloved Sahaydri ranges were reduced to the size of anthills in comparison.

The Lancers marched through a valley bordered by jagged, splinter-tipped mountains, the skyline broken by sharp-edged spurs and deep brooding crevasses. The rain had gouged deep grooves into the mountain-side, exposing veins of black lava like tear-stains. All around the soldiers, a primordial stillness, pierced now and again by the keening of eagles high above their heads.

The battalion pushed forward at a steady pace, skirting the few villages that dotted the landscape. The villages were the most basic possible, not much more than a few huts cobbled together with livestock corralled to the back, and the rough-hewn turrets on the house of the local Khan. Nature, in contrast, had donned her loveliest colours. The soil of the valley was immensely fertile, fed every year by the silt washed from the mountain-sides. Poppies, lilies and knots of polyanthus nodded in the coarse grass. Peat-trimmed lakes glistened with fish, and pomegranates dangled ruby red from the trees. The locals maintained a wary distance from the soldiers, except for a few rosy-cheeked children who peeped at them from behind the rocks.

Despite the cautionary call to arms and Mrs Anderson's misgivings, the atmosphere in the North West remained peaceful over the next few months. The army base at Chikdara was especially tranquil. The men, Machu included, settled into a monotonous routine of guard duty and field exercise. Recces were conducted faithfully every evening and status reports filed, followed by sundowners at the officers' mess, with mince cutlets from local mutton and slabs of chocolate sent by family back in England.

Officers applied for permission to allow their wives to visit, and permission was granted. The Colonel's wife, with typical efficiency, lost no time in organising a bazaar every Saturday in the camp grounds, where the locals could show off their wares. Polo matches were conducted under kingfisher skies, and Sunday picnics held in the shade of the Chinars. 'So pretty really, these trees. Eastern cousins, don't you think, of the plane trees one finds along the esplanades of London and Paris?'

Even the Afghans seemed to relax and become more accustomed to the presence of the battalion. The men were especially friendly to the native soldiers, calling to them with a ready smile and wave whenever they happened by. Most could speak rudimentary Hindustani; it had been an association of many innings after all, between the two countries.

Machu was roaming the bazaar one evening, the real, sprawling thing in the tribal settlement that lay beyond the army camp, not the sterile stalls erected in the camp each week. Here, chickens scrabbled in wooden crates and goats stared saucer-eyed as prospective buyers tugged on their horns and pinched the fat of their necks. It was an unusually warm day, the heat coaxing an earthy noisomeness from the animal sheds. The livestock reminded him with a sudden pang of Coorg. He had bought a few chickens before he left, hopefully they had grown into good egg layers by now. Perhaps he would buy a cow this time when he was home.

He wandered into a carpet seller's shack. Rolls of carpet lay stacked on the wooden floor, and in the corners. 'Here,' the seller exclaimed, 'see this, and look at this one,' rolling them out in the dust. Machu laughed, mopping the sweat from his brow.

'No,' he said, shaking his head, 'only looking.'

He walked on, past the tea vendor, to a seller of wooden toys. He picked up a horse, turning it this way and that in his hands. Would Appu like it, he wondered.

The shopkeeper watched from the interior as he fanned himself. 'Inside,' he called. 'Too much hot there, come inside.'

Machu hesitated, trying to adjust his eyes to the darkness inside. It was hard to tell who else was back there. The soldiers had all been given strict instructions.

Do not place yourself at risk.

Do not be in a situation you cannot control.

It had been in a bazaar such as this, Machu supposed, that the officer whose attack had triggered alarm signals throughout the Empire had been ambushed. He really should remain outside. 'Too hot,' the shop-keeper repeated. The weight of his revolver felt reassuringly solid against his hip. Ducking under the canopy, Machu entered the shop, the wooden horse still in his hands.

There were more toys inside, and pretty blouses like the ones the local women wore. 'You take one, heh?' the shopkeeper said, nudging a pile towards him. 'Good for your woman.'

247

A delicious aroma wafted from the curtained-off back of the shop and to his embarrassment, Machu's stomach rumbled out loud. The shopkeeper laughed, his eyes almost disappearing into heavily wrinkled cheeks. Turning his head he called out to whoever was there. A few moments later, a delicate hand appeared through the curtains, bearing a steaming plate. Machu gazed longingly at the naans and lamb kebabs, then shook his head. It would not be right.

'What? No. You must.'

Machu did not want to offend the old man, but it was Mohammedan fare after all. He shook his head regretfully again, and the shopkeeper sighed. 'From where do you come? Which part of Hindustan?'

'The South. In the mountains.'

'Very far from your home, I see. Well, sit. Talk with us a while, heh, even if you will not eat with us.'

Machu hesitated again, but the shopkeeper was already clearing the bales of goods, dragging a small stool in their place.

'Chillum?' Machu nodded, taking a deep drag of the hookah. He opened his mouth, letting the smoke drift leisurely from his lungs.

'I have been to Hindustan. Many times. Not recently, these legs have grown tired, but I have been. Great cities you have in your country, heh? Dilli. What a jewel. And Bombay. What a dariya the city has. I used to sit for hours on the rocks, watching the water. This home of yours, is it near Bombay?'

Machu shook his head. 'No. Much further south. Although I remember seeing your countrymen in my land as a boy. They used to come to sell us horses.'

'Ah, our horses. El Kheir, they are called, in the Koran.' The shop-keeper drew on his hookah. 'El Kheir, the supreme blessing. It is said that before Allah created man from the dust, first he made the horse from the wind.' He waved his hand expansively in the air. '"Condense," Allah ordered the south wind, "I wish to make a creature from your essence." The wind condensed and such a creature Allah made from it! "I shall make you supreme among animals," Allah said to his creation. "You alone shall fly without wings. The blessings of all the world shall reside between your eyes and victory be eternally bound to your forelock."'

The old man smiled. 'There are beautiful horses in my village.'

'Where is it, your village? What is your tribe?' Machu asked.

'A small one, some miles from here.' He waved his hand. 'That way, through the mountains.'

Machu knew that the Pashtuns were made up of many tribes. 'It'll come to nothing,' Lt Balmer maintained. 'There are so many tribes, it won't take much for the allegiances to break.'

'So what do you think, sepoy?' Balmer had asked Machu as the latter drew his bath. 'Am I not right? There is much infighting within the tribes, it will take only the slightest pressure from our forces to scatter them apart.'

Machu had hesitated, choosing his words carefully. 'Where I come from,' he said finally, 'there was much fighting too, in the old days, between the clans. Still, when the Mohameddan armies came from Mysore, we always stood side by side. War, forced circumcisions, abductions, mass executions . . . the sultans of Mysore stopped at nothing as they tried to break our spirit and tear us apart. It only served to bring us together. We fought off their armies, year after year, through generations of war.'

Balmer had yawned sleepily. 'They will not band together,' he repeated. 'Mark my words. Two tribesmen might clasp hands, looking deep into each other's eyes and then the very next evening, why, there they might be, hacking each other to pieces.' He shook his head, unbuttoning his shirt. 'They will not stand together long,' he repeated.

Machu had said nothing more.

'We have clans too,' he said now to the shopkeeper. 'In the old days, there was much fighting between them.'

'And now? Do they all walk together?'

Machu laughed. 'Yes, for the most part. Now our guns are used to hunt. Although, every now and again, when there are disputes that cannot be settled otherwise . . .' Shrugging, he looked down at the horse still in his hands, running a thumb over its rich red coat. 'How much?'

But the old man was interested in continuing the conversation. 'Disputes? Over what?'

'Honour. Sometimes a woman. Land.'

The Afghan's lips parted in an infectious, gap-toothed smile. 'Land!

Do you know how we settle disputes over land in this part of the world?'

Both claimants, he told Machu, were asked by the village elders to walk across the land in question. A copy of the Koran was given to each, to hold in his hands as he walked across the land, swearing on the holy book that the land he walked upon belonged to nobody but him. The usurper always slipped a little dust from his own fields into his shoes. He could thus walk comfortably across his neighbour's fields, swearing hotly all the while that it was his own land his feet rested upon.

Machu laughed out loud, slapping his knee.

The shopkeeper grinned, squinting at Machu through the smoke from the hookah. 'Of course,' he added, 'since both sides are fully aware of this practice, it usually comes down to a good fight in the end.'

Machu laughed again and nodded. 'A good fight indeed. So what do you think, are we all headed for a good fight soon, in these mountains?'

The shopkeeper sighed. 'Who can tell? They say many things, the leaders, blowing this way one day and then that way the other. In the old days, when the blood still ran hot in this body, I would have been there myself. But now ... when a man has seen enough mornings, fighting starts to lose its lustre. Honour, paradise ... these things are for the young. Old age has fewer demands. A few more mornings I would like to see, bas. See my family again in the village. And once, just once more, maybe the dariya in Bombay before I die.'

His tone grew wistful. 'I would sit for hours upon the rocks, looking at the water. Such a blue, like the sky had spread over the earth. A man could travel for ten lifetimes over its expanse and still not find the outer shore.' He shook his head. 'I am a simple man, heh? Only an old shopkeeper, near the end of his time. I do not know which way the wind will blow. All I can do is sell my wares and hope that Allah has set aside a few more mornings for me.'

Machu looked down at the toy in his hands. 'The horse,' he said finally, holding it in front of him, 'how much for this?'

The old man smiled gently. 'Nothing. You are my guest. Give it to your child with my blessings.'

'I'll make a bargain with you,' Machu countered. 'How about I take this, that blouse – there that one, in red and blue – for my wife, and that jacket for my little boy. These, I must pay for. However,' he pulled the plate of food that still lay untouched before him, 'I would be honoured to share your meal.' Wrapping the kebabs in the warm naans, Machu began to eat.

The days grew steadily hotter and spring melted into the rolling boil of summer. The flowers were burned from their stalks, and the landscape acquired a bleached, desolate appearance, broken only by gossamer-winged butterflies whose colours shone in the sun like filaments of pellucid metal. And still the frontier remained peaceful.

Machu was granted permission to avail himself of his annual furlough. He headed back to Coorg, with the gifts he had bought at the bazaar and two slabs of melted but precious Cadbury's chocolate that Lt Balmer had sent for Appu.

He paused for a moment at the entrance to Coorg, stripping off his shirt and rolling out a kupya from his pack, trading pleasantries with the men at the outpost as they gathered about him in welcome. The men caught him up with the news of the past year – the paddy had grown well, and coffee prices were also up. A calf with six legs had been born in Makkandur village and two men had been gored by wild boar on a hunt. 'Watch out for elephants,' they cautioned, 'there is a herd this side of the forest. Not two days ago, we saw one going that way. A huge boulder, we thought it was, and then we saw it was an elephant, sitting on its haunches and sliding downhill.'

He listened happily, his heart gladdened by the leafy, river scent rising from the soil of his land. Here too summer had arrived, the ferocity of the heat, however, tempered by the forest cover that dappled its glare. He looked up at the sky; it was clear as lake water, smudged at its edge by faint rills of white. His ancestors, come to welcome him. Something shifted inside him, a piece falling into place once more as, adjusting the pack about his shoulders, he quickened his pace towards home.

The next weeks passed in a pleasant blur. Machu could hardly stop marvelling at how much his son had grown in the past year. 'He looks just like me,' he whispered to his wife as they stood watching Appu sleep. She laughed softly.

'Down to his dimple. He is very good at sports, wins all the races in the village, even against much bigger boys.'

She watched as Machu opened the high neck of Appu's jacket a little wider so he might breathe more freely. The child insisted on wearing his father's gift all the time. His mother had scolded him at first, couldn't he see it was getting dirty? Machu had intervened. 'It doesn't matter,' he said, 'I will bring another one the next time.'

'He misses you a great deal,' she said now. A shadow passed over Machu's face as he smoothed the hair back from Appu's forehead.

'It isn't easy to be away. But what must be done must be done.'

'Yes . . . Did you hear by the way about that woman?'

Machu's eyes flickered towards her, but his voice was even. 'Which woman?'

'Who else? Devi. People say her crop is extremely good this year as well. All kinds of things I have heard about her. That she called tantric magicians from Kerala and they have buried secret talismans in the soil. That she has had to pay for it with no more children, just the one boy.'

Machu chuckled. 'Come now. People talk, that is all.'

'Some say that she has lain with white folk, and that is why they give her handsome prices.'

'Don't talk nonsense,' Machu said shortly. 'She has worked hard and it has paid off.'

His wife's lips trembled. 'Yes, take her side, why don't you? I am just telling you what people say. Don't other people work hard? Why is it that their crops have not been as good? Still, what am I to you, only your wife . . .'

Machu hooked a placatory arm about his wife's waist, drawing her to him. 'Enough, woman. Why waste time talking when there are other things we could be doing?' He grinned. 'The other children you keep talking of, how about we go make some now?'

That night, he lay in bed, staring out at the stars, his wife's body heavy against his chest. 'So she has done well?'

'Who?'

'Devi . . . she has done well? What do people say?'

His wife stirred and looked at him. 'Three estates she owns now.

Three!' She paused, trying to read his face in the dim light.

'And,' she added, 'it all began with those first hundred acres.'

Machu said nothing more, but three days later, after he'd been to Mercara to buy a peechekathi as a gift for Lt Balmer, he impulsively goaded his horse west. The gulmohar trees were in bloom, exploding along the dust road in brilliant bursts of red and yellow. Machu barely noticed as he galloped along. 'It has nothing to do with her, my visiting the estate,' he assured himself. He would pass by, just glance at the property. Surely he was entitled to this much curiosity?

'In all likelihood, she will not even be there,' he thought, even as he spurred his mount faster down the road.

He drew in at the entrance, patting the horse's neck as he peered at the estate. A new gate had been installed, replacing the rough bamboo slats he remembered from years ago. Tall it was, the gate, handsomely carved and obviously expensive. He reached a hand towards its bars, and it gave under his touch, swinging slightly open. His horse tossed its mane, impatient to be off again, and he stroked its flank. 'Ayy, El Kheir,' he murmured dryly, 'you may have foresight in your forehead, and victory in your mane, but a little patience in your hooves would have been fortuitous as well.'

He rubbed its forehead, calming the animal, suddenly unsettled himself.

The estate lay quiet and seemingly empty but for the low whirr of dragonflies. Rows of neatly pruned coffee bushes gleamed a deep, glossy green in the shade, disappearing into the distance. Dismounting, Machu tied the reins of the horse to the gates and walked in. The overhead canopy was a lot thicker than in other estates, Machu noted, and yet this appeared deliberate, not a case of neglect. The path was meticulously trimmed, the earth beneath the coffee bushes denuded of weeds. She had done well. He walked on, heading deeper into the cool, silent plantation.

He spotted Tukra an instant before the Poleya saw him. 'Who is it?' Tukra called sharply. Recognising Machu, he lowered the bamboo pole he was brandishing. 'Mistake happened, anna,' he said, relieved, 'I could not see you clearly.'

'It is no matter,' Machu said genially. 'My wife tells me that I have become brown as tree bark and quite unrecognisable. I was passing by, and thought I would . . .' He cleared his throat. 'Is anybody else here?' he asked nonchalantly.

Tukra shook his head and sullenly looked at the ground.

'Oh,' Machu said, unaccountably disappointed. 'Well no matter, I will have a look around and leave.'

'You should not be here,' Tukra blurted. 'He . . . Devanna anna . . . it is not right.'

Machu turned around, his eyes cold. 'What did you say?'

Tukra took an involuntary step back. 'Nothing, nothing . . . anna, you should not be here!' The words came tumbling out, bumping against each other in his anxiety. 'This is Devanna anna's property. Devi akka and you . . . I know that the two of you . . .'

Machu stepped very close to Tukra, his features set. Sticking the barrel of his gun under the latter's chin, he forced his face upwards. 'Do you know what I can do to you Poleya? I could shoot you right here for your impudence and all of Coorg would applaud me. If you ever, *ever*, make the mistake of using your mistress's name improperly again, I will. Do you understand?'

Tukra crumpled in panic. 'Mistake happened, anna, big mistake from Tukra's doings. I fall at your feet . . . it is just that Devi akka . . . she hardly even talks with Devanna anna . . . I too have a wife, of course she talks *too* much, a fisherwoman she used to be, and now she keeps talking, talking, talking, but shouldn't Devi akka at least talk sometimes to Devanna anna? Devi akka . . . I used to dance in the grass for her as a boy, no place for that here in Mercara, but I am precious to her, I know. Why it was *me* she wanted to send after you, nobody else but me to go find you before their wedding. Of course you can walk through the estate, mistake happened.'

'What? What? Stop!' Machu shouted at Tukra. He lowered his gun. 'Look. I am not going to harm you.'

Tukra collapsed in a snivelling heap.

'She *sent* you after me? When?'

'She wanted to. That morning. The day before the wedding. Tukra overheard them, Tayi and Devi akka. Tayi was crying, and Thimmaya anna, how he shouted. He *never* shouts, not like his son, always shouting, Tukra do this, do that . . .'

He had left that morning for Kerala, Machu remembered, with grain for barter. 'Why?' he asked, his voice flat as a stone. 'Why did she want to send for me?'

'I don't know. She . . .' Tukra paused. 'No, no, Tukra is always talking nonsense, that's what everyone says. Come, I will show you the estate. Please anna, don't tell Devi akka I told you, I was never supposed to have heard. How Tayi cried that day, and Devi akka, so many tears . . .'

Machu was gone.

'Devi.'

She stopped dead in her tracks, the breath knocked from her. It had been nearly four years since they had said a word to one another, even stood within speaking distance. The sun had deepened the teak of his skin, into a deep, forest-tree brown. The old ache immediately started again, her hands clamouring to reach up, to touch, to feel, to lay themselves against his jaw. She curled her fists inward, the nails digging into her palms. 'I heard you were back.'

He was staring at her, a wildness in his eyes. 'Why didn't you wait for me?'

'What?' His voice, his *voice*, a river stone, sun hot, skimming her skin. The strands of grey in the whorls of hair just apparent through the open neck of his kupya, the minuscule bump on each earlobe where the skin had grown over the pierced holes. The Army did not permit earrings, she had heard. She swallowed, glancing about to see who might be watching. The alley to the bank was often crowded with people. She laughed, a small, skittering sound like a marble rolling across a floor. 'How . . . how did you know I would be here? How long will you be in Coorg?'

Machu smiled mirthlessly. 'This time, you will answer me. Devi. Why didn't you wait for me?'

Devi shakily raised her hand to her face, as if to shield it from the sun. 'Please Machu. It doesn't matter any more. It has been *nine* years, you are married.'

'Answer me,' he said, his jaw taut. 'Why did you want to send for me before your wedding?'

Her eyes grew huge with shock. 'How? Who ... how did you ...' She looked away, trying desperately to steady herself. A passerby called out to her in greeting but she did not notice. 'How did you find out?'

Machu stepped forward even closer, and her eyes filled with tears. 'Don't,' she whispered. The smell of him, of wood and musk. To touch him once more, just *once* more, time standing still, the feel of his arms about her again.

'Answer me. For if you will not, I go straight to your family. Your father, your grandmother, your brother – I don't care who, but *someone* will tell me what truly happened.'

'No! No, not them, not after so many years.' She began to cry soundlessly, helplessly, tears slipping down her cheeks. She tugged at the veil binding her hair, pulling its ends higher so they shielded her face. 'I wasn't allowed to,' she said, and he had to strain to hear the words. 'If ... if you know so much, it won't be long before you learn the rest. My son,' she began to shake. 'My son, he ...'

The dreadful words stuck on her tongue.

'What? Your son *what*?'

She lifted her tear-streaked face to his. 'My son was not born of consent.'

Machu went very still, his face white. 'Your son was not ... Devanna? Did he ... *Devanna?*' He slammed a fist into the wall.

'You will hurt yourself, stop, don't.'

He turned to her, his eyes stormy. 'Why didn't you tell me? Over and over I asked, "Why, Devi? Why did you not wait for me? *Why*, when there was so little time left to the vow?" You *knew* how you were tearing me apart with your silence, and yet you did not say a word.'

'Tell you, and then what?' she asked despairingly. 'You would have wanted nothing to do with me after that.'

'What?' Machu reached for her and then remembering the very public setting of their conversation, drew back his hands and furiously raked through his hair instead. 'How could you have thought that I would not have stood by you?'

'Tayi ... she said that ...' Her voice faltered. She shook her head, weeping soundlessly, a bottomless grief marrowing her bones. 'It was too late.'

'You ...' Machu ran his fingers through his hair and stared at her, then laughed hollowly. 'All this while. For all these years, despite everything that has happened, despite Devanna's blood that I believed stained my hands. No matter how far I have tried to go from you. No matter how I have tried to forget, or how much I deny it, I carry you within me like a hook in a fish. Like a bullet Devi, a bullet that has worked its way permanently into my flesh. And yet you didn't trust me enough to tell me?'

'For you, I would ...' His face twisted. 'Devi. *I forsook my vow for you*. For a few snatched moments with you, *I forsook my God.*'

That night, the North West erupted. An attack was launched on the army camp at Nowshera, the locals startlingly well equipped with Martini rifles and even grenades. War was officially upon them; the radios telegraphing with the news. Machu grimly threw his things together as his wife fretted. 'Why must you go? You're on leave aren't you? Why must you return, why now, when there's so much danger?'

'Don't be foolish. It's my duty.'

'But what if ... what if you told them that you simply hadn't heard? It's so far away after all, just tell them you did not hear the news.'

Machu said nothing and continued to pack.

She nodded then, trying not to cry. 'I see how it is. You have to go.' She went to the prayer corner and bringing out the sacred ash, dabbed some on his forehead.

'Well, no matter then,' she said, attempting a smile. 'Go. And return to us soon, even more of a hero.'

Chapter 22

The battalion marched relentlessly forward under the intense glare of the sun. Already, three soldiers had succumbed to the intolerable heat. It was becoming routine procedure to carry the collapsed men to the side of the road where the medic would sprinkle such water as could be spared upon their twitching faces. He knew it would do precious little and yet he persevered, staying by the side of the dying men with his orderlies as the battalion pushed on. It was draining work. Barely would he catch up with the battalion than it seemed another soldier would fall, frothing at the mouth, his eyes rolling back into his skull. Even the pack mules and horses had been pushed to the limits of their endurance.

Machu squinted tiredly at the sun. It seemed to blister the back of his eyes, cauterising all thought, all memory in a haze of blinding white. Such fury. Surya the Sun God shoulder to shoulder with Agni, the God of Fire. Mounted upon their war chariots and blazing forth in combined, diamond-armoured splendour. Nothing, it seemed, could compare with the naked might of the Afghan sun. Heat seemed to radiate off every surface, from the corrugated mountain-sides and the treacherous, stone-filled ravines, blazing from the bald, cloudless sky. A spark shot out from beneath the hoof of the horse immediately in front of his own and the animal jerked its head. 'Hurrr . . . hurr . . .' Machu stroked the sweaty neck of his beast, calming it.

This was not the way to travel, in the oppressive heat of the day. He glanced behind him, wiping the sweat from his eyes. The battalion undulated along the trail in a long line of khaki and steel, as plainly visible in the chalky pass as bugs on a white bedstead. He looked about him uneasily, at the jagged spurs lining the pass, but the outcrops of rock remained deserted. For now.

This was not how the enemy travelled. They used the coolness of the evenings and nights, moving swiftly through the familiar mountain passes under the cover of darkness. The battalion, however, was desperately short of time; Lt Balmer had said as much as Machu had laid out the officer's belt, khaki breeches and pith helmet that morning.

Machu had headed back to the frontier in a daze. Three days ago now, or was it four? He wasn't entirely sure. The train had steamed north towards the frontier, carrying its load of troops, ammunition and grain.

He had stared out sightlessly as it sped through the countryside, the image of her fixed in his mind. That lovely face, tear-streaked as she had looked up at him, such despair in her eyes. 'It was too late.'

He had leaned his head against the bars of the metal-shuttered window. 'It doesn't matter any more,' he had told himself. 'It cannot.' He had thought of his son, his wife. She was a good woman, he was lucky. Then why this pain, Ayappa Swami, why this grief like a red-hot hammer battering his insides?

The train had charged forward, the insistent clank of its wheels the only constant in the formless, changing world pouring past its windows. Machu had shut his eyes, his face lined and drawn.

Rules of conduct. They talked in the army of rules of conduct. But the truth was that there were none. Men made them up, these rules, to bring some semblance of order, a notion of control to their lives. A compass by which they might map out their existence.

Honour.

Retribution.

Redemption.

Did any of these truly matter?

His life seemed to lie about him in hollow disarray. All these years lived, the distance covered, bridges crossed, the rivers forded. All of them, meaningless.

The code of honour he had believed betrayed. The loyalty that was due a kinsman, the loyalty he had believed breached by his own hand. The crushing guilt he had carried all these years, so acid that it had corroded everything that had followed in its wake. All that he had forsaken, to make up for a crime he believed he had committed.

Everything he owned, everything he had ever been.
And all the while . . .
Who was the true victim, who had truly been wronged, and at what price redemption? If he had but known what had really happened. If Devanna's hand had fallen on any other gun. The only gun in the entire rack that listed to the left. *The tiger killer's gun.*

If only she had told him. If *only* he had believed what he had known all along, deep inside. Such guilelessness in her eyes as they had stood side by side on the Bhagamandala mountain, all of Coorg spread before them. 'You are mine,' she had said to him, 'I will wait for you forever.'

The train rushed on, its wheels turning, clanking forward. The sound of its wheels seeming to him to contain but a single, insistent note. 'Mine,' they seemed to lament. 'You. Were. *Mine.*'

He had joined the battalion at base camp. War was in the air, the adrenaline-charged musk of it, the mood of the camp severely changed since he had left. The wives were gone, dispatched immediately to safety as soon as the news of the insurgency had broken. Tension hung thick in the barracks, some men pacing back and forth as they boasted about the number of Afghans they would bag, others cracking overly loud jokes or sitting lost in thought upon their bunks.

There were two new officers who had been assigned to the battalion, both volunteer officers, pasty faces agog at the prospect of seeing action. As soon as the trouble had begun in the North West, they, like their peers all over the country, had rushed to be part of it. They had tracked down dusty connections, pulled all possible strings and dashed off voluminous letters to the authorities, begging to be drafted into action.

The stakes of war were high, the upside huge. A citation of bravery, a medal of honour, even a mention-in-dispatch could potentially be career defining, the catalyst needed to propel them from their dull, desk-bound jobs in the outposts of the Empire into something of true merit. A man with no family connections to speak of, no wealth with which to buy a career, could rise to respectable heights with the aid of a little battle action. The volunteer officers with the 20th knew how fortunate they were to have been drafted, even if they were not entirely sure whether it was anticipation pumping through their veins, or fear.

Machu looked at them as they entered Lt Balmer's tent. He could not understand what they said, but the unnatural squeak of their voices, the way they glanced anxiously towards the pass that led to the mountains, told him all he needed to know.

'It doesn't matter,' he wanted to say to these skinny lads. 'None of this does. The glory you seek has no meaning. Who truly is the hunter and who the hunted? We draw our mortal lines in the dust, map our inconsequential battles. While the Gods watch amused, mocking us from the distant mountains.'

Even Lt Balmer grew tense as they waited for the attack to commence, but for the next two days, nothing happened. Only Major Climo seemed his usual brisk, unflappable self. The daily recces increased in number and frequency, the garrison and the trenches were fortified, but the pass remained deserted.

And then the orders came. Afghans had collected in vast numbers at Mohmand, thirty-six miles to the north. Typical of their particular brand of gallantry, they had approached the native syces a couple of days ago, urging them to flee the mountains. Trouble was coming, they warned. They had no issue with the soldiers, only the white men who commanded them. 'Go,' they urged. 'Return to Hindustan, this is not your war.'

By the next morning, the hills around Mohmand were crawling with Pashtuns. Pennants of every shape and colour fluttered from the rocks, still in the distance but edging closer. Telegraphs had spun urgently from the camp confines, seeking reinforcements, and in response, the 20th Lancers had been ordered in immediately.

The Lancers marched all day, their throats afire, their feet blistered and bleeding inside their boots. At last the sun began to slide westward. They reached the Mohmand camp shortly after sundown. The signs of impending battle were unmistakable. The pennants of the enemy surrounded the camp in a rough crescent, vast daubs of deep blue, white and red across the dusty hills. The robes of the Pashtuns, the white of the tribes from the East, the blue of their neighbours, the red and the mustard of still more, announcing the many thousands of men gathered for the fight.

The bazaar in the middle of the camp had been levelled, and the trees blown up, offering a clear line of sight. The garrison had been fortified with any materials to hand; logs, sacks of sand, even biscuit tins filled with dirt, shepherdesses and preternaturally rosy cheeked milkmaids smiling seraphically from the lids.

The officers of the 20th reported in and shook hands with their exhausted compatriots, cracking feeble jokes about the champagne they would pop once these upstarts had been taken care of and this tamasha laid to rest. It was forced laughter; the memory of the three men lost en route to Mohmand weighing heavily upon them. The volunteer officers, their noses peeling painfully from the march despite the broad pith helmets, laughed loudest of all.

Battle plans were shared and vetted, and camp duties divided among the men. The soldiers who had been on guard duty for the past thirty-six hours were relieved for a few hours of sleep, and despite the gruelling march of the day, the men of the 20th fell in to take their place.

Slowly, the night deepened. A watchful silence enveloped the camp, interrupted now and again by the shuffle of the transport mules in their enclosure, or the uneasy whicker of a horse. Machu was on guard duty, stationed on a small outcrop of rock that bounded the camp to the left. The stars shone clear, casting a cold, precise light on the desolate landscape. The fires had died to a few glowing specks, while all along the boundaries of the camp, bayonet points glittered blue-white in the night. 'Beautiful isn't it?' The hulking Sikh soldier assigned guard duty alongside Machu cleared his throat and spat into the dust. 'Pristine as a fucking virgin, that's what this country looks like at night.'

Machu nodded.

'It is not like this in my village. Green. Very green. Wheat,' the Sikh added by way of explanation, 'we have wheat fields.'

The hours dragged by. 'Did you hear about the deserter bastards?' the Sikh suddenly asked. Machu nodded again. Two Afghan soldiers had disappeared from the camp earlier that evening.

'Can you blame them? It is their country after all.'

Machu had asked Balmer about it that evening. What would happen if the deserters were found? 'They will be shot,' Balmer had said simply. He had been strangely pensive. 'It's their land Machaiah. Their country. Once we were at odds with their own countrymen, what else could we expect? It is too hard a test of their loyalty.'

The Sikh, obviously hankering for conversation, cleared his throat again. 'Did you hear about the deserters from the previous war?' Without waiting for a response, he continued. 'Well! Do I have a story for you.'

Five Afghan soldiers had deserted during the Frontier Wars a decade ago, he said, taking with them their rifles and quota of ammunition. The Commanding Officer had been apoplectic with rage. Summoning the two remaining Afghans in the battalion, he had stripped them of their uniforms, telling them the conduct of their compatriots left him no choice.

When they had protested their loyalty, he threw down a challenge. They would be taken back, he said, with full back pay, provided they tracked down and returned to the Quarter Guard those five stolen rifles.

Well! The weeks passed, and then months. Lives were lost, the war won and the border normalised, and still there was no sign of the two soldiers. It was obvious that they, too, admittedly more from circumstance than from choice, had deserted.

And then nearly three years later, a pair of painfully thin, bedraggled Afghans showed up at the battalion and demanded to see the Commanding Officer. It was the two soldiers. All this time, the poor sods had been waging their own private war. Enduring God knows what hardships to recover *those very same five stolen rifles.*

Machu laughed, low and long.

They were silent for a while and then Machu stirred. 'You know, I had an ancestor who lived, oh, I don't know, maybe two hundred years ago. He was a great sportsman, a hunter without peer. Very tall. The family has preserved the tunic he wore. It barely holds together now, but it is there, in the ancestral home. In all these years since he passed on, not one other man has managed to fit into it. He was a fearless warrior they say; they still talk about his feats during the wars we waged against Mysore.

'This mighty ancestor, though, was only too human. Many years after his first marriage, when he was far past his prime and the age when these things are considered acceptable, he fell headlong in love with a young woman. He tried at first to stay away, telling himself he was being foolish.

'But no matter how far he went, no matter how he tried to forget, the memory of her was burned in his flesh. Like a bullet that had wormed its way into his heart, like a hook that had pierced his gut.

'Like the faint traces of snake poison he secretly believed still swam in his blood.

'Finally, unable to fight this any more, he did the only thing he could. He wed the lovely maiden, convincing himself that his first wife would understand. She would sympathise with his obsession, embracing the newcomer to her bosom like a sister.

'Besides, he said to himself, he was the head of the household, was he not? Who was to decree how many wives he could have? Bolstering himself thus, he made his way home decked in his wedding regalia, his blushing bride by his side. And there was his first wife to greet him, standing on the steps of their home – arms akimbo, eyes flashing with fury, and brandishing a sword.'

Machu grinned, his teeth gleaming briefly in the dark. 'Our women, they are tigresses. No matter how our fearless hero begged, no matter how much he threatened or pleaded or how many jewels he promised her, his wife refused to let him into the house. Finally, the hapless bridegroom had no choice but to build an identical home, right next to the first. It was there he housed his second family.'

Machu paused, his eyes distant. 'It all worked out eventually,' he added. 'They lived harmoniously enough after that, or at least that's what people say.'

He tilted his head and looked up at the stars. 'I am done with the army,' he said abruptly. 'After this war, I am putting in my papers and going home.'

'To your village, huh? Is it green?'

'Lush. She is beautiful, sardarji, so beautiful, my heart aches each time I look at her.'

*

The hour of the second watch began and the guards changed. Machu fell exhausted into his bedroll. He lay there for a moment, utterly still. *He was going home*. A gradual peace descended upon his drawn features. He shut his eyes, and slipped almost immediately, and for the first time since he had left Coorg, into a deep, dreamless sleep.

It felt as if he had barely closed his eyes when he was being roused again. It was time for the recce. A handful of men under the command of Lt Balmer were to go up to the pass that led to the mountains to find out how far the insurgents were from the camp. The Sikh from the previous guard leaned forward as they assembled by the quarter guard. 'I will rip their arses apart,' he whispered enthusiastically to Machu, stabbing his fingers into the air, 'let even one of them come into sight.'

Machu grinned in spite of himself, the dimple flashing in his cheek. He glanced around at the rest of the men. One of the volunteers had been assigned to the party and was looking a little green as he turned towards the pass.

They slipped from the camp under cover of this last hour of darkness. The stars were slowly receding, faint pinpricks of light in the purple sky. The air was cool, the final breath of freshness before the dust devils started to blow again, filling eyes and boots with sand.

They moved up the pass in silence. It was bounded on both sides by sharp-edged spurs of rock that could tear a man's bare feet to shreds if he wasn't careful. The camp fell rapidly out of sight as the pass twisted and turned upwards. Nothing moved. Even the fat-bellied lizards that slithered across the rock face in the heat of the day were missing, curled still asleep in their holes.

Machu walked steadily on in the fading moonlight, the stillness about him solidifying his thoughts. This was not his war. This was not his land. He would give in his papers, he thought again to himself. He had some money saved, they would get by. Devi . . . his heart quickened.

A chill breeze blew through the pass and, despite himself, Lt Balmer shivered. 'No cymbal clash'd, no clarion rang, still were the pipe and drum . . .' The line from the poem ran through his mind. For the life of him he couldn't remember what followed after. '. . . still were . . . still were . . . still were the pipe and drum . . .' It suddenly seemed of paramount importance that he remember.

Ah! 'No cymbal clash'd, no clarion rang, still were the pipe and drum. Save heavy tread and weapon clang, our onward march was dumb.' Shifting the strap of his rifle, he continued silently forward at the head of the recce party.

The mountains, crystalline shadowed, gazed meditatively down at their passage.

They were now at least a mile from the camp. The pass narrowed to a sharp-edged defile ahead, barely wide enough to fit two men standing shoulder to shoulder before turning sharply to the left. Through there, Balmer decided, they would reconnoitre just beyond the turn, then head back to the camp. He signalled to his men and they moved up the defile.

For a split second, the silence continued, both sides too stunned to react. And then, a fiendish yell, bestial, bloodthirsty, ricocheted from the ancient crags into the velvet-cloaked valleys below.

The recce party had stumbled on the enemy, thousands upon thousands of men creeping stealthily through the gorge and towards the sleeping camp.

The 20th opened fire at once, letting loose volley after volley of shots into the enemy at close range. They were met with howls of rage from the Pashtuns who quickly shouldered their own rifles.

'Fall back, fall back,' Balmer cried. They moved back, pace by pace, still firing. The noise bouncing off the rock face was deafening.

The 20th retreated, taking up position before the turn and the narrow defile, behind a rough outcrop of rock; the first line of defence kneeling, the second standing upright behind them, reloading and firing, reloading and firing into the enemy as they tried repeatedly to breach the turn. Shrapnel flew as bullets thudded into the rock face, bodies began to litter the defile, and still the Afghans pressed forward. They clambered over the bodies of their fallen comrades, letting loose wild volleys of bullets before being mown down themselves. Still they came: for each Pashtun fallen, two more to take his place. Their bullets, too, began to find marks – a soldier immediately to Machu's left, another, hit in the neck, gurgling blood and clawing wild eyed at his throat as he fell.

The recce party shot a rocket into the air to warn the camp, the acrid stink of the shell burning their nostrils. As the shell flared high above

266

them, it highlighted for an instant the desperate scene before them. The Pashtuns were gaining ground, Machu saw. They were being cut down steadily by the 20th, but there were too few soldiers to hold them at bay for much longer. And when they did breach the corner and get into the pass . . . He glanced at Balmer, saw the anxiety in his face. 'Stay strong men, stay strong,' Balmer shouted over the din, 'not long now before they send us reinforcements. Sepoys, hold steady.'

Balmer glanced behind him towards the camp. 'Come on now.' Why were the reinforcements taking so long? Lady Luck had dispensed her favour on them momentarily with the fortuitousness of their position past the defile, but Balmer knew that her affections were notoriously fickle. The recce party held the pass for now, but not for much longer. Not with the sheer numbers of the enemy.

Another soldier cried out, the rifle falling from his hand as he slumped forward. 'Get his bullets,' Machu shouted, but there was barely time to reload. The Afghans were pushing forward, leaping around the pass.

Balmer reached into his belt pouch, but there were no more bullets. 'We need ammo,' Balmer thought desperately, searching behind him in the still empty pass. *Where were the reinforcements?*

The volunteer officer stood next to him, firing wildly. There were so many of the enemy rushing around the corner, it did not matter that his aim was unpractised; he shot erratically into their numbers, and with each bullet, someone fell. And then his rifle, too, fell silent. Machu saw him turn to Balmer, gesticulating wildly. 'The camp,' he shouted into Balmer's ear, 'we must retreat.' Balmer shook his head, not bothering with words. They would never make it, Machu knew, not with the mob that would tear after them.

'I'm out, no more ammo,' the volunteer cried again. 'What do we do?'

The last rifles of the 20th sputtered to a halt. For just an instant, the pass fell silent again, the Afghans listening intently around one corner, the soldiers searching behind them on the other, willing the reinforcements to arrive. Balmer stared at his men, momentarily at a loss. Machaiah was looking steadily at him. Balmer saw, the tight resignation in the older man's face speaking plainly of what must follow.

Balmer shut his eyes for a brief, calming instant. A vast bank of rhododendrons flashed through his mind, the enormous hedge of it that lined their garden back home. His mother sitting in the shade, in a white wicker chair, her favourite tabby purring on her lap. '*I'm sorry mother.*'

Taking a deep breath, he pulled his revolver from the holster. 'This is it, men,' he said. 'Remember, glory to the 20th.'

The Sikhs pulled their turbans from their heads, their hair tumbling wild and loose down their backs. 'Wahe guru ki khalsa, wahe guru ki fateh!!' they cried, thrusting their bayonets ferociously in the air. And alongside them, another voice that echoed from the mountains.

'AYYAPPA SWAMI!' Machu roared, leaping with what remained of the recce party from behind the outcrop into the pass.

Machu thrust his bayonet through a Pashtun, skewering him, but even as he fell, the man slashed at Machu's shoulder. He stepped aside, the blade of the sword nicking his skin then falling away. He turned, pushed his bayonet through another man, removed it cleanly, thrust again. Duck, move, thrust, parry, thrust, remove, step aside, turn, thrust, remove, thrust. Something hit him on the head, he staggered for a moment as a warm gush of liquid streamed down his face, then righted himself, *thrust.*

Back and forth his arm moved, no time to think, just this fluid dance, the hunter and the hunted. His blade turned dark, slicing through muscle and sinew. Thrust and remove, thrust and remove, the odikathi, digging deep into the tiger's guts. Dust rose thick in the air from beneath the churning feet, the screams of men echoing from the rocks. A foul stench of involuntarily voided bowels from among the fallen mingled with the acrid sting of gunpowder and the mineral smell of blood. From the corner of his eye, Machu saw the volunteer officer go down. 'Balmer,' he thought, 'where is Balmer?'

He turned just in time to see the lieutenant fall forward. An Afghan stood over him, both arms raised high as he prepared to bring his sword crashing down. 'SWAMIYÉ AYYAPPA!' Machu smashed his bayonet into the man's spine, viciously twisting the blade. He was pulling it free when a man came rushing up to him and brought his sword down on Machu's arm. Machu shouted in agony. Bending his head, he butted the man ferociously in the nose, felt, rather than heard, the cartilage crunch apart. The man staggered back, clutching at his face. Grabbing his bayonet in his left hand, Machu stabbed it through the Pashtun's throat.

In the distance, the blare of bugles. The reinforcements, at last. From behind them, the faint roar of men, the war cries of the Sikhs. Machu grinned, a wild, wolfish grin, the dimple dancing in his cheek. It would not be long now.

He stood over Balmer, not sure if the lieutenant was alive or dead, his right arm nearly sliced through, dangling uselessly from his side. His face was wet with blood, it was dripping into his eyes, so that he could barely see. No time to think, just this dance, this eternal, exhilarating dance, thrust and parry, thrust, remove, thrust. The hooves of horses, thundering up the pass. Machu laughed out loud. 'El Kheir,' he roared, *'El Kheir!* "May victory be eternally bound to your forelock . . ." *I am going home.'*

He could hardly see through the blood, he was fighting more from instinct than anything else. Thrust and remove, thrust . . . a bullet hit him square in the chest. Machu jerked backwards from the force of it; to his great surprise, he found his legs would no longer hold him. He fell hard to the ground, the breath knocked from his body.

Everything went silent, as if wads of cotton had suddenly been plugged in his ears. The flash of swords about him. The blue white glint of their tips, as if the stars hung lower this morning. The unbound hair of the Sikhs whirling about them as, one by one, they too fell.

Machu was filled with an inexplicable urge to laugh. It was all so ridiculous. Honour, glory – all trampled underfoot in some misbegotten pass. The battle would end soon, he knew, and eventually, the war. The world would turn. Men would forget. And then, as sure as the sun was rising even now in the East, the very same battles would be waged again, for reasons that would not matter. Who would remember the blood staining the dust; who would mourn hope, lost forever?

A man was poised above him, his sword lifted. Machu gripped his bayonet. The Afghan raised his arm high and Machu stabbed the bayonet upwards, into the man's groin. The man dropped like a stone and, suddenly, Machu's hearing returned. The cries were louder behind him, he could hear the horses pounding up the pass. The Afghans began to falter. How many, he wondered idly, had the sardarji killed?

Ah, but it did not matter. None of this did.

He was going home.

The pop of gunfire, the whistle of bullets above him. Or was that the breeze, rustling through the rushes? The air was still, so clean it hurt his chest to breathe. The paddy, just turning green, the jewelled flash of a kingfisher among the crab pools. And look there, just beyond the crest of that hill, a flock of herons, graceful as the wind. Machu watched them soar, his heart taking flight along with them, cresting into the sky.

'It feels like a pair of wings,' she had said to him. 'Loving you, it is like being given the gift of flight. To have all of the sky at my disposal, to soar where I will.'

A numbness was slowly descending on him. He gripped his bayonet closer, fighting the darkness, forcing his eyes to stay open. Pennants of golden silk danced before him, rustling in the air. The snorting of horses, the thunder of their hooves. Cold, arrogant steel, slicing through his flesh. The fiery orange of the tiger as it turned roaring to face him, the tint of the early morning sky that was even now staining the mountain tops. She was calling out to him, her laughter tinkling in the breeze. He shook his head, smiling, reaching for her, but it was like reaching for quicksilver. '*Wait, I am coming home.*'

He tried to say her name then, as liquid flooded his chest. He struggled, coughing, but when he finally did say it, *De-vi*, it was but a sigh, slipping unheard into the stones. He struggled again, feebly trying to draw air into his lungs. The reinforcements were upon them Machu realised, the Afghans in full flight beyond the defile. 'Over here,' someone shouted, 'Lt Balmer is here. He's alive!'

Machu grinned, the dimple flashing briefly, and a fierce elation flooded his chest. 'I am headed . . .' He coughed again, a great gush of blood spilling from his mouth. 'I . . . am . . .'

And then the tiger killer was still, his eyes open, staring unblinking into the rising sun. His grip slackened and the bayonet slipped at last from his hand, raising a brief puff of dust as it fell.

Hundreds of miles away, a woman, heartbreakingly lovely, woke with a start, her heart contracting with nameless dread. The fields erupted in an explosion of white as a flock of herons suddenly took wing. Water rolled off their wings, their beaks and their claws in minute

270

droplets, catching the first rays of the sun as they hurtled towards the earth. And it was as if the birds were weeping, crying a shower of diamonds over the still-sleeping town below.

'I am yours forever.'

Chapter 23

Devi stood in the vegetable patch, trying to make sense of the tomatoes. They had seemingly grown overnight, the plants very nearly the height of the wooden stakes to which they had been bound.

'I had Tukra treat them with lime,' Devanna said softly, pointing towards the stakes. He waited, and when there was no response forthcoming, 'See? Here, and here, so that the termites wouldn't get at them.'

She looked about her in a daze, his words barely registering. How had they grown so quickly? Why, she clearly remembered planting them not one week ago. Barely the length of her palm they had been.

'Devi, come, we should head inside. It looks like rain.'

She said nothing.

Such ripe, juicy fruit. She reached a hand towards an especially voluptuous specimen, testing the springiness of its flesh.

'The tomatoes . . .' Devi said vaguely, still not looking at him.

'Do you want some with your lunch? Tukra – pick some.'

She shook her head, suddenly irritated. Really, he could be so obtuse sometimes. 'The *tomatoes*. Can't you see how they have grown? I planted them just a couple of days ago and already . . .' The tomatoes swayed fatly on their stalks.

'You planted these three months ago,' Devanna said gently. 'Don't you remember?'

'Three months?' She whipped around. '*Three months?*'

'It is almost October, Devi. Look at the sky.'

It was a soft, rain-washed blue. The colour of a myna's egg, Machu used to call it, the sky after the rains.

'October?' Confusion washed over her, and she took a faltering step backwards.

Tukra jumped forward, ready to assist, but stopped as Devanna shook his head. 'Yes. Soon it will be time for the Kaveri festival,' Devanna said, his eyes fixed on her face. He limped cautiously towards her. 'It's been three months.'

Devi shook her head disbelievingly. 'No.' It could not have been ninety days already. She knew they were watching her, she could sense the wariness in their gaze. 'Go away,' she wanted to shout, 'go *away*,' but she said nothing, staring at the shiny redness cupped in her hand. She squeezed the tomato, and it gave slightly under the pressure.

'Devi...'

Her hand closed tightly over the fruit and it burst, squirting through her fingers. Devi backed away from the plant, staring in horror at her red-stained palm. Three months, it could not have been three months since ... since ... She turned at last to Devanna, her face crumpling.

'It's OK Devi, it's OK.' He was by her side, wiping her fingers clean. Just like when they were children. He was saying something and she tried to reply but her throat was choked with grief and she folded against him sobbing.

'It's OK,' he said against her hair, holding her tight. 'Come, you need to rest. Nanju will be home from school soon, you don't want him to see you like this.'

When Devi finally awoke, it was in that in-between hour between night and morning, when the forest was silent and the animals returned to their lairs, when ghosts sighed wistfully into sleeping ears and the breeze lay coiled and waiting in the hearts of the trees. Her head was clear at last of sound, the ringing in her ears silenced. He was gone. She tested this truth, tracing the cold steel of the words. He was gone and there was only one thing to do. Devi lay unmoving in her bed, lying perfectly still as she waited for the dawn.

Devanna tried to dissuade her. 'Devi, what on earth will you tell his widow?'

'That she has no money and I do. That I can give her son a far better life than she ever will. Tukra,' she shouted. 'Are the horses harnessed yet or must I walk all the way to the Kambeymada village?'

'The boy is her only child,' Devanna tried again.

'All the more reason that she look after his interests.'

'Devi . . .'

'Enough.' Devi turned on him, her eyes glittering, whether with nervousness, excitement or a slight madness, Devanna knew not which. 'This is not your concern.'

She refused to let him accompany her, sitting ramrod straight in the carriage all the way to the village, her hands folded in her lap. Once again Devi had lost weight, her figure now almost girlish, the collarbones prominent under her blouse. Where grief might have tarred another, it had only enhanced the translucence of her skin, rendering her face almost ethereal. Only the eyes, dark as coal, betrayed the fragility that lay beneath.

With Machu's passing, it was as if a fulcrum had gone missing from the world. A reaction so physical that barely would she place her feet upon the ground than it would buckle. The memory of his eyes, golden, so filled with pain. '*I would have stood by you.*' The dark walls of a well spinning about her, a subterranean vortex of loss bottomless in its tow. Until the previous night, when suddenly, there had been stillness.

Appu.

Devi realised then what she must do, felt the rightness of it in the *stillness* of her bones. Machu was gone. But *Appu.* The child was always meant to be hers, he should have been *their* son. She was only bringing him home.

The house was shockingly small. Devi looked at the dust smudging the table and the widow reached self-consciously to wipe it away. The woman flushed then, colour tingeing her cheekbones at being caught in this small act of pride. 'So why are you here?' she asked, her voice tight.

The child wandered in just then, dragging a wooden horse. Devi's heart constricted. *So* much like Machu. He spotted Devi and stopped, sucking noisily on his thumb. The widow gathered him into her lap and gently removed the offending appendage from his mouth. When he promptly tried to put it back in, Devi leaned forward in an attempt to distract him. 'Kambeymada Appu, is that not your name?'

He looked curiously at her. 'Who are you?' he demanded.

'I am . . .' She paused, at a loss.

'My father died.'

Devi swallowed. 'I know, kunyi.'

'I have to take care of the house now. He told me to, when he left for the mountains.'

'Yes.' She smiled shakily. 'See, here. Would you like a sweet?' She pointed to the box she had brought with her.

'Sweets! What kind?' He reached eagerly for the box, but the widow pulled his arm away.

'No.' She set him down on the floor. 'No Appu, go and play outside for a while, there's a good child.'

A disappointed Appu looked for a second as if he might argue but then he stoutly nodded. Devi bit her lip, unable to take her eyes off him as he left the room, his little horse clattering behind him on its string.

'Appu looks *so* much like . . . he looks just like his . . .' she began huskily.

'He used to say your name,' said the widow, cutting her short.

Devi went very still. 'What?'

'Machu. He used to say your name.' The eyes she raised were lifeless. 'In the nights, in his sleep. Once, even while we . . . He used to call your name.'

Devi looked at her, stricken, and the woman laughed humourlessly. 'Of course, he never guessed that I knew. Men!

'So,' the widow continued. 'Why are you really here, so many months after my husband has passed away?'

Devi drew a breath, trying to collect herself. She forced herself to look the widow in the eye. 'You're right,' she said, 'I didn't come here just to offer my condolences. Appu. Why don't you enrol him in the mission school? It's the best in Coorg, my own son goes there.' Despite her attempts to appear composed, the words were spilling out nervously, her hands jerking, punctuating the air. 'I will, of course, pay all of his tuition. I know the school is too far to travel to from here, but he can stay with me.'

'You want Appu to . . .' The widow threw back her head and cackled, a sound like a chalk being dragged across a slate. 'So it wasn't enough that you sank your claws into my husband, now you want our son too?'

'Machu was an honourable man! While he was married to you . . .'

'While he was married to me, thanks to whatever black magic you spun, he never stopped dreaming of you.' The widow rose abruptly. 'I have work to do. You must leave.'

'Wait!' Devi searched frantically for the right words. 'Think of the child. Even on the army pension . . .' She gestured towards the dusty table. 'I can offer him a much better life than you can.'

The widow tilted her head and there was something in the gesture that reminded Devi of a cat.

'Is that so? Well, the school has a hostel, doesn't it?' she asked silkily. 'Why don't you just pay for my son's room and board as well, and I can then enrol him there?'

'No! He needs a home. With me, he will . . .'

The veins stood out on the widow's forehead, accentuating the gauntness of her face. '*This* is his home. *I* am his mother.'

Devi began to panic, at being caught out so effortlessly. She began talking even faster than before. 'He and my other son, they will grow up as brothers. And you could visit whenever you wished.'

'Of course. He gets a brother, your husband can fill in for his father, and he gets not one, but *two* mothers. Two mothers fighting over him, making him choose between them. Me, his birth mother, the one he will always remember as having given him up, and you the saintly surrogate. No. Never.'

'Please,' Devi said desperately. 'This is for Appu's own good, you cannot give him the life I can. Machu would have wanted this for his son.'

The widow's face darkened. '*Our* son,' she spat. 'He is my son too, don't you ever forget that. So your money can buy him the life I cannot? Let me tell you something. The means that you speak of with such confidence? It is *borrowed* land that you till.

'Oh come,' she said bitterly, at Devi's nonplussed expression. 'Don't look so surprised, we both know you are a canny woman. Nari Malai estate, is that not what you have named the land that belonged to my husband? Tiger Hills, for the tiger killer himself?'

'It has nothing to do with him.'

'You're lying. It has everything to do with him.'

'No,' Devi began, but then she stopped, the colour draining from her face as pieces from the past began at last to fall into place. '*I will see to it,*' he had said to her, '*that you get your share.*'

'No,' she whispered, 'it cannot be, the elders, it was they who . . .'

'The land was his. He insisted that they give it to you. He had the elders concoct the story of the donation to the temple so nobody would know the truth.' The widow sat down abruptly at the table. And then, holding her head in her hands, she began to laugh once more.

'It was *his*. A hundred acres, and he gave it all to you.'

Devi sat dazed in the carriage as they headed back towards Mercara, the widow's awful laughter echoing in her ears. *He had given her his land.*

'Nari Malai,' she said abruptly to Tukra. 'Drive me there.'

Tukra turned to look at her in alarm. 'Aiyo, it is getting dark, the elephants . . .'

'Nari Malai,' she ordered again, her voice rising.

Telling him to wait for her at the entrance, she opened the gates to the estate. *His* estate.

'My roots,' he had said, pointing to all of Coorg laid out before them.

The wind shifted direction and the horses tossed their manes, whickering softly. Devi walked into the darkening estate.

His heart lay here, she had always known. Weighted with this black, beloved soil, contoured by the forests, marked permanently by these hills. 'Your heart is here, you would wither away anywhere else.'

And yet he had signed away his land to her. 'What did you go and do,' she whispered in anguish. He need never have joined the army, had it not been for her demanding Devanna's share of the Kambeymada assets; *he might still have been alive*. Right here, walking this very piece of land.

The evening mist was rolling in, clouding the surrounding mountains and wreathing the path in grey. She stubbed her foot against an exposed tree root, faltered, walked on. A full moon was rising, casting a slanted sheen upon the mist. She moved deeper into the estate, navigating by instinct rather than sight. At last she stopped, in the heart of the silent plantation.

'Machu,' she cried. 'Machu!'

The mist moved closer, slipping through the coffee, wrapping itself around her. 'Machu, I know you must . . . your roots, your heart is *here*.' She stood there waiting but there was only silence in reply. 'Machu,' she called again, casting about her in the mist-shrouded estate. A chill rain began to fall. 'You . . . without you . . .' The rain dripped down, gumming her hair to her scalp, forming rivulets down her back. 'I *know* you are here,' she said despairingly. 'I *know*.' Falling to her knees, closing her fists about the damp earth, *his* earth, digging her nails deep, deep, as far as they could go into the black, loamy soil, Devi began to weep.

It was Nanju who saw them approaching the Mercara house a couple of days later. 'Avvaiah,' he called, 'look!' He pointed to the two figures, barely visible through the rain as they made their way to the door. The water whipped at them, slashing down hard, but the widow refused to enter the house. 'You promise to give him his birthright?' she asked cryptically, but Devi knew exactly what she meant.

Nanju peeped curiously around his mother's sari. The widow had her arm around the boy's shoulders. Nanju couldn't see his face; he was wearing a slit-open gunny sack across his head and over his back to protect him from the rain. 'Nanju, go inside,' Devi ordered, and reluctantly he withdrew indoors.

She turned to the widow. 'Yes,' she said, careful not to stare at the boy, trying to keep her voice from trembling. 'I promise.'

'I entrust him to you. You take care of him now or else . . .'

'Come visit,' Devi said, the brightness in her tone sounding false even to her own ears. 'Whenever you want.'

The widow gave a veiled smile that did not reach her eyes. 'Appu will never have to choose between us.'

She dropped to her knees and hugged her son to her, stroking his head, whispering endearments into his ear. Then pushing him gently into the house, she turned and disappeared into the rain.

Devi shut the door with hands that shook. She stood transfixed, still not believing what had just transpired, staring blindly at the door and the whorls in its grain. Slowly, she turned, very slowly, as if not yet certain that this wasn't a dream. Appu was silent, his eyes wide with apprehension. '*He has your eyes, Machu*'. Something began to stir within Devi, a breeze hitherto dormant. Hot, primal, a love born of jungle caverns and animal mothers. Not merely the love she bore towards Nanju, no matter how deeply that ran, but a fierce, tender, erupting love, uncoiling from her navel and towards this child. Gently she untied the sack from around his neck, carefully picking apart each knot. 'Will you have some hot milk?' she asked.

He stuck his thumb into his mouth in response.

'Come,' she said, 'I will give you some milk, hot-hot, my kunyi will enjoy it . . .'

Appu turned towards the door, as if assessing the absence of his mother. His beautiful tawny eyes welled with tears.

'Now, now.' Devi picked him up in her arms. 'Aren't you a big boy?' He nodded miserably. 'Then why the tears? Big boys don't cry, do they?' She kissed his cheek, hugging him close.

Later that evening, after the children had been put to bed, when Nanju heard Appu crying into his pillow, he rolled over to pat him on the shoulder. 'Don't cry,' he said earnestly. 'My Avvaiah is very nice. She'll take care of you, you'll see. We're to be brothers now, she told me. Brothers! Go to sleep, and in the morning I'll show you my toys.'

The widow had the last say in the matter after all, ensuring in one fell swoop that while Appu would be provided for as she never could for him, she would always have the upper hand. They found her three days later, washed ashore in a paddy field, her body bloated and foul with gas. The cremation was a hurried affair, the corpse bursting with a loud pop on the funeral pyre.

Devi said nothing when she heard about the suicide, drawing Appu into her lap, her arms tight about him as she rocked him back and forth. Her horror and guilt over the widow's suicide turning now to anger at the other's actions, *such cowardice*, then back to shock and pity. She looked at the child, trying to steady her breathing and it hit her then, with visceral force. He was hers. Appu was *hers* at last.

Poor soul, people tut-tutted over the widow. She had always been so much in love with her husband, she had never been able to be apart from him. His long absences in the army had been hard enough on her, and his death had been just too much to accept. She had leapt to her death, from a rickety bridge over the Kaveri. What a goddess, people said of her, deified on the altar of love.

Devi kept her counsel, but despite having sole claim over Appu now, their words rankled. Devanna could read the heartache in her eyes. 'It is easy for the dead,' they railed, 'it is the *living* who suffer the ache of loss.'

Many years ago at the mission school, Reverend Gundert had told them the story of Christ and his supreme sacrifice. The entire class had been silent, enraptured by the images he conjured of Christ bleeding and transfixed on the cross, all except for Devanna who had sat there, troubled. 'Yes, Dev?' the Reverend had asked. 'Do you have a question?'

'It's just ... what about Mary? What happened to her after Christ sacrificed himself?'

He still remembered the expression that had crossed the Reverend's face, how bereft he had suddenly appeared. 'Ah Dev,' he said softly, 'it is only a few who ask that question. What about Mary indeed? The ones who pass on suffer but briefly; it is those they leave behind who must truly bear the weight of the cross.'

Аррu

Chapter 24

≈ 1913 ≈

'Nanju! Where have you disappeared to? Ayy, Nanju!'

Devi turned exasperated from the kitchen door. 'This boy! Where does he keep wandering off to? Rambling around goodness knows where. Fourteen years old, whiskers beginning to sprout on his face, and still he has no sense of time at all.'

Appu was lounging against the window, engaged with a huge brass seer measure of milk. 'He's probably somewhere close,' he said, cheerfully jumping to Nanju's defence. 'The piglets, maybe he went to check on them.'

Devi pursed her lips, but before she could say anything more, he slammed the empty measure with a thunk on the sill and belched. 'Cheh,' Devi chided, tugging his ear. 'Is this what I have taught you, to make these rude noises?'

Appu forced a deliberate belch through his throat again and grinned.

'Donkey child.' Devi shook her head, amused in spite of herself. 'Go find Nanju,' she said, smoothing the thick spring of hair back from his forehead. 'Take him his milk. And don't you drink it,' she added, 'you've had quite enough already.'

Appu strolled into the vegetable garden. Tukra had killed a bandicoot rat that morning, by the drumstick tree. It had been huge, the size of a suckling pig. Appu looked around hopefully as he skirted the pumpkin pit, but there were no more rats to be seen. Vaguely disappointed, he whistled at the dogs tethered in the kennels. They cocked sleepy eyes at him, wagging a desultory tail. He took a sip of milk and ambled on, behind the chicken coop and the cattle shed, emptied now of the cattle that had been taken to pasture. He poked his head over the wall of the sty, sending the piglets into a squealing, curling, whirling frenzy of excitement. He took another sip of milk, whistling at the old sow lying on her side, and she grunted softly. Where *was* Nanju?

'Ah,' he thought, 'the birdhouse.' He headed into the plantation, through the coffee bushes that surrounded the bungalow.

The birdhouse lay a little way into the estate, by the side of the massive stump of a jackfruit tree. Appu sauntered down the rough trail that led to it, thinking wistfully about the elephants. It was because of them, really, that the birdhouse had been built.

A herd of them had run amok through the estate two summers ago, drawn by the scent of ripening jackfruit. They came at night, crashing about the plantation as the workers trembled in their shacks and the dogs barked futilely. They circled the jackfruit trees, this way and that, as they reached with their trunks for the spiky, pendulous fruit, and in the process ended up trampling scores upon scores of coffee bushes. Appu had thought it was all rather thrilling, but Devi had cursed the elephants long and hard. She hired watchmen to stand guard at the perimeter of the estate where it abutted the forest, arming them with rifles. 'Unload them into the air at first sight,' she ordered. How Appu had begged her, Avvaiah *please*, to let him stand guard with them, but she would have none of it. He frowned as he remembered.

At first it appeared as if the watchmen had succeeded. The elephants lumbered away at the sound of the guns, ears flapping in fright. For the next few nights, the men stood guard, but of the elephants, there was no sign. It was not a week later however, that following Friday to be exact, that the watchmen were waylaid. It had been their weekly day off and a host of them were returning drunk and merry from the shanty. The elephants had stood in the middle of the road, the terrified workers told Devi later, like the minions of Ganesha the Elephant God himself. Mammoth ears, like the fronds of some monstrous palm tree, flapping to and fro, massive tusks gleaming as they raised their trunks up high and trumpeted into the sky. Devi had spotted Nanju and Appu then, listening open mouthed from behind the door. 'Go inside,' she had said to them sharply. 'At once.'

It was Tukra who filled them in on the details later. The elephants had charged the workers, goring two of them to death and flinging three more into the rain ditch that flanked the road.

Devi tried talking sense into the workers. What had happened was tragic. However, she pointed out, elephant encounters happened all the time in these parts, it was bound to happen with the estate lying as close as it did to the jungle. No, shivered the survivors, this was no chance encounter. It was retribution, precise and pointed. How had the elephants known to target *only* those of the party who had stood guard in the estate? They refused to stand guard any longer, and nothing she said could sway them.

She had barbed wire installed, reinforced with sharpened bamboo and broken glass. The next morning, the elephant tracks spoke for themselves. The beasts had uprooted two athi trees that bordered the fence. When the trees fell, they had dragged a section of the fence down with them. The elephants had then calmly crossed once more into the estate. Before leaving, they had left Devi a parting gift – tracts of trampled coffee bushes, wrenched from the soil and flung contemptuously aside.

She knew when to concede defeat. She had the workers cut down the jackfruit, every single one. Some fruit she bade them take home to their families. Twelve of the fattest, she saved for the pantry, a few to be set out at teatime with honey, some to be made into jam, and the rest to be julienned, sun dried and then crisped golden in hot oil and tossed with salt and red chilli powder. The majority of the fruit she had heaped in piles by the side of the estate. It was a conciliatory gesture that the elephants seemed to accept; by the next morning, the fruit was gone. Devi nodded with satisfaction as she surveyed the mess they had left behind, of stubbled green jackfruit skin, seeds and chunks of unripe fruit. 'Burn this mess,' she ordered the workers. 'And now that the elephants know there is no more fruit to be had, cut down the jackfruit trees, every last one of them.'

That afternoon, the boys had returned from school to the crash of timber. Appu had hurried at once towards the sound, Nanju but a footstep behind. Appu watched spellbound as the workers sawed back and forth, the sweat running down their backs, two men to a tree. 'Ayy,' he called, eyes shining. 'Here, let me have a go as well.'

When Nanju, however, saw the trees trembling under the assault, and the sticky ooze of sap from their torn bark, he had turned pale. He backed slowly away from the workers, his ears filled with the awful groaning the trees made as they crashed to the ground. Turning abruptly, he had raced towards the house. 'Nanju,' Appu had called surprised, 'where are you going?' He had started to follow him, but just then another tree had fallen. With a whoop of excitement, he had turned back to the workers. 'Didn't you hear me? Give me the saw, let me have a go!'

Devi had looked up in surprise as Nanju burst into the kitchen. 'What is it?' she asked. 'Why has your face become small as a rat's?'

'The trees,' Nanju mumbled. 'I . . . I don't like to see them fall.'

Devi turned back to stirring the jam. 'It's necessary kunyi,' she said amused. 'Do you want the elephants to return next season?'

'They look . . . the trees look like old men being cut down.'

'Oh, don't be silly!' It came out sharper than she had intended, but really, sometimes Nanju could say the most foolish things. 'Old men indeed.'

He stood there, biting his lip and fiddling dismally with the pile of double beans that Tukra's wife was shucking. Devi sighed. 'You can be *such* a child.' Unlocking the doors to the pantry, she took out two laddoos and set them before him. 'Here,' she said, 'eat.' He shook his head and she could see he was close to tears.

'Nanju,' she began, trying to keep the exasperation from her voice, when Devanna limped into the kitchen.

'What's this? Why the long face?'

Nanju told him about the trees. 'Ah, the felling.' Shifting his walking stick, Devanna bent forward awkwardly to ruffle Nanju's hair. 'Your mother is right, you know, we need to fell them. I'll tell you what, though, let's make a birdhouse, Appu, you and me. We'll use wood from each and every tree that has been cut down today, a memorial of sorts, to remember them by. What do you think?'

Nanju looked at his father. 'A birdhouse? How?'

'Ah, let us see now, we need to plan. I have just the book to help us ...' Still talking, Devanna led Nanju from the kitchen. Devi stared at the laddoos lying untouched on the granite counter, reminded suddenly of an afternoon long ago. It had been a jackal, hadn't it, that had got into the hen coop? Those poor chicks, how she had wept for them. And the funeral that Devanna had organised later that afternoon. The sparkling crab stream, a coffin, fashioned from leaves and lined with silk cotton.

Suddenly upset and not knowing why, she picked up the laddoos and flung them into the rubbish.

Devanna sent both boys through the estate to find the oldest tree that had been felled, the one with the most number of rings on its stump. 'By its side,' he told them, 'that's where we will build.' The birdhouse had taken nearly seven weeks to fashion, a large, ornate structure fitted with multiple birdbaths and feeding stations. Devanna had Nanju and Appu fill the basins with water, corn and seed, and placed a small nugget of copper in each of the baths to stave off algae. After only a few hesitant runs past and through the birdhouse, the visitors had come. Onyx-tailed drongos and white-rumped mannikins, purple-winged coucals, red-whiskered bulbuls and olive-backed woodpeckers, thronging the basins and filling the area with song.

That's where Nanju would be for sure, thought Appu now as he made his way into the estate. 'Nanju!'

'Shh.' Nanju turned half frowning, half smiling towards him, a finger on his lips. 'Stop crashing about like an elephant, you'll scare away the birds.'

'Didn't you hear Avvaiah calling for you? Here's your milk.' Appu flung himself on the grass beside his brother.

Nanju noted the depleted contents of the glass and gave Appu an affectionate cuff that knocked the latter's cap off his head 'What?' Appu exclaimed, reaching for the cap as it rolled in the grass. 'I didn't take any!' He dusted it off and perched it jauntily on his head once more. 'Well, maybe just a little,' he confessed, grinning.

Nanju shook his head with amusement. He took a sip, then wiped his lips with the back of his hand and handed the glass to Appu. 'Here.'

Both brothers leaned companionably against the jackfruit stump, soaking in the sunshine and passing the milk between them as birds cooed and called overhead and splashed in the baths, sending droplets of water shooting into the air.

It had been almost four years since they had moved permanently to Nari Malai, soon after Machu's widow had left Appu with Devi. Everyone marvelled at the change the child had wrought in her, his arrival snapping her out of the stupor of the previous months. Fired with a renewed sense of purpose, she had had the Mercara house repainted, and ordered a new set of furniture from Mysore. Nonetheless, something had been lacking. And then she had had an epiphany – why, it was the house itself! Devi had disliked the house from the moment they had moved there, but somehow, in all these years, she had never entertained the thought of leaving. At first there had been little money to afford a more suitable home. And later, when there was more than enough, she still had not moved. Partly, it was apathy, stemming from the sheer familiarity of the house, grown in these intervening years around them like a cocoon. And partly, it was a deliberate embracing of her distaste for the house, her contempt for its dim, cramped rooms. She had clutched this to herself, thorn-like, the daily discomforts a perverse marking of all that had passed, everything that was never to be.

Appu was the charm that broke the spell. Devi had looked at the house with renewed disgust as she held him in her arms. Dark as an abattoir it was, she thought uncharitably, thanks to that butcher landlord of theirs, the smell of fish and chicken fat seeming to permeate its very bones. Why, she wondered astonished, had she not thought of moving before?

'Nari Malai,' she had announced brightly to the family, 'we will all move to the estate. Did you know your father was a tiger killer, kunyi?' she asked, turning to Appu. 'Killed a tiger practically barehanded, he did.'

'Devi ... what about Nanju's schooling?'

She hadn't looked at Devanna as she replied. 'It's all arranged. I have ordered a new automobile from Mysore. We can hire a driver who can take him into Mercara each morning.'

Nari Malai! The boys had been tremendously excited at the notion of living on the estate but nonetheless, when it was actually time for them to leave Mercara, Nanju was suddenly sad. It was Devanna who had found him, lying curled on the floor under the bed. He had thrown back the covers and laughed. 'Now, who do we have here? Come out you little fugitive, come on, before your Avvaiah finds you.' He had drawn Nanju towards him. 'I know how you feel,' he told him gently. 'After all, this is the only home you've known. But we're going to a new home now, there's the estate for you and Appu to romp about in ...'

'Are you happy to go, Appaiah?' Nanju had asked.

'Your mother is happy,' Devanna had replied simply, 'and that is all that counts.'

And indeed, after a very long while, Devi was happy. This was *happiness*, not merely the absence of unhappiness or the shuttering of grief, like an iron cover dragged across the yawning mouth of a well. This was HAPPINESS; unexpected, unwarranted, a counter, partial but a counter all the same, to everything that had happened before. Joy unfurled within her until she would stop abruptly, mid laugh, terrified it would all be snatched away from her again.

In the early days, she would hurry to the boys' bedroom, heart pounding. There she would stand, by the side of their bed, frightened out of her wits, filled with the mad certainty that just like that, Appu would stop breathing, like *that*, in a snap of the fingers, he would be taken from her. 'I know it, I know it ...' and then Appu would turn in his sleep, smiling at some dream. Slowly her panic would subside. His chest would rise and fall, rise and fall, her eyes lulled by the hypnotic rhythm of it; Devi was filled with a love so fierce that the breath caught in her throat.

She had managed very nearly to forget that Appu was born of another woman; it was only sometimes, when he turned his head suddenly or looked up at her in that way he had, that she was reminded of his mother. However, even that sharp burst of angst was quelled when Appu began to call her, none other than her, Avvaiah.

Once, soon after he had arrived, she had been returning from the estate when Nanju had run out to welcome her. 'Avvaiah is here, Avvaiah is here.' Caught up in the general excitement, and mimicking Nanju, Appu had shouted along with him. 'Avvaiah is here!'

Nanju had suddenly, uncharacteristically, turned on Appu. 'She is *not* your Avvaiah,' he'd cried. 'Don't call her that.'

Devi didn't admonish Nanju, had only laughed as she scooped Appu into her arms. She kissed his cheek. 'This silly Nanju. Not your mother, he says, of *course* I am your mother. And you, my sun and moon, are my precious, darling child.'

The move to Nari Malai was for Devi the final piece of the puzzle. It was Machu's land. It was as it should be that his son grew up there. It was important that Appu learn every fold and turn of the property. That the trees recognise his footfall, that the breeze that blew through the coffee bushes should know the contours of his hands, the timbre of his voice.

The family had settled so fully into the estate, it was hard to imagine that they had ever lived elsewhere. Devi had the bungalow repaired and a new roof put in. The old wasp-ridden rubbish pit had been filled in and she had had an outhouse built in its place, fitted with blue-rimmed chamber pots. She commissioned an artist from Mysore and had him paint a huge mural of a tiger in the nursery; it watched fiercely over her boys as they slept.

Nanju and Appu had taken to country living like two fish released from a pond into a flood. Off they'd run into the estate as soon as it was light, scampering through the coffee until the plantation pulsed with their laughter. Devi would listen from the verandah and smile. Sometimes when she looked at the sky, she imagined she saw the faint outlines of a warrior, his rifle resting in one hand, his odikathi raised high in the other. 'Your son is home Machu,' she'd whisper then. '*Our* son . . . he is where he belongs.'

She talked often of Machu to Appu. 'He died fighting,' she would say as they walked through the verdant acreage, her boys and she. Nanju and he grew very quiet as she talked of the battle that had been waged in the mountains far away. 'A death most honourable, the death of a warrior. Your father . . . he died a hero, kunyi.' Little Appu would walk very straight as he listened, his shoulders unconsciously drawn back, his fists taut at his sides. She would take his hand then, gently prising the fingers loose as she gestured about them. 'He is one of them now, the veera that protect this land.'

When Appu turned six, Devi had arranged for him to be admitted into the mission school as well. 'Talk with the Reverend,' she had said to Devanna. 'I don't know why you have not stayed in touch with him. Contacts matter.'

Devanna had remained silent but at her urging, he finally sat down to write to the Reverend. It was a difficult letter. Draft after discarded draft later, he had opted for a formal tone, one that merely pointed out the unfortunate circumstances under which Appu had fallen into their care. He talked of the heroism of the boy's father, even offered to get a reference from the battalion if it would help. His nib hovered for a while over the letter as he signed off. In the end he chose:

'Thanking you sincerely.

Your former student,

Kambeymada Devanna.'

Devanna stared at it, and then tearing it in half, he threw the letter into the wastepaper basket. When Devi asked that evening if it had been posted, Devanna hesitated an instant and then gestured noncommittally with his hand.

When weeks passed with no response to the never-posted letter, Devi tried a different tack. She dressed Appu in his best clothes, the brand new shorts and shirt she had bought from the English clothing store in Mercara. She smoothed his hair down with coconut oil and water, as Devanna coached him how to greet the Reverend in English. Devanna was reticent about accompanying them, but Devi was having none of it.

'You have to come,' she insisted, 'you were close to the Reverend. You *must* speak with him on Appu's behalf.'

The former novices, now nuns, flocked around Devanna like plump, greying pigeons in their habits. Devi watched, a strange softness in her eyes as the nuns cooed over him. 'I am well, I am well,' he assured them, smiling, the gauntness in his features suddenly dissipated. 'Look,' he said, removing his hand from the cane, 'I can stand unaided, even walk a few steps.'

'Where have you been child?' they wanted to know. 'You have completely forgotten us. So close you live, and not once have you come to visit us in all these years. Did you not want to see the Reverend? Old he has become now, he needs young people around him.'

'I heard he had a stroke . . .' Devanna said hesitantly, and one of the nuns shook her head.

'Two. Two strokes, one after the other. He survived both with the Good Lord's grace, but what a scare he gave us each time.' She sighed. 'Hardly ventures out now, stays in his office working. But what am I chattering on for? He will be so thrilled to see you.'

She hurried down the chessboard-tiled corridor, calling out to Devi as she left. 'Devi, your son Nanju, he is a sweet boy. Reminds us so much of his father, he does.' The softness died abruptly from Devi's eyes. She smiled briefly and looked out the windows at the nodding gerberas.

The nun returned, fussing with her habit. 'Child,' she said, embarrassed, 'the Reverend, he . . . he is busy right now. Can you . . . do you think you can leave him a letter?'

'He has already sent one,' Devi interrupted, 'and we are still waiting for a reply. Oh, this is ridiculous.' Without waiting for a response, she swept down the corridor.

'Devi! Child! You cannot just go in.' Squawking in alarm, the nuns fluttered around Devi trying to dissuade her, but she was already knocking on the door to the Reverend's office.

He turned in surprise from the bookshelf.

'Who . . .?'

'Devi. You don't remember me perhaps, but surely you remember my husband? Kambeymada Devanna. Dev, you used to call him.'

The Reverend looked past her at the nuns. 'It's all right,' he said to them. 'Shut the door behind you, please?'

'He wrote you a letter, why did you not reply?'

Gundert frowned, puzzled, but before he could comment, Devi rattled on. 'He is waiting outside. Why did you not come out to see him?'

Gundert looked down at the book he held in his hand. Sunlight poured into the study through the starched curtains, their crocheted edges casting serrated circle and heart patterns on the walls and the floor. The light bounced off the Reverend's bowed head, a patchwork of pink scalp visible through the thinning silver hair. 'I am busy.'

'Too busy to say hello? He used to look up to you so. I should know, all he would talk about was you. All he thought about was what you taught him. Trees and flowers and poetry, that's all the man still thinks about, to this day. And you will not even come out and see him?'

Gundert was grasping the book so tight, there were faint indentations in its leather-bound cover from his fingers.

'I see how it is,' Devi said when he did not reply. 'So be it, let's get down to brass tacks then. You're building a new wing to the school are you not? I hear you're seeking donations to fund the construction. How much do you need?'

Gundert looked up at her. His voice, when he spoke, was flat. 'One thousand.'

'Done.' Devi turned to go. 'I will have my bank arrange the funds. In return, there is a boy who must be admitted.' She dropped an elaborate curtsy. 'Good day, Reverend.'

Devi swept out of the school, but Devanna halted by the gates, shading his eyes against the sun to scan the windows that lined the Reverend's office. He stood there, his heart pumping painfully as he searched, but of the Reverend, there was no sign. He turned away, the pinched expression settling back into his features, failing to notice the slight shifting of the curtains in Gundert's office. The sort of movement an old man might cause as he stood there, heavy hearted, then stumbling hastily back from the windows lest he be spotted.

In the coach on the way home, Devanna asked after the Reverend. Was he looking well?

Devi shook her head. 'Frail, he looked. Shrunken. Eyes all watery. I can't believe how scared I used to be of him.'

'Did he . . . I mean, did he . . .'

Devi hesitated only briefly. 'He asked about you,' she said then, briskly. 'Wanted to know how you were, how you were doing. He would have come out himself, but he had people there in his office.'

Devanna had nodded, knowing she was lying, but was strangely comforted all the same.

Chapter 25

The years that followed passed gently over them all, cloaked in the easy language of youth and two thriving sons. While neither boy came close to duplicating Devanna's academic prowess, Appu at least showed an early and outstanding athletic ability, becoming the youngest student in the history of the mission school to try out successfully for the junior cricket team. When a craze for hockey swept through Coorg, ten-year-old Appu was at once enchanted; the following year, he was effortlessly selected for the junior outdoor XI. The team forged its way through the district tournament, generating so much local excitement that on the day of the finals, there was not even standing room to be found around the field. All of Coorg, it seemed, had turned out to watch the game and judge for themselves the prodigious talent of the Kambeymada lad they had heard so much about. Appu did not disappoint, scoring two crucial goals.

Devi could barely contain her pride as he went up to collect his Player of the Tournament trophy. 'Look at him, just *look* at him!' she whispered jubilantly to Tayi, and the old lady smiled.

'What a game!' someone said, stopping to congratulate Devanna. 'The boy is a natural, you must be proud of him.'

'I am, very,' Devanna replied, beaming.

'Lucky child,' the man continued, glancing enviously at Devanna's brogues. 'If it weren't for you, where would he have been today? No parents, no land, no prospects . . . it was a fortunate day for him when you took him in.'

'Nanju and Appu, they are equally my sons,' Devanna said embarrassed. 'We as parents are the fortunate ones.'

'Well, he is very lucky to be your ward. Such largesse . . .'

'Appu is no ward, he is my son,' Devi interrupted coldly. 'His father was a tiger killer. A war hero. That game Appu just played? As you say, he is a natural. It's in his blood. No amount of *largesse* can substitute for that.'

'Why do you say such hurtful things?' Tayi admonished her later.

Devi frowned. She was still upset by the man's comments. All these years, and yet people refused to accept that Appu was hers. The day had been a muggy one, the threat of a storm brewing in the oppressive air; the headache that Devi had been ignoring all morning had painfully flared up. 'What did I go and say now?'

'You're so quick to point out at every instant that Devanna isn't Appu's father. Think how Devanna must feel when you do so. He's treated Appu as if he were his own child, from the day you brought him home.'

'Appu is *Machu's* son,' Devi said flatly.

'And you, his mother? I see. So where does that leave Devanna? Or Nanju?'

'What do you mean? Nanju is my child too.'

'Come Devi. You know you favour Appu, you always have. And yet, has Devanna once voiced his objection? Never, despite the hurt it must cause him.'

'*Voice his objection?*' Devi pressed her fingers to her throbbing temples, suddenly filled with anger. 'On what grounds? You want to talk about Nanju? Let's. Take a long look at him, Tayi, remember as I do, every time I see him, just *how* his father's seed was planted in me.'

Tayi blanched and turned to the sink.

'No, why do you turn away from me now? Is this too bitter a truth for you?'

Tayi began to sort the pots and pans with a great deal of clattering. 'Enough. Why do you insist on raking up the past? It's gone, Devi.'

'That's right. Let's shut it tidily away, pretend that nothing happened. Yes, the past is gone. *Machu* is gone, forever. While Devanna limps about this house, a . . . a constant reminder of everything I have lost.'

It grew dark outside, the birds suddenly quiet as they hurriedly flew towards shelter. 'He has always loved you,' Tayi said distressed. 'From the time you were little.'

'Love. It must be a misbegotten love indeed, to have caused me so much grief.'

Tayi's hands trembled. 'Whatever happened, happened. The past *is* gone. Look ahead, to the future. This bitterness . . . My flower bud, my darling child, be like a *flower*. The beauty of a flower lies in the sweetness it carries within, in the fragrance it shares with the wind.'

Thunder rumbled as the first drops of rain splattered into the dust, a cooling whiff of petrichor rising from the estate. Devi massaged her temples again. 'My head,' she said tiredly. 'I'm going to rest for a while. You're right, Tayi, I should look ahead. Iguthappa has been kind, and I am blessed. Machu's son. Appu . . . I've been given the future.'

From the other side of the kitchen door, Appu detached himself from the shadows and melted silently into the house.

Devanna awoke in the middle of the night, smiling. He groped about in his mind, trying to replicate the fragrance that had perfumed his dreams, but it slipped through his fingers, note after tantalising note. He had been jumping, he remembered, across the crab stream, his legs bounding off the wet mud. She was laughing, her laughter the very colour of the water, a clear, unaffected silver. He turned his head, still half asleep. Fireflies hung flickering outside the bedroom window, tracing patterns across the velvet of the night. Now on, now off, shifting and rearranging themselves in a myriad sparks of code.

The bamboo flower! His eyes flew open. The flower the Reverend had shown him all those years ago. He recalled the fragrance still trapped in its dried petals, the heady roundness of it.

Deeper than a rose.

Muskier than jasmine.

Bambusea. Indica. Devi.

How had he forgotten all these years?

He slept no more that night, thumping his walking stick impatiently on the floor for Tukra to help him out of bed as soon as the first light streaked the sky. 'Quickly Tukra, we have a flower that is waiting to be discovered.'

When Devi came downstairs, she found to her surprise the coffee workers gathered earnestly around Devanna as he held court upon the lawn. He was searching for a particular flower, he told them, large as his fist and divinely perfumed.

It was rare, very rare, and grew hidden among the bamboo thickets. 'Find one for me,' he told them, 'and you will be richly rewarded. But remember, I want the plant, roots and all.'

The workers waggled their heads, bemused by this odd request but keen to please this master who always had a kind word for them and their children as he patiently attended to their cuts, sores and various fevers. They would ask their relatives too, they assured him, those who worked on other plantations as well as those who still lived among the forests. Someone would definitely find the flower.

Nanju and Appu clamoured to be included in this project. They went traipsing eagerly through the estate and poked at the bamboo thickets that grew by the lake, but apart from two petrified rat snakes that the dogs promptly tore apart, there was little else to be found. 'But *where* is it?' Appu asked impatiently and Devanna smiled. He raised his cane and pointed towards the mountains, hazy in the distance. 'Probably there. But it would be foolish, wouldn't it, to overlook the possibility of our own estate?'

Devanna began once more to maintain records of the plants he found, pressing the specimens when his fingers were too stiff to paint. He spent hours referencing and cross-referencing his books, inscribing the species and genus to which each specimen belonged in a copperplate script that sometimes lifted and jerked midway no matter how hard he tried to control his hands.

When he had exhausted the possibility of finding so much as an undocumented spore on the grounds of Nari Malai, Devanna looked to the neighbouring forest. Every Friday afternoon, on the workers' weekly day off, Tukra drove him to one of the trails. By this time, the boys' interest had waned. Devi saw the disappointment on Devanna's face when he called to them and not even Nanju wanted to accompany him.

'Go with him, donkey boys,' she chided. 'So much time you spend roaming around the estate like ragamuffins, why can't you go with Appaiah?'

Devanna smiled. 'It's all right. If they don't want to come, don't force them.'

Devi shrugged elaborately as if to distance herself from the support she'd just demonstrated. 'As you wish. I can't understand these obsessions of yours. Going to the forest! Be careful. Or have you forgotten there are elephants there?'

Devanna smiled again and began to say something, but Devi had already disappeared into the house.

Yet again, the bamboo flower refused to reveal itself. Nonetheless, the forest yielded rich bounty. Devanna found scarlet-tipped orchids that he draped over the trees surrounding the house. He came across vast, secret meadows of wildflowers that he and Tukra brought back by the armful for Tukra's wife to thread through the links of the prayer lamps and place in brass urns through the rooms. One time he found a hollow filled with sampigé saplings that he transplanted along one side of the lawn at Nari Malai; another time, he came back with masses of wild roses. Slowly, despite no concrete plan to do so, almost by accident, the gardens of Nari Malai that would be marvelled at for decades to come began to take shape.

They were a thing of strange, wild-edged beauty; not for Devanna the manicured perfection of flowerbeds and trellises. Here there was a wall of the fragrant Night Queen, and by its side a loose-fisted medley of wildflowers. They spread untamed around the base of the large banyan tree that was allowed to reach its vast, parrot-adorned branches across the lawn. There was a rambling rockery, peppered with bonsai miniatures of loose-jacket oranges and wild mango. He had the workers bring him the smooth black stones to be found in the rivers and with these, Devanna fashioned an astonishing, many levelled pond. It started at a height, in a large oval that narrowed at its base into a series of smaller, evenly spaced scallops meandering down. He trained lotuses across the different levels, the flowers pulsing with colour against the deep black of the stones.

He designed an arbour, hewn from timber to his specifications over which he trained not roses but brilliant spumes of bougainvillea. If you knew where to look, up at the very top of the arbour, you would see a faint inscription carved into the wood and all but obscured by the flowers:

> *In my old griefs*
> *And with my childhood's faith.*
> *I love thee*
> *With a love I seemed to lose*

There were wild orchids with musky scents and variegated colours draped over the branches and he had two more birdhouses built, until the gardens of Nari Malai, throbbing with birdsong, became the talk of every social circle, Indian or otherwise. There was only one spot in the garden that was left bare, at the very apex of it. 'A flowering plant,' Devanna said when quizzed about it. 'One day, that spot will house a very special flower. Some day.'

'What a thing of beauty,' Tayi marvelled, gazing at the grounds. She glanced at Devi. 'You do know he built it for you, don't you?'

Devi grimaced and did not reply, hunched over the accounts.

'Haven't you realised? In his choice of flowers, in everything . . . this garden is *you*, Devi.'

Devi looked then at the garden. 'There, kunyi,' Tayi pointed. 'Did you notice there is no jasmine? He knows you hate it. Look, there. Sampigé instead. And see the rockery – filled with your favourite fruit. And there.'

Tayi pointed out all the little touches that made up the gardens, things that Devi had been oblivious to.

Why, there was the wheelbarrow they had played with as children, converted now into a vast freestanding pot of lilies. There, in the rockery, the small purple stones that could be found in the Pallada village. And look there, a sapling from the mango tree that had grown in her father's home. Devi looked around, amazed, and then the ends of her mouth began to twitch with laughter.

'What?' Tayi asked smiling. 'What is so amusing?'

Devi began to laugh, louder and louder as she looked about her, laughing so hard that tears spurted from her eyes. 'Look at us Tayi,' she gasped, 'just look at us.' She gestured towards the flowers. 'He toils here all day, all for me it seems. While my world lies just beyond, there, in the estate. A fine pair we make! Nails filthy from the same soil, each creating our own memorials to the past.

'Nari Malai! Taj Mahal estate, that's what we should have called it.' She laughed again, pressing her palms to her eyes.

'Ah, Devanna, Devanna. He built this garden, he built it for me, he thought of everything it seems. But you know the one flower he missed, Tayi? Laburnums. Butter yellow laburnums, twisting in the breeze.'

Chapter 26

≈ 1915 ≈

'I'm sorry Reverend,' the police commissioner said. He spread his paw-like hands in front of him.

Gundert stared at him, giving no quarter, his eyes like two chips of blue ice.

The police commissioner was new to Coorg. 'We have orders,' he said, and this time there was a slight sharpness to his tone. 'Our countries, after all, are at war.'

War had indeed mushroomed in the West, casting Europe into shadow. The continent lay divided, trenches furrowing their way like scar tissue across its soil. War, most momentous, the papers called it, unprecedented in the history of mankind. World War I. A war so far reaching that its reek permeated the globe, its bony fingers stretching, grasping, as far away as Coorg.

As soon as the war began in earnest, the British Government had closed India's borders, denying all access to Germany. The Mission was headquartered in Switzerland, not Germany, its officials had protested, *we are neutral*, but nonetheless, no more of its men, supplies or funds were allowed into the country. The edict had largely been met with sympathy. The Coorg planters rallied amongst themselves, organising raffles and tombolas to raise funds, and sending anonymous donations to the local mission. Gundert had looked on, touched, as the donation tray after the Sunday Mass came back week after week

301

so loaded with coins it had taken two nuns to haul it into his office.

The war dragged on, brutal and unrelenting. The German government, seeking to unseat Britain from its colonies, began to fund Indian insurgents. They colluded with them in secret meetings held in Berlin, America and London, supplying them with arms and money with which to oust the British from India. Furious, the British Government responded by issuing a clampdown on all imports from Germany. Declaring the Industrial Establishment of the Basel Mission to be a German organisation, they confiscated all of the factories and industrial works that the Mission had set up in India – the weaving looms, the terracotta tile factory, even the printing press that Gundert had worked so tirelessly to set up. All Mission personnel were to be interned immediately.

The police commissioner had made his ruddy, reluctant way to the Mission, where he had attempted to explain to Gundert that it was a mere formality, but all things considered, it would be best if the Reverend did not travel outside of Mercara for some time.

'Yes.' Gundert smiled frostily. 'Your uniform, Commissioner,' he said, and the commissioner glanced startled at his trousers. 'Your khaki breeches. Did you know that khaki dye was invented by a predecessor of mine from the Mission? The very first khaki cloth to be used anywhere in the world, spun on our looms. The weaving looms that *we* set up here in India, the very same looms that your compatriots now see fit to usurp.'

'The war,' the commissioner began, but Gundert reached for his walking stick, pulling himself up from the chair.

'Thank you for your visit,' he said haughtily.

That afternoon, he made his way to the trading shop, where Hans was pacing the floor. 'Reverend,' he exclaimed, the worry on his face dissolving into a grin. 'We haven't seen you in a while. Here, sit, would you like some water? It's a long way to walk.'

Gundert waved away his ministrations, although he was breathing heavily from the exertion. 'Have they been here too, the police?'

'I must report in every morning to the garrison, they say. Roll call.' Hans shook his bear-like head.

'Perhaps it is better you keep a low profile for some time Hans,' Gundert said, troubled.

'Ah, do not worry. They need this shop in Mercara, ja? They will do nothing to me. Besides,' he said simply, 'you are here to look after me.'

Gundert blinked, then looked away at the interior of the shop to mask how touched he was with this proclamation. He pointed his walking stick at the sparsely stocked shelves. 'Are imports coming in?'

'A few. From my supplier in Malaya, mostly. Difficult to get things from home these days. Still,' Hans said sardonically, 'there is so much money here, business has been good.'

Wartime had proved a boon for Coorg and her coffee. The Allied Armies could scarcely get enough of the stuff it seemed. They ordered vast quantities of coffee beans for their troops, Kona from Hawaii, Robusta from Brazil and quintal upon quintal of smooth, rich Arabica from Coorg. Coffee prices had already been healthy; they shot to unprecedented heights during the war and there they would remain for the next decade.

A new elite emerged in Coorg on the wings of this prosperity, like stripling green underbrush beneath a stately jungle grove. These were the progeny of some of the most respected local families, boasting ancestral histories as long and deep as the Kaveri in flood. They had been educated in Madras and in Bombay and some, even in England. One among them had studied papermaking in Japan, two others had visited New York.

They returned home with modulated accents and trunks full of porcelain, fine cigars and back copies of *Racing News*. They demanded their share of the family properties and built on them European-styled bungalows surrounded not by the lush banana, areca nut and orange groves of their youth, but cropped lawns perfect for an afternoon of croquet. They pored over catalogues from Jermyn Street and Savile Row, ordered shiploads of Chippendale furniture and frequented Hans' store, picking up vast quantities of turntables, painted lamps and pink-cheeked dolls.

Husbands badgered their wives to become 'modern' and the women obliged by shearing off their waist length plaits in favour of the latest bobs. Theirs was a shandy-sipping, cigarette-smoking, air-kissing set that threw fabulous teas and knew how to dance the tango. Crinkling their noses at the old Coorg names – très old fashioned, non? – they rechristened themselves, sometimes with mixed results. Dechamma, Kalamma, Neelamma and Nalavva became Polly, Kitty, Titty and Pussy; their husbands, Jack, Joe-boy, Tarzan and Timmy.

Their new-found prosperity was not lost on the pragmatic English. So it was that the committee of the Mercara Club, while unanimously voting to continue the Reverend's membership despite his Germanic origins – he is a *Christian* missionary, dash it – also passed an unprecedented motion to allow into its fold select members from among the locals.

It was a stringent process. Any hopeful and his wife had to survive three separate evenings at the Club where they were subjected to intense scrutiny – everything from the way the husband pronounced his aitches and held his goblet of brandy to the manicured tips of his wife's fingers. If the couple was deemed to be cultured enough, the husband was then invited to a two-hour interview in the King Edward room. The committee sat with their backs to the window or to the roaring fireplace, depending on the weather, and grilled the hapless applicant on politics, moral integrity and his ability to contribute – in cash or in services – to the welfare of the Club. Still, despite the stringency of admission, no fewer than fifteen couples became members of the Mercara Club that first year of 1915.

The committee also approached Devanna. He was one of the wealthiest locals, after all. They sent him an invitation, on thick cream stationery embossed in burgundy. Would he and his wife like to attend an evening at the Club, two Wednesdays from now, at six in the evening? RSVP.

To their astonishment, Devanna turned them down. Devi pursed her lips, but said nothing. Gundert frequented the Club; after the way he had refused to acknowledge Devanna when they had gone to seek Appu's admission into the mission school, she knew Devanna was trying to spare his old mentor the embarrassment of a chance meeting. Besides, Devi had little in common with the Coorg women who spent their evenings there. 'A flock of sparrows,' she thought, 'tittering in their borrowed feathers.' Her world was here, in the estate and with the children. Clubs and such like, where was the time for such frippery?

Coorg had the loveliest summer it had enjoyed in years. The ficus hybrid that Gundert had planted all along the wall of the mission was in full bloom, carpeting the stones in pink and mauve. The White Elephant sale that the Church ladies organised against its backdrop was a roaring success, with everyone getting quite silly, really, on the home-brewed gooseberry and ginger wines.

The war, meanwhile, burned on. 'Sentiment is turning increasingly ugly,' the concerned Home Board of the Mission wrote to its stations around the world, summoning its missionaries home. Gundert refused to leave.

'My work,' he wrote to the authorities, with painful, arthritic fingers, 'is here.'

Devanna was limping towards the house one sunny, golden evening, carting a bag of eggshells that he had been crushing into the rose beds, when he stopped, shading his eyes as he looked towards the drive. An Austin stood parked there, the black gloss of its chassis evident despite the dust. He sighed. Yet another guest come to remark on the garden. He made his reluctant way to the verandah, where Devi's expression told him at once that the guests were discussing something entirely different.

'Mr Devanna.' It was Gordon Braithwaite, a beefy stranger by his side.

'May I introduce you to Colonel Bidders?'

Devanna shook the gentleman's hand, murmuring a welcome and easing himself awkwardly into a cane chair.

'Surely you've heard,' Braithwaite was continuing, 'of Bidders Academy?' Indeed Devanna had. It was a school for boys, very prestigious, located in the low hills of Ootacamund about a hundred and fifty miles south of Coorg. He nodded and looked curiously at the Colonel.

Bidders, it turned out, was on a quest. The school had been in operation for some time now, with the last five graduating classes having done rather well for themselves at Trinity and Balliol. However, he said, taking a large swallow of freshly squeezed orange juice, he wanted more Indians to enrol.

'Captain Balmer,' he said. 'I don't know if you're familiar with the name?' Devanna shook his head, bemused. 'Retired now. Early retirement from the army after the Frontier affair of 1908. Saw action at Mohmand with the Lancers. Quite a battle from all accounts. He was promoted immediately after, but war injuries prevented him from serving much longer. He's back in England now. Decent chap, met him in London earlier this year.' He had another go at the juice.

'Told him about my upcoming trip to Coorg, which is when he talked to me about his orderly. Also from Coorg . . .' The Colonel fished about in his pocket for a square of paper. 'Ah. Sepoy Machaiah.

'Balmer is convinced that the only reason he is alive is because of the Sepoy's actions. Says he tried to get the man a citation of bravery after the battle. Unfortunately too few survivors, no eye witnesses except for Balmer's account, and he had been grievously wounded himself, hard even for him to know what was true and what he'd imagined . . . Still, when I told him about my plans to visit Coorg – superb hunting in these parts,' the Colonel added, beaming, 'took down two bison last week – Balmer talked to me about the Sepoy's son. I hear you have taken the orphan under your wing. What do you think about enrolling the boy in my academy?'

Devanna glanced troubled at Devi. She was sitting ramrod straight in her chair, her hands twisting the ends of her sari.

'No need to decide now, of course,' Bidders added, fanning himself with his sola topee, 'but do give it some thought. Our academy can offer the boy so much more than a local school can, no offence to the Mission.'

'Well,' Braithwaite slapped his hands on his thighs. 'A pleasure as always, Mrs Devanna,' he said, beaming. He turned to Devanna. 'May I trouble you for a quick look at your phlox before I take my leave? The wife has heard so much about it, it would behoove me well to give her an account.'

'Yes, yes, of course . . .' Devanna stood up, fumbling with his walking stick. He took a step forward, starting as there was a loud crunch underfoot. 'It's nothing,' he said as Braithwaite shot out a hand, 'eggshells . . . for the roses, I forgot they were here.'

Devanna showed them around the garden, and seeing them off with cuttings of phlox and orchids, waited, a hand raised in farewell as the Austin turned out of the gates. Devi was sitting on the verandah where they had left her, staring unhappily into space.

'Devi,' he said, 'he doesn't have to go.'

'You heard what he said,' she responded heavily. 'It's one of the finest schools available.'

'The hostel ...' he began, as Martin Thomas' face loomed suddenly from the past. He swatted at a bee that had drunkenly followed him in from the phlox. 'The hostel,' he repeated, trying to keep his voice even. 'The ragging can get ... it can be hard.'

She gave a small noncommittal shrug, her eyes clouded. 'You know he can take care of himself.'

'No. You don't know, you have *no idea* how bad it can get. He doesn't need to go.' His voice was sharp now. 'The mission school is fine, at least we have him here with us.'

She turned to look at him then, still abstracted.

'The ragging,' Devanna said again. 'If they give him a rough time there ...'

'*Everyone* likes Appu,' she said wearily, standing up to leave.

She announced the decision at the dining table a week later.

'The Bidder Academy? *Really?*'

'Yes. She tried to smile, placing another otti on Appu's already full plate. 'You will join them next term.'

'The *Bidder* Academy? Avvaiah, they have sports coaches for hockey and tennis, *and* they have a swimming pool.'

'Yes, yes ... Nanju,' she looked wanly at him as he listened to the exchange. 'I know you have just one year left to complete at the mission school, but since your brother is going to Bidders ... if you want to go as well ...'

'Yes, oh yes Nanju,' Appu interjected, 'you have to come too.'

Nanju shook his head in alarm. 'No,' he spluttered, 'I'm not leaving Nari Malai!'

A deep pall of gloom settled over Devi at the thought of Appu leaving. She lay in her bed that night, unable to sleep long after the lamps had been extinguished. Even the house, with little creaks and groans, like an old man settling down to rest, fell at last into slumber while Devi remained awake.

Throwing off the blankets, she went to the window. The moon was so bright that even the colours of the flowers were visible, the night tinted an otherworldly blue. Her thoughts drifted to the dead soldiers once more. Devanna read aloud from the newspapers each morning, visibly distressed as he recounted the number of casualties. India had contributed in large numbers to the war; over forty thousand Indian soldiers were dead. Turkey, Kut, Africa, France . . .

It had affected Devi deeply, the thought of those lost men. 'Who will cremate them?' she would wonder to herself. Their mothers, their wives, how they must grieve . . .

Her eyes wandered over the hedge, abloom with masses of fragrant Night Queen, past the arbour of bougainvillea and the small grove of sampigé trees. So many lost, she thought again. What would become of their ghosts, she wondered, the veera trapped in foreign lands not of their choosing? At least, she reminded herself heavily, they had sent Machu's remains home.

She gazed disconsolately at the lotus pond and the silver-lipped lotuses trailing its length. From the upstairs windows, the pond was no longer an abstract, its design clearly apparent. Devanna had shaped it in the image of a woman's head. The back of it, with a long, winding plait cascading down. Devi unconsciously touched a hand to her hair. Would the school wardens feed Appu enough eggs in the morning? He liked his eggs scrambled, with ginger and tomatoes. Seven ottis the boy could put away at one sitting, with three, sometimes four pats of fresh butter . . .

An owl swooped past the window. Devi froze. It was said that if the cry of an owl sounded like *tikki-per, tikki-perrr*, it was a good omen. *Kuttichood, kuttichood*, on the other hand . . . pierce and burn, it meant, *pierceandburn*. She watched, her heart racing as the bird flew silently over the lawn and disappeared. Wandering to the dressing table, she fiddled with the jar of cream that sat gleaming in the moonlight.

For many years after Machu died, Devi had lost all interest in her appearance. Her monthly blood had stopped immediately after he had passed. It had seemed only fitting; a private marking of grief, an internal

308

tombstone for the past. It had not even occurred to her to seek medical counsel.

Slowly however, traces of the old vanity had resurfaced. Tukra's wife massaged warm coconut oil into her hands and feet every day before her bath. There was a small earthenware bowl at the edge of the washbasin, filled with gram flour for washing her face; when the workers hauled in honeycombs from the massive beehives that hung from the shade trees in the estate, Devi always reserved some of the honey to dab onto her skin.

It had been Devanna who had ordered that first jar of face cream for her, years ago, from the Selfridges catalogue. He had said nothing about it, merely bidding Tukra to leave it, shellac pink and perfumed with roses, by her bed. Devi, too, never acknowledged the gift, but months later, she made a point of remarking at the breakfast table that she was nearing the bottom of the jar.

She had not objected when Devanna ordered a replacement, nor when he had begun to do so faithfully, one every six months. Devi carefully washed out the empty jars. A couple she kept on her dressing table to hold safety pins and hair clips, three more she had pressed into use in the prayer room, to store vibhuti, camphor and sandalwood powder. The remainder she saved, every last one of them, in the trunk that lay beneath her bed, telling herself that the only reason she did so was that their crystalline exteriors were *far* too pretty to discard.

She tossed the jar now, from hand to hand, pressing her fingers into the starbursts etched into its sides as she continued to fret over Appu. Would the school know how to tend to the nosebleeds he suffered from during the monsoon, to have him lie down with a cold spoon against his back? What about the fresh buffalo milk the child so liked to drink? On and on she worried as the grandfather clock downstairs called out the hours, until, laying the jar down at last with a sigh, Devi curled up in her bed and tried to get some sleep.

The weeks passed. Devi insisted that she escort Appu to the school, brushing off Devanna's suggestion that it might be more appropriate for him to accompany the child.

'Devi, if you must go, I will accompany you, it is not proper for you to travel all that distance without a chaperone.'

'Don't be foolish. If you come too, then who is to look after Nanju?'

When it came time to leave, for an instant it looked as if both boys might tear up as they bid each other farewell. And then boxing Nanju on the arm, Appu dimpled. 'You are going to regret this, you know. When I come back and tell you all that I have been up to in Ooty . . .'

Nanju in turn cuffed him on the head. 'Huh. I am looking forward to some peace and quiet without you crashing about here at Nari Malai.'

'Tell me at once, remember,' Devanna said to Appu, his face drawn. 'If *anybody* there gets tough with you, don't retaliate. Just let me know and we will handle it, you hear?'

'Cheh,' Devi spluttered, 'what rubbish are you teaching him? You listen to me Appu,' she said fiercely. 'If anyone gets tough with you, you get even tougher with them!'

So militant did Devi look that Nanju and Appu glanced at one another, then burst out laughing.

They drove down to Ooty, Devi and Appu, in the new Austin. Devi talked brightly all the while, falling finally silent as the car turned a corner and the red brick buildings and sprawling lawns of the school came into view.

'Bidders!' Appu whooped, thrusting his head from the window of the car, the wind ruffling his hair.

The chauffeur carried his trunks up to the dorm as Devi and he walked the grounds, inspecting the pool, the tennis courts and the sports fields. Appu ran his hand lovingly over his new hockey stick, barely listening as Devi told him yet again to 'eatwell-brushregularly-studyhard-sayhisprayerseverynight-andwritehomeoften'.

'Yes Avvaiah,' he agreed. He was itching to try out the stick. He swung it gently back and forth, testing the heft of the wood against his palm.

A bell rang somewhere in the recesses of the hostel. The teachers began to make polite noises and parents, taking the hint, reluctantly began to leave. Devi smoothed Appu's hair back from his forehead. 'Be good, now you hear, kunyi? And write often, I'll be waiting for your letters.'

'Yes Avvaiah,' he said, scuffing the dust with the stick.

'My darling child. My sun and moon, my sun and moon,' she said, turning away so he wouldn't see her tears.

Chapter 27

Barely had the car pulled out of the drive than Appu took off at a loping run towards the grounds. 'Oy,' one of the boys called after him, 'didn't you hear the warden? Attendance in fifteen minutes, he said.' Appu grinned, not bothering with a response as he disappeared round the side of the hostel towards the sports field.

'Stop,' he ordered the sweeper who was leisurely clearing the field of leaves. 'Move, I want to play.'

The sweeper looked doubtful for an instant, and then setting aside his broom, he ambled to the edge.

Appu set down the ball and glanced briefly about him as he straightened up, taking the measure of the field. He swung the stick experimentally from side to side, absorbed in the weight of it in his hands. Fixing his gaze firmly on the ball, Appu began to dribble. Slowly at first, as he got acquainted with the new stick. Gradually he picked up speed, dribbling faster and faster, breaking into a wide, unconscious grin as the stick responded to his touch. Up and down the length of the field Appu ran, weaving this way and that, effortlessly driving the ball before him.

When the warden spotted him from the hostel windows and bellowed out, 'Come in at *once*, youngster,' Appu did not even look up, focused solely on his game. The irate warden came rushing down the stairs and out to the field.

Half the new class hung out of the hostel windows to watch. 'Crazy bugger!' they commiserated, watching the warden descend upon Appu. 'He's in for it now!'

Appu barely turned a hair, however, as he turned to smile pleasantly at the warden. 'No sir, I did not hear the bell,' he said, quite reasonably. 'No sir, I did not know the field is closed at 6 p.m.'

'Yes sir, of course, at once.' Scooping up the ball with a flick of his stick, he put it in his pocket and loped back to the hostel, whistling.

The warden stared irritably at his retreating figure, aware that the wind had been neatly taken out of his sails, but uncertain quite how that had happened. 'You,' he shouted, turning his annoyance towards the sweeper. 'Oaf. What were you doing encouraging the boy? Don't you know sports are not allowed this late?'

'Saar, yes saar,' the sweeper mumbled, picking up his broom and whisking it smartly, double-quick across the field.

Captain Balmer posted Appu a fat package of Cadbury's chocolate and, with the parcel, a letter congratulating him on his admission to Bidders. 'Your father was a fine man,' he wrote. 'Should you grow up to fill only half his shoes, I would still know you to be head and shoulders above most men. I shall be following your progress at Bidders with interest; should there be anything you require, do not hesitate to ask.'

The year passed in the most amiable fashion. It was a casual, natural leadership Appu exuded, and there was no sport, it seemed, that he did not excel in. He became the centre forward of the junior hockey league. He was a star cross-country runner and a critical part of the swim and tennis teams. All of which served, in a sports-mad school such as Bidders, to propel him to the forefront of popularity.

It did not hurt either, that he had access to eye-poppingly large sums of pocket money. All he had to do was telegraph Avvaiah – for tennis lessons, he explained at first, or a school trip, but soon, even those explanations stopped. They were not needed – twenty rupees, his telegraphs would say, or fifteen, or thirty, and within the week, the money appeared magically in his account. It never occurred to Devi to ask for an explanation. What could the child spend the money on after all? A few more cakes at the tuck shop perhaps, but where was the harm in that?

And indeed, Appu was generous, treating anyone who asked to chocolates and milk sweets, but he soon discovered the far more exciting privileges that money could buy. The school had in its employment a roster of youngsters from the local villages to tend to the school grounds, to clean the masters' quarters and man the gates. It was an open secret in the hostel that for the right price, any of these enterprising fellows, the watchmen especially, could be persuaded to smuggle in ciggies, comics and even booze. Appu promptly pressed them into service. It was an unthinking authority that he imposed on them, the same that Devi might employ with her own workers, a superiority so rooted in obvious privilege that the watchmen automatically obeyed.

Many of the coffee pickers at Nari Malai came from regions outside Coorg and, along with the Kanarese that he spoke fluently, Appu had also absorbed a smattering of Malayalam and Tamil. The watchmen were thrilled that the young sir could converse with them in their own tongue. 'Come to our hut, anna,' they invited, and Appu visited often after school hours, squatting on his haunches and smoking their beedis.

After each term ended, Appu headed immediately back to Nari Malai, his trunks loaded with sports trophies that Devi polished to a shine with tamarind paste and placed in a custom-built rosewood cabinet in the foyer. She fretted incessantly over him. 'How thin you have become, legs like a chicken's! Such fat fees I pay and still they can't feed you properly?'

'I've grown taller Avvaiah, that's all,' Appu would point out amused, but this Devi would ignore as she hurried to the kitchen. Nanju would glance at Appu then, half jealous of all the fuss. It was hard for him to remain irritated though, not with Appu winking comically at him behind their mother's back – '*Like a chicken*? Not even a cockerel, but a *chicken*? More like it is Avvaiah who is the funny old hen, huh Nanju? Pwuuck, pwuuck, pwuuck . . .' and generally doing such a perfect imitation of Devi's lamentations that Nanju would burst out laughing.

The idyll of holidays ended, Appu would return to Bidders, pockets heavy with cash and his trunks loaded with tuck. Devanna wrote to him regularly and every once in a while, there was a laboriously written affair from Nanju. He wrote about the college he would be attending next summer. The forms had been filled in; it was a fine institution, people said, one of the few in the country to have been chartered by the State.

Devanna sent Appu the details of Nanju's leaving. Nanju would be graduating in agricultural studies at the University of Mysore, he wrote. The King of Mysore had sent his experts on a five-year field trip around the world, he wrote, and the university had been established based on the promotion of original research (University of Chicago), the extension of knowledge (University of Wisconsin) and the promulgation of an educational system that would train its students for political and social life (Universities of Oxford and Cambridge).

Devanna's letters always ended with the same: Your mother sends her love and her blessings. She asks that you make sure to eat properly and not be shy in asking the masters for more tiffin should you be hungry. Please, son, keep us informed of your progress. Let me know at once should anyone treat you roughly.

It was while he was in his second year at Biddies that Appu learnt of the KCIO programme. When he returned to Coorg in the summer of 1918, he had an important announcement to make. 'Avvaiah,' he said excitedly, 'I am going to apply for the King's Commission.'

Devi looked bewildered. 'The what?'

'The KCIO programme . . . King's Commissioned Indian Officers.' Devanna elaborated. 'The war – with so many Indian soldiers sacrificed to its cause, Indian politicians have been pushing for Indians to be allowed into the Army as officers of rank, not just as troops. It's been all over the newspapers. The programme is very selective, only a few seats to be released each year, and there is a strict interview process. The chosen few will receive the King's Commission, and be allowed to command even British troops.'

'Yes!' Appu nodded vigorously, his hair falling into his eyes. 'The KCIO, Avvaiah! I could be a general in the Army one day!'

Devi smiled. 'The Army, is it? Like your father? We'll see, we'll see . . .'

'A *general*, can you imagine? Ayy Tukra,' he called to the Poleya who was pottering around the dining room, wiping the afternoon dust from the window sills, 'did you hear? You better learn to salute me.'

'Saloot?' Tukra asked interested. 'But how do you do this saloot?'

Appu leapt from his chair and, spinning Tukra around, raised the latter's hand to his forehead. 'There. Like so, *this* is a salute. Now stand still so we can admire you.'

So ridiculous did Tukra look, standing stiffly to attention, fingers splayed in an awkward salute, the ubiquitous dust cloth hanging from his shoulder like some faulty epaulette, that they all began to laugh.

'Oh, don't listen to him Tukra,' Devi said amused. 'Mr General Sir,' she said to Appu, 'sit down and finish your lunch.'

So insistent was the political pressure on the Government that the KCIO policy was promptly implemented, and in October 1918, the first batch of Indian cadets was initiated into the programme. Devanna sent Appu a clipping from the newspapers. Only fifty seats had been released. There had been seventy applicants from all over the country, scions of the finest families in the land, even royals from the houses of Kapurthala, Baroda, Jamnagar and Jind. Despite the fifty vacancies, just forty-two candidates were deemed promising enough to be admitted into the programme, and among them, there was a Coorg. 'Nineteen-year-old Cariappa,' Devanna wrote, 'will be among the first KCIOs in the country. Should he set a strong example, it will only bolster your own application.'

Balmer was highly supportive of Appu's ambition. 'Nothing would make me happier, and, I suspect, your father, if he were alive, more proud. If you should need recommendations,' he wrote, 'I would be honoured to provide you with mine.'

A month later, the war ended, a ceasefire coming into effect at 11 a.m. on the 11th of November 1918 – the eleventh hour of the eleventh day of the eleventh month, and almost mid way through Appu's third year at Bidders. The principal gave the boys a half day to celebrate the Allied victory. Restless and irritated because it meant that there would be no hockey practice that evening, Appu wandered over to the watchmen's hut. He took a deep puff of a beedi, the acrid smoke searing his lungs. Suddenly a thought struck him.

'You all, what is it that you do for fun?' he asked the watchmen, squinting at them through the smoke. 'No, not gilli danda. What do you take me for, an idiot? Not childhood games, what do you do for *real* fun?'

The watchmen looked at one another, hemmed and hawed for a bit, and then told him about the cockfights held in their village.

They were not *actually* held, mind you, how could they be, when they had been banned by the local magistrate? They were a respectable, law-abiding lot. Ask any of the villagers and they would vehemently deny ever having laid eyes on a fighting cockerel, let alone having had anything to do with attending or organising a fight. Still, when the moon was high, and the locally brewed arrack flowed freely ... now and again, something might be arranged.

The local policemen were invited to share in the booze and partake of the winnings from the fight, and by the next morning, cockfight? What cockfight?

When it became known in the hostel that Appu had somehow arranged an illicit cockfight, his already prominent star rose among the seniors. He greased the palms of the watchmen generously and their collective conscience prickled only briefly. It was a sizable contingent of boys that slipped out of the school gates the evening of the fight. 'Quickly, come,' the guide sent from the village urged them nervously, leading them to a natural dip in the land that lay to the side of the settlement. A makeshift ring had been demarcated by sticks, illuminated by a single, reedy lantern. Two stringy looking cockerels were pushed squawking into the ring and with a low whistle from someone, the fight officially began.

At first the birds tried to escape, desperately flapping their clipped wings, but they were pushed unceremoniously back inside the ring. Resigning themselves at last to the fact that there was no way out, they flew viciously at one another, clawing, pecking and ripping with their specially sharpened beaks. The boys stared transfixed, some ashen, some with faces flushed, each unable to tear his eyes away from the torn feathers, the trails of dark blood that ran thicker and thicker down the cartilaginous legs of the birds. They shouted too, along with the villagers, hoarse cries of excitement and encouragement, urging, cursing, willing the exhausted, faltering cockerels forward, until at last one of them keeled over into the dust.

A cheer went up through the crowd and money swiftly changed hands as, with a final, swift wringing of their necks, the bodies of both cockerels, the vanquished as well as the victor, were tossed aside.

Later that night, when one of the seniors reached into his pocket, it took Appu some seconds to grasp fully what it was that had been placed in his hands.

He had heard about it of course, every boy in Biddies had. One of the seniors had filched the miniature from his father's library. It featured a woman, Appu knew, in a wondrous state of undress. One of his classmates claimed he had even got a peek at the painting before the senior, whose room he had been cleaning, had spotted him and soundly boxed his ears. Unfortunately, the painting had been lying face down and he had not seen very much.

It was an old Mughal miniature, the ivory on which it was painted dulled and yellowed with the years, the lapis lazuli along its rim missing here and there.

The artist's muse was a young woman, luxuriating in her bath, her head arched to expose the single strand of pearls looped about her throat. He eyes were shut, her lips, a rosebud red, partly open. A gauzy veil lay across her body, revealing more than it hid. Apart from that, she was unabashedly naked.

Appu's heart began to race as he devoured her with his eyes, the tips of her breasts, the alabaster whiteness of her belly. The whorls of hair peeping from between her legs.

'Down boy,' the senior snickered. 'Never seen one of *these* before, have you?'

Appu was struck dumb. He barely slept that night, consumed by what he had seen and sweating uncomfortably in his bed. The next evening, he went to the watchmen's hut with a proposition. They must have family working in the tea plantations in the area. Erotica, he told them. Smut. It would likely be in the master study, or in the bedroom. 'Check the drawers,' he told them. 'Filch some for me and I'll pay you well.'

They had gaped at his request. 'But what if we are caught?'

Appu laughed. 'Don't worry. This is one theft that will never be reported to the police. Think of the shame. Don't worry,' he repeated insouciantly, 'I'll make it worth your while.'

Christmas came around and Appu left for Coorg once more. 'Avvaiah,' he said suddenly one afternoon at lunch, 'we should change the name of the estate. Nari Malai is so provincial. Let's call it Tiger Hills instead. English.'

'What? Come on Appu, we are going to do no such . . .' Nanju began, but Devi looked fondly at this fancy son of hers.

'Machu,' she thought, 'you would be so amused.'

'No,' she said to Nanju, 'he's right. We should move with the times. Tiger Hills it is.'

Nanju said nothing more, but he was especially quiet when Appu found him later that afternoon, sitting beside the birdhouse. When Appu finished a long and especially wicked story about one of the boys at Biddies and Nanju didn't so much as crack a smile, Appu looked at him quizzically.

'Nanju,' he said lightly, 'if it means so much to you, call it Nari Malai. It was just a thought, that's all.'

Nanju shrugged, apparently absorbed in the birdhouse.

'C'mon man, you're . . .'

'Is there *anything* she won't do for you?' Nanju said suddenly. 'Ask her for the sun the next time, why don't you, along with the moon and all the stars in the sky?'

Appu chuckled and, throwing back his head, began to sing the ditty they had come up with at Biddies. It was an ode to the draconian nurse who manned the infirmary. He had taught it to Nanju and they substituted certain key words whenever Devi and Devanna were in earshot; not that Devi would understand anyway.

> *A rich girl uses vaseline,*
> *A poor girl uses lard*
> *Nursie likes axle grease,*
> *Her* punt *is old and hard.*

Despite himself, Nanju's lips began to twitch. He sighed, and then, cuffing his brother lightly on the head to acknowledge the blatant change of subject, he joined in the ditty as well.

It was the following spring, almost at the tail end of the school year, when the watchmen finally sent word to Appu. A tea boy in one of the plantations had found something that would interest the young sir. The wait had been well worth it, Appu discovered, stunned at the prize the watchmen delivered.

It was a stack of daguerreotypes, each lovingly framed in gilt. There were two women, gently disrobing each other. A creamy shoulder exposed in one frame; a flutter of fingers, a length of leg in the next. A corset, coming delicately undone, until soon, they were spread-eagled on a lace bedspread, frolicking with abandon under the hearts and knots carved into the headboard above.

The daguerreotypes passed into legend at Biddies. For years to come, they would be handed from one graduating class to another, lovingly fondled by so many hands that the gilt frames grew dull, the identities of the two beauties infused by a hundred active imaginations.

They sealed fifteen-year-old Appu's standing at school for good – Dags, the boys now called him, the deliverer of the daguerreotype legacy, and Dags he would forever remain to a certain social circle, even when they were old and grizzled, with barely the strength to walk.

The summer of 1920 dawned especially hot and dusty. Coorg lay parched under rainless skies. Twice already that year, there had been jungle fires. A gooseberry had withered perhaps, somewhere in the arid jungle. The fruit had burned under the relentless sun until, deadened, it had snapped free of its bough and spiralled to the ground below. Maybe it had hit a rock, and so hard was the dried berry, the effect was not unlike a catapult being aimed at the boulder from a considerable height. The impact of its fall set off a spark, which caught the surrounding grass. The undergrowth was as dry as kindling and the ensuing fire spread far before finally being contained by the Forest Department.

People would talk for years afterwards of the detritus the fire had left in its wake. The swathes of soot that had hung in the air for weeks; the black, twisted corpses of animals too weak or too small to have escaped. Some even claimed to have seen the tantric, dancing triumphantly in the flames, but this of course was never proven.

The heat wave continued, shrinking the rivers to trickles of muddy water. Birds dropped dead from the trees. The Coorgs sliced open vast heaps of tender coconuts for their sweet, cooling water while the white-folk relied on pitcher upon pitcher of iced tea.

A large jugful stood on the table in the Reverend's apartments, and his guest sighed as he poured himself another glass. He was a fellow missionary from the region; with the war ended, he had made his way back to India. 'Berlin has become a city of ghouls, Hermann. Hardly any men left from the war, and those who are left are on the street corners. Most are missing limbs, an arm, a leg, sometimes more. There are no jobs for them, the factories are shut. Our soldiers sell whatever they can – matchboxes, hairbrushes, shoelaces, flowers robbed from freshly dug graves, gasoline from parked automobiles. It breaks one's heart to see them. "Me," they shout, "buy from me."'

Gundert listened, filled with a profound sadness. The weekend after the armistice, he had held a midnight mass at the Church. 'For all the lives lost, for all those torn asunder.'

'Amen.'

The Club had thrown a dance afterwards, to celebrate the Allied victory. They had politely sent Gundert an invitation, but he could not find it in himself to attend.

'You did not leave I heard, all through the war?' his colleague continued. 'Was it . . . have things been all right for you here?'

'Ja.' Gundert turned to look at the garden, the lawn turned a parched, dusty brown.

He thought suddenly of his own village, of the fir trees tipped with frost. His mother used to mull wine with orange peel and spices, filling the house with the delicious aroma of nutmeg and cloves. During the holidays, Gundert was allowed a cup now and again. It was one of his happiest memories: Olaf and he, coming in laughing from the sleet, the air so cold it hurt to breathe. His fingers stiff, frozen from the cold, and then the wine, warming his hands as they cupped the gently steaming glass.

'The ice cubes have all melted,' he said heavily. He reached forward to swirl the pitcher of tea, the light mottling his skin. 'Shall I ask for more?'

*

Appu came home for the holidays once more. A school chum invited him to join the family at the Club one evening.

'Come along, don't you want to see what they get up to in that fancy schmancy club?' Appu urged Nanju, but the latter was having none of it.

'No, certainly not, whatever am I going to do there? No Appu, you go.'

Appu walked into the Club, the easy swing of his stride, the width of his shoulders and his impressive height all serving to belie his seventeen years. Even Devi had been startled at how much he had grown this past term. She barely came up to his chest now, needing to reach up on her tiptoes to brush his hair back from his forehead and that, too, only when he indulgently tilted his head towards her. Nonetheless, the gangliness that so afflicted boys his age had passed Appu by. He carried the extra inches well.

He glanced about him, affecting a blasé expression, as if he had been frequenting the Club all his life. He took in the thick red curtains, the pall of smoke that hung over the card tables, the waiters standing ready just beyond the light of the lanterns. 'The billiards room,' his friend's father suggested, 'would you boys like to give it a go?' Appu bent over the billiards table, and from the way the balls sped across the green baize, one would have been forgiven for thinking that he had been playing the sport forever.

There was a hearty round of applause at the end of the game. Someone offered to buy both boys a drink. 'Ah, it's OK laddies, you're old enough. Not so long ago, youngsters your age were getting drafted, weren't they?'

Liquid fire. Appu held the glass of whisky up to the lamps, examining the pale golden swirl of the alcohol. Suddenly aglow with bonhomie, he threw back his head and guffawed. His voice had cracked the previous year and already it was baking into a deep, rich baritone.

So penetrating was his laugh that it carried into the ladies' cloister. Kate Burnett glanced towards the sound. Who was that, she wondered, as she took in the spreading hulk of Appu's shoulders. There was an air of *youth* about him, like the scent of a new leaf in spring.

Appu caught her looking at him, the frankness of her appraisal making him flush. He turned away in confusion, then, annoyed at how easily she had punctured his composure, he swivelled on the barstool back towards her. Taking a long, iced swallow from his drink, he returned her gaze, his eyes boldly raking over every inch of her, from the bob that shone like polished mahogany, to the pointed tips of her shoes.

Kate arched an eyebrow at his insolence, the corners of her lips contriving to lift slightly at the same time in amusement.

She turned back to the women, ignoring him. To his annoyance, Appu found his eyes returning to her again and again through the remainder of the evening.

He had been unable to get her out of his head, when his friend invited him to the Club again the following week. Appu eagerly accepted. He dressed with care, setting Tukra to polishing his oxfords for a good hour, but to his disappointment, she was nowhere to be seen that evening.

'Mrs Burnett? The pretty, brown-haired one? I suppose she must be home – her husband travels a great deal I've heard,' his friend said vaguely.

Appu was surprised at how let down he had felt by her absence. He thought of Mrs Burnett a great deal over the next days, showing Nanju the package of FLs he had bought, *just in case*.

'French Letters. You do know what these are for, don't you?'

Nanju nodded sheepishly. 'Yes.'

Appu boxed him on the shoulder. 'So you do want a few? For the lovelies in your college? It's OK, I have more.'

It took three more visits to the Club before he saw Mrs Burnett again. He looked anxiously at her and to his enormous relief, she remembered him. She tilted her head in a mock salute, her earrings swinging delicately against her hair.

Midway through the evening, a bearer handed him a note. Appu excused himself to visit the men's room where he unfolded the note. 'BELVEDERE ESTATE,' it said simply. 'Tomorrow. 3 p.m.'

The paper smelt faintly of her perfume. Appu held it to his nose, eyes shut, as he took in its fragrance. And then scrunching the note into a ball, he threw it into the chamber pot.

Chapter 28

~ 1920 ~

Catherine Burnett was bored. It was nearly five years since she had first come to Coorg. She had met Edward at a social in London where the bulk of his frame had immediately caught her eye. It had not been long before they were affianced, and soon he was writing to her from his estate in India, describing cool, lush Coorg, the thick jungles and ancient, forgotten stone temples, the waterfalls that spilled down mountainsides and evenings filled with fireflies. Kate had been enchanted, a spell that would last well into their marriage. And then gradually, she wasn't even sure exactly when or why, the bloom had begun to fade from the rose.

'The coffee,' she would correct herself in a private, wistful joke, 'the aroma has begun to fade from the coffee.'

Edward had bought another estate, this time in South Coorg where the soil was particularly fertile and coffee yields were said to be exceptional. Unfortunately, it meant that he was gone for days at a stretch, leaving Kate to her own devices in their sprawling bungalow. At first she hadn't minded – she had been planning to redecorate anyway, and besides, the separations brought a certain . . . *frisson* to their marriage. But after she had finished refurbishing, and with the gardens landscaped and manicured to perfection, an ennui had crept in.

Edward would come home, tired and laden with the frustrations of a new estate; he would kiss her absently on the forehead, oblivious to the new dress she had put on especially for him. They went to the Club regularly when he was in town, but even that had grown dreary. The same faces every time, the same gossipy conversations.

The evening that she noticed Appu, Edward and she had had a '*disagreement*', as he preferred to call their fights. She had been, oh, she didn't know, a trifle on edge perhaps, brought on by the fact that he was leaving for the other estate again in a couple of days. He had patiently explained, yet again, that the estate was not quite there yet, another year perhaps and then . . .

'Another year?' she had protested. 'Edward, another year is simply too long for us to carry on like this. You are hardly here, we hardly ever meet . . . it is simply *far* too long.'

'Come Katie,' he had said, in that calm tone that so deflated her. 'Must you exaggerate so? We spend a great deal of time together, why, I have been here all this past fortnight.'

She had stared at him in frustration and then she had sighed. When he put it so rationally, her outburst did seem a little ridiculous. Still, she longed to do something, smash some porcelain perhaps, or fling the china against the door. Maybe *then* he would raise his voice.

A vague restlessness had remained within her as they motored down to the Club and she barely noticed the sunset washing in through the windows of the car. She had smiled wanly at Edward as he escorted her to the ladies' room, 'Thank you darling,' and joined the women who were busy dissecting the shoes someone had worn at the summer picnic.

'Worn down at the heels, did you notice?'

'One can always tell good breeding – just look at the shoes, my mother always said, they will tell you everything you need to know about a person . . .'

Kate glanced surreptitiously at her own patent T bars. She made sure the servants kept a flannel cloth in the glove compartment of the car at all times, but she had been so preoccupied this evening that she had quite forgotten to brush off her shoes after the drive here, and their tops were clearly dusty. With a fluid movement, Kate moved her feet under the sofa, contriving to turn and look at the billiards room as she did so.

He had laughed then, right at that moment. 'Who is that?' she had wondered interestedly. Definitely not one of the regulars. Very young of course, but there was something about the set of his jaw, the shape of his head . . .

He had turned, and catching her eye, had quite adorably blushed in confusion. Something had sparked within Kate. The realisation, perhaps, of the power she wielded over this not quite boy, not quite man, the ability to make the blood rush to his head merely by looking at him.

The women around her were still prattling on when he returned the favour, twisting around at the bar to stare at her. Kate knew she should look away, but she didn't. She held the lad's gaze, unflinching as he took her in slowly, from head to foot. When she finally turned away, to her surprise, her pulse was racing.

'Five years,' her cousin had said to her once in London. 'Five years is how long it takes to develop an attraction for the natives. And, oh Katie, once you do, there's no going back.' Kate had laughed nervously, looking over her shoulder to make sure her mother was nowhere near, before pressing for more details. Her cousin lived in Kenya – 'a continent apart, but we are both bound by coffee,' she had pointed out to Kate.

'It happens gradually in Africa,' she confided. 'At first glance, the natives appear crass. So sooty skinned that, really, they seem almost alien, a completely different species from you and me. All one sees is the crookedness of their hair and the flatness of their noses. And then slowly, one's eyes adjust to the African light and they open to the beauty of the natives. You begin to marvel at the gloss of their skin. You see the nobility in their features and envy them the whiteness of their teeth. You see how gracefully they move against the open landscape, how deeply rooted they seem to the earth until it's *us* who seem not to belong there. Ah Katie, Katie. Before you know it, like an itch that blossoms from the very root of you, you begin to *yearn* for their touch.'

It had happened slowly with Kate, just as her cousin had predicted. When Kate first arrived in Coorg, while she had not been *repulsed* by the locals, she had not been attracted to them either. In the past months, however, she had begun to notice things that she not before. She watched the husbands of the Coorg women at the Club; the fluidity of their movements, the hair that sprang thickly from their foreheads. The unfreckled skin, tinted tea and clotted cream, honey gold, or a rich, brooding coffee. She stared at their hands, at the shape and girth of them, guiltily imagining them moving over her. She began to flirt with them, just the odd glance, leaning in just a shade closer than was warranted at dances, as she whispered in their ears.

All harmless, of course, and perfectly discreet; she was just keeping herself amused.

So it was that she sent Appu the note. 'Just tea,' she told herself, 'there's nothing wrong with being hospitable to the lad. What does it matter, really, if Edward is away?' Still, to ease her qualms, she told him about it, casually, that evening.

'Hrmm?' he said, preoccupied with his accounts. 'Yes, of course dear, as you wish . . .'

Maybe it was his utter lack of jealousy that irked her, but Kate took especial care with her appearance the next day, staining her lips a deep shade of oxblood and dabbing eau de parfum behind her ears and in the hollow of her throat.

If anything, Appu had taken even greater pains. He informed nobody of their tryst, merely telling Devi he was going into Mercara. He commandeered the Austin that he had taught himself to drive the previous summer, nodding impatiently through Devi's implorings to be careful. He was giddy with excitement, lightheaded almost. He knew how these things worked – why, hadn't Bobby MacGowan come back to Biddies last year full of goondah stories about his next door auntie?

His heart thudded painfully as he thought of Mrs Burnett. He knew what to do of course, he had practised puckering his lips against his arm, and his pillow, but still . . . He dragged his sleeve across the beads of sweat forming on his forehead, glancing once again at the package resting on the seat of the car. It was a set of lace handkerchiefs that someone had given to Avvaiah. She wouldn't even notice they were gone. It would be OK, he told himself, patting the FLs in his coat pocket.

She was there in the doorway, shushing the dogs and raising a cupped palm to shade her eyes from the sun as she called a playful greeting. She looked devastating, her dress of some devilish material that sparkled as she moved. She kissed him on the cheek as she accepted the hankies, a light touch that tied his stomach in knots. She sat him in the piano room, asking him numerous questions about school, how old he was – 'eighteen,' he lied – and his family. Appu dutifully answered all her questions, shifting uncomfortably in the thin-legged loveseat as he sipped his coffee and tried not to stare at her legs. And then, to his utter confusion, she stood up, and extending a cool hand into his, led him to the door. 'We must do this again,' she told him gaily, 'it has been *ab-so-lutely* lovely.'

Kate invited Appu over for tea thrice after that. Each time, she personally supervised the menu, making one of her rare appearances in the kitchen. Cucumber and tomato sandwiches, crusts removed and cut into triangles. Raisin scones and custard. Coffee marble cake, jam tarts and tiny cocktail sausages, the kind that came in a tin at Hans' trading shop. Eggy hot pots, and a summer fool with mulberries from the estate. 'Remember now, *moisten* the tea cloth before you wrap the sandwiches in it,' she instructed the cook. 'Oh and you can take the afternoon off, tell the other servants as well.' He threw her a look, so filled with knowing insolence that her voice had faltered for an instant. 'What is this?' she had snapped then, pointing at an overflowing pail of vegetable peels. 'I don't pay you to keep my kitchen like a pig sty. Clean up around here *at once*.'

He had scurried to do her bidding, 'Yes madam, doing now only, madam,' but even so, when she had marched from the kitchen, her cheeks were hot.

Appu had accepted each invitation with alacrity, sweating under his collar and thrusting a sprig of wildflowers from the Tiger Hills gardens into her hands one time, a tin of violently coloured sweets the next. She toyed with him, just a little bit more each time, letting the hem of her dress ride up ever so slightly, the sequins at her knees catching the light as she leaned across him for a spoon. *The scent of his skin, like freshly mowed grass. The scent of spring.*

Each time, temptation moistening her legs, sliding through her insides, as she debated taking that final step across the line.

Finally, Appu took the decision out of her hands. He had grown increasingly angry with her questions, with this silly game they seemed to be playing. After the umpteenth pointless query, he slammed down his cup, sending the coffee sloshing into its porcelain saucer. Striding over to Kate, he hauled her from her chair.

'Oh,' Kate began, startled, and then his mouth came down on hers.

For all of Appu's practice, that first kiss was still more ardour than skill. Nonetheless, despite the wetness of his mouth, Kate's breath came hard and fast as she pushed him away. Raising her arm, she slapped Appu across the face with all her tennis-toned strength, so hard that he rocked back on his heels, his hair flopping onto his forehead. She turned towards the door. 'Mrs Burnett,' Appu began shakily, and then he stopped as, rather than storming off as he had expected, she shut the door all the way and locked it.

So young.

Taking a deep breath, she lifted her arms again, this time as if in supplication. 'It's Kate.'

He was at her side in an instant, fumbling as he tried to undo her shift, then pulling it up and over her head instead. He flung it from him and it floated down, a whisper of chiffon and silk pooling on the floor. He looked befuddled at her brassiere and she laughed nervously. *Her mouth felt so dry.* 'The Symington Side Lacer,' she whispered, moistening her lips, 'just the thing to flatten one's bosom into the proper silhouette.'

Her heart was racing, her legs so weak she could barely stand. *His lashes were so ridiculously long.* She took his hands in hers, gliding her thumb over the half moons of his nails and the veins throbbing in his wrists. She raised his palms to her chest, staring deep into those dark, fringed eyes.

'Here,' she said. 'The lacings, untie these.'

If more than a week went by without him seeing Kate, Appu was unable to sleep, rubbing against the sheets for relief and snapping irritably at everyone, a bewildered Devi included. Nanju tried to draw him out, but he was even less inclined than before to join him in his wanderings around the estate or to help clean the birdhouse.

'We need a club membership,' Appu declared suddenly one evening at dinner, and Devi was so relieved that he had finally said something that she immediately acquiesced.

He haunted the billiards table at the Club since it enjoyed the best view of the ladies' corner. He scarcely knew which was worse: not seeing her, or the knowledge that if she was there, then so too was her husband.

And then without warning, one of the bearers would slip a note into his hand. 'THURS. 10 A.M.', and his heart would soar.

'Play for me,' he said once, and she seated herself at the piano, revelling in how comfortable it felt to sit naked upon the stool. It was a short grand piano that Edward had imported from London two years ago for her birthday. He had asked her, as he did every year, precisely a month before the actual day, what it was that she wished for as a gift.

'Surprise me darling!' she had exclaimed. 'Get me something, anything, just surprise me!'

He had pointed out quite reasonably that there was little point in that, what if she did not fancy what he got her?

'Simpler if you just tell me what you'd like, Katie,' he had said. 'That way I can get you exactly what you want.'

Telling herself that he was right, and she was being silly, Kate had eventually suggested a piano. It had taken six men directing the ox cart to bring it up the winding drive, and she had had it installed in the drawing room, overlooking the lawns and the rabbit hutches that bordered it.

It became a ritual of sorts, for Appu and her. She would play for him as he lay there spent, whatever took her fancy. Dreamy, distracted sonatas, crashing chamber pieces and intricate waltzes as the skies changed colour and the clouds shifted shapes beyond the diamond-paned windows that opened onto the grounds.

'Tell me about your parents,' she said once as he lay sprawled across her. Appu shrugged. 'Not much that I haven't told you already – he wanted to be a doctor before his accident, and she runs the estates . . .'

She ran a hand over the warm silk of his back. 'I meant your birth parents, silly. Tell me about them.'

'Not much there either. Father died at the Frontier.' His voice was cool. 'Mother died soon after, and my parents . . . my aunt and uncle, took me under their wing.'

'How did your mother die?'

Appu stiffened imperceptibly. 'She was taken ill,' he lied smoothly.

He raised himself on one elbow, and looked down at her. 'And now, no more questions.'

'But . . .' He trailed a finger down her stomach, making her gasp. 'No more questions,' he repeated, bending towards her.

Kate never quite knew how Edward found out, whether it was that shifty-eyed cook, or one of the other servants. He never actually said anything outright, but one day, when she came in from the garden, something was just . . . different. She had placed the trowels in the gardening basket and reached to kiss his cheek. 'Hello, you. I didn't hear you come in.'

'How long?' That's all he asked, without even looking at her.

They talked then, as they had not in some time, as dinner grew cold and the peas congealed in their gravy. She was free to leave, he said. 'Obviously I have failed you. You are free to go, I shall not prevent you. Do you . . .' His hands shook slightly, the fork he held clenched in his fist clattering onto the plate. 'Do you love this other person?'

Kate burst into tears, astonishing herself. 'You!' she told her husband then, 'it is *you* I love.

'Please,' she begged, kneeling by his chair and taking his face in her hands. 'Please darling, look at me. I love you so much, I miss what we had. This . . . it means NOTHING to me. It was . . . I don't know . . . I've missed you so. Oh *God*, Edward, I love you.'

Appu suffered terribly. There was no word from Kate at all. He took to his bed, only perking up in the evenings when it was time once more to go to the Club. He haunted the billiards table with its view of the ladies' corner, but of Kate there was not a sign. Devi grew so alarmed by his lassitude, she even summoned the doctor. 'There's nothing the matter with him,' the doctor pronounced. 'Adolescent languor, that's all.'

At first Nanju left him alone to brood, but when it seemed that there was no letting up in Appu's melancholy, he tried another tack. 'You look like a water buffalo,' he pointed out. 'Lying here all day long . . .' He flung open the curtains, flooding the room with light. Appu flinched and pulled a pillow over his head.

'Well, buffalo,' Nanju said, seating himself upon the bed, 'it's a beautiful day out there. Shall we go fishing?' He waited, but there was no response.

'Ayy,' he said gently then, 'did something happen at the Club? It's that woman isn't it, the one you talked about?'

Appu said nothing, hardly even seeming to breathe.

Nanju sighed. 'Appu,' he began, and then he shook his head. 'It *is* a beautiful day,' he repeated simply. He started to get up and that is when Appu moved at last. Face still buried under the pillow, he pushed his foot forward. Not saying a word, the rest of him lying there unmoving, mutely propelling his foot under the sheets until it touched Nanju's leg. Nanju looked at his brother, a mix of fondness, anxiety and a mild exasperation on his face. And then he shifted position, moving slightly sideways, so that when his leg settled again, his knee lay stoutly over Appu's foot, warm and comforting, as if sheltering some burrowing, vulnerable animal.

Finally, unable to bear it any more, disregarding Kate's warning to *never* contact her directly, Appu drove to Belvedere estate.

'Dags,' Kate gasped horrified. 'Why are you here?'

Appu listened as she explained that she could not see him any more. 'Why?' he asked and she shrugged, a delicate movement that set her bob swinging as she stared out towards the lawn.

'Why?' he asked again. 'Why?' he shouted then, without giving her a chance to reply, sweeping the bric-a-brac from a side table and sending it crashing to the floor.

Kate's hand flew to her throat. 'Dags! Come on now, *surely* you didn't think . . . surely you knew this was temporary?'

'I *love* you,' he said desperately, his voice cracking.

'Love? *Love?* What we had was not love, it was lust. I mean, look at us for God's sake. We come from two different worlds, why, I must be at least ten years older than you, that's not . . .'

He tried to kiss her then, and she wrenched free from his grasp.

'For God's sake. Are you not listening to me? This is over.'

He stood there in her silk-frilled parlour, struggling for the right words and to keep from crying in her presence. 'You . . . you . . .' and then he turned and ran for the door. 'Whore,' he shouted over his shoulder, 'fucking white whore,' as he leaped into the Austin and tore down the drive.

Kate and Edward Burnett left Coorg not long after that. Rubber, they told their friends, they had heard rubber was going to be huge, and after selling their estates, they sailed for Malaya. There was talk of them in the Club for a couple of weeks. All those rumours that Kate was seeing someone behind Edward's back. Nothing ever proved, of course, but still, where there was smoke . . . Quite the coquette she was, flirting with all their husbands beneath their very noses.

Soon, even the gossip died away and there was little to indicate that the Burnetts had ever been there.

Still, there were legacies that Kate left behind. It was she who completed Appu's introduction into society. It was she who had taught him how to hold his glass properly and to tell crystal by the *pinggg* sound it made when you flicked a nail against it. It was she who had shown him to keep a pocket square ready at all times, ironed to flatness and dabbed with eau de cologne in case a lady ever had need of it.

It was she who had schooled Appu in the slopes and curves of a woman's body, guiding his hands over the secret places that most men never truly discovered. A tender earlobe. The hollow behind a knee, the delicate skin along the inside of a forearm.

It was she who taught Appu how naïve it was to expose one's heart at all.

Nanju sat beside him as he was packing to leave. 'You all right?'

'Why wouldn't I be?'

'Come on Appu. I know something happened.'

Appu continued to stuff shirts, trousers and shoes into his trunk. 'No. Nothing.'

Nanju sighed. 'As you wish. Take care now, you hear?'

'I'm fine,' Appu said, still refusing to meet his eye. 'Don't know why you should think otherwise.'

And indeed, once he was back at Biddies, Dags seemed more than fine as he regaled the boarders with his escapades. He described Kate in detail, every minute aspect of their trysts. When he had ripped apart every shred of her dignity, after he had stripped her naked through his words, *that* was when Dags finally started to feel better. She was right, he told himself. It had been only lust. He forced Kate from his memory like water through a sieve, until all that remained was a coarse sediment. An essence, as it were, distilled from their time together, fashioned solely from the pleasures of the flesh. He even came up with a sonnet to commemorate their affair, belting it out to the tune of the school song.

> *Katie, Katie, show me your thighs,*
> *A yard above the knee*
> *Spread your legs and arch your buns*
> *The better for me to see*

Now when he sneaked to the village, Dags knew what to ask for. 'Women,' he said, 'older women, young girls, whatever you have available. I will pay well.'

In Appu's final year, Biddies flew into a tizzy over the headmaster's daughter. Rosemary D'Costa was slender, and almond eyed. She had arrived at the school with her mother who was too sickly to stay any longer in Madras; Rosie would be schooled at Biddies, it had been decided. The students naturally fell over themselves, vying for the affection of the only girl at the school. They left pastries in her desk, and love notes and flowers of every kind, all of which Rosie accepted with a sweet smile, bestowing her affections neutrally upon everyone and no one.

Of them all, it was Dags alone who treated her with a distant cordiality, opening the door politely for her but looking above her head when she turned her eyes up to his with her softest, most melting smile. Naturally, of them all, it was he who intrigued Rosie the most. She began to place herself in his path, to visit the hockey training sessions and cheer the swimming team, until it was plainly obvious to anyone who cared to see, that Rosie D'Costa had eyes only for swimming captain, hockey captain, moneybags Dags.

He became an obsession for Rosie. The more the other boys hankered after her and the more Dags stayed away, the more she wanted him, until he was all she could think about. He timed it perfectly, goading her almost to fever pitch so that when he finally did make his advance, she was as sweet and yielding as a ripe guava.

Appu enjoyed Rosie for nearly the entire term, their mutual she-nanigans driving the boarders mad with envy and making the poor saps who were truly in love with her sick to their stomachs. What he overlooked though, was her stolidly middle class upbringing. When one afternoon he informed her casually that they were over, Rosie had been shocked. Her copious tears, her vehement pleading, had served only to make Appu's lips tighten slightly in distaste. 'There, there,' he said as he patted her shoulder, looking surreptitiously at his watch and wondering how much longer before he could get back to the hockey field.

When it became obvious that there would be no changing his mind, a wailing, distraught Rosie collapsed into the arms of her mother. That good lady, of course, ran to her husband and a horrified Devi rushed to Ooty to prevent her darling from being summarily expelled.

It took a great deal of negotiating, a lot of string pulling and donating to the school, but finally, Biddies agreed to let Appu finish his year. A shaken Devi gave Appu an earful, refusing to be mollified even when he dimpled winningly at her and cracked a weak joke or two. Rosie was whisked back to Madras, and when she got her next period, her mother wept from relief. All things considered, the entire episode was hushed up rather well.

It was only when Appu began his application to the KCIO pro-gramme that the full repercussions of the previous term really came to light. When he wrote to Captain Balmer for a recommendation, the captain wrote a sombre letter back, expressing his regrets. He had heard from Colonel Bidders about the unfortunate incident at the school. No doubt, there were always two sides to every story; however, under the circumstances, he could not, with a clear conscience, recommend Appu. He was truly sorry – he had had high hopes for him, but as things stood . . . the KCIO programme included a rigorous selection process, and it was certain that, given what had happened, Appu would not be considered for admission. If there was *anything* else he could do for him, he would be only too happy to help. There were other fields besides the Army.

Devanna wrote to Colonel Bidders on Appu's behalf, only to be met with a rebuttal. The boy had very nearly been expelled. It was only on account of his track record at the school in all the previous years that he had been allowed to finish. 'I'll have you know, sir,' the Colonel wrote, 'that the cornerstone of the school is its unflagging commitment to the development of sterling character in our youth. I do not see, given all that has transpired, how you expect me to recommend your ward to the admissions committee of what is the most prestigious programme in the Army today.'

Still Appu did not lose heart. It would all blow over, it had to. 'Come down Avvaiah,' he urged. 'Talk to the headmaster, he won't refuse you.'

Devi went once more to Biddies, but to no avail. 'He won't budge, the old fool,' she said angrily to Appu. 'You've brought this mess squarely upon yourself Appu. The *headmaster's* daughter?'

Appu pushed a hand through his hair. 'What does this mean? The K CIO programme . . .' It hit him then at last, that do what they would, this time he was not going to get his way. The K CIO door had been shut in his face.

Devi bit her lip, her anger dissolving at the stunned disbelief in his eyes.

'Appu,' she said gently. 'There are other things besides the Army.'

'There *must* be a way Avvaiah. Maybe if you *met* Colonel Bidders, instead of just a letter . . .'

'Appu. Listen to me. It's done. Move forward.'

'No.' His voice trembled. 'The Army. I have to get in.'

'Why?' she asked softly. 'Because of your father? No, you don't. Your father joined the Army because he had no other choice.'

'He was a hero.'

'He was a hero long before he joined. He was a tiger killer Appu. A tiger killer.'

She waited, but he said nothing.

'Your father's heart, even when he was far from Coorg, was always there. Tiger Hills – that is your legacy Appu. And Tiger Hills, you shall have forever. Forget this K CIO business, they don't know what they are missing not to have my son.'

'My father gave up his life in the Army.' Appu's voice was tight. 'Captain Balmer wrote to me about how well he fought.'

'He joined only because he had to,' Devi repeated. 'His roots—'

'Oh stop, for God's sake, just stop Avvaiah.' He whirled on her, cutting her short. 'How would you know? You were *not* his wife, you are *not* my . . .' He stopped short of saying it, you are not my *mother*, but the word hung unspoken between them.

Devi swallowed, trying to quell the bright stab of pain flaring within her.

He saw her to the car and bent down to touch her feet. She hesitated a moment, as if wanting to say something and then changing her mind, she got wearily into the car.

He waited as the car pulled away and when it was finally out of sight, he turned, squaring his shoulders as he stared at the red-bricked sprawl of the school.

It spread like wildfire through the hostel, the news that Dags, *Dags*, was not going to be allowed into the KCIO programme. 'Pshaw,' Appu said airily to his commiserators. 'Who cares about the Army anyway? All those stuffed shirts – thank you, but no thank you.'

He said as much to Nanju, when he returned to Coorg, but Nanju was not fooled. 'What happened, happened. Why don't you go abroad instead? England. Study there. With your sports record, I am sure you will get in someplace good. Forget this Army business.'

Appu brightened. Yes. He would go abroad, show them all. He sent a flurry of telegrams to his classmates – 'Send Oxbridge applns. immed.'

'The application deadlines, Dags,' his friends wrote back, 'have all passed.'

'What does it matter?' Devi asked. 'Stay here at Tiger Hills for now, you can apply next year. We'll tell everyone you had to defer your application by a year for personal reasons.'

Appu stared silently out of the dining room windows. A wave of disappointment rose within him. If things had gone according to plan, he would have been preparing for the KCIO interviews.

'Appu? Are you listening? Just stay home this year.'

It was as if he could hear the march of boots in his head. He stared at the estate with its endless, orderly rows of coffee bushes. The sound of boots in his head, marching forward, away into the distance. The coffee rustled briefly in a sudden wisp of breeze and then became still once more. Appu felt choked, hemmed in, as if a band of iron were pulled tight around his chest.

'Madras,' he said abruptly. 'Never mind going abroad. I'm done with all of this. I'll go to Madras instead. Presidency College.'

'All right,' Devi said. 'As you wish. Go to Madras, study hard. Next year, we can see about the foreign universities again.'

Chapter 29

The banyan tree seemed blown from smoke and shadow, its contours blurred, watermarking the early morning mist. Charcoal and slate, Devi thought, the colours that lay between night and dawn. Cold fire, forgotten stone. Drawing the shawl tighter about her shoulders, she touched her fingers to her temples.

This was usually her favourite time of day. When the garden lay half asleep, orchids secretly unfurling, the grass shivering and weighted with dew. The veera watching from the shadows as she silently walked the grounds. Machu's presence seemed to be everywhere, there, just there, standing straight and tall among the trees, a fluid truth discernible among the moist, shifting shapes of the dawn.

Today, though, a headache flicked cruelly at her temples, pressing needle-fingered through her scalp. She moved gingerly about the garden as the parrots in the banyan tree began to stir. Raising a hand to massage her forehead again, she turned towards the house. 'Devanna,' she called fretfully, 'Devanna.'

'Zeuzera coffeae,' Devanna read aloud. 'The coffee berry borer is the single most damaging pest to plague plantations across India, Malaya and Brazil. Also known as the cocoa pod borer, the tea stem borer and the coffee carpenter, the beetle has even been known to infect teak, eucalyptus and grape. The newly hatched larvae enter the young twigs of a coffee bush, migrating as they grow to larger branches. As the

339

beetle bores its way through the plant, damage is evidenced by holes mottled with frass . . .'

Devanna paused to glance at Devi over the half moons of his spectacles. 'Insect excreta,' he explained helpfully. 'Now where was I . . . mottled with frass and characterised by overall brittleness and withering. Larvae pupate in the tunnels, with each adult female laying between 190 and 1,134 eggs. Serious damage results ultimately in the death of the coffee plant.'

'All useful information, I'm sure,' Devi said tartly. 'Now can you please come up with a solution?'

She was worried for the coming crop. Coffee seasons alternated in quality; a bumper crop one year was typically followed by a lighter one the next. Usually even the lesser yields had been good, but for the first time, Devi's estates had faltered last season.

The crop had been adequate, but not nearly enough to pay for the Strawoniser spray engines that she had installed after the previous harvest. The bank manager had been good to her, extending the loans for another year, however Devi knew that the discussions would not go nearly as smoothly a second year running. She had crossed her fingers and waited anxiously for the blossom showers. The rains, thank Iguthappa Swami, had been plentiful and Devi had heaved a sigh of relief. Still, unwilling to leave anything to chance, she had bolstered the soil in all three estates with a compost of manure and cuttlebone as an extra precaution. The coffee blossomed in profusion, thousands of the tiny, honeyed white flowers dotting the estates.

And then, just when all was looking well, the coffee borers had struck.

Coffee borers had been a menace all across Coorg that year. Encouraged by the unusually warm weather that had followed the monsoon, insects of all kinds had proliferated, harmless grey rubber bugs that confabulated on walls and squeezed plumply into the cracks in photograph frames and wooden floors, red velvet boochies that children picked from the grass and stored in glass bell jars, furry-legged caterpillars and long-waisted centipedes in the exact colours of the Indian Railway.

Unfortunately, the reviled coffee borer had thrived as well, multitudes of the pest infesting the coffee plants, boring their way relentlessly through plantation after plantation.

It had been just a couple of bushes at the periphery of Tiger Hills at first, their stems riddled with holes, the odd borer beetle hovering nonchalantly in the air. And then suddenly, in scarcely more than the blink of an eye, the borers were running rampant across the entire estate. It was stunning how rapidly the pests had bred and it was not long before another of Devi's estates was infected as well.

She had the estate workers shake down the branches of the coffee bushes, in the hope of dislodging the larvae. When the insects still multiplied, she placed a bounty on their steel-jawed heads, offering two rupees for every hundred of the borer fly. The workers performed vast massacres with alacrity, but for every hundred of the flies they killed, still more eggs were hatched. She had then, on Devanna's advice, applied a wash of alkali vat waste at five rupees an acre. Still her bushes continued to wither.

So acute was the distress in the Bamboo district that already many of the European estates had embarked on the final, desperate step of burning down the infected bushes. She had heard that in some estates as much as fifty percent of the land had been cleared and replanted with 'supplies' – immature coffee saplings. It was a desperate step. The new saplings would take at least seven years to reach maturity and begin to yield. 'No,' Devi thought stubbornly to herself, 'there must be a better way.'

She went over the numbers again in her head. Two of her estates, including Tiger Hills, had been infiltrated by the borers, which put just over half of her annual produce at risk. Luckily, the third estate, a sprawl of two hundred acres in South Coorg, had been unaffected. The beetle, it seemed, preferred the open stretches and rolling hills of the north over the thickset forests of the south.

If the crop at the South Coorg estate was good, and they contained the spread of the borers in the other two properties, they could make it through the year.

It would be tight for the next few months, but there were ways to cut corners. She would not hire the temporary pickers she usually called in to help, that would save some rupees. The family could help oversee the picking, especially Nanju and Appu. She would speak with Appu as well, to have him cut down his expenses ... Devi sighed.

It was over a year since Appu had come back for good. Devi bit her lip as she stared out across the lawn. That KCIO business ... the very year after Appu had graduated from Biddies, two more Coorgs had been selected for the programme. Appu had no doubt come to hear about it as one of the admitted boys, Timmy, was also a Presidency College graduate. Appu, however, had said nothing; indeed he had never spoken of the Army again. All the boy seemed interested in was his horse racing and partying. While at college in Madras, he'd become so thoroughly entrenched in the local social life that he had dropped the idea altogether of studying overseas. Three years later, when he graduated, he had taken up an apprenticeship with a tea exporting company. Rapidly growing bored, he had tossed up the job not five months after he'd joined, and had wandered back to Tiger Hills.

Devi had not objected. Nanju had graduated from agricultural college some years earlier and had headed eagerly back to Coorg. She had assigned the South Coorg estate to him to manage. The boy was a hard worker, and anxious to please. 'Appu will learn,' she had thought. He would watch his industrious older brother, and would soon tire of his own lotus-eating ways. To her chagrin, however, Appu had showed not the slightest inclination to anything more taxing than visiting the Club.

She twisted her plait around her fingers, oblivious to the softness in Devanna's expression as he watched from behind his book. At forty-eight, Devi looked to him even lovelier than before. The years had colluded to burn away the soft comeliness of youth, but in its stead they had laid bare a spare, whittled beauty. The hair that sprang free to curl about her temples had barely any grey, her skin still supple as silk, despite the faint lines around her mouth. Her cheeks had hollowed, but this had only accentuated the bone structure of her face, with its promontory of proud, jutting cheekbones.

'I don't want to have to burn the infected plants,' she said suddenly to Devanna, almost pleadingly. 'Find another way, there must be one.'

He sighed and reached for his walking stick. 'Let me look,' he said to her, 'I have a book on ayurveda, maybe ...'

'Careful you don't fall,' she said distractedly as he hobbled across the verandah. 'The tiles are slippery with dew.'

Gundert's senses had become so dim and unreliable that he did not realise at first that he had fallen. He had often, in recent days, found himself addressing shadowy figures that, on closer inspection, proved to be nothing more than a billowing curtain or a trick of the light. His hearing was failing too; Gundert knew from the way the nuns started when he spoke with them louder than he had intended. It was slowly giving way, this body, like a sack that had weathered too many seasons.

Some weeks ago, he had woken smiling. Olaf and he were fishing by the village lake, searching for the fat bass that huddled beneath the stones. The water lapped warmly against his legs, making him smile.

It had taken him some minutes to realise that it had been a dream, that it was not the lake of his boyhood but something else entirely that had made his legs so wet. He had pushed the blankets away with a cry of disgust, struggling to be free of the sodden sheets. His leg, unaccustomed to the hurried movement, had given way under him. Gundert had fallen to the floor, cracking his elbow against the table as he tried to regain his balance.

He had gritted his teeth against the pain as he tried to hoist himself upright. The sheets kept slipping from his grasp until at last he had been forced to concede defeat.

'Sister Agnes,' he had called, hating how his voice quavered. 'Is anyone there?'

They had bustled in, exclaiming in concern. They helped him into a chair, pretending not to notice the nightshirt that had ridden high during his fall, laying bare his shrunken thighs. 'Please don't worry, Reverend,' the Sister had said, briskly changing the sheets, 'this used to happen to my uncle too. Happens to a lot of us, what to do? Not to worry.'

He had said nothing, breathing heavily as he cradled his aching elbow. His ankle hurt too but it was nothing compared to the unending humiliations of old age. Agnes bustled out of the room with the soiled sheets, still talking. 'Just a minute Reverend, and I'll be back. We'll get you back into bed in no time at all.' He was precariously close to tears.

After the bed-wetting incident, Gundert had stopped his nightcap of milk for fear the liquid would encourage his unruly bladder. He took special care to move deliberately and always in easy reach of a wall or the back of a chair as he hobbled between his apartments and the chapel. He knew the sisters pitied him, he could hear it in their voices. Why didn't he return to his own land, they wondered. His work here was done, he had devoted his life to the Mission. Surely Jesus would not begrudge him spending his final days in the company of his family? In that familiar way the natives had, they asked him why he did not leave, without the slightest trace of embarrassment or the notion that his decisions might be none of their business.

It hurt him that the sisters talked of his land and theirs as two separate constituencies. All these years he had spent in India. His youth, his middle years and now, his decrepitude. Not a furlough had he taken; not a single day off. *Andere Länder, andere Sitten*; he had believed, when in Rome, do as the Romans do. Had he not embraced this country, its ways, its customs, and taken its causes to his heart? So many lives he had believed moulded under the eaves of this school, *his* school. And still they talked of him returning to his own land. As if all he had been was an interloper, a stranger passing through.

There was nothing in Schwarzland for him any more. His parents had long since passed on; he had been an only child as his father had been before him. Everything he had, everything he had ever loved, was here.

The Mission sent a new priest to stand at the helm of the school, a robust, enthusiastic sort with large yellow teeth and a braying laugh that could be heard all over the school. The mission committee had sent an official to explain the replacement. 'You have done well here,' the man had said, clapping Gundert on the shoulder, 'but it is time perhaps for new blood, ja?'

Gundert had braced himself for just this encounter, he had gone over in his head a dozen times how he would frame his arguments. When he opened his mouth, however, his voice sounded reedy, petulant. 'New blood? Does the Mission not see how many years I have spent here?'

'Of course we do. You have done well,' the man reassured him, 'but your work here is over. Go home. God knows, if I could, I would leave tomorrow.'

Gundert had been unable to remember any of the rebuttals he had so painstakingly prepared. He sat distraught in his chair and when the mission official took his leave, the man had clearly noticed the tremor in his fingers as they shook hands.

They had let Gundert remain in his apartments for now, but it would not be long, he knew, before the request came, politely worded, for him to move. Nagged by a persistent fear that someone, somewhere at the Mission would seek to send him back to Germany, Gundert began to pray for release. Every day in the morning and at dusk, he limped painfully to the chapel where, clutching his rosary and prayer book, Hermann Gundert pleaded for benediction. 'Enough,' he whispered. 'Take me to you while I still have control over my senses.'

He had been shuffling towards the altar when he had fallen again, tripping over a section of the jute linoleum that had mildewed and frayed along one edge. So befuddled was he by the sudden loss of balance, it had taken him some moments to realise that he was lying on the floor. A shooting pain swept up his lower back and Gundert fainted.

The news of his fall spread like jungle fire, amplified by distance and third party accounts until people began to throng to the Mission, convinced that the Reverend lay on his deathbed. Hans shuttered his trading shop and insisted on stationing himself at the foot of the Reverend's bed, weeping noisily and blowing his nose as Gundert feebly patted his arm and tried to comfort him.

The doctors pronounced the patient weak but essentially stable, however, and as the days went past, the stream of visitors trickled to a close. They sent him get well soon cards though, which the nuns glued to the walls of Gundert's bedroom with rice paste, and jam preserves and fruit cakes that were distributed among the students. As more time went past, these too came to an end. The nuns even managed to reassure a bleary eyed Hans, and to the collective relief of the town, he reopened his store.

Gundert remained confined to his bed. It was as if the fall had jarred something loose within him, as if overnight the iron resolve he had always managed to tap within himself had turned porous and weak. The doctors said he was lucky not to have suffered any broken bones, but nonetheless, it was a terrible effort to lift himself from the bed.

The nurses brought him a bed pan and he could not summon the energy to object. When they noticed the stale, unwashed odour of his body, they insisted on bathing him each morning. Gundert lay still as they sponged him down, turning his head so he would not see their pitying faces. This loss of control over one's limbs, this newborn dependence on the kindness of others. It was God's way, he knew, of softening the cocoon of the body. 'Thy will be done,' he repeated silently, railing at the indignity of being turned over like a baby, at the hands dusting his back with talc. 'Lord, call me to you.'

The rose apple trees that he had planted in the mission garden were in bloom; sweetly scented and buzzing with honeybees. '*The flowers are two to four inches wide, consisting mostly of about three hundred conspicuous stamens. There are usually four to five flowers together in terminal clusters.*'

'You must turn Reverend,' the nurses said.

The flowers fell from the rose apple trees and their boughs grew weighted with ripening fruit that gave off the delicate fragrance of rose water. The nuns picked some fruit for the Reverend, to double boil with egg yolks, milk and sugar into the custard that he had always been so partial to. His face brightened as they brought him a bowl, and he cupped the warm custard in his hands, savouring its rose-scented steam. He was able to take only two spoonfuls, however, before his stomach heaved and he vomited onto the bedclothes.

Mild foods, the doctor advised. Baby food – fruit and mashed vegetables with very little salt and no seasoning. No dairy, no eggs.

'Aren't you going to see the Reverend?' Devi asked Devanna. She had felt a pang of sadness when she had heard about the fall. Her own father had passed away six years before, unexpectedly, in his sleep. Devi had wept bitterly, but nonetheless she had been grateful that Thimmaya had been spared the abuse of old age. Poor Reverend, with only strangers to care for him. 'Go,' she urged Devanna, 'he will be happy to see you.'

'No,' Devanna mumbled, clutching his book so tightly that the veins stood out in his wrists. The Reverend had made it abundantly clear that he wanted to have nothing to do with Devanna. If he wanted to see him, Devanna knew the Reverend would have sent for him long ago.

Gundert's body continued to decay, his bowels spluttering to a halt.

His stomach grew taut and bloated with gas, the nuns frequently having to worm a gentle finger into his crusted orifice to dig out the pebble-like excreta he was unable to pass on his own. One by one, the moorings that had held so steadfast for all these decades slipped loose and Gundert began to drift in and out of the past.

He started to conduct conversations with the ghosts that lurked in his room, greatly upsetting the nuns, but Gundert had ceased to care. Could they not see his mother, sitting there in the chair, knitting by the fire as she always did in winter? *Schnee von gestern.* It was snow from yesteryear, Gundert knew, but did that make it any less real?

There, look, his father, fiddling yet again with his eyeglass, trying to seat the lens more firmly in its frame. Once or twice, he had even thought he had caught sight of Olaf, there, just beyond the curtains, but no . . . not yet. Not yet.

And there. The Korama, fiddling with Gundert's desk. The priest chuckled to himself. The wily tribal knew, oh he recognised all right, the value of the bloom that lay within. His thoughts drifted. How he had tried to find the flower. *Over hill, over dale, through bush, through briar, through blood, through fire he had wandered* . . . Not always alone though. Dev . . . *his* Dev. Gundert turned his head towards the windows, lost in happier times.

It had been a productive morning, Devanna remembered, despite his fall. The Reverend and he had been exploring the low-lying hills to the west of Mercara. They were returning with masses of promising plants when, with a great thunking of bells, a herd of cows had appeared round the bend of the trail. Heads lowered, they cantered in front of a skinny cowherd who was clearly in a rush. 'Come Dev,' the Reverend had said amused, 'let us move aside before we are trampled.'

Devanna had slipped on the loose gravel. Luckily he had fallen forward, onto his hands and knees, and apart from a nasty looking scrape on one knee, he had been all right.

Still, the Reverend had been concerned. They were at least two hours from the town, and it did not take long for cuts to become infected here. He cleaned the wound as best he could with his handkerchief. 'Do you have any water?' he asked the cowherd who, quite forgetting his earlier hurry, had halted to observe the proceedings.

The boy shook his head, the bubble of green snot protruding from one nostril threatening to shake free at any instant. He had bent to examine Devanna's wound, and then abandoning his cows, had raced into the adjoining thicket.

He reappeared moments later, carrying in his grimy hands five bulbs yanked freshly from the soil. 'Wild turmeric!' the Reverend had exclaimed. 'Of course. It is a natural antiseptic, why did I not think of it?'

'*Jeder Jeck ist anders*,' he had said ruefully, as the cowherd smashed the turmeric bulbs against a rock and smeared the paste onto his protégé's knee. 'Every lunatic is different. Never forget Dev, that every idiot is special, and might yet surprise you.'

Turmeric! Devanna thought to himself now, jolted from his reverie. Mightn't that work against the coffee borers? And what if he bolstered this with leaves from the neem tree, another natural antiseptic? Devanna devised a paste of turmeric and neem that the workers applied to each infested coffee branch. They watched the plants anxiously for the next two days but there seemed to be little change. The third morning, the workers called excitedly for Devi. She hurried into the estate. Around each treated coffee bush, there lay what appeared to be fat white droppings. 'What . . .?' Devi bent down, peering through her glasses. 'That boy,' she said, to no one in particular, 'he has gold in his brains, that's what.'

The turmeric paste had achieved the impossible, poisoning the larvae until they had tried desperately to crawl from their nests, collapsing at the base of the plants. A huge sense of relief surged over Devi. The crop that year would be saved. She looked up at the cloud-crowded sky. '*We will be fine.*'

She ordered two chickens to be cut that evening, grinding the coconut herself for the curry.

The estates steadily recovered. Devanna, however, found little comfort in the role he had played in salvaging them. He limped miserably about the garden, as news continued to drift in from Mercara and the mission.

The Reverend was withering away, it was as if he had lost the will to live.

'Poor Reverend,' the nuns whispered among themselves, wiping the tears from their eyes.

Gundert lay all day with his head turned towards the windows and the gates of the Mission. 'Where is Dev,' he wondered fretfully, 'why hasn't he been to visit?' He would remember then, with a pang, that he was not permitted to see Dev again. His part of a bargain, he vaguely recalled . . . the memory would drift into the cobwebbed recesses of his mind and his eyes would turn once more towards the gates.

'The Reverend is dying,' Nanju commented, 'that's what they're saying in Mercara.'

'Call me to you, Reverend,' Devanna begged silently, 'send me a sign. Please, just the smallest sign you have forgiven me.'

The nuns brought the school choir to the Reverend's bedroom. 'Look, Reverend,' they said to him, cradling his head in their arms. 'The choir would like to sing for you.' The nun conducting the children raised her baton and their voices, clear as bells, swirled about the fragile priest.

He had known at once, as soon as he had looked at Dev, that the child was exceptional. Here was the student he had been searching for all these years. Here his hope, his legacy. 'One day, surpass me. As I know you will.'

An image rose before his eyes. Dev's tortured, tear-stained face. The terrible confession, the searing heat of it. 'Foolish Hermann. He is not yours, he never was. Foolish awkward Hermann, abandoned again.' The all-encompassing rage at the realisation that Dev, *his* Dev, was not his at all. A spasm shook Gundert's body and he shuddered in the nun's grasp as he remembered. A fury such as he had not known himself to be capable of, and in its passing, the smooth, black casing of bitterness.

The gunshot, cracking the carapace wide open. It was an accident, people had said, that the gun had gone off as Dev was cleaning it. He knew better. His boy was too gentle of heart to be interested in guns and the like. It had been no accident.

'You can come to me with anything, child,' he had promised him. And when he did . . . How he had failed him.

349

The choir sang on, the hymns soaring and cresting, spilling out over the steps to the garden and the walls of the mission, such beauty in the voices of the children that passersby stopped entranced to listen.

He had given up all claim, as penance. 'I will never lay eyes upon him again, please, just let him live.'

The nun wiped the tears dribbling from Gundert's eyes, rocking him back and forth as if he were a baby. 'Der Gott, bitte nicht mehr, no more, I cannot. Please Lord,' Gundert prayed, 'have mercy. Let me lay my eyes upon him one last time before You call me to Your side.'

It was Appu who found the bamboo flower.

Egged on by his cronies at the Club, Appu had discovered a voracious appetite for the hunt. They would drive into the jungle, armed with new smooth gauge rifles, with cheroots tucked in their shirt pockets and silver flasks of brandy to celebrate the kill. Nobody was surprised when at this sport, too, Dags proved to be a natural.

They had left Tiger Hills early that morning, but the hunt had yielded little except two meagre waterfowl. Appu impulsively decided to change the hunt into an overnight affair. 'It'll be fine sport, chappies,' he said. 'Let's leave the jeep here, the terrain's too difficult for a vehicle in any case. We can camp somewhere, and continue the hunt tomorrow. Mother has packed enough provisions for an army – we'll have more than enough food for the night.'

He sent two of the servants back to Tiger Hills to inform them of the change in plan, and then shouldering his rifle, he plunged into the jungle. Buoyed by his assurances and confident stride, the hunt party straggled behind him, but despite a crashing in the undergrowth that suggested a wild boar, they found little to show for their labour. They camped, before it grew too dark, by a clot of bamboo where the servants built a large fire and set about roasting the fowl.

Appu awoke early the next morning. A band of sunshine, still tentative in its assault, had nonetheless managed to slip through the tree cover and now shone directly onto his eyelids. He muttered under his breath, turning his head, but his sleep was broken. He lay there for a while, and then sighing, opened his eyes. It was then that he spotted the flower, protruding from a slender shoot of bamboo. Rolling to his feet, he crouched before the bloom, using the blade of his pocket knife to push the petals this way and that. The flower was massive, larger than anything he'd seen. And the perfume . . .

With a deft movement, Appu sliced the flower from its stem and wrapped it in his pocket square. It would be a handy trifle at the Club later that evening, he thought, a gift for one of the pretties.

'Come on you lazy arseholes,' he hollered, kicking over the embers of the campfire, 'time we got out of here.'

They were nearly ready to leave, when Appu thought of Devanna. Mightn't the flower interest the old man too? Going back to the bamboo, Appu tugged repeatedly at it, finally managing to yank it from the soil, a single, barely opened bud shivering on one of its nodes.

When he arrived at Tiger Hills, he found an irate Devi waiting for him at the gate. She had barely slept from worry. All night in the jungle, had he gone mad? Was he trying to send her to an early death? Just because his father had been a tiger killer, did Appu think he too could saunter into the jungle as he pleased? Had he not heard that a rogue elephant had killed one of the workers on the neighbouring estate not two weeks ago?

'Come Devi, he's returned safe and sound,' Devanna began, trying to deflect her anger, and then he stopped cold, staring at the plant that Appu casually held out to him.

The flower lay upon its shroud of white silk. Devanna longed to reach out and touch its faded petals, but he knew the Reverend would not approve.

'Maybe you, Devanna,' the Reverend was saying, 'will be the one who will help me find it.'

'The bamboo flower,' Devanna whispered hoarsely. 'Reverend . . . the sign . . .' He smiled then, a smile of such absolute happiness that it dissolved the shadows from his eyes.

The palsy in his hands was even more pronounced than usual as he prepared a pouch filled with earth and gently placed the root of the plant into its temporary home. Along with the plant, he enclosed a note, one that would need no explanation, containing only three words.

He sent the driver to the Mission, with express instructions to hand

351

the plant to a nun and *make sure* that it got to the Reverend. He could barely focus that afternoon, half-heartedly weeding the garden before giving up and limping back and forth along the drive, waiting for the summons that would surely come.

The nun who opened the door of the Mission had obviously been crying. The embarrassed driver looked at the floor as he held out the plant. She accepted it mechanically, tears streaming down her cheeks when he explained that his master had sent it for the Reverend. His master had told him to wait for a message, he said.

'Tell him . . . tell Dev . . . not good . . .' She broke down again as the driver shifted uncomfortably from foot to foot, unsure how to respond. The nun shut the doors and, not knowing what else to do, the driver retreated to the car. He waited there for an hour and when nothing else was forthcoming, revved the engine and turned back towards Tiger Hills.

The nun took the plant into the Reverend's room, wiping her eyes. 'Reverend?' she said. He had suffered a third stroke some time during the previous night. When the nuns came to bathe him that morning, they had found him in a deep coma, his head still tilted towards the gates.

'See Reverend, our Dev, our little Dev has sent you something.' She opened the note, her brow furrowing in confusion. '*Bam . . . bambusea . . . Indica . . . Olafsen*,' she read laboriously. '*Bambusea Indica Olafsen*,' she repeated, wondering what it meant. The comatose priest lay still, the breath rattling in his lungs.

She placed the note on the bedstand, propping it against the lamp. She stroked the bud that Dev had sent; even through her puffy, swollen eyes, the nun could see how beautiful it was. Cutting it carefully from the stem, she went to the chapel where she placed the bloom on the altar. 'Lord, have mercy.'

The remainder of the plant – stem, roots and all – she had the cleaning boy throw on the rubbish heap.

The driver returned to Tiger Hills. No, he said defensively, in response to Devanna's frenzied questions, he was sure that there was nothing else. Yes, he had given the plant to a nun. No, there was no other message.

Gundert continued to wheeze in his bed. The bamboo flower bloomed in the dark, cool chapel, slowly unfurling until it was as large as a man's fist. It perfumed the pews for days and on the ninth day, when the bloom was just beginning to fade, Gundert died.

The church bells pealed out over Mercara and eyes turned sombrely in the direction of the Mission.

He had been a good man, the Reverend. May his soul rest in peace.

Reverend Hermann Gundert, 1840–1927, was buried in the Mercara cemetery. The cross that rose above his grave was as simple and unadorned as he would have wished. The eleventh day after his passing, the very same day coincidentally, the regulars would marvel later in the Club, that the Thames grew so uncharacteristically swollen with rain that it completely flooded the moat at the Tower of London, a vicious, unseasonable rain lashed all of Coorg. It rained that way for an entire week, so hard that bridges were washed away and snakes dislodged from their holes; an unceasing downpour that tore the heads of young paddy from their stalks and caused an epidemic of fevers to rage up and down the hills.

The rains were especially severe in South Coorg. Nanju caught a high fever from working around the clock in the estate, trying to lash together sheets of tarpaulin above the coffee, but his efforts were in vain. The wind whipped away the covering and when the torrent finally ended, Devi's estate, along with those of her neighbours, lay flooded in four and a half feet of muddy water.

However, what was worse, much worse, was the damage to the godown. Nanju had been so busy trying to shield the plants that he quite forgot to check the godown where the harvested coffee berries were stored. Its roof had held only for a couple of days before caving in. When Nanju finally checked the place, the berries had been rotting in water for days, their surfaces coated with the black fuzz of mould.

Devi listened, stony faced, as Nanju told her the extent of the devastation. There would be no crop from South Coorg that year. The buffer she placed her hopes on, the stellar crop that should have come from that estate, was no longer a reality. With the damage already

353

caused by the borer insect, there was little left with which to pay back the bank.

After all the years of relentless hard work, despite all her planning, Devi found to her shock that she was ruined. The bank managers were sympathetic but firm. They had already refinanced her loans twice, they reminded her, and Mrs Devanna, they simply could not do it a third year running. Besides, she was actually asking them for more loans so that she could tend to her flooded estate. No it was simply not feasible. They could defer the interest on her borrowings, they told her, but unless she found a way to come up with at least a third of the capital she owed, they would be forced to foreclose.

The only concession Devi managed to wring from them was a brief window of time. 'Fifteen weeks,' the bank manager told her, 'and this is only because you have been a client of such high standing.'

It was drizzling when she left. She stood in the street, dazed from the conversation. 'Devi akka!' A young couple crossed the street towards her, beaming, and Devi fixed a smile on her face. She watched as the husband placed a protective finger – anything more would be inappropriate in public – under his wife's elbow, holding the umbrella over her head as he guided her carefully through the mud. Devi felt a sharp, bitter pang of envy.

They bent down to touch her feet and, suddenly acutely aware of her wet sari, Devi made her excuses and left. She drew a deep breath, straightening her shoulders as she walked to the car. She would find a way.

She devised a plan to sell the other two estates, but the prices she was quoted were ludicrous. Nobody wanted to buy an estate infested with the borer fly. She explained that they had the pest under control, it was this turmeric paste, you see, but the instant that potential buyers spotted the tell-tale holes in the branches, they backed off. The buyers agreed with her that the estate in South Coorg would have rich yields; not for another three years, however, they pointed out. The rains had washed away much of the fertile top soil; it would take careful nurturing, likely even expensive applications of jungle mud, before it began to yield anything.

However . . . the buyers turned their beady eyes towards Tiger Hills.

Now that was a fine bungalow. And the gardens. Why, everyone knew about the gardens, from Mercara to Mysore. How much would Mrs Devanna want for *this* property?

'More than you could ever afford,' Devi replied flatly. 'Tiger Hills is not for sale.'

They sold both cars over the next months, and Appu did not settle his dues at the Club. Nanju grew silent and despondent, sure that his mother held them responsible for their difficulties. Devanna tried to cheer him up. 'There was nothing you could have done, monae,' he said gently. 'These things happen.'

After waiting in vain for more reasonable prices to prevail, Devi let both the other estates go to a wizened old coffee magnate from Mysore. She pawned all her jewellery, keeping only her mother's bangles, and the tiger brooch that Machu had given her. Still their cash continued to dwindle until Devi finally had to stop all work at Tiger Hills. 'Take a holiday,' she told the workers, 'this is only a temporary stoppage.'

'But akka, will you still pay our wages?' they asked alarmed. Devi looked shamefacedly at the ground.

They let the servants go, everyone except Tukra and his wife who wept when she counselled them to think about leaving. 'Go where akka?' Tukra asked tearfully. 'This is our home.'

The fifteen weeks that the bank had granted Devi drew to a close. They sent an appraiser to value Tiger Hills.

'No,' Devi told the man. 'This is still my home; I won't have you here.'

'But madam,' he began, and something in her snapped.

'Leave now,' she said, her voice hard. 'Before I set the dogs on you.'

'You're being foolish,' he warned. 'Less than a week, that's all, and I'll be back. And then, madam, there will be nothing you can do about it.'

He was right, Devi knew. It was meaningless, her act of bravado. Three more days, that was all they had left, and then the bank would foreclose on Tiger Hills. Three days more before they were pushed from their home. She retreated to her bedroom and sank onto her bed. *Tell me what to do Machu, I have tried everything.*

355

The curtains rustled impersonally and Devi began, at last, to cry. '*I have failed you, I have failed us all.*'

Two days later, Mr Stewart came to visit.

He had taken the coach from Mysore to Mercara, he explained, and then a carriage to Tiger Hills.

Devi nodded. 'The bank? You are with the bank?'

'Bank? No, madam,' he said puzzled, mopping his forehead. 'Our firm is an independent one, in no way affiliated with a financial institution. Er . . . is Mr Devanna home? I need to consult with him.'

Devanna reluctantly came out to meet him but he had not come to tour the gardens, nor offer a price for Tiger Hills. 'The will, Mr Devanna,' he said, 'I am here to discuss Reverend Hermann Gundert's will. Did you not receive the telegram I sent you?'

'The deceased,' he explained, as a bewildered Devanna shook his head, 'had rather a lot of property in Germany. Black Forest region, rather picturesque I am told. He left instructions in his will, to liquidate the holdings.' Devanna looked at the papers the lawyer was holding out to him.

'You, Mr Devanna, are named in the late Reverend's will as his sole and unequivocal beneficiary.'

Devanna stared at him, stupefied. 'I am . . . what did you say?'

'Reverend Gundert's beneficiary,' the lawyer repeated patiently. 'He has bequeathed all he had, sir, to you.'

It had taken some time for the Reverend's affairs to be put in order, he explained, or he would have been there sooner. He rustled through his papers. 'The details are set out in these documents. A sum of one hundred and thirty thousand pounds sterling is to be wired to your designated account from the holding bank in Berlin. There is one thing though. You,' glancing surreptitiously at Devanna's cane, he continued smoothly, 'or a person authorised by you must visit the bank in person before the monies can be transferred. Oh,' he added, 'and here.' Reaching into his briefcase, he withdrew an oilskin packet. 'The deceased also left this for you.'

Devanna nodded blankly, taking the packet.

Appu leaned forward. '*Ours.* You mean, all this money is ours, no strings attached?' His eyes were gleaming.

'Mr Devanna's, yes. It belongs to him to use as he deems fit. So, Mr Devanna, if you would sign here ... and here ... wonderful. Well, I should get going then.'

Devi saw the lawyer to the door and made her way back to the verandah, where the family sat stunned at the news. Devanna was staring out at the garden, turning the oilskin package this way and that. She ran the numbers through her head again. One hundred and thirty thousand pounds. One *hundred* and *thirty thousand* pounds.

It was enough to take care of all their financial troubles, with a great deal left over. Tiger Hills was safe – it was more than safe.

'Well ...' she said shakily. 'This ...' She began again searching for words. Then Devi simply threw her head back and laughed out loud. Nanju and Appu leapt from their chairs, everyone seemed to be talking at once, and Tukra and his wife came rushing from the kitchen to see whatever was the matter.

In the melee that followed the lawyer's visit, none of them noticed that Devanna had gone missing. He limped into the garden, clutching the oilskin package in his hands. His sole beneficiary. Him, the Reverend had named *him* his only beneficiary. He sat down on the wooden seat of the arbour. The Reverend had chosen *him*.

He hugged the package to his chest for a long time before he could bring himself to open it. The first thing he pulled out was a book from the Reverend's collection. Devanna immediately recognised the handsome cherry leather binding and the gilt-edged lettering along its spine. The thick, creamy pages reeked faintly of naphthalene, transporting him across the years. *A sun-filled classroom. The guttural sound of the Reverend's voice, bringing the words to life.* Devanna swallowed, a catch in his throat.

The calotype lay pressed under the front cover. The two men within its frame stood beaming. One swarthy, the other slim and tow haired, their faces alive with promise. Devanna picked up the calotype and then saw that a dedication lay beneath, on the front page of the book. It was a quotation from the Bible, inscribed in the Reverend's precise copperplate. '*Sons are a heritage from the Lord,*' he had written, '*children a reward from him.*' Devanna's eyes filled with tears.

One more thing lay inside the oilskin, a package of silk, soft and yellowing from the years. He unwrapped it with hands that shook. A dried flower, large as a book, thin as tissue. He traced the delicate stamens with his thumb, running his fingers back and forth along the parchment petals, and then Devanna began uncontrollably to weep. A faint, desiccated perfume rose from the bamboo flower. It lingered in the air; sweeter than a rose, richer than jasmine, with the musky undertones of an orchid.

Chapter 30

Nanju was apprehensive at the prospect of visiting Germany. First of all, he had only ever been as far as Bangalore. More importantly, he was anxious that everything with the visit go exactly to plan. After the debacle of the waterlogged godown, he was determined to do his mother proud.

Going to Germany would entail a journey by rail from Bangalore to Madras, then passage on a steamer bound for Europe, followed by rail or coach to Berlin. He had visited the mission library, where he found an old German to English phrasebook that was coming apart at the seams. 'Guten Morgen, guten Tag, guten Abend, gute Nacht,' he mumbled to himself in his bath. 'Wie heissen sie? Ich heisse Nanjappa, ich komme aus Indien.' He pored over the posters displayed in Hans' store, advertisements extolling the pleasures of the Seine and the Rhineland. He even bought himself a new hat for the trip, a grey fedora in the exact style that the gentlemen in the posters so nattily sported.

So anxious was he to get everything right that it had not even occurred to him that Devi might choose Appu instead.

Dusk had fallen over Tiger Hills. Lizards were skittering onyx-eyed along the walls and across the ceilings, tracking the moths fluttering about the lamps. The family was gathered for the evening prayers. Devi rang the little brass bell, to dispel foul spirits who might be circling, and passed her palms over the flame of the prayer lamp. She dipped her forefinger into the crystal jar of vibhuti and dotted Appu's forehead with it. 'Swami kapad,' she murmured as Appu bent to touch her feet. 'God bless. Don't forget the photographs kunyi,' she added as he straightened. 'You must get them taken tomorrow, the lawyers said they absolutely require those for the travel documents.'

Nanju was sure he had misheard. 'Travel documents?' he asked, his eyes going from Appu to Devi. 'What travel documents?'

'Swami kapad,' his mother said as she blessed him. She sighed as she fastened the lid of the jar and returned it to the shelf. 'The documents need to be in perfect order. So much paperwork for this boy to go to Berlin.'

Nanju's voice sounded high even to his own ears. 'Appu is going to Berlin? *Appu?*'

'Well, yes, someone needs to represent your father at the bank, remember?'

'You chose *Appu?* But what about me?' he asked shocked. 'Why not me?'

Devi looked at him, half smiling, half surprised. 'It's best that Appu goes,' she said. 'You know he can handle all those white folk better than any of us.'

'*I* should go. I'm the elder son, am I not? I should represent the family,' Nanju said tightly.

'Nan-ju. Come, what is all this?' She spread her hands before her. 'You never even want to go to *Bangalore*, let alone on such a long journey. It didn't even occur to me that you'd want to go to Berlin. Why didn't you say anything to me before?'

'No harm done Avvaiah,' Appu interjected lightly, 'why don't the both of us go together?'

'Yes, very fine, and where's the money for tickets going to come from? I've barely managed to scrape together enough for yours, where am I going to get the money for the second? Until the bank releases the funds in Germany . . .' Devi shook her head. 'No, only one of you can go this time.'

'He's *my* father,' Nanju said then. He turned to Devanna, his eyes full of mute appeal. 'Appaiah is *my* father.'

'Oh come now, Nanjappa,' Devi snapped, losing her patience. 'Stop. If you are so keen, when the money comes in, I will send you abroad as well, wherever you want to go. This time, however, it's your brother who is going to travel.'

Devi turned from him, and waving her palm over the prayer lamp, snuffed out the flame.

Devanna found him by the lotus pond. Nanju held his new fedora in his hands, mechanically twisting the brim back and forth between his fingers.

'Nanju,' he began, hesitatingly. 'Monae...'

Nanju looked down at the hat. He ran a thumb over the silk lining, caressing the olive softness of it. 'The floods,' he said to his father, 'the damaged coffee. I know she is still angry with me. One thing she asked me to do, did she not? To look after the crop. And even that, I couldn't do. How can she entrust me with going all the way to Berlin?'

'No, it's not like that. Your mother, she...'

'It doesn't matter, Appaiah,' Nanju interrupted. He tried to smile. 'Like she said, there will be more visits.' He rose abruptly and, with a small, indeterminate sound, flung the new fedora away from him. The hat soared into the air, a smudge of grey arcing against the night, and then it fell straight into the pond. It bobbed on the surface for a minute or two as if still coming to terms with this abrupt change in circumstance, then sank burbling into the water.

Devi harboured no illusions about Appu. She knew that once he left for Europe, unless she gave him very good reason to, he would be a long while returning. So well did she understand her son that she knew perfectly well the hook with which to bait him.

Chengappa's daughter, Baby, had grown into a spectacularly beautiful young woman. It must run in the Nachimanda family, people conjectured, for hadn't Baby's aunt Devi been one of the loveliest women of her time?

Despite her frequent visits to the Nachimanda home, Devi had not spent a great deal of time with her niece. When Baby was eleven, her maternal grandmother had suffered a debilitating stroke. Chengappa's wife had departed for her village to care for her ailing mother and she had taken the four younger children, Baby included, with her. Once there, she had realised the local school was far superior to the one in the Pallada village, boasting a full time master who spoke fluent, if singsong, English. They had decided to school the younger children there, and

Chengappa's wife had spent most of the school year away from her marital home.

It was only after Baby had finished her schooling that her aunt became reacquainted with her. Devi was visiting Tayi one afternoon, when Baby came out with a tumbler of coffee. Even the normally critical Devi was taken aback by how pretty the girl was. 'How she has grown!' she exclaimed after Baby had bent shyly to touch her feet and then disappeared inside the house. 'Why, I remember her at Appaiah's funeral, she was just a little child.'

Tayi coughed as she drew the blankets closer about her. 'You forget how quickly children grow. Why, it seems like only yesterday that you were running about in the courtyard, streaked with dirt and getting up to mischief.'

Devi laughed. She reached for her grandmother's hand. 'And you are just the same. Always talking to me as if I were still a child. Tell me Tayi,' she continued, 'what do you think of Baby for Appu?'

'Appu? Don't you mean Nanju? He is older, is he not, he should be married first.'

Devi sighed. 'Nanju's shown little enough inclination whenever I bring up the subject of his marriage, but it's high time I found him a wife, I know. Still, it's Appu who is my immediate concern. I want to get him betrothed before he leaves for Europe – we can have the wedding when he returns. That will give me plenty of time to find someone lovely for Nanju.'

Appu had looked incredulously at her, just as she had anticipated. 'Engaged? Come on Avvaiah, have a heart,' he exclaimed, 'I'm only twenty-four.'

'That's all well and good,' Devi said, 'but I've already confirmed the alliance with my brother.'

'What? Avvaiah! No, I will not be party to this, you cannot simply . . .'

She refused to listen. 'Kunyi, just wait till you see her,' is all she would say.

His heart stopped. Appu was convinced that the first time he laid eyes on Baby, his heart actually stopped beating for a moment. Never, not at the Club, not in Madras, nor Bangalore, nor all of Coorg had he laid eyes on someone this exquisite, her ivory skin so translucent that when she lifted her glass to drink, he could almost see the water slipping down her throat.

Nanju stared alongside, equally thunderstruck. Baby sat before them in a sari of the palest blue, a coral sprig of wild roses in her plait. 'Just like a cloud,' Nanju thought in a daze, 'or a pearl, wrapped in a light blue sea.'

They sat as if turned to stone, gawping at her. 'Wait till the fellows at the Club lay eyes on her!'

'Such purity, such untainted innocence – even the flowers in her hair seem tawdry in comparison.'

'Slender too, I can't wait to see what she looks like in a dress.'

'Those eyes, Iguthappa Swami, those eyes.'

'We'll make a fine looking couple alright.'

'Like a pearl, an incomparable pearl.'

'So, kunyi,' Devi asked Appu, with a perfectly straight face. 'Do you approve of my choice?'

Baby blushed and looked down at her feet but there was a smile fluttering on the full, cupid's bow of her lips.

'Kunyi?' Devi asked again, her tone solemn but her eyes dancing. 'Is something the matter? You *do* approve, don't you?'

'Yes,' they both said then, Nanju and Appu together, still staring at Baby.

It was Appu who continued. 'Yes. Yes, *yes*.'

Appu and Baby were formally betrothed to one another, Nanju watching silently as the village priest consulted his almanac and suggested the twelfth of November for the wedding date. Devi slipped the gold earrings from her ears, a pair of simple studs, the only jewellery she wore any more apart from the tiger brooch. She put the earrings into her niece's hands. 'Here, kunyi. They belonged to my mother. Your paternal grandmother. I don't have much else to give you at the moment, but,' she pulled Appu's ear as if he were a little boy, 'after this fiancé of yours returns from Germany, there will be more. A *lot* more.'

*

As the date of Appu's departure drew closer, Devanna tried speaking with Devi on Nanju's behalf. Maybe it would be better if Nanju went instead of Appu ...

Devi was incredulous. 'Don't you want this to go smoothly? You *know* Appu will be better at handling the lawyers and the white folk.'

Devanna then tried intervening with Appu, fiddling with the knob of his walking stick as he suggested that Appu might consider abdicating in favour of Nanju. But despite being starry eyed over his fiancée, love – or lust – had not yet befuddled Appu's judgement. 'Not go! And miss the Olympics?'

He grinned. 'I'm sorry Appaiah, but nothing, and I mean nothing, could keep me from going to cheer on our team in Amsterdam. Come on Appaiah. It's the Indian *hockey* team. At the Olympics, for the very first time ever! I *have* to go.'

Appu left for Madras in April. The prospect of his departure threw Baby into such a black depression that she took to her bed with a fever, but not before sending three hundred and thirty-three holigés, each fried to perfection and wrapped painstakingly in banana leaves, as sustenance for the voyage. Devi insisted Appu pack them with the rest of his luggage. He did as he was told, giving away the hefty package to the first beggar he saw in Bangalore. How on earth did they expect him to carry holigés on the steamer? He could just see himself now addressing his fellow passengers. 'I say, care for a holigé with your cigar, old chap?'

Still, touched by Baby's intentions and even a little awed by the apparent intensity of her feelings for him, Appu placed an order for a stunning and ridiculously expensive pair of sapphire and black pearl earrings for her in Madras. 'These,' he said airily to the proprietor. 'Keep them on hold for me, I shall be wiring funds to you from Europe.'

He boarded the Arcot, a steamer bound for Cologne by way of Colombo, Karachi, Suez, Djibouti and Port Said. It was a nearly identical retracing of the journey Gundert had made more than sixty years ago. 'Diji-bou-tee, Kar-achi', he had read aloud from the lists of ports of call as Olaf had stood grinning over his shoulder.

At each port, Olaf had thrown a pfennig into the harbour. 'So that one day, Hermann, we will be back.' They never had come back of

364

course. Unbeknown to Appu, most of the coins still lay where they had been thrown all those decades ago, rusting apathetically amid the muck and silt as the shadow of the Arcot passed high above them.

He arrived in Berlin on 18 May 1928. Summer in Berlin was like a balmy November morning in Coorg. The city was at her best, the wide, tree-lined avenues, the flowering parks and the vast, elegant sprawl of buildings displayed to advantage in the lambent light. It was the Jazz Age and the peak of the cabaret, the last full-blown hurrah of the Weimar Republic before Hitler would come to power. Olaf had looked to India for a jolt of excitement all those years ago but had he experienced Weimar Berlin, he might never have left the country. It was a city of artists and intellectuals, of philosophers, wanderers and fortune seekers, attracting from all corners of the developed world the bright, the damaged and the most beautiful.

Revellers spilled from the cafés on every street corner, smoking and laughing, throwing handfuls of coins towards the musicians playing beneath the open windows. Appu stared open mouthed at the monocled, trouser-clad women strolling arm in arm down the streets and making no secret of their affection for one another. Posters beckoned from walls, fences and lamp-posts. He could make out the word Kaberette again and again, the rest of the words he didn't understand, but the illustrations on the posters told him all he needed to know. Couples of indeterminate gender lay entwined on park benches and pressed against alley walls. Appu coloured as a woman caught him staring and winked at him over her paramour's shoulder. He hastily looked away, then laughed out loud. Anything went in Berlin it seemed, everything was acceptable.

'In der Luft,' people said wonderingly of Weimar Berlin, it was in the air, and Appu was at once caught up in its swirl.

He checked into the hotel that the lawyer had recommended, a sensible, no frills place, but even the modest deposit required at the front desk all but exhausted the money Appu had brought with him. He hurried to the bank early next morning, where, after a weary, soul-destroying day of filling in forms, signing documents and producing affidavits, the proceeds from the Reverend's estate were finally released into his custody. He wired the funds home at once, after setting aside a thousand Reichsmarks for his own enjoyment. Then, his shoes clacking against the marble as he raced down the steps of the bank, Appu set out to explore the city. 'A drink,' he mimed to the hotel concierge, 'I need a drink,' and that good man pointed·him at once in the direction of the cabaret.

Appu sat in a corner of the smoke-filled club, mesmerised by the long row of dancers shimmying across the stage. He strummed his fingers on the table, keeping time, as the music rose in a crescendo. The girls stomped faster and faster, undoing bits and pieces of their clothing as they twirled. A bodice here, a garter belt there, their tiny skirts flying about their thighs. Appu watched breathlessly, the blood pounding in his ears. The orchestra came to a halt with a last, triumphant crash of cymbals and he leaped to his feet.

'Bravo,' he roared, along with the rest of the crowd, 'BRAVO!' The girls came back twice to take a bow and when they finally left the stage, Appu fell back into his chair with a guffaw. Clicking his fingers at the waitress, he ordered another drink.

'Do you speak English?'

The woman who spoke into his ear had chosen the brief lull in between acts to address him. Appu turned merrily towards her.

'I do indeed.'

She was an aspiring actress. 'Motion pictures, darling,' she explained, blowing smoke rings into his face. 'Lots of money to be made. I need one big break and then . . .'

He laughed and ordered another round of drinks. 'Motion pictures! Well, when you make it big, *darling*, I shall certainly come to watch.'

Ellen Antonia Hicks she said her name was, *Lady* Ellen Antonia Hicks, looking puckishly at him, as if daring him to question her statement. Appu bowed solemnly before her. 'My lady Hicks. A pleasure.'

'From London,' she said to him. 'Five years ago.' She gestured about her. 'Can you blame me for staying on?'

Appu looked at the elaborately dressed crowd, drinking, smoking, laughing, petting, as if without a care in the world. He grinned. 'In der Luft, isn't that what they say?'

He raised his glass to his lips, scanning the crowds again. A particularly comely face caught his eye, the oval cast of it reminding him, with a sudden pang, of Baby.

'Oh, I wouldn't bother,' Ellen shouted in his ear. 'That is no lady, my friend, but Baron Ludwig. Fond of pretty boys and silk lingerie.'

Appu blinked in shock as he realised she was right; the comely lass was no lass at all. 'Everywhere,' Ellen pointed helpfully. 'Him. Head of one of the largest banks in Berlin. And him. Officer with the Reichstag. Yes, all men.' She tapped a long, painted nail to her throat. 'The Adam's apple darling, you have got to look for the Adam's apple. No amount of make up can mask that on a man. There, you see that gentleman? Now *he* is actually a she.'

She took a drag on her cigarette. 'Who is the cock, who is the hen? Where are the women, which are the men? What is taboo, what is a sin? Nobody cares, welcome to Berlin!

'Sex.' The word gusted from her mouth on a cushion of air. Appu glanced at her lips, at the fire-red stain of them, then looked away. 'Anita Berber used to dance not far from here you know, completely starkers darling, to the strains of Debussy, Strauss and Delibes. Snorting cocaine and morphine, having all sorts of very public affairs with men and women alike. Sex,' she repeated, pursing those soft, engorged lips. 'Neither money nor social standing required, given freely and for gain. It is the great leveller in Berlin. Look.' She gestured about them. 'The richest and most influential, rubbing shoulders with artists, homosexuals and transvestites. Women dressed in men's clothing, men haunting clubs and boxing matches in women's garb, their make up so perfect that if it weren't for the Adam's apple . . .'

Appu began to feel lightheaded, whether from the alcohol, the effects of his journey or the newness of it all, he wasn't sure. Struck by a sudden notion, he looked doubtfully at Ellen's throat but no, she was unmistakably female. She leaned closer, and Appu started as the necklaces wound about her throat brushed against his shoulder.

There was an acrid stink to the air. Someone had lit up a reefer. 'In der Luft, for sure,' Appu thought, 'the smell of sex, and ganja fumes, that's what floats in Berlin's air.'

Suddenly he felt very alone, cut adrift in this shape-shifting city. Coorg, Avvaiah, Baby . . . they all seemed so distant. This was a different world. Downing his glass, he turned to Ellen.

'I leave for Amsterdam in two days,' he said simply. 'The Olympics. Come with me.'

Ellen smoothed the newspapers in her lap, resisting the urge to use them to fan her face and squeeze some little breeze from the morning. The Olympisch Stadien was full to capacity. The stadium had been built especially for the Games with an unprecedented 34,000 seating capacity. For the hockey finals that were about to begin, not a single seat remained unoccupied.

For days on end, the newspapers had been filled with accounts of the startling prowess of the Indian hockey team and its astonishing centre forward, Dhyan Chand.

'*Indians wear celestial blue jumpers with white sleeves, white Byron Collars. Seen from above, they are Revue girls, but from below they are men of steel. When they play, their stick is in turn their spoon, their fork and their knife. At times it becomes their waiting tray as well. The Indian ball seems also ignorant of the laws of gravity. Up whistles the ball and they catch it on the outside of their stick and there it lies, as if it is tucked away in a lady's work-basket, and they run away with it at express train speed. Up whistles the ball and they give it a wink and it departs from its straight course, deviated or attracted by a superterrestrial influence to the left or to the right and there it sits on the stick like a canary on its back, because there is* always *somewhere in the field an Indian stick waiting.*'

Appu shifted impatiently in his seat, drumming his fingers on his knee. Ellen grinned. He had been like a child all day, bubbling with anticipation over the match.

He had told her the stories over and over, of how the Indian team had struggled to obtain permission to play. The British government had been reluctant at first, but then had realised that it would be a public relations coup of sorts, for a colony to participate in the Games. A testimony to the benevolence of British rule. The team had played at the London Folkestone Festival the previous year, where they had won all ten matches. 'Seventy-two goals they scored,' Appu told her. 'And

Dhyan Chand!' The slender Chand, it seemed, dripped glue from his hockey stick, so precise was his control over the ball. He had scored no fewer than *thirty-six* of India's seventy-two goals.

The team had continued their impeccable showing at the Olympics. Ellen even knew their score to date, so thorough had been Appu's briefing: Played: 4, Won: 4, Goals For: 26, Goals Against: 0.

'What's taking them so long?' Appu complained, and she shrugged, smiling as she slipped her hand through the crook of his arm. He held his drink to the sun, the light turning the liquid into a dark, gently fizzing red. He took a sip and burped, the bubbles rising up his nose. 'Sorry. Strange drink, this,' he mused. 'I can't decide if I like it or not. Still, the name has rhythm, don't you think? Co-ca Co-la.' He held the bottle up to the sun again, turning it this way and that, and then jumped to his feet with a sudden roar, nearly spilling the drink into Ellen's lap.

The gates to the ground had opened and the two teams, Netherlands and India were filing out. 'Come ON India!'

A great cheer went through the stadium, followed by a thunderous round of applause. 'COME ON INDIA,' Appu roared again. 'DHYAN CHAND, Come ON Dhyan Chand.'

Even Ellen could recognise the artistry of Chand's game. He scored two of India's three goals, taking the team to an elegant 3–0 victory. Appu leaped into the air at the end of the match. He jumped, he yelled, and he swept Ellen off her feet, scooping her into a bear hug and crushing her to his chest.

They spent some days carousing in Amsterdam, then made their way back to Berlin. The first thing that Appu did was book them both a room at a hotel on the Dormendstrasse. They stood in the middle of the square, Ellen clutching her hat against the breeze and laughing as they tried to decide which hotel appeared to be the most appealing. 'That one,' Appu pointed. 'The one with the blue awning. Der . . .' He squinted, trying to read its name. 'Der Blaue Bast. The Blue . . .'

'Velvet,' Ellen chimed in, smoothing the hair back from his forehead. 'Der Blaue Bast, The Blue Velvet.'

She proceeded to introduce him to Berlin; they rapidly became a fixture at all the hotspots of the city. She had friends all over, raffish artists, struggling revue girls, officers in the Reichstag, Polish émigrés and banking fat cats. Any number of them were always available to attend boxing matches and bicycle races, opening nights and petting parties, and spend drunken, raucous hours at the Spiegeltent and the Eldorado.

Appu was welcomed into their circle with open arms. The 1920s had brought about a resurgence of interest in all things Eastern. The daily newspapers were filled with columns penned by expatriates from Calcutta to Penang, offering perspectives on everything from the Kama Sutra to the Buddha. Hermann Hesse had published his magnum opus, *Siddartha*, to widespread acclaim. Audiences thronged to the Winter-garten for hot dogs and cold beer and to marvel at Indian 'holy men' reclining on beds of silver nails. Ellen's friends had looked at Appu with genuine interest, quizzing him about life in India.

'I sleep in a tree house,' Appu informed them gravely, 'and my butler sends me my meals by means of a rope swing. When I need to step out, all I have to do is whistle and my pet elephant ambles right up to the tree. Dashed convenient.'

Ellen kicked him under the table, but Appu continued unabashed. 'Snakes? Of course there are snakes. I sleep with a knife by my side always. And there is the snake charmer who keeps a nightly vigil at the foot of our tree.'

The proceeds from the will arrived in the bank account in Mercara and Devi began to clear her debts. Devanna suggested that she buy back the two estates that had been sold, but instead she invested two thirds of the capital with an insurance company in Bombay, and in a textile and tea conglomerate in Calcutta. 'Those estates brought us bad luck,' she told him. 'I don't want them in the family. I will buy one more property, a good piece of land to bequeath to Nanju. But beyond that and Tiger Hills, I have learned my lesson. We will not be left so vulnerable again. No more coffee.'

The workers were called back to Tiger Hills, and the pathways cleared of the weeds that had advanced in the intervening months. Devi bought Tukra's wife a pair of gold bangles and a thin gold chain. For Tukra, she bought a pair of trousers and dark brown, leather sandals from Mysore. Tukra was immensely touched by the gifts, especially the footwear. He held the pair of sandals to his nose, breathing in their new-leather smell. He rubbed his thumb over their thick soles, marvelling at their sponginess, squinting with pleasure at the steel buckles. The next morning, however, Devi spotted him ambling barefoot once more about the courtyard. 'Ayy Tukra,' she called, 'where are your new shoes?'

Tukra looked sheepish, but before he could say anything, his wife cut in. 'Where do you think, Devi akka? By our bed, that's where he has kept them. Refuses to take them out of their box, says they are too beautiful for his feet.'

No matter how they laughed or how much Devi tried to cajole him into wearing them, 'I will get you another pair when these wear out,' Tukra refused to budge. The sandals lay unworn in their box, right beside his mattress where he could see them each morning.

In preparation for the wedding, and as a surprise for Appu when he returned, Devi decided on a massive overhaul of the Tiger Hills bungalow. It would be transformed, with a new façade superimposed upon the present foundation; it would be the largest, most modern home in all of Coorg.

The renovations were a source of endless gossip, both at the Club and among the Coorgs. An architect had been summoned from Bangalore, to design the two-storey structure. It was going to be built entirely from materials found on the estate. A vast kiln had been erected to make mud bricks. Maistries had been employed from Kerala to develop a special wash for the walls with lime, and the yolks of no fewer than *twenty-eight thousand* eggs.

'Quickly, quickly,' Devi urged the workers. 'My kunyi will be returning soon, all of this must be completed by his return.'

She began to hunt in earnest for a bride for Nanju. 'Find me someone,' she urged her family and acquaintances. 'The prettiest girl you can find, the kindest and the most accomplished, nobody but the best for my eldest son.'

Devi began to hum again as she went about the house, hopelessly out of tune as always. Listening to her from the open windows as he pruned his bonsai, Devanna smiled.

Baby leaned against the window, letting the night breeze cool her forehead. The moon was barely a sliver, but the rains had momentarily stopped and the air was so clear, she could see all the way down to the paddy fields in the light from the stars.

She missed Appu terribly. She knew that he had wired the funds from Germany; Devi maavi had been so relieved when the monies arrived that she had had two goats butchered and the mutton distributed in the village, along with coconuts from the palms at Tiger Hills. Nanju anna had told her that Appu had watched the hockey finals. Some other country he had visited to watch the game, it had a name that she kept forgetting . . . Amsta something. And then he had returned to Germany. This is what made Baby unhappy. Did he not miss her? Did he not want to rush back home, to be by her side?

'Did he ask after me?' she had wanted to ask Nanju, but the words had stuck in her throat.

'He'll come back soon,' Nanju had said quietly. 'He can't possibly . . . He knows what a treasure he has in you; he'll be back.'

The breeze tugged on her chemise. 'What a lucky girl you are,' everyone kept telling her. 'She is very rich, that aunt of yours. And that new house she's building – you'll be living in a palace.'

It was a bad omen for a woman to lay eyes upon her marital home before she was wed, but Baby had listened so closely to accounts of the house she could see it clearly in her mind. The bricks were a deep red, each brick painstakingly outlined with a white lime wash. The rosewood for the doors had come from the estate, and above each door there were panels of stained glass that threw coloured patterns on the floor. The verandah lay to the left of the house, with a sweeping view of the gardens and flanked by the traditional brass water pots that Baby would make sure to keep filled with fresh flowers. Kanakambara or rajakirita, she wondered, which would be prettier in the water?

There was a set of cane chairs and a coffee table for white-folk visitors. The Coorgs would consider it beneath themselves to sit there, preferring the traditional aimaras cut from thick slabs of wood and bordering the entire periphery of the verandah. One entered the house by way of a foyer; there was a cupboard beneath the stairs where Baby would store Appu's walking shoes, ready for when he wanted to step out. The dining room was to the left. There were panes of bevelled glass set into its doors, coloured blue on one side and dove grey on the other. The sitting rooms lay opposite, two large rooms separated from one another by means of a small divider. The floors were of wood, Baby had heard. She wondered how her anklets would sound as she moved over them. She must be careful not to get splinters in her feet, the slightest pressure and her skin tended to tear.

And then upstairs ... Despite the fact that she was alone, Baby blushed. Upstairs were the bedrooms. First though, was the library at the head of the stairs, with large windows that overlooked the grounds. Six bedrooms branched off in either direction. She blushed again as she pictured the bed, a large four poster that Devi had had custom built. Appu would sit here each night, on pristine white sheets, Baby thought to herself, and she would massage his legs with arnica oil and feed him milk and cardamom ...

She smiled and smoothed down her chemise. He would be home soon.

Tiger Hills Estate, Murnad, Coorg

23 August, 1928
My dear Appu,
Where are you? We have sent you three telegrams and the lawyer tells me that all three have been forwarded to your hotel by the bank. But there is no reply from you.

Avvaiah is wanting to know — when are you headed back? It is now more than four months since you left. Think about Baby. If not for us, you must show her some regard. You must return.

Everything else is well. One of the coconut pickers fell while climbing the trees. Silly fellow broke his collarbone and fractured his ankle but otherwise there is nothing to worry about.

Really Appu, this is not right. Think of Baby. Every time I see her, she has only one thing on her mind. How is Appu, where is Appu, when is Appu coming back. Show some sense. Come home.

Your loving brother,
Nanju

Ellen read the letter aloud to Appu who was lying diagonally across the bed, his eyes closed.

'Baby . . . your fiancée, I assume?'

He said nothing.

'The beetle-wing earrings. Are they for her then?' They had picked out the earrings together, about a month ago, at a little boutique. They had been making their tipsy way back to the hotel after a champagne lunch, when the shop caught Appu's eye. 'A bauble for my lady,' he exclaimed, holding the door open and bowing as she swept in.

They had examined row after row of jewellery and then Ellen's gaze had fallen upon the earrings. 'Why, how novel.'

They were made from real beetle wings, the proprietress told them. She leaned forward, the lapels of her blouse falling open to reveal an impressive cleavage. 'For you,' she murmured seductively to Appu, 'I give a good price.'

Appu had grinned but Ellen was unamused. 'The earrings,' she snapped to the woman. 'Pull out a mirror, I would like to try them on.'

They were a cascade of iridescent, blue-green wings, laced together with thin gold wire. 'Lovely . . . Like something from a fairy tale, Dags, don't you think?'

'Ja, ja,' said the proprietress. 'Fairy earrings, for a fairy princess.'

Ellen laughed, mollified by the flattery, then stopped. Dags was staring at the earrings, a distant look on his face. 'Dags? Hellooo, Dags?'

He looked at her, the expression already gone from his eyes, so fleeting, she thought she might have imagined it. He reached for the price tag and shook his head. 'Not nearly expensive enough for someone as priceless as you. Come darling, we can do better.'

She had hesitated and then tried on the gemstone encrusted pendant he was holding out to her.

He had bought it for her, the pendant, but he bought the beetle-wing earrings too; when she looked questioningly at him, he had lightly kissed her forehead. 'For someone back home,' he had said insouciantly. 'For you however . . .' He slipped the pendant and its chain from the box and fastened it about her neck.

'It's beautiful,' Ellen had said, her mind still on the earrings and their faceless recipient. She had looked down, trying to control the tremor in her voice, shocked at how upset she was. 'Beautiful, darling, I love it.'

'The earrings, Dags,' she said again now, 'were they for Baby?'

Appu gently rubbed her leg. 'Mmhmm . . .'

'Are you . . . will you be leaving, then?'

He was silent for a while, then rolled over, scratching his stomach. He reached across her for a reefer. 'Not just yet.'

Later that week, they were out with a boisterous group, Appu as usual, being the life of the party, when Jürgen Stassler pulled him aside. 'You come from money, ja?'

Appu raised an eyebrow.

'You do not have to reply, it is evident enough from your manner of speech. Tell me. You have heard of Adolf Hitler? Are you interested in learning about his Youth Party?'

Appu went along with Stassler to one of the meetings, as a lark. Stassler talked all the way there. 'Germany was a proud country once,' he said. 'One of the finest in Europe.' He gestured contemptuously at a whore leering at them. 'Look at us now. A city of the desperate. Berlin is now an ageing whore. Her legs, they are parted wide, her brassy charms wearing thin.'

Appu was startled. Stassler was paraphrasing something that Ellen had said the previous evening, waving her cigarette about as she pontificated. 'Berlin is an ageing cabaret dancer,' she had said. 'A woman ever so slightly desperate, but there's an enduring magic to her tawdry charms. They still come by the hordes, her admirers, to dance to her tune and inhale her gold dusted dreams.'

'Well,' Appu began, but Stassler had stopped abruptly and was knocking on a massive wooden door. They were ushered in without fuss, and pointed in the direction of a large, well-lit hall. The congregation was strictly male, youths aged roughly fourteen and upwards. An officer came up to them, and pointing his riding crop at Appu, barked something in German. Apparently satisfied with Stassler's response, he nodded and walked stiffly away. Someone stepped up on to the podium and a hush fell on the room. The speeches began. Appu could not follow most of it, but every so often, an officer would grab the microphone and scream 'Sieg!' into it.

'Heil,' the crowd shouted in unison.

'HEIL,' Appu roared along with them.

'A drink,' Appu cried to Stassler when the speeches were over. 'Brilliant stuff, this Youth Party. Heil! Didn't quite follow what they were going on about but it sounded dashed exciting.'

It was the Jews, Stassler translated for him over beers, them and their greedy, money-grabbing ways. He seemed to think that the Jews were somehow responsible for the post-war bankrupting of Germany. 'They bought our land. The land that had been in our families for centuries. Sold in desperation, for next to nothing to these . . . these . . . *foreigners*.' Stassler spat out the words.

Appu wondered idly how Stassler would react if he knew that Reverend Gundert had sold his lands and bequeathed the proceeds to a *foreigner*. 'I say . . .' he began, but Stassler was ranting on.

Ellen was troubled when Appu later recounted the evening to her. 'Keep away from Stassler,' she said to him. 'I don't even remember how he became part of our crowd, but he's always given me the creeps, the way he stares at me with those bulbous eyes.'

Appu yawned as he unbuttoned his shirt. 'Well, do us all a favour and bed him then,' he said lightly. He grinned, the dimple cutting a deep groove in his cheek. 'Sex resolves a lot of issues. Forget Stassler, we should let *you* loose in one of those Youth meetings and let you work your magic.'

Chuckling, he turned to fling his shirt on the sofa, and missed entirely the look of raw hurt on Ellen's face.

Chapter 31

Devi nodded in satisfaction as she took in the new library. The renovations were nearly done, the piles of loose gravel removed from the courtyard, the walls lustrous with their wash of lime and egg yolk. 'Never will be flaking, akka,' the maistries had assured her, 'cent-percent guarantee.' It was an ancient recipe, they explained, handed down from their forefathers. Rain or shine, not a crack would appear in these walls, they would remain good as new for the next three generations and beyond. Devi ran her hand along a section of wall and her fingers came away clean, with not a flake of lime wash on her skin. For once the maistries appeared to be right.

She had ordered the jewellery for the weddings, from the goldsmiths in Mercara and Mysore. Nothing but the best for the brides of her sons. Diamonds, of course, and the ruby adigé, the coral pathak and the crescent-shaped kokkéthathi. There was a jadau set that the jeweller had shown her, studded with uncut gemstones and ludicrously expensive. 'All the way from the North, akka,' he had protested when Devi had scoffed at the price. She had bullied and cajoled until he had agreed to a marginally more reasonable sum, and then she had ordered another. There were Victorian cameo brooches, ivory hair combs, muslin saris so finely spun that they fitted, all nine yards of them, into the palm of a woman's hand, silk scarves (it was the rage these days, for the young to tie an ascot at their necks above their saris), satin chemises bordered with lace, silk nightgowns, dressing gowns of flannel and velvet, and handkerchiefs embroidered in the convents of Mangalore, each stitch so fine that it was impossible to tell which was the right side.

For the boys, white and gold wedding turbans lined with thick cream silk, white kupyas tailored to their measurements, individual sets of fifteen shirts and five trousers each ordered from London, suits from Hardings and Sons in Bangalore, custom-made shoes from Connaught Circus in Delhi, pocket watches encased in gold filigree, hair pomade, bottles of eau de cologne, silver-handled shaving brushes and, the coup de grâce, an order placed with the dealer in Bangalore for two brand new Austins.

Just last week, she had finally found an estate for Nanju. She had driven the brokers mad these past months, rejecting one estate after another. The soil on one property had felt too dry to the touch, there was obvious waterlogging in another. The well had been inauspiciously dug in the northern-most part of another property, and in another, the entire estate had been planted to the West. The property she bought had to be flawless. It was for her eldest child after all. And then finally she found it, a beautiful parcel of land in the South.

Now all she needed was to find Nanju a bride and for that rapscallion son of hers to return home. She looked at the clouds drifting across the sky. Somewhere under the night-stained edge of that very sky, her child lay asleep. *Iguthappa Swami, send Appu home*. Devi leaned her forehead against the window. From here, she could see the mountains, their tops hidden from view. There, the mighty Bhagamandala and the Kaveri temple. She stared into the distance, a catch in her throat. It seemed like a different lifetime now, the Kaveri festival, climbing up to the peak . . . all of her life still lying ahead of her.

She would go again, Devi resolved pensively. She would take her sons and their brides to the temple, seek Kaveri amma's blessings once more.

A movement below caught her eye and Devi brightened as she spotted Nanju on the lawn. 'Nanju,' she called, smiling. 'Come upstairs kunyi, I have something to show you.'

They had not spoken again about his unexpected outburst, when he had questioned her for sending Appu to Germany. There was no question in Devi's mind that she had made the right decision. Still, she knew she had ended up hurting him. He had said nothing more on the matter, hugging Appu fondly when he had left. Nonetheless, she had noticed how withdrawn Nanju had become over these past months and she had been anxious to make amends. She beamed as he came up the stairs.

'Avvaiah?'

'Here.' She held out a sheaf of papers.

'Oh, are we buying again?' He looked through the papers and whistled softly. 'Six hundred acres? This is a large property.'

'Yes. And it's yours.'

He looked at her, not understanding, and she laughed with delight. 'Take a look at the papers, go on, see, the land is registered in your name.'

'Mine?'

Devi laughed again. 'Yes, my slow thinking son, yours, all yours. See here, this is your name, is it not, at the top of the papers?'

'But . . . Tiger Hills?'

She shook her head, still smiling. 'What of it?'

'Tiger Hills, Avvaiah. *This* estate. What . . . I'm the older son.'

'Yes, of course. Which is why you get the larger property. *Six hundred* acres, monae. I even had a soil sampling done, very good they tell me, the coffee will—'

'No, Avvaiah. Give this to Appu.'

'What is this nonsense? Do you know how hard your Avvaiah has searched to find you this? This is the best property that has come on the market in years, the shade trees are excellent, and look at its size. With six hundred acres, a person could—'

'I don't *want* six hundred acres. Not six hundred, not even ten thousand, all I have ever wanted is Tiger Hills. Give this to Appu, buy him two more if you want, but Tiger Hills . . . Tiger Hills is mine.'

'Kunyi, what is this? Tiger Hills is Appu's.'

'It goes to Appu,' she repeated, distressed when he said nothing. 'Tiger Hills has to be Appu's.'

'Like breathing.' The words were barely audible and Devi wasn't sure she had heard correctly at first. 'Like *breathing*,' he said again, staring at the title deed in his hands. 'This estate, even as a boy . . . This land, it's like breathing for me, Avvaiah. He looked helplessly at his mother. 'Appu will never love it as much as I do, you know he won't.'

379

'In the name of all the Gods. Nanju, please. Don't make matters difficult.'

The memory of Machu's widow rose unbidden in her mind. '*You promise to give Appu his birthright?*' the woman had asked.

'Tiger Hills goes to Appu, it has to. Look, just *look* at this property I bought you. Six hundred acres. It is much larger than Tiger Hills, you ought to be bursting with joy!'

'Thank you Avvaiah,' he said then. 'Tiger Hills . . . thank you,' he repeated heavily. Bending down, Nanju touched his mother's feet.

Devi bit her lip, unsettled by the exchange. 'Swami Kapad. God grant my son all happiness. And now that you have a property with which to support a wife, I'm going to find you one. Someone really lovely, really good, nobody but the best for my son.'

He looked at her, a strange, tight smile on his lips. 'As lovely as Baby?' he asked.

Devi was more disturbed than she cared to acknowledge by what Nanju had said; so much so, that she went the very next day to visit Tayi.

'Kunyi, please stop. You make me dizzy.' Tayi feebly patted the side of the cot. 'Come sit.'

Devi ignored the summons, although she halted her pacing to stand by the window. She glared at the chickens pecking in the mud. 'Not one word from Appu, Tayi. Is he all right? When is he coming home? Nothing. Has he no concern for Baby? And I am his *mother*. Does he not understand how I must worry?'

Two of the hens got into a tussle with one another in a loud screeching and squawking and Devi banged on the window bars. 'Shoo!' she shouted, 'Shoo,' and they subsided with a disgruntled puffing of their feathers. She turned to Tayi, suddenly frightened. 'He . . . he will return, won't he? Appu will come home, won't he?'

Tayi sighed. 'Of course he will.' She patted the side of the bed again. 'Sit.'

Talking with Tayi had lent her some modicum of comfort, but nonetheless, Devi remained upset on her way back to Tiger Hills. She raised a hand to the tiger brooch, running her fingers absently over its smoothness. Maybe it had been a mistake after all, sending the boy abroad. She knew, she knew with a mother's instinct, that he was getting up to no good there. 'All these white girls,' she thought uncharitably, 'no thought of maryadi.' No sense of what was proper, and what was not. Appu was *betrothed* was he not? And still they must be making eyes at him . . .

The car rounded a bend and the valley below came into view. The paddy was growing, a brilliant green fuzz over the soil. Herons skimmed the crab pools; all around, the emerald hills.

'These are my roots,' Machu had said to her, when they had stood looking out over Coorg from the Bhagamandala peak. And *still* he had given her his land. She stared unhappily out of the window. Tiger Hills had always been Appu's. How had Nanju ever assumed it would go to him?

Like *breathing*, Nanju had said to her, that was what being at Tiger Hills felt like to him. Her normally reticent child had suddenly turned into a poet it seemed.

A heron took solitary wing, floating from the fields in a spool of purest white. Devi watched its flight, gripped by melancholy.

To love so fully, to be so completely immersed in someone or something, yes, that love ran deep; it could feel as natural as breathing. But what Nanju did not yet know was that there was a deeper dimension to such love. A rootedness brought alive only by loss.

'Love is breath, yes, but also what follows after, when all breath is done, when all that remains is silence. Love is water, yearning for the sea. It is the tree that must remain rooted while reaching for the sky. It is shadow, freighted with absence, the recesses where joy blossoms no more.

'Love is what endures, through the years, the bastard aftermath of a loss I cannot even mourn as my own.'

The car turned another bend. The heron soared, banked, flew on.

Appu tilted his head and looked at the sky. Here in Berlin, the stars seemed distant, out-dazzled by the lights of the city.

There had been an air of suppressed excitement about Stassler all that evening. They had first met for drinks in the lobby of the Blue Velvet and had then proceeded to the cabaret. Midway through the evening,

Stassler had leaned forward and whispered in Appu's ear. 'You must come with me afterwards.'

Appu gazed thoughtfully at him. Stassler's eyes had seemed to bulge even more than usual, a vein bulging on the side of his forehead. He shook his head, as he drew on his reefer, swallowing a mouthful of smoke. 'Not tonight, Ellen is tired.'

'Not Ellen. Only you. You *must*.'

Despite himself, Appu was curious. He took another drag of the reefer, feeling his lungs expand. 'And where are we going?'

'You must come,' is all Stassler said again.

Appu was even more mystified at the end of the show when he realised Stassler had invited along only two others from their party, Henrik and Gustav, a flamboyant fashion plate of a couple with start-lingly perfect skin. Henrik looked about them as they headed away from the Dormendstrasse and down one of the lesser-known alleys.

'So where is this dashing new club then, Jürgen?' he asked.

'Ahead,' Stassler mumbled.

'Well slow down a little, won't you, my pretty,' Henrik said, 'the heels on these shoes are entirely too high for such abuse.'

Gustav laughed gently but Stassler said nothing and hurried along.

Appu ambled beside them, listening with only half a ear to Henrik prattle on about the show that evening. He looked dreamily about him, the reefers he had smoked all evening filling his lungs. *Such* lights there were in this city. Green . . . yellow . . . blue, red, orange, and colours he did not even know the names of, diffusing from the street lamps and the cabarets, reflected from the earrings of the women . . . men? who passed by. Appu raised a hand and it seemed translucent, the bones jointed in a webbing of colour.

They walked on, turning down this alley way and that. Appu noticed that the lights swirling about him were slowly dimming. Still they walked, down increasingly quieter streets. There were no clubs here; in fact, now that Appu thought about it, it was awfully deserted. They turned yet another corner, and he was filled with a fierce longing for another reefer.

'Stassler,' he began, irritably, 'where in God's name . . .' Then he saw them.

About fifty paces ahead, four or five figures were standing under an unlit streetlamp, waiting. Appu shook his head, trying to clear it. No, it was no mistake, those men in the shadows ahead were watching out for something.

'Stop,' he hissed. 'I don't like this.'

Henrik and Gustav huddled together, suddenly nervous. 'Stassler?'

'Come on!' Stassler cried then, his voice harsh. His hands flew in the air, beckoning to the waiting men. 'Over here!'

Appu stood frozen as the figures peeled themselves from the shadows, one, two, another, then two more, and charged towards them. They were shouting something but he couldn't make out their words. Henrik screamed in fright, or was it Gustav? The useless pattering of their heels as they tottered back up the street.

'Get them,' Stassler was screaming at Appu, his mouth twisted with hatred, 'don't let them get away.'

Appu raised his fists drunkenly, still not understanding, but the men were already streaming past him. He stood like that for an instant, fists bunched in front of him, then turned, watching, as if in a dream, as they overtook the two flamboyants. He saw them fall, Henrik-Gustav-Henrik, hard to tell who was who, a muddle of shrieking silk and velvet. The *tshack-tshack* sound of fists, marring that pampered skin. A picture floated into his head, of the goat meat that hung from hooks in the butcher's shop at Mercara. Great slabs of flesh, skinless, coloured red and purple, such vivid colours, marbled with creamy veins of fat. *Tshack-tshack-tshack*, the sound of fists hitting skin, like meat being pounded.

They were screaming for help, 'Dags! Bitte bitte, mein Gott, bitte.'

One of the men pulled out a vicious-looking truncheon and began laying into the figures. Stassler had run over as well, and was laughing as he kicked ferociously at the two shapes on the ground.

Still Appu stood frozen. 'Dags.' The cry was feebler now, he could hear an awful crunch, bones being broken. A dark stain was spreading from the bodies, red, or black or maroon, he couldn't tell, seeping into the street.

Appu turned on his heel and *ran*, ran for his life, away from Stassler and the Hitler Youth.

He was shaking when he reached the Blue Velvet, the coins slipping through his fingers as he tried to tip the doorman. Ellen had fallen asleep. He sat trembling on the sofa and, uncorking the decanter of brandy, downed its contents.

'*Dags. Bitte, Dags.*'

He should have done something, he should have done *something*. He tilted the decanter to his throat again, but it was empty. *It was not your place. It was* not. *This is not your problem, this isn't your home.*

He stared at Ellen, as if seeing her for the very first time. What was he doing here? He looked at the tautness of a thigh flung across the bedclothes, the thin blue veins that lay in the hollow of a knee. How tawdry she seemed. So easily had.

He shut his eyes, willing away the horror of the evening, and Baby's face floated suddenly in his mind. Appu thought of his waiting fiancée, was reminded of the bone-jolting beauty of her. Pristine, so pure. The certainty that no man had ever feasted his eyes upon her thighs, that no man other than he ever would.

Dragging open his trunk, he began to pack, throwing in piles of smoking jackets, shoes, shirts, bow ties and felt hats, whatever came to hand.

Ellen awoke startled by the noise. 'Dags?' she asked woozily. 'Dags?' she asked again, her voice now high with alarm. 'What's going on? What . . . Where are you going?'

Her mascara had smudged along one cheek, giving her the look of a frightened clown. 'Dags! Whatever is the matter? Why aren't you saying anything? Please, Dags, *where* are you going?'

'Home, darling,' Appu said, without even looking at her. 'Home.'

Chapter 32

Mist swam up the sides of the hills, blanketing the mourners. A three-legged stool had been placed in the centre of the courtyard. It too was wreathed in grey. A brass plate rested upon the stool, heaped with raw rice harvested from the Nachimanda fields; atop the rice, the flame from a gleaming brass lamp flickered and dipped as if in time to the dirge. The drums beat slowly, wistfully as the Poleya funeral dancers, arms entwined, undulated in a circle about the stool. Now appearing, now vanishing, treading in and out of the fog.

A reed mat had been woven by the village mat maker especially for the funeral. It had been laid upon the floor of the verandah and the women of the house sat here, their hair unbound and hanging to their waists, yards of white muslin draped and knotted about their shoulders. Gravely, in time with the drums, the funeral singers sang the requiem.

> *You are ruined, Tayavva, ruined like never before*
> *The loss you suffered, Tayavva*
> *O! What a terrible loss*
> *You are defeated, Tayavva, defeated like never before*

Devi sat as if carved from marble, barely, it seemed, even breathing.

Tukra kept pace with the drums. He seemed to dance instinctively, not really listening to the throbbing beat. His face was contorted with grief, his features blurred and running into one another; whether this was from the mist or the film over her eyes, Devi was not certain.

He had insisted on dancing at the funeral, even though his wife had warned him it would not be easy on his knees. 'You're old now; leave the funeral dance to the young,' she had counselled, but he had been adamant. 'It's for Tayi,' he had wept, 'Tayi.' He circled the lamp now, one step forward, one step back, the voices of the singers washing over the mourners and the sombre hills.

> *Like the Lord's seven strings of gold beads*
> *Snapped and scattered, Tayavva*
> *So too you have snapped*
> *Just as His looking glass*
> *Slipped from his hand and shattered, Tayavva*
> *O! So too are you shattered Tayavva*

Devi stared at the corpse lying on the verandah. They had washed the body that morning and wrapped it in white. She had stoppered the nostrils, earlobes and slack belly button with plugs of cotton; a gold sovereign gleamed from the centre of the wide forehead.

> *Just as His golden needle*
> *Broke at its eye, at its eye, Tayavva*
> *O! So too are you broken, Tayavva*

Tayi was lying there. *Tayi*. Her Tayi. Gone. First Avvaiah, then Machu, then Appaiah and now Tayi. A great weight settled on her, like a millstone rocking slowly upon her chest, constricting her lungs. Devi rose to her feet and stumbled into the house.

It lay quiet and deserted. The hearth would not be lit for eleven days after Tayi was ... after the cremation. Devi stood facing the soot-darkened walls.

'*Devi kunyi. Flower bud! Here, a hot otti.*' The high pitched, carefree sound of a child's laughter. She started, but it was nothing, nobody. Ghosts from the past.

'*A story, Tayi, tell me a story.*'

'*A story, is it, my sun and moon? Well, let us see now ... It is said that years ago, many, many years ago, before the Kaveri temple was built, when the mighty trees of the forest were still curled upon themselves in dormant seed, there was a great war. It was waged over a king's daughter, the most beautiful princess you ever did see. Yes, my flower bud, just like you.*

'*Such a war was fought, the likes of which our people had never seen.*

386

When it was over, our brave lay unmoving upon the battlefield, their eyes open to the skies, and our queens had vanished into smoke. It is said that our people fled then, the few who remained, leaving behind the rocks and golden sands, stained now by pillage and carrion. And that when they left, there sounded an unearthly sigh, like a gust of cold wind. It travelled the length of the battlefield and blew past the smouldering remains of the fort, and the sky grew dark with cloud.

'*Far they travelled, down rivers, through the plains and steaming jungles, shadowed always by the sorrowing clouds, until at last they halted in wonder. Such a land lay before their eyes. A land of sparkling waters and shaded hills, a place of fruit and milk and honey. They stood there marvelling, at the edge of the hills, when a maiden appeared before them. "Halt," she said, and her voice was like the murmuring of a brook. She was Kaveri, she said, the caretaker of the hills, and none might pass without her command. She heard their story then, of the terrible war just waged, and she tilted her head, her tresses flowing like water.*

'*"You may stay," she said, "in this incomparable land, but first, you must promise me something. Every year, when I emerge anew into this world from the Bhagamandala mountain, you must be there to greet me. Float flowers and coconuts into my waters and in return, I will give this land to you for all time. I shall flow through your holdings in rivers of sweet-fleshed fish and fat black river crabs. I shall water your fields, filling them with brooks and puddles that shall host the graceful white winged birds of your birthland. I shall tumble through these hills in a thousand waterfalls and see to it always that the forest teems with life."*

'*Our people promised the beautiful maiden that they would do as she said. She smiled, and it was like the sun shining through a stream. "Yours shall be a blessed race," she said, "a pearl-like race of valiant men and women of honour. May your fields be always ripe with grain, may your flowers always bloom."*

'*She looked at them. "Why do you still look so sad?"*

'*They told her then, of the dead, of all those left behind. Her eyes grew tender and they were the colour of a shaded jungle pool. She pointed a finger to the skies, and lightning flashed through the clouds. "Your veera shall live on. In the skies, in evening mists, in the shadows behind the trees. Your ancestors," she blessed, "shall watch over you forever."*

'There was a great sigh at her words, like the gusting of a breeze. The clouds above their heads parted and shadows flitted through the trees. The leaves on the trees rustled, despite there being no wind, and then once more, there was silence. When they turned back to the maiden, she had vanished.

'They settled here, our forefathers, in this land of sparkling water and open skies. And now and again, it is said, when the clouds part and the rain falls like silver, now and again, the veera step forth from the shadows to take root among us once more.'

The drums continued to beat outside. Devi stood silent as a statue, the white of her sari and her skin seeming almost to shimmer in the dim light, her hair curling about her shoulders.

Word had come to Tiger Hills the previous evening. Tayi was poorly, and the doctor had said it would not be long. Devi had flown, shocked, to the Nachimanda house. A fever, Chengappa told her, his eyes weary. A stubborn fever had taken root inside Tayi and left her weakened. He had thought it best to summon all the family. 'Where have you been, Devi?' he chided. 'She's been asking for you.'

Tayi lay in her cot, her shrunken frame almost swallowed by the blankets. 'Tayi?' she whispered. 'Don't worry about a thing, all will be fine.'

She took Tayi's hand in her own. How frail Tayi seemed, barely a handful of skin and bones.

Tayi stirred. 'Devi kunyi?'

'Shhh.' Devi stroked Tayi's hair. 'Try not to speak, the doctor has said you must rest.'

'Rest is all there is left for me now kunyi . . . Water . . .'

Devi poured a tumbler of water from the clay pot. 'Don't talk like that, you have a fever, that's all.'

Tayi shook her head. 'This is the end for me. I feel it in my heart.' She lay back against the pillows, breathing heavily. 'Where . . . So many days you did not come?'

Devi bit her lip. 'I know, it was just that . . .'

'Appu. He has returned safely?'

Devi nodded unsteadily. 'He has.'

He had wired a telegram from the ship – 'Arr. 20th Madras, Coorg immed. after'. Predictably, it had already been the 19th by the time the telegram had reached Tiger Hills. There had barely been time to marinate the chicken for the pulao and buy fresh fish from the shanty, to send the servants foraging for the umbrella mushrooms Appu so loved, when there he was, framed in the doorway.

'Avvaiah.'

Devi had promised herself she would be aloof and distant when he arrived. Teach him a lesson, she would, for all those months of silence. One look at his face though, tired and travel worn, and her heart had melted. She had flung aside the ladle, still steaming from the pulao. As he had bent to touch her feet Devi had pulled him to her, cupping his face in her palms. 'I was afraid that you would never . . . It's good, kunyi,' she said, 'it's good to have you home.'

He had stood before her, remaining strangely withdrawn when touching Devanna's feet as well. It was only when Nanju had walked in from the estate that any real emotion had crossed Appu's face. His eyes had unexpectedly welled with tears and he had flung his arms about his elder brother in a tight bear hug. 'Nanju.'

Nanju awkwardly patted Appu on the back. 'So you came home. You came back after all.'

He had slept. How he had slept, for almost an entire day. And then he had awoken in the middle of the night, as hungry as a horse. She had stayed up with him, sitting across from him at the table as he ate. Just watching him eat, filling his plate again and again until at last he was sated. He had wanted to set out immediately to visit Baby, and Devi had laughed. 'So impatient. No, kunyi, not when there are hardly any weeks left until the wedding. It's not auspicious for the groom to see the bride before the wedding day.'

She had thought he might argue, but he had nodded. 'Let's have the wedding as soon as we can then,' was all he said in reply.

Devi rubbed Tayi's hand between her own, trying to get some warmth into the stiff fingers. 'I meant to visit sooner . . . anyway, I am here now, and I am not leaving until you get up from this cot.'

She brushed off Chengappa's suggestions that she get some rest, it could be a long day tomorrow. 'No.' She sat by her grandmother's side, moistening her forehead with cloths soaked in rosewater as the hours wore on and Tayi continued to wheeze in her bed. Now and again, there was a snuffle from the dogs outside, the only other sound.

Devi silently bargained with the Gods. 'Fifteen gold sovereigns,' she offered Iguthappa Swami, 'fifteen sovereigns to your temple, or fifty, I don't care, just let my Tayi be well. Two pigs,' she promised the veera, 'the fattest, largest sows in all of Coorg I will have shot in your name, and any number of fowl.'

'All I ever wanted was for you to be happy.'

'What?' Devi sat up startled, rubbing the sleep from her eyes. 'Tayi, did you say something?'

'"Let all her sins come on my head, Iguthappa Swami," I used to pray, "give her nothing but happiness."' Tayi started to cough, her lips so pale they seemed almost blue.

'Get some rest Tayi, please,' Devi said tremulously.

'How is she doing?' Chengappa's wife softly entered the room. 'Here, do you want me to take over for a while?'

'No, it's all right,' Devi said. She forced a smile and looked up at her sister-in-law. 'Get some rest.'

Chengappa's wife squeezed Devi's arm briefly and left, shutting the door behind her.

Devi turned back towards the bed. Tayi's cataracted eyes were filled with tears. 'If I could do anything, anything to change the past . . . When I think of that morning, your face . . . I thought, if we all forgot, if we *never* spoke of it again, it would give you a way to go on. That what happened would be buried. Perhaps it was foolish, but it seemed the right thing to do.'

'Tayi, hush,' Devi said huskily. She pressed her grandmother's hand to her lips.

'I know you are still very angry inside. Angry with what happened, angry with me for not allowing you to send word to Machu.'

She went into another paroxysm of coughing.

'Each . . . each of us has sorrow allotted to us, and happiness too. Iguthappa Swami doles out both. The past is gone kunyi. Look to the future. Be happy, make others happy. Devanna, he has suffered too.'

Despite herself, Devi began to bristle. 'Tayi, enough, I don't want to . . .'

390

Tayi placed her palm on Devi's cheek, her fingers trembling uncontrollably. 'Forgive him kunyi. So many years . . . forgive him.'

'Forgive him? *Forgive* him? Do you know what it is like Tayi, to mourn someone, each and every day, and not even be permitted to acknowledge the loss? In the world's eyes, I have no claim to Machu, he was nothing to me. Only I know . . .' She brushed her hands across her eyes. '*So many years*, yes, but it does not become easier with time. It just grows heavier and heavier, this loss of which I may not even speak. Like a stone about my neck, with nowhere to put it down. And you tell me to *forgive* Devanna?'

'He has suffered too.' Tayi closed her eyes. 'The sorrow you bear, he carries a weight within him too.'

Her voice grew faint. 'My flower bud . . . I have told you so often, the true beauty of a flower lies not in the size or colour of its petals, but in its fragrance. Listen to your Tayi. Be like the jungle flower that despite blooming unseen, untouched . . . still gifts its sweetness to the breeze.

'My darling child,' she whispered, 'my precious sun-and-moon, be the orchid that perfumes the wind.'

'A thousand gold sovereigns,' Devi bartered desperately in her head, even as the men of the family lifted Tayi from the bed and placed her upon a mat on the floor. The bamboo bottle of Kaveri water was brought down from the prayer corner. A little was poured into a silver tumbler and tufts of garike grass and tulasi leaves floated in it. They poured some of the sacred water into Tayi's slackened mouth as, in low voices, Chengappa and his wife began making arrangements for the funeral dancers.

As the shadows shortened on the ground and the sun climbed higher in the sky, Tayi slipped finally from them all.

Devi stood alone now in the dim kitchen. She shut her eyes and leaned against the door, so racked, so torn apart with grief that it was impossible to weep.

A chill wind gusted about the courtyard, slicing through the mist; women shivered, and drew their shawls closer. Devi's lips moved with unspoken prayer, her face utterly drained as she watched the men of the family ready the bier. Devanna limped across the verandah, anxious to be by her side. She looked up briefly as he approached; their eyes met for an instant, clouded by an identical grief.

Tayi's corpse was lifted gently onto the bier and one by one, the men of the household came forward to shoulder it. Nanju was at the front, his eyes swollen from weeping. Appu, sombre and drawn, stepped alongside him but as he bent to lift the bier, Nanju thrust out a hand.

'No.'

A single word, and hardly loud, but in the momentary hush of the drums, it sounded like the crack of a cattle whip.

'What?' Appu bent and tried to shoulder the bier once more.

Nanju's hand shot out again. 'By blood, Appu. By *blood*,' he said tautly. 'Tayi was *my* blood, not yours. You know the tradition. Only blood relatives may touch the bier.'

Appu looked around at the startled, watching crowd. He turned to Nanju and tried to smile, but his muscles felt stiff, frozen. 'Nanju, come now . . .'

'By blood,' Nanju repeated. His lips twisted. 'This is not yours to have.'

'She was my grandmother too,' Appu said bitterly, but his voice lacked conviction, as if he was not fully convinced of the words himself. 'She was just as much mine, as she was yours.'

Devi watched, shocked from her stupor, as her two boys, their heads shaven, squared off in the fog. 'As lovely as Baby?' Nanju had asked. *As pretty a wife as Appu's?* Her face grew tight with anger.

'Move aside Appu. Don't make me . . .'

'Make you what? Make you *what*?' Appu grabbed the front of Nanju's shirt, suddenly so angry that he forgot the watching mourners. 'You think you're above me, is that it? Me, the orphan taken in, while you are to the manor born? Let me educate you on your bona fide origins.' The words that Appu had overheard all those years ago danced on the tip of his tongue, hot as coals.

'Take a long hard look at him,' he had heard Devi say to Tayi in the kitchen. 'Remember, as I do every time I see him, *just how his father's seed was implanted in me.*'

He had not understood the implication of Devi's awful revelation, not until many years later. Appu had hugged the knowledge to himself, shielding Nanju from the devastating hurt he knew would follow. But now . . . he stared furiously at Nanju, the words trembling on his lips. Then abruptly, his anger turned to confusion. This was *Nanju*.

Nanju.

After that long journey back from Berlin, after all that had happened there. Despite that first, welcoming sight of Tiger Hills, despite Avvaiah and Appaiah, it had only been after Appu had laid eyes upon Nanju that it had truly sunk in that he was home.

And now it was *Nanju* who was laying him out naked. He looked at the rows of gawking faces. 'My father was the tiger killer,' he wanted to shout. 'The *tiger killer*. I am no abandoned orphan, I am the son of Kambeymada Machaiah, bravest, most honourable, the last tiger killer of Coorg.'

His ears filled with that sound again, of mutton being pounded. *Tshack tshack tshack*. The sound he had been trying to get out of his head ever since . . . He had stood by, the son of the tiger killer, and watched them pound the pretties to a pulp. He had stood by, and done *nothing*. Appu looked desperately around him, his breath coming fast despite the chill in the air.

'Nanju,' a distressed Devanna intervened. 'What are you doing? Appu is your brother.'

'Tayi was my blood, not his.'

'Nanju!' Devi's voice cut sharp as a knife. 'Have you lost your mind?' She stalked towards her sons, head flung high but still barely even reaching their chests. 'If you don't know better than to create a scene, to pick a fight with your brother now, the most inopportune of times, then blood or not, *better he a son of mine than you*.'

Nanju flinched, as if she had reached up and physically slapped him. He looked about him, taking in the shock on all their faces – Appaiah, the uncles, aunts, numerous cousins, and there, Baby, *Baby*, bright as a pearl.

The expression on her face, shock, distaste and something else, something unbearable . . . the *pity* as she glanced briefly at him and then looked away at Appu. Nanju's mouth opened, he tried to say something to his mother, '*why* do you do this to me, over and over,' but the words were locked in his throat.

'Have you gone deaf? The *bier*. Appu and you together . . .'

Looking neither to his left nor his right, Nanju stepped away from the bier.

The two boys left immediately after the funeral, tension lying thick and unfamiliar between them all the way back home. 'I need a drink,' Appu said tersely to Tukra as soon as they reached Tiger Hills. 'Tell them I've gone to the Club.'

Devi and Devanna stayed a few hours longer with the family before returning. He looked worriedly at her as she sat silently to one side of the Austin. The windows of the car were rolled down. Usually she hated even a breath of air to pass through the glass; it blew her hair in a dozen different directions, she complained. Today though, when the driver leaned to roll up the windows, she had lifted her hand. 'No,' she had said quietly. A brisk breeze swept through the car, carrying with it the promise of an early winter and whipping Devi's hair about her face.

'Avvaiah.'

Nanju was waiting for them in the portico.

'Nanju,' Devanna began anxiously.

'Avvaiah,' Nanju said again, cutting off Devanna as the driver leaped to open the car doors.

'Avvaiah,' he said a third time, and at last Devi heard him. 'You insulted me. In front of everyone, talked to me as if I were a servant.'

Devi looked at him wearily and then, shaking her head, walked inside the house.

'Don't you walk away.' The words were like bullets, ricocheting off the hallway and stopping Devi in her tracks. 'I am your son, Avvaiah, your son. Your blood. Is that not important to you?'

'Not now Nanju,' she said tiredly.

His voice cracked. 'I know you've always loved Appu more, even when we were children. I used to lie awake in bed, did you know that? Pretend to be asleep and watch as you came into our room and stood by our cot. Always on the side where Appu slept, standing over him and watching him sleep. What about me, Avvaiah? What about me?'

'Nanju, please. All this drama . . .'

'This drama? Every single time, you think first of Appu. *I* am your son. Me.'

'You are both my sons, equally,' Devi said tersely. 'Appu is your brother, or have you forgotten?'

'Nanju, monae, what is all this, what's got into you?' Devanna pleaded. 'Calm down. We've barely bid Tayi farewell, this is hardly the time.'

Nanju turned towards his father, the words bursting from him. 'This isn't the time, it never *is* the time. Quiet, Nanju, hush, Avvaiah has a headache. Hush Nanju, Avvaiah is busy. And you, Appaiah, what about you? She has no time for you either, she has never cared for either of us, don't you see? Not you and never me, no matter how hard we try. Why do you just sit there and do nothing?'

Something snapped within Devi. 'Yes, Devanna, why don't you answer our son?' she spat. Tell him why you take it, tell him why you do nothing, tell him just how and why we were married, why don't you?' She whirled towards Nanju. 'You want to know what you are to me, Nanjappa? You are a *curse*. So that every day when I look at you I am reminded of all that is lost.' The words flew like poison from Devi's mouth, festering with grief. 'Every time I look at you, I am reminded of what could have been. A curse, a punishment, that is what you are to me.'

They stood shocked in the aftermath of her outburst, all three of them still for an instant, and then she reached for him, realising just what she had said. 'Nanju,' she whispered.

He was staring at her, ashen. The shadowed meaning of his mother's words shifting, twisting over his skin. 'Tell him,' she had said, 'just *why* we were married.' He turned towards Devanna, as if for support, looking to this father, so cherished, so beloved, surely so beyond reproach, and saw the anguish, the *guilt* in his eyes.

'Kunyi,' Devi pleaded. 'I did not mean . . .'

Nanju's face crumpled. He thrust out a hand, as if to hold her at bay, and rushed up the stairs.

Devi retreated to her room. The things she said, the *things* she had said. She sat on the edge of her bed and reached shakily for the jar of cream. She twisted it in her fingers, but the light was dull and the starbursts in the glass seemed blunted and opaque. It slipped from her grasp, rolling on to the floor.

Devi began to weep then at last. For all that had happened, all that was lost, for Tayi, *Tayi*, don't leave me, not you as well, *don't go*. She drew her legs beneath her, curling small and bereft upon the woollen blankets. Clouds moved across the sky, thick and amorphous, and a soft rain began to fall.

A visibly unstrung Devanna tried to reason with Nanju. 'Monae, please, everyone is very upset right now, we've just lost Tayi, your mother is hardly in her right mind.' Nanju couldn't bear to even look at his father.

'She never wanted me.'

'She loves you. She always has. You are her son.'

Nanju shook his head, trying valiantly to hold back his tears. 'I have to leave. I have to.'

'Where? Monae, please . . .'

'I don't know. I don't care. I cannot be here any longer.'

He left that very afternoon, his face white and drawn as he bent to touch his father's feet. Devanna pressed something into his palm. 'If you will not change your mind,' he said miserably, 'then at least keep this.' It was an old silver amulet.

'It was your mother's, she wore it as a child. She gave it to me many years ago.' The amulet lay gently glowing, light and shadow pooling in the faded prayer that scrolled across its face. 'There hasn't been a day since that I have not kept it near me. Take it,' Devanna said shakily, 'as a token of both our blessings.'

Nanju looked as if he might refuse but then mutely placed the amulet in his pocket. He left then, walking out into the fitful rain. The trees sighing as he went down the drive, as if bidding farewell to this beloved son, this quieter brother who had always loved them the most.

A songbird began to trill somewhere in the estate, fluting into the falling rain.

When Appu returned from the Club, his lips tightened when he heard what had happened. Without a word, he turned the car about and raced after Nanju, tracking him down in Mysore.

'I am done with Tiger Hills,' Nanju said quietly. 'You should leave.'

'Done with Tiger Hills? Don't be a fathead. You know that you of all people will *never* be done with the place. And where are you going to go anyway?'

'Bangalore. Bombay. The university there . . . it doesn't matter.'

'You're upset. We all are.' Appu stopped, trying to find the right words, still hurt by Nanju's actions at the funeral. 'Just come home.'

Nanju said nothing, a lump in his throat as he looked away.

Appu shook his head. 'Have it your own way then. I know you'll return soon enough.' He forced a grin. 'As you embark on this moment-ous journey to unknown shores, I shall impart sage advice.' Wagging a solemn finger at Nanju, he began to recite:

> *Beware the Jabberwock, my son!*
> *The jaws that bite, the claws that catch!*
> *Beware the Jubjub bird, and shun*
> *The frumious Bandersnatch*

Nanju tried to smile. 'Yes. The Bandersnatch. I hear Bombay is full of them.'

They stood looking at one another. Appu punched him lightly on the shoulder. 'Come on man. This is all . . .'

Nanju turned away. 'You should leave.'

Appu was getting into the car when Nanju called out behind him. 'You take care of her, you hear? Baby. You take care of her.'

Appu's eyes narrowed. He started the engine without a word, and turned back for Tiger Hills.

It was almost a month later before they received any news of Nanju. He wrote to Devanna, a short, formal letter. He had applied for a teaching position at the agricultural college in Bombay, it would be some weeks before he heard, but he was hopeful. It was obvious to all of them that Nanju had no immediate plans to return.

Devi did the only thing she knew how to – she lifted her head high, put one foot in front of the other and marched on. She went ahead with the preparations for Appu and Baby's nuptials; although it was tradition to wait a year after a death in the family before hosting a celebration of any kind, Tayi had made them all promise that they would not postpone the wedding.

Devi brought home the jewellery from the safe deposit box in Mercara. She laid the velvet boxes on the bedspread, their bijou contents winking in the sun. Two of each gemmed bauble, one for Baby, and one for Nanju's future bride. She unhappily stroked a gold sovereign. Was this any way to behave with one's mother? What did the boy expect, an apology? So she had said some things in the heat of the moment, had she not tried to tell him that she had not meant those things? A lump rose in her throat as she shut away the gold.

The day of the wedding dawned crystal clear, the arrangements so opulent that they set an altogether new standard against which weddings in Coorg would be judged for at least the next decade. There was talk about Nanju's absence, of course there was, but for once, the rumour mill ran in Devi's favour. Poor woman. Look what he had done, that elder boy of hers, just upped and ran away to the city. The quiet ones were always the ones who got up to mischief. He was in Bombay, so they had heard. The boy had got some teaching job, or was he studying? They weren't sure . . .

Devi remained stoic through all the commiserations. Masking the unhappiness in her eyes, she deflected the questions with talk of the weather and the quality of the coffee crop expected that year. Nobody noticed how tightly she held herself, or the way her gaze flickered time and again to the driveway, as if trying hopelessly to conjure up her missing son.

The gossips at last shifted their attention to the wedding at hand. The bride was ethereal, they exclaimed. She had the look of her aunt, those same cheekbones, the same delicate skin that looked as if it might bruise at the slightest touch. And what a welcome she had from the groom's family! There were two sets each of every gemstone imaginable – diamonds, sapphires, rubies and emeralds – ropes of pearls, chokers and chandelier earrings, silks, linens and gold sovereigns aplenty for all the days of her life.

Baby demurely kept her eyes downcast as women lifted her veil to ooh and aah at her beauty. She was so completely, sublimely happy, she could have sworn her feet were floating a few inches off the ground.

'You have a long night ahead of you,' her friends whispered mischievously as they seated her in the car that would take the newlyweds to Tiger Hills. 'The bridegroom looks as strong as a bull, he will not allow you much sleep tonight.'

'Goodbye then,' Appu called from the window and the car began to pull away from the courtyard. A pang shot through Baby and she turned her head, squinting through the windows as her family grew small and doll-like then finally faded into the distance. Her eyes moist, she searched delicately for the handkerchief that her mother had folded into her blouse.

'Are you all right?'

Glancing shyly at the uncle seated in the front seat of the car who was designated as chaperone to the newlyweds, she nodded.

'That's my girl,' Appu said and leaned back against the seat.

Baby cast about desperately for something to say, but the words felt sticky, all jumbled together. Filled with a sudden impulse, she shifted her veil. Just a discreet fluttering of spangled silk, but when the fabric settled it rested lightly over his fingers. Her hand moved unseen beneath the silk, and shocked at her own daring, Baby reached out and placed her fingers on her husband's.

She knew, even without looking at him, that Appu was smiling. They rode that way for the remainder of the journey, saying no more to one another but with their hands tightly entwined beneath the folds of her veil.

Devanna had taken charge of the decorations at Tiger Hills in anticipation of his new daughter-in-law, gilding its walls with dozens of oil lamps. Hurricane lanterns swayed from the boughs of the banyan tree and the flames of a thousand candles danced along the walkways of the garden and from the walls until the house and its grounds were molten with light.

Baby watched spellbound from the window of the Austin as they drove through the grounds. The estate workers had gathered for a glimpse of the bride and she smiled beneath her veil as they erupted in a loud cheer as the car swept past them up the drive. The portico and verandah were swarming with guests. The driver drew to a halt and Appu stepped from the car, extending a gallant hand to his bride. Baby stepped out shyly and touched a beaming Devi's feet.

'Swami kapad, kunyi.' She kissed Baby's forehead. 'May you live long, may you die a married woman.'

The bride was taken to the well to draw the first pail of water and then right foot extended, once, twice, a third time over the threshold, Baby entered her new home. Devi smiled. 'There will be time enough tomorrow to show you through the house, but for now, come, the prayer room first, and then let us take you to your room.'

They seated Baby on a vast four poster bed draped in silk and brocade. More innuendoes and giggling, and then the women left her alone to await her groom. Baby sat patiently on the bed for what seemed like hours, while the merriment below showed no signs of abating. Now and again, someone checked in on her. 'Patience, patience,' they told her grinning, 'your groom is busy hosting his guests, you may as well get some rest while you can.'

Devanna stopped by to see her, then, shortly after he had left, Devi knocked and entered. 'Kunyi?' She smiled as she re-arranged the veil about Baby's face. 'You looked so beautiful today. I cannot count the number of people who congratulated me on my exquisite daughter-in-law.'

'Everyone says I look like you,' Baby said shyly.

Devi laughed with pleasure. 'Maybe so, maybe so, but I lost the flush of youth some time ago.' Seating herself on the bed next to Baby, she cocked her head to one side, listening to the raucous sounds of merrymaking below. 'Appu and his friends. Such a boisterous lot . . .' She patted Baby's cheek. 'Still, now that you are in the house, he will improve his ways. You give me a grandchild soon, you hear?'

Baby blushed and Devi smiled. 'God bless you kunyi,' she said again. 'God bless the both of you with all happiness.' Her eyes grew clouded. 'I only wish . . . I wish all of the family had been here.' How she had hoped that Nanju would return for the wedding. 'Your great grandmother,' Devi said. 'If only Tayi had lived to bless the wedding.'

'Don't be sad, maavi,' Baby said softly. 'Tayi is here with us.'

'Yes, kunyi, I know.' Devi straightened her shoulders and tried to smile. 'They all are. Tayi, my parents, Appu's father – our ancestors, watching over us.'

Baby nodded, anxious to ease the other's hurt. 'Yes, they are, Tayi especially. *I saw her today, maavi.*' She looked earnestly at Devi. 'Right at the back of the guests when we were leaving for Tiger Hills. Tayi. Standing there and waving at me, bidding me farewell.'

Devi looked startled. The girl was gazing wide eyed at her, her eyes clear and limpid. A faint misgiving began to uncurl in Devi's chest. 'It is very late,' she said abruptly, rising to her feet. She patted Baby on the cheek again. 'Try to get some rest. From the sound of it, it will be a good many hours before your husband comes to you.'

Baby bit her lip as Devi left the room. Her mother had warned her not to talk of spirits and the dead, people did not understand, she said. But Baby had only been trying to help. She knew how sad Devi was over Nanju anna's sudden departure . . . besides, Tayi *had* been there.

Troubled, Baby rose from the bed in a rustle of silk and went to the window. Light spilled from the drawing room, casting patches of gold onto the lawn. She could hear the sound of glasses clinking. Laughter, much laughter, the high pitch of a woman's voice. Baby frowned. When would Appu come upstairs? She was filled with a sudden, fierce longing. She turned her palms upwards, holding them towards the light. The dabs of bridal henna had stained her skin a deep, vibrant maroon. She turned her palms this way and that, examining them, and her lips curved in a smile. The richer the stain, it was said, the stronger the love a husband would have for his wife.

It was almost four in the morning when Appu finally entered. 'Baby?' he said softly. 'Where . . . there you are, my lovely bride. What are you doing by the window?'

She looked at him, reproach in her kohl-rimmed eyes.

'Come. What is this? You saw my friends, they have come from Madras, from Bangalore, a few even from Bombay. I couldn't very well leave them and disappear could I?' He smiled and lifted the veil from her head. 'Ayy, wife. You were all I could think of downstairs.'

She looked at him again, with those sooty black eyes. 'Wife,' he said softly again, savouring the roll of it against his tongue.

The first light of day was filtering wispily in through the lace curtains when Baby laughed out loud. Appu cupped her mouth with his hand.

'Hush.' He grinned, the dimple flashing in his cheek. 'Do you want the entire household to hear?'

She shook her head, her eyes dancing beneath his palm, but as soon as he removed his hand, she laughed again.

She ran a hand down his back, the damp warmth of it. The two of them, entwined like this, limbs and trunks and skin, hard to tell where she ended, where he began. The smell of him, like moss in the rain. She turned her head, tucking her face into his neck, breathing him in. Her friends had been entirely right, she thought happily, she would get very little sleep.

'Again,' she whispered, moving slowly under him, 'again.'

Chapter 33

⁂ 1930 ⁂

Baby gazed enchanted at the toe rings that she had first slipped on as a bride. They flashed silver in the sun, their intricate whorls broadcasting to all the world that she was now somebody's wife.

'Admiring them again, kunyi?' Devanna asked, amused.

Baby blushed and sheepishly shook her head. Devanna chuckled as he turned back to the flower beds. She glanced surreptitiously at him and then touched a finger to the black beads about her neck. *Married*.

Devanna and she were picking flowers for the house, in what had become their weekly ritual. The garden was fully in bloom; a riot of colour in every direction, an artist's palette upended on the soil. Baby sighed, a soft, contented sound.

The leaves of the sampigé trees rustled in the breeze and she frowned, reminded suddenly of Nanju. It had been his birthday three days ago. Devi had picked a perfect sampigé blossom to place in the prayer corner. 'Thirty-one,' she had said at the breakfast table, staring at her plate. 'Nanju is thirty-one today.' Neither Appu nor Devanna had said anything in response.

It hung over them, the pall of Nanju's leaving. 'Why don't you just go to Bombay and bring him back?' Baby had once asked Appu.

'Because my mother can be as stubborn as a mule,' Appu had replied, 'and it seems that in this regard at least, Nanju has taken after her. He'll return, but only when he is ready.'

Baby looked at Devanna again. She had grown very fond of her quiet, gentle-mannered father-in-law and it distressed her to see the sadness that sometimes seemed to envelop him like a shroud. Nanju would return, she knew in her heart that he would soon be home for good. And then they would *all* be happy.

'Baby!' Appu's voice carried over the lawn, startling her from her reverie. 'Baby, look at the time, we have to leave!'

'Here,' Devanna said affectionately, 'hand me the flower basket. You had better hurry, you know how he gets with his hunts.'

Calling out to Appu, promising to be ready in *two* minutes, no more, Baby hurried towards the house, toe rings twinkling all the way.

When they returned later that morning, dusty and grimy, a deer and two pheasants slung in the back of the jeep, Appu was brimming with laughter. 'You should have seen her, how I wish you'd seen her,' he recounted to Devi and Devanna. 'Barely had I downed the deer than our lady here was off and running. "I am bal battékara," she yelled, scaring the living daylights out of the other women as she raced towards the kill. Were it not for my bullet, her screams alone might have put paid to the poor animal!'

'It wasn't like that at all,' Baby protested. 'I—'

'You streaked like a flash of lightning before anyone else stood a chance!'

'Oh hush now, stop troubling her,' Devi said as she sprinkled teli-neer on them both to ward off the evil spirits. 'It's in Baby's blood,' she stated proudly. 'When I was a child, I was *always* named the bal battékara at my father's hunts.'

> 'The beautiful girl is finally here, come to visit her near and dear.
> Rubies glittering about her neck ... anklets shimmering like the sun ...
> The beautiful one has come, drenched in a rainstorm she has come.'

'What?' Devi asked Devanna surprised. 'What are you muttering there in the corner?'

'Baby,' Devanna said softly to his daughter-in-law, patting her cheek, 'at times you remind me very much of someone I used to know.'

*

'Devanna!' Devi called urgently some days later as she hurried through the house. 'A letter, there's a letter!' In the seven months that Nanju had been gone, now and again there was a letter from him, bearing some little news from Bombay. Devi had pounced on the letter as soon as she saw it in that morning's post. 'A *letter*,' she said when she found him. 'Here, quick, read it to me.'

She stood there rapt as Devanna read the brief letter aloud, disappointment clouding her face when he had finished. Once again, there was no mention of a visit, no hint of a reconciliation.

'Is that all?' she demanded. 'Are you sure there isn't any more?' Without waiting for his response, she took the letter from Devanna, holding it to the light, turning it backwards and forwards, this way and that, as if searching for some indication, some hint of Nanju's return that Devanna might have overlooked.

'No matter,' she said then, a lump in her throat. 'No matter. He never was much of a one for words.'

She walked slowly down the foyer. She had hoped that in this letter at last . . . A burst of laughter drifted in from the dining room. Baby was arranging a vast armful of flowers as Appu watched, leaning against the wall, his hands shoved in his pockets.

'At least Baby,' Devi thought wanly, 'has brought laughter with her to Tiger Hills.'

Baby murmured something and Appu laughed out loud again; Devi turned, suddenly desperate for a pocket of quiet. She made her way to Nanju's bedroom. It was the old nursery; Appu had long appropriated one of the larger rooms on the first floor, while Nanju had chosen to remain here, in this room of his childhood. She stared unhappily at the mural of the tiger that still sprawled across one wall. When Appu had left for Biddies, she had braced herself for the pain of his absence. A mother's pain at being separated from a child – it had felt like a missing limb, a phantom pain that cut deep.

It was different with Nanju. A slower ache, but unexpectedly insidious. Like a leg turned stunted, just a little shorter than the other, dragging perpetually behind. The letter today . . . how she had hoped that at least now, after all these months, there would be a sign that Nanju was coming home.

Devi sat there, on the perfectly made bed, brooding over her son.

'Dags!' Timmy Bopanna called. 'Who do you wager will win then?'

'What, the Aga Khan prize?' Appu wandered over to the bookie table, Baby in tow.

In the winter of 1929, almost exactly a year to Appu and Baby's wedding, the newspapers had been agog with the Aga Khan's challenge. It had been thrown to Indians everywhere – the first Indian to pilot a solo flight between England and India would be awarded a prize of £500, the Aga Khan had declared. The journey could start from either end, whether in England or in India, but must be completed in six weeks from the date of commencement. The contest would remain open for a year, beginning January, 1930. There were three contestants entered. Jehangir Tata, amateur aviator, and scion of one of the wealthiest families in Bombay, Man Mohan Singh, a graduate from Bristol, and Aspy Engineer, another hopeful from Bombay.

Bets were being placed enthusiastically in the Mercara Club with the odds strongly in favour of the Sikh, 'Has to be Man Mohan, he is the most experienced of the three.'

Appu shook his head. 'Jehangir, I wager. Met the chap once at a dinner in Madras. Impressive fellow. If anyone can do it, I think it will be him.'

'Come now, surely not! Mohan Singh all the way, he is the most pukka, he has the most flying experience . . .'

Appu grinned, taking a drag of his cheroot. 'I defer to my lovely wife,' he said. 'Darling? Who shall I place my bet on?'

Baby blushed as the focus of the group shifted to her, secretly delighted to be singled out so publicly by her husband.

'I think . . .' She looked at the photographs of the three contestants placed on the table, cut from a newspaper and stuck neatly on the back of a menu card. 'Him,' she pointed, smiling.

'Aspy?! Baby, the boy is not yet eighteen!' Seeing how her face fell at his words, Appu bowed gallantly before her. 'So be it,' he announced to the watching crowd, 'if my bride favours Aspy Engineer – and lucky the lad is, to have so brooked favour with her – then here! Two hundred says that Aspy shall indeed be the victor.'

Baby's face lit from within.

The three contestants began their flights in the spring of 1930. Man Mohan took off from Croydon, the other two from India. Every twist and turn of their flights was reported in the media, then dissected in the Club.

'Single engines, all the aircraft.'

'Gipsy Moths, no radio aids.'

'Here Timmy,' Appu called, grinning, 'your Man Mohan doesn't look so smart now, does he, with his Miss India?'

The Sikh had named his aircraft Miss India. Unfortunately, twice after leaving England's shores, he had had to turn the aircraft around and restart his journey. His vessel was aptly named, the newspapers pointed out. Miss India, she was named, and that was *precisely* what she seemed to be doing.

On his third foray out, Man Mohan Singh made steady progress. He was Eastward bound via Lympne, Paris, Rome, and Gaza, with Jehangir Tata and young Aspy Engineer flying furiously in the opposite direction. Singh landed at Drigh Road, Karachi on 12 May 1930. 'Victory!' the papers trumpeted 'The Sikh is the victor!' Aspy, trailing Singh by a day, landed in England the next morning.

However, news of Singh's victory was premature. A forced swamp landing of his Miss India in France had resulted in a day's delay, the authorities discovered. His flight had taken six weeks *and a day*. It was Aspy Engineer after all, the long shot and Baby's pick, who was finally declared the victor.

'I told you so!' Appu said exuberantly at the Club as he scooped up his winnings. 'This bride of mine is a winner!'

He bought Baby a diamond sunburst brooch to celebrate, and a matching armband. It cost a great deal more than his takings, but that was hardly the point, was it?

Appu got Baby pregnant. Or at least Baby thought she was, twice in quick succession, over a span of five months. Each time, her face had crumpled when the monthly blood arrived, cruelly delayed by a few days, just late enough for her to have got her hopes up.

'Don't worry,' Devi comforted her, when Baby wept. 'Do not fret, kunyi, you are both so young, there is so much time ahead of you.'

Appu sat beside Baby on the bed, and took her in his arms. He kissed the top of her head. 'Ayy, my lovely. Stop now, hush. How about I recite you a poem?'

> *'There was a young girl,'* he began, tone solemn,
> *'Who begat three brats named Nat, Pat and Tat*
> *It was fun in the breeding,*
> *But hell in the feeding,*
> *When she found there was no tit for tat!'*

Baby was silent, puzzling through the words and then, despite herself, she giggled. She pummelled Appu's chest with her fists and they both started to laugh.

Nanju's letters continued sporadically, growing ever more erratic, in frequency as well as content. Once there was only a paragraph, devoted entirely to the sound of the sea, the way it crashed and tugged against Bombay's shoreline. Another time, he fretted over the lack of the night. 'There are always lights here,' he wrote to Devanna. 'It is impossible to rest.' Not once did he talk of returning.

The next year, when Appu's twenty-seventh birthday came around, Devi made an offering at the Iguthappa temple in the name of all three children – Appu, Baby and Nanju. Appu sat on one enormous pan of the balancing scale, pulling a blushing Baby on to his lap, as the priest loaded up the corresponding pan with sack upon sack of raw rice. Devi folded her hands in prayer, watching as the two pans of the scale were finally in perfect balance. 'Iguthappa Swami, protect my children.'

They donated the rice to the temple, and Devi gave an additional hundred rupees to the priest. 'Pray for my sons,' she asked, 'both of them ... let them both be home.'

She was in pensive mood on the way back to Tiger Hills, barely noticing as the car bumped along the pitted roads. Appu, who was driving the car ahead, slowed and, pulling to the side, flagged them down. When Devi rolled down the window, he pointed to his left. 'The Kambeymada village, Avvaiah. I told our lady here that it lies along this road, and she wants to visit the old Kambeymada house.'

Devi was about to point out that it was getting late when Baby leaned across Appu, her eyes shining. 'May we?' she asked. 'Please, just for a short while, I promise we won't be long.'

'Oh, all right,' Devi capitulated. 'The two of you go. No, not us, it's late and we're tired.'

Devi sat at her dressing table that evening, combing out her damp hair. It was hard to believe how long it had been since she had last visited the Kambeymada house. Appu and Devanna went each year for the Puthari celebrations, but she refused to go. The house, its grounds ... there were too many memories.

She put down the comb, and stared at her reflection in the mirror. She touched a finger to the hollows under her eyes. When had these appeared? She shut her eyes, suddenly weary. The ceremony at the temple had upset her more than she realised. Nanju should have been there. And then, this visit of Appu's to the Kambeymada house. It had immediately brought up memories of the past, rocking her already fragile mood.

An image swam before her, of yellow laburnums glowing against a bald, turquoise sky. She sat still for a moment, trying to gather herself and then reached unhappily for the tiger claw brooch. It lay in her palm, a smooth, worn comma gleaming faintly in the dusk. Tiredly, she pinned it to her sari, and then, raising the comb, began once more to untangle her hair.

She heard the honking of the car, the lights from its headlamps flaring through the windows as it swept up the drive. Appu and Baby were back. Devi twisted her hair into a knot, and slowly headed downstairs. Appu was unlacing his shoes on the verandah, grinning as Baby excitedly showed Devanna a large frame.

'Avvaiah, see what we found. My lovely wife,' Appu explained, 'discovered this in the attic. Only she, of course, would even think of scampering up to the attic, but there you have it.'

'I went up, just to have a look, and there it was, lying against a wall,' Baby explained. 'Right at the very back, covered in dust. One of the old men in the house, he remembered that it had been put there years ago. It was meant to be reframed he told me, soon after Kambeymada Nayak passed away. But then, with the division of the property and so on, everyone somehow forgot about it.'

'It's a family photograph, Avvaiah,' Appu said. 'Here, see for yourself.'

'A photo . . .?' Devi's heart skipped a beat. She sat on the sofa next to Devanna, pushing her glasses onto the bridge of her nose. It was an old sepia print. White ants and termites had burrowed into the rickety black frame. From under the clouded glass, faces from the past stared solemnly back at her.

'Mysore,' she said, her voice tight. 'Kambeymada Nayak had brought a photographer from Mysore.'

'*So many years, Machu.*' She raised a hand to the frame, a slight tremor in her fingers as she traced the figures that lay silent beneath the glass. One by one, saving the face she most longed for until last.

'Look.' Baby was less patient. 'Here you are, with Nanju anna.'

He had slipped so easily from her. One push, then another and there he lay, at the edge of the straw mattress. Such little fingers, such perfectly formed feet. 'Such a good child,' they said of him, 'hardly even cries, doesn't want to trouble his mother at all.'

Devi reached towards the slender young woman and the round-faced toddler who sat on her lap. How *young* she had been. 'Such a sweet-natured child, he was,' she said to Baby. 'Hardly cried, always smiling . . .' Devanna said nothing, but she knew, even without looking at him, that he too was finding it very hard not to cry.

Devi began to point out the others to Appu and Baby, choked with emotion. 'Here. Kambeymada Nayak. Your great grandfather, Appu. What a moustache he had!'

'And him?' Baby pointed at a man standing in the very last row. 'So tall – this is Appu's father, is it not? It has to be, Appu looks so much like him.'

Devi's eyes lifted to where Baby was pointing.

Your face. To rest my eyes just once more upon your face.

'He . . .' She stopped, trying to regain her composure. 'Look monae,' she said then to Appu, trying desperately to sound light hearted, 'didn't I always tell you that you look just like him?'

Baby twisted the photograph towards her. Only Devanna noticed the involuntary twitch of protest as Devi tried to hold on to the frame.

Baby stared at the photograph. 'How strange.' She turned it around again so the others could see what she meant. 'Appu's father. He isn't looking at the camera at all. Why,' she continued, as she peered at Machu's face, then she laughed and looked up at Devi.

'The way this photograph has been taken, it almost seems as if he is staring straight at you!'

Devi began to cry then, tears rolling from her eyes. Appu looked at her startled and shuffled his feet as Devanna dug his hand into his pocket and quietly handed her his handkerchief.

They had the photograph reframed with a square of new glass and hung it in the drawing room. Every morning now, on her way to the garden, Devi stopped to touch her fingers to Machu's face. The grim, worn cast of it, his eyes contriving to be at once dark with anger and yet hollowed with unhappiness as they stared not at the photographer, but at the back of her head.

'Such things I said to you that day. Half a man. I called you half the man you were. How angry I made you. And then you went and won the paaria kali match . . .'

She would stand there, reliving the past, 'all these years, so many years, Machu,' drinking in that beloved, long-lost face as the plantation stirred and the mist swirled dreamily about the garden.

The photograph was a sign, Devi knew. She felt it in her bones. It was a good omen, an indication that the family would soon be together again. Sitting on Nanju's bed one afternoon, she came to an abrupt decision. This was foolishness. All this drama over nothing. She would wait until next year. Until the Puthari festival, no longer. If this donkey son of hers had not returned by then, she would send for him. Why, maybe they could *all* go to Bombay together, make a visit of it. 'I will twist his ear hard,' she promised herself, 'and smack him on that stubborn forehead of his. And then I will bring him home.'

It was as if a weight had lifted from her chest. Devi was smiling as she shut the door of the room behind her.

'Ayy, old man,' she said to Devanna the next morning as they sat on the verandah. 'No need to be so forlorn. Just you wait and see, I will bring your son home.' Devanna looked at her quizzically and she nodded. Then, cocking her head to one side, Devi began to sing. On

411

and on she sang, as tunelessly as ever, waggling her eyebrows comically and only stopping when Devanna at last began to laugh.

The coffee yield was especially rich that year, attracting a host of jackals that prowled the estate at night. The chicken coop was reinforced with wire, and the dogs, despite their yipping, were shut indoors where the jackals couldn't get at them. The jackals were drawn to the ripening coffee, sniffing out the sweetest, most succulent berries. It was a well-known fact that the seeds of these berries, passing undigested through the stools of the jackals, consistently produced the best flavour of the crop. The Coorgs would not touch the droppings of course, nor use the seeds themselves, but they had their Poleya servants pick through them and collect the seeds for sale. At Tiger Hills too, Tukra and the other servants followed the tracks of the jackals each morning, picking through the droppings. Devi akka was in a generous mood that year it seemed; she had told them to sell the seeds and keep the proceeds for themselves.

Jehangir Tata, the third contestant in the Aga Khan's challenge, established the first air mail carrier service in the country. He piloted the first flight himself, a Puss Moth that flew from Karachi to Bombay and onwards to Madras via Ahmedabad and Bombay. Appu's face lit with excitement at the news. 'This is only the beginning,' he exclaimed. 'Now that the country has air mail, can passenger carriers be far behind?'

His eyes shone as he stared at Tata's photograph in the papers. 'What it must feel like! To fly like a bird, so free, nothing around but wide open sky.'

The rains came once more, a series of warm, gentle showers rimmed with rainbows. The forest mushrooms that year were so plentiful, the shanty was filled with baskets of them for weeks. Thick, fleshy mushrooms the size of a man's fist, so intensely flavoured that one had no need for meat.

There arrived one more letter from Nanju, this time containing not a word. It was an unsettling, single page of foolscap, covered entirely with tracings of the amulet that Devanna had given him. It was as if he had placed the paper over it, and run his pencil furiously across. Right side up, upside down, horizontal, vertical, along this side of the page and that, tracing after tracing of the rounded rectangle shape of the amulet and the prayer it contained. Devanna stared at the strange letter, his face pinched. 'It's nothing,' Devi said to him, trying to mask her own worry. 'He was probably at a loss for what to write.' She smoothed the unsettling drawings under her fingers. 'We'll go to Bombay,' she said decisively. 'Let the rains be done, we'll all go to Bombay and bring Nanju home.'

Baby believed she was pregnant again. This time, she did not tell Appu in case it was yet another false alarm. A full week passed, and still she hugged the news to herself. Her legs seemed to grow more leaden with each passing day and there was a strange cotton fuzz taste in her mouth, yet Baby didn't say a word.

'Are you well?' a concerned Devi asked, noting the pallor of her face. Baby nodded, trying to smile, but the ache in her legs grew so severe that finally that afternoon she took to her bed, drawing the blankets as close as possible. Her head felt heavy, so unbearably heavy. She shifted this way and that, trying to get comfortable, and at last fell into a fitful sleep, a hand draped across her stomach. Almost immediately she began to dream.

She found herself tiptoeing through a large building, careful, so as not to wake any of the people in the series of dank, dimly lit rooms. Someone moaned, and Baby realised that the building was a hospital. The person moaned again. 'Avvaiah,' he whispered, and a pang shot through her as she recognised Nanju's voice. He moved gingerly and grimaced in pain. 'Avvaiah,' he repeated, stopping short, as if embarrassed that someone might hear. He lay there, a look of such unbearable hurt in his eyes that Baby wanted to cry. It was as if she could feel it herself, the crushing weight of his despair. He sat up, wincing. She watched helplessly as he lowered his feet to the floor and shuffling past her, disappeared through the door.

Baby awoke in a sweat; she lay there for an instant, her heart racing. So vivid had the dream been that it took a few seconds for her to register the dampness that lay pooling between her thighs. 'No,' she panicked, all thoughts of Nanju dashed from her head. She knew, she *knew*, even before she thrust her hand downwards, and her fingers came back murky with blood.

Devi sighed as she sorted through the post. Two days now since Baby had taken to her bed. Once again the monthly blood had come; the child had been so crushed that she had developed an alarmingly high fever. How the poor girl had wept. 'It's OK kunyi,' Devi had consoled her, masking her own disappointment. 'Hush now, it isn't as if the mountains have fallen or the Kaveri run dry. It is not the end of the world. I'm sure that next month . . .' But still Baby had wept, as if her heart would break. A distressed Appu kept pacing the bedroom, back and forth, back and forth, until Devi had practically had to order him downstairs.

She looked absently up at the ceiling now. The upstairs wing was silent. 'Keep her sedated,' the doctor had advised. Baby was sound asleep, despite the gramophone that Appu was playing in the drawing room.

There was at last a break in the rains, the sun aslant through the sampigé trees, the flower beds gently steaming. The very kind of day that Nanju would have loved. Off he would have disappeared, poking about goodness knows where in the estate, checking on his beloved birdhouses.

She looked at the telegram in her hand. It was addressed to Devanna. 'Here,' she said, 'for you.' Something from one of the stores from where he ordered his books, she presumed.

'Ah?' Devanna patted his pockets, searching for his glasses.

The cat on the verandah yawned and began licking its fur. 'Around your neck,' Devi said without looking up, 'they're around your neck.' Devanna looked sheepishly at her and began to tear open the telegram.

It was only when he dropped it, with a hoarse cry that so startled the cat outside that it jumped into the air, that Devi twisted towards him.

'What? What is it?'

Appu bent to pick up the telegram. He scanned its contents, his face turning ashen. 'There . . . there has been an accident.'

The telegram was from Bombay, from the university where Nanju taught. There had been a terrible accident, it informed them. 'Monsoon; road having potholes. Mr Nanjappa is no more.'

The cat outside stalked stiff legged and disgruntled to the window and leaped on to the sill. Slowly it began to lick its fur once more. A butterfly flew in just above its head but the creature was too engrossed in its grooming to notice. The butterfly wandered into the room on bright yellow wings barely the span of a fingernail.

Devanna was saying something, but there were not so much words as sounds. Syllables of grief, of the harshest bereavement. A litany of loss.

Devi reached up and pulled her hair loose from its bun. It spilled about her shoulders, still thick, streaked here and there with silver. 'My son,' she whispered. 'My *son*.'

The butterfly hovered above them all, bright as a laburnum petal, adrift in the breeze.

Appu rushed to Bombay. A friend of his, engaged to a cousin of Jehangir Tata's, pulled some strings on Appu's behalf. He clambered aboard Tata's single-engined mail carrier in Madras, folding himself amongst the mail bags, the only available space in the place.

'*Post* haste, I suppose,' he said wanly to the pilot, casting desperately about for a joke.

The pilot glanced soberly at him and nodded. 'I heard of your circumstances. My condolences.'

Appu fell silent. He sat hunched on the bags, his knees drawn almost to his chin as the Puss Moth pointed her nose into the sky. The roar of the engine all around him, loud, blessedly loud, driving all thought from his mind. He sat there, on his first flight after all, but hardly noticing as the Puss Moth ducked and wove her way through the billowing, powder puff clouds.

Bombay was sweltering; so muggy that Nanju's body had already been cremated. 'Too much smelly, saar,' they explained helpfully to him at the morgue.

There was nothing left of Nanju to bring back home at all.

Chapter 34

Tiger Hills was steeped in mourning. Devanna had lapsed into silence. Not a word did he utter, not a sound did he make, sitting as if turned to stone in the planter chair. The garden grew wild and untended. He did not seem to notice. He had worked like a man possessed for the first few weeks after the news had come, lashing together the tips of rose bushes, pulling this one from the soil, grafting those three together. And then he had collapsed, exhausted. Nobody understood the magic he had wrought, the lamentations he had poured into the soil, but when the roses bloomed, they were the darkest scarlet imaginable. So sootily red, they were very nearly black. He had filled the garden with them, in every available patch of soil. Red-black roses, like clumps of clotted blood, as if the entire garden had turned fissured and bleeding.

The roses eventually withered and fell to the ground. The stems that should have been pruned lay neglected. They grew long and wild, crowned with thorns. Tukra faithfully watered the plants every morning and evening, but it was not enough. 'What shall I weed today?' Tukra would ask. 'Are there any cuttings to be done?' Devanna sat unheeding.

'Come maava,' Baby urged. 'Let us go pick some flowers. You and me together.'

He looked then, at the photograph of Nanju that was hung outside the prayer room. His smiling, open face framed so incongruously, so cruelly, with the garland of fresh flowers that marked the dead. Devanna's eyes filled with tears.

If Devanna was silent the house, on the other hand, was filled with music. Sheets of it, swinging, thumping, twirling through the rooms.

Appu seemed to play the gramophone without a break, as if this false gaiety would somehow compensate for the silence. 'Baby, get dressed,' he would call, 'we're going to the Club.'

At first Baby had thought her husband strangely stone-hearted. When the terrible news had arrived, Appu had not shed a tear. Devi had, for once, seemed at a complete loss; it was Appu who had called for the barber to shave his and Devanna's head, it was Appu who had sent the servants to the Nachimanda village and beyond, bearing tidings of the tragedy. It was he who had made the travel arrangements to visit Bombay. All the while dry-eyed, almost offhand.

It was weeks later when Baby had woken with a start. At first she had not been able to place the sound. A muffled choking. Had she imagined it? No, there it was again, that strange, smothered noise coming from the bathroom. She tapped on the bathroom door – 'Appu?' and when there was no reply, she had entered. He was leaning against the mirror, arms wrapped over his head. 'Appu?' she had repeated, and he had turned towards her. It had taken the breath from her, the look on his face. Such a hunted, hopeless expression, the look of a man who had searched within himself and recognised that something was irreparably lacking.

'Appu,' she said softly again, and he had shaken his head. 'Here darling, here,' she said, pressing forward and slipping her arms about him. That strangled sound again and Appu began to cry. She covered his face with gentle kisses, on his lips, his neck, his forehead, that shaven head, then led him back to their bed. He had put his face in her lap, like a child, and wept so bitterly she thought her heart would break.

'Nothing . . .' She bent forward, the better to hear what he was saying. 'I did nothing. I should have called him back, should have insisted . . . I did nothing Baby, once again *I did nothing*.'

Finally he had fallen asleep. The next morning it was as if nothing had happened. When she tried to talk with him about it, he whistled even louder, drowning out her words.

He had not spoken of Nanju after that.

The Indian hockey team left for the Los Angeles Olympics. Appu contrived to be at once absorbed in their progress. 'I knew it!' He pumped his fist in the air, listening closely to the wireless broadcast of the finals. 'Ah, Dhyan, Dhyan, what would we do without you!' He spoke the words almost reverentially. The four years since Amsterdam had scarcely blunted the prowess of the Indian team and his beloved Dhyan, it seemed.

'Appu,' Baby chided, glancing at the verandah where Devanna sat. 'He might be asleep.'

'What, at ten in the morning? What's the matter with this bloody household? This is the Olympics, Baby. The *Olympics*.' He turned the volume even higher.

Baby glanced unhappily outside, but despite the racket, Devanna did not so much as stir.

It was Tukra who finally intervened. 'Devi akka,' he said, standing in the doorway of Nanju's room and twisting the ends of his dish cloth. 'You must come down. This is not good. Devanna anna, he doesn't speak at all, his garden, he doesn't care any more, he hardly eats, and the plants, look, just *look*.'

Devi blinked, taking in the garden as if for the first time. Where had all the flowers gone?

'You must talk with him,' Tukra repeated. 'He doesn't talk to me. I ask him, "shall I weed under the banyan tree, shall I rake the leaves?" and he doesn't even speak.'

'You have four children, don't you Tukra?' Devi asked. Three girls and a boy; she had helped to get all of them married. 'You are blessed,' she said simply.

'Nanju anna . . .' Tukra's voice wobbled. 'You still have a son. You are Appu anna's mother,' he said tearfully. 'You still have a son.'

Pain sliced through Devi, so sharp that the bile rose in her throat. She pressed her forehead against the window. That last terrible exchange of words . . . 'Watching Appu sleep, Avvaiah,' Nanju had accused her. 'Not me, never me, but *Appu*.'

Devi flinched as she remembered. 'Not true,' she whispered. She squeezed her eyes shut, conjuring an image from the past. Nanju kunyi, asleep in the nursery. Both her boys, swaddled safely in their dreams.

All that came forth was a confused medley of images. The light from the oil lamp spilling about her feet, casting spirit shapes upon the windows and wooden rafters. The tiger snarling from the wall. An owl, hooting low and long somewhere in the night. And there, look, her sons. Brothers both, lying sound asleep. There was Nanju, curled in a ball . . .

And right here, Appu. Arms flung wide and smiling at some dream, his dimple so deep it made her want to cry.

'Iguthappa Swami,' she used to pray, unable to take her eyes off him, 'keep him safe. Take me, take whatever else I have, but spare me this child.'

'*Watching Appu sleep, Avvaiah. Appu.*'

Devi's eyes flew open. 'I watched over you too, kunyi,' she whispered anguished. 'I watched over you too.' A light breeze flitted through the windows, making the curtains billow. Devi shivered.

That night too, Devi barely slept, but as dawn broke, she at last gathered up her hair, left so long unbound, and fastened it into a bun. She opened the door and, clutching the balustrade as if she might lose her balance, went downstairs. The house was silent, a thin grey light seeping through the rooms.

Pausing by the old photograph, she touched her fingers first to Machu's face, then to the baby on her lap.

She had asked Baby once, soon after the news arrived. 'You told me you see those who have passed on, that they reveal themselves to you,' she said tersely. 'Have you seen my Nanju?'

Baby had slowly shaken her head.

'I knew it!' Devi had turned towards the garden, a fierce light in her eyes. 'He isn't dead, he cannot be.' For if he were, she had reasoned, surely his spirit would have found a way to return home? 'It's like breathing,' he had said to her, that was what Tiger Hills had meant to him. Abruptly the light had died from her eyes, as she recognised the absurdity of her hope.

She laid her palm now over the photograph. *Nanju kunyi.*

Devanna was on the verandah, slumped as usual in his chair. She seated herself beside him as shadow melted into light and the parrots in the banyan tree began to glide down to the grass.

'Forgive me,' she said then, her throat tight.

'He had your smile.' His voice was rusted, hollow. 'You always said he looked just like me, but it was your smile he had.'

'Devanna, I . . .'

'It should have been me. Not him. Me.'

Devi's eyes filled with tears. 'You? *I* was the one who said those things and drove him away.'

He turned to her with haunted eyes. 'Should I hate you Devi? For saying those things? Or should I thank you for keeping the circumstances of Nanju's birth from him all these years? I was the one responsible for his birth, I am therefore responsible for his death.'

'"*I am poured out like water,*"' he quoted, his voice so raw, it seemed to cut into her, '"*and all my bones are out of joint. My heart has turned to wax; it has melted away within me.*" He was the distillation of all that was good in you and in me. If he too is gone, then what's left? What's left but these sorrowing bones?'

Birds began to throng the garden, marmets and sweet-voiced koels, filling the estate with song.

'You're forgetting something,' she said huskily. The sun began to move in the East, staining the clouds rose. 'You have *another* son. Appu. He needs his father. If you give up like this . . . You . . .' She paused, fighting back her tears. 'Devanna, *we* have another child.'

He started to cry then, soundlessly, tears streaming down his cheeks, the tic in his hands so pronounced he didn't even attempt to wipe them away.

They sat down to breakfast that morning, all of them together at the dining table. Devi pulled out her chair and hesitated. Then, instead of at her usual place at the head of the table, she sat in Nanju's chair instead.

'Appu,' she ordered, to mask the sharp stab of pain even this simple action had wrought, 'stop dawdling and drink your coffee before it grows cold. And turn down the gramophone for goodness sake. Is this a home or a hotel?'

Baby thought he might object but Appu grinned. 'Yes, Avvaiah,' he agreed, getting up at once, the relief obvious in his voice.

In the summer of 1934, Gandhi came to Coorg. Despite the sweltering sun, the crowd that turned out to hear him speak was nearly ten thousand

420

strong. He talked almost exclusively that morning of the lower castes. How heinous a notion it is, Gandhi said, the concept of untouchability. That a man may or may not be granted entry somewhere just because of his birth. In God's eyes, all are one . . .

Fired by his words, the local nationalists demanded that the ancient temples of Coorg be open to everyone, regardless of birth. All of Coorg flew immediately into a tizzy, the Coorgs firmly divided in opinion as the British looked on, amused.

'It's only fair,' the nationalists said. 'Be he Poleya or Coorg, every man has equal right to the home of God.'

'Bloody fools,' retorted the old guard. What was the world coming to that a Coorg now had to treat the Poleyas as equals, the very same Poleyas who had served them for generations?

Finally, a compromise was reached. The Poleyas were allowed into the temples, albeit through a separate entrance. Under *no* circumstance would they be allowed into the sanctum sanctorums. Both nationalistic and feudal sentiments were appeased, but it was an uneasy truce.

Some months later, Timmy Bopanna approached Appu at the Club. 'Have you considered running for office, Dags?'

'Politics and me?' Appu chuckled. 'My dear chap, have you paid no heed at all to the politicos of today? One needs to be clad in a loin cloth and weigh no more than a hundred pounds to be taken seriously.' He shook his head. 'Politics and me, you must be joking.'

Timmy smiled. 'Not quite such a far-fetched notion, I'd wager. Gandhi is only the face of the nationalists Dags. The austere, humble hook that reels in the votes. Behind the curtain – ah, it's a stage filled with people like you and I.' He leaned forward to make his point. 'Educated. Cultured. From old, established families, of a certain . . . *standing*.' He gestured about the billiards room, lowering his voice. 'When the English leave, to whom do you think they will entrust the reins of government? Homespun nationalists? Or men like us, men of the world who can smoke a cheroot with them and talk to them as equals?'

Appu clicked his fingers for the waiter. 'Another gin.' He turned amused eyes on Timmy. 'And why ever would we want to meddle with all that?'

421

'Because,' Timmy said slowly, 'money without power gets awfully dull. The old days are gone Dags. You and I, we each come from some of the most venerable families in Coorg, but nobody gives a damn. It's all this nationalistic rubbish – land owner and worker, both equal. Bloody nonsense. And it'll only get worse, mark my words. Unless people like us stand up and fight for what is rightfully ours.

'Look what happened after Gandhi gave that speech. Our temples, thrown open! And this is only the beginning,' warned Timmy. 'If we don't stand up for what is ours, we stand to lose all of Coorg.'

Appu was unconvinced. 'Come, Timmy. Nothing of the sort will happen. Never mind money without power, *you* are the one being awfully dull.'

Timmy flushed. 'What's the matter with you Dags? Don't you want to make a name for yourself?' He gestured again at the smoke-filled room. 'Is this enough for you then? Well, it certainly isn't for me.' Rising to his feet, Timmy walked away in a huff.

Appu looked around him as he nursed his gin. The same old room, hardly changed through the years. The billiards table, the velvet curtains. Glasses tinkling, women laughing. He thought of Kate. Where was she, he wondered, the wanton Mrs Burnett? He had been in the billiards room, hadn't he, when he first spotted her? Suddenly restless, he downed his drink in one swallow and clicked his fingers at the waiter. 'Another.'

'Dags!' someone called to him from across the room. He pretended not to notice. At least that KCIO fellow, that Kipper Cariappa chappie, was not here this evening. He was in Coorg for a month's holiday, and Appu kept running into him at the Club, him and his blasted Staff-College-graduate, army-man, KCIO stuffed shirtedness.

'Don't you want to make a name for yourself?' Timmy had asked incredulously.

'*My* father,' Appu thought blackly to himself, 'was a tiger killer. An army hero . . .' His thoughts trailed away, the prick of superiority that they induced not lasting long.

'Make a name for yourself', if you please. Suddenly he longed to be far away, where, he didn't know, just away from all these clowns. 'Dags,' someone called again. With a muttered imprecation, Appu drained his drink, slammed the glass down on the side table, and strode to the bar.

'Even if we wanted to get into politics, where would we begin?'

Timmy turned around, a satisfied expression on his face. 'Ah,' he said, 'I'm glad you asked.'

'The Viceroy?' Devanna asked, astonished. 'The Viceroy, here in Coorg?'

Appu nodded. The family was gathered in the library before dinner. It was a new ritual begun on Appu's insistence, 'a little music Avvaiah, some civilised conversation.' He reached for an LP record, blowing on it as he slipped it from its cover.

'Yes,' he confirmed. 'The reigning Viceroy of all of British India, his importantness Lord Willingdon, or Lord Willie Ding Dong as some of us have, with the utmost affection, christened him. The word is that he may be convinced to visit Coorg. I suggested to the chaps at the Club that we should build a hall in his honour in Mercara. Get him to inaugurate it, they do seem to love that sort of thing, these fellows.'

'And if he does come . . .'

'Well, if he does come, then we host him at the Club, and press our case for renewed coffee subsidies and a railway link from Coorg to the rest of the state.'

Devi looked startled at her son. Since when had he started worrying about coffee subsidies?

'Too little too late,' Devanna said slowly. 'Subsidies can only help us so much . . .'

Coffee prices had tumbled, impacted by the Great Depression. Unless a planter had vast holdings, it had become a tricky business to run a coffee plantation profitably in Coorg.

Appu grinned. 'Well, it isn't solely about coffee, is it now?' He tapped a finger to his temple. 'This country is going to be independent of British rule sooner or later. The question is, to whom are they going to leave the reins of administration?'

Devi shook her head. 'Since when have you become interested in politics, Appu?'

'Well, *Coorg*, Avvaiah. We must get more involved with its administration, otherwise once the British leave . . .'

'I see. And this Viceroy of yours, you think he is going to look at this hall and name you his successor in gratitude?' She sighed and shook her head again. 'How much is this hall of yours going to cost?'

He shrugged, a little hurt by her dismissiveness. 'Ten, fifteen thousand? Hard to tell just yet. I have promised to contribute five.'

'Five thousand?' Devi exclaimed in dismay. 'That is a lot of money.'

'Oh, I don't think we will have to part with even half of that. People are already clamouring to be part of the donor pool. *Everyone* wants in, Avvaiah.'

He placed the needle of the gramophone on the record, and music filled the room.

'Whatever is Coorg coming to?' Devi said bemused. 'People are happy to spend fifteen thousand rupees without blinking an eye, and all for the privilege of shaking this white man's hand . . .'

Appu had risen to his feet. 'Enough politics for the evening,' he said, lifting Baby gracefully to her feet. 'How about a dance then, my lovely, before we head to the Club?'

Baby glanced shyly at Devi and Devanna as he drew her close. Laying his cheek against her hair, Appu began to sing along.

Devi swirled the snifter in her hands, the brandy sloshing golden against the crystal. It had become a habit with her now, this daily peg in the evenings. Ever since Nanju . . . she took a hasty swallow of the brandy, grateful for its heat against her throat. Without the liquor, it was hard to sleep.

She turned slightly, to look at Devanna. He was watching Appu and Baby dance, not *smiling*, no it was far too soon for that, for either him or for her, but nonetheless, there was a softness in his expression, smoothing the lines in his face.

Appu twirled Baby around in his arms, still singing along, Baby's earrings flashing green and gold as they caught the light.

Such a beautiful couple. 'Please Iguthappa Swami,' Devi sent up a silent prayer as they glided about the drawing room. 'Let them . . . let no more . . . let us . . .'

She stopped, fumbling with the words, unsure any more of how best to petition the Gods for their protection.

*

It was touch and go for a while, with the Viceroy. His military attaché insisted his schedule was simply too tight to accommodate a trip to Coorg. It was Appu who had come up with the idea of the races. The planters sent the Viceroy a gift, a finely tooled silver peechekathi, its hilt inlaid with gold. The dagger was wrapped in muslin and placed in a brass trunk filled nearly to the brim with rich brown, perfectly cloven coffee beans. Together with the gift, there was an invitation printed on heavy cream stationery.

The coffee planters of Coorg are honoured to invite His Excellency to inaugurate the Mercara Derby.

And while he was their guest at the races, the invitation added, it would be their privilege to share with him the finest coffee in the world. Intrigued, the Viceroy informed his disgruntled attaché that they would be stopping for two days in Coorg.

Once the Viceroy's attendance had been confirmed, the funding for the hall was completed within a matter of weeks. So plentiful were the donations that Appu contributed no more than a few hundred rupees from his promised five thousand. People kept coming, despite being told that no more donations were being accepted, citing connections, demanding to be allowed to contribute, so that their names would be listed in the founding annals of the hall.

The day of the visit drew closer and preparations intensified for the Derby. The organisers raised a massive purse of fifty thousand rupees and the finest jockeys had signed up, from Madras, Calcutta and Bombay. The horses came in and were stabled at the Club. Extra help was hired for the ball from the sister club in Bangalore and Appu cajoled Devi into funding new brass-buttoned tunics for all the waiters.

Women bought new saris, veils and ball gowns for the event and sent their best jewellery to be polished. Appu selected Baby's wardrobe, and not a word of protest did she utter over the low-backed gown he had chosen for the ball. This visit was important to him, she knew. She must look her absolute best.

On the morning itself, she dressed carefully in the drop-waisted chiffon frock he had laid out for her. She fastened the diamante edged buckles of her heels, and smoothing her hair into a chignon, looped a strand of perfect pink pearls around it. Appu was pacing back and forth in his suit, practising his spiel. 'It is an honour, your Excellency. We are delighted to have you with us. And may I present my wife . . .'

He stopped mid-stride as Baby walked out of the dressing room and then Appu grinned. 'Perfection. What a vision. Baby, you're going to knock his socks off.'

With a blare of horns, the Viceroy's entourage drew up. He was handed a pair of scissors and with a graceful flourish, the Viceroy cut the ribbon draped over the entrance to the hall, inaugurating it to thunderous applause. His Excellency turned and waved, a cheer rippling through the crowd.

The queue moved quickly and soon it was their turn to be introduced. His Excellency glanced appreciatively at Baby as Appu introduced himself. 'And this,' Appu said proudly, 'is my wife, Baby.'

Baby smiled shyly at the Viceroy. 'How do you do?' she asked.

'Quite well my dear, for such an early start. So tell me, do you think this coffee is indeed the finest in the world?'

Baby stared at him flustered; she should respond, she knew she should. The pressure of Appu's arm increased ever so slightly on her back. She should say something. 'Yes, your Highness,' she stammered. 'I mean, yes, your Royalty . . . yes, it is, Sir Willie Ding Dong.'

The row later in the car was the worst they had ever had. 'How could you,' Appu said. 'How *could* you? Wiped my face in the mud, that's what you did. Didn't I tell you how important this was to me? I'm trying to make something of myself Baby, or don't you care? Yet there you go, insulting the *Viceroy*, the blasted VICEROY of India to his blooming bloody face. *Willie Ding Dong?*'

'It was a mistake Appu,' Baby said tearfully. 'You were the one who called him that.'

'Not to his face.'

'It was a mistake,' she wept. 'I just got so nervous—'

'Nervous? About what? Can't you speak, don't you have a mouth? Look at Daisy, look at all those other women, how gracefully they conducted themselves. They looked like queens. While you . . .'

'Then why did you take me along? You know I am not that comfortable with these things. And did it not go off well regardless?'

Despite her awful blooper, the morning had indeed gone well. The Derby had been a thundering success and the Viceroy had even seemed to enjoy himself. But Appu was still shaken. They fought all the way back to Tiger Hills where Devanna took one look at Baby's tear-stained face and asked alarmed, 'What happened? The nationalists . . .'

'Oh, there was no trouble from the protestors. But your daughter-in-law more than made up for any damage they could have caused. Ask her, just ask her what she did.'

'Come now, Appu,' Devi said, her lips twitching when she heard what Baby had said. And then, for the first time since Nanju's passing, she started to laugh. '*You* were the one who called him that!'

Her blasé response only fuelled Appu's anger. Baby tearfully said she couldn't possibly go to the ball that evening, everyone would be staring at her.

'Fine,' Appu barked. 'Do as you bloody well please.'

Changing angrily into his white tie and tails, quite forgetting, in his temper, the orchid in the icebox meant for his buttonhole, Appu left alone for the ball.

Devi sighed. 'He's being silly, child,' she consoled Baby. 'Give him time, he will calm down.'

Chapter 35

⚜ 1936 ⚜

Devi bit her lip, watching anxiously as Baby spread banana jam on her toast. There was a fixed expression on Baby's face, lines creasing that once smooth, perfectly arched forehead. She moved her knife absently across the bread, back and forth, back and forth.

'It has come out well this time, the jam,' Devi said, in a bid to distract Baby. 'It's all in the bananas of course. The red neindra variety – they're good only for steaming. Medium-sized mara bananas are the ones to be used, but even so, too sweet a fruit and the jam will be nothing but sugar; too ripe and it will turn out runny. These were just right, the flesh firm, the correct amount of sweetness. Came from the grove at the back of the estate.' She paused, waiting for a reaction, but Baby's attention was fixed on the stairs.

'Baby!' Devi cried, so startling her daughter-in-law that she dropped her knife with a clatter.

Devanna glanced at her across the table; Devi sensed the disapproval in his gaze and forced a softness into her voice, but it still sounded high, worried. 'What are you doing, kunyi, making bread pudding? *Look* at your toast.'

Baby cast her bewildered gaze down at the toast, so loaded with the moreish jam that it was beginning to fall apart. She flushed. 'I didn't realise ...'

'Kunyi, eat your breakfast,' Devanna gently interjected, 'Appu will

428

be down soon enough, you know that he sleeps in after a late night out.'

'Late? How late?' Devi asked ominously. 'How many times must I tell him, enough of these late nights? Baby, you must . . .' She paused, struggling to keep her voice even, then reached across the table and took Baby's hand in hers. 'Keep him in your sights, have I not told you that? How often must I tell you, kunyi? He is a *married* man, don't let him forget that.'

Baby stared unhappily at her plate.

'Tukra,' Devi said, 'go wake Appu.'

Tukra shuffled his feet in alarm. 'Aiyo! Appu anna gets angry if I wake him up, says he will wring my neck, not that he would, but still, that is what he says, Tukra, he says, I swear I will wring your . . .'

'Oh, for . . . Appu! *Appu!*' Devi waited, listening for some movement, some sound of footsteps perhaps, or an answering call, but the upstairs wing remained stubbornly silent.

'This boy! Not two drops of alcohol down his gullet and he would snore through the floods.' She turned to Baby, visibly upset. 'Why do you let him go out without you? You must accompany him, be by his side at all times.'

'His friends . . .'

'So, his friends are all fancy types. So what? You are prettier than them by far. But . . .' Devi pointed at the clothesline weighed down with the morning's washing. 'These blouses of yours! Fit not so much for a woman as for a she elephant!' The offending garments swayed decorously on the line, with their full sleeves and high necklines.

Baby shot a mortified glance in Devanna's direction. He had retreated behind his newspaper, gallantly pretending he had not followed a word of this last conversation.

Devi was continuing her tirade. 'All the young girls wear these small-tiny blouses, and here you insist on wearing clothes that Tayi would have approved of. I am not suggesting you run about indecently dressed, but *really*, kunyi!' She pressed a hand to her aching head. 'This is what we will do. I'll call the tailor home. Let him stitch you a few blouses, modern types.' She ran an appraising eye over her daughter-in-law's form. 'You're so young, at your age, a woman ought to flaunt her charms.'

Too embarrassed to even look up, Baby nodded silently.

Appu used to make fun of her blouses too, and the chemises she liked wearing underneath. 'What the . . .?!' he would say incredulously, holding them up. 'Aren't you hot under all this fabric?'

'I'm a married woman now, am I not? I have to maintain my decency. Or would you rather I walked about showing skin to every man who comes my way?'

He would pull her into his lap, laughing. 'Not *every* man, no. But how about wearing something a little more exciting now and again for your husband?'

She had tried. Worn the frocks he bought her, gone with him to the parties and tried making conversation with the impossibly glamorous wives of his friends. They had all exclaimed over her, how pretty she was. Dag's blushing rose, they used to call her. A few of them had tried drawing her into their circle, but they spoke so fast it was hard to follow their conversations. She knew English of course, had studied it at school. Nonetheless, it took her time to speak in the language, needing to translate the words in her head before pushing them carefully off her tongue.

The Coorg women – they were the worst of the lot. She had migrated towards them, confident of the common ground they shared, but when she spoke with them in native tongue, they always replied in convent-accented English – a subtle rejection that made her flush.

'Do we have to go?' she had pouted one day at Appu. 'Why don't we stay home, instead? Let me cook, I will make you mutton stew with pearl onions, and hot ottis, soft as butter.'

Appu shook his head and laughed. 'No ottis tonight my darling. Crumb chops and caramel custard, or so the Club secretary has informed me.' He smacked her cheerfully on her bottom. 'Come on now, hurry up, or we shall be late.'

She had made a genuine effort that evening, trotting out the sentences she had been practising in secret. 'How are you feeling, Ethel? Why, you are looking very pretty today, Daisy.'

Daisy Bopanna laughed. 'Nothing like a bit of nooky to bring colour to one's cheeks. Timmy was quite in the mood this afternoon. What is it with these Coorg men, all a woman needs do is touch their elbow or nudge a toenail even, and bang! Off they are to the races!'

Baby had gone bright red. 'Come now darling!' Daisy exclaimed. 'Don't look so shocked, you make me feel *wicked*!'

Appu had sauntered towards them, snifter in hand. 'Wicked? Baby, whatever have you been saying to my sweet Daisy to make her feel so?'

'Appu . . . that . . . she . . .'

Daisy had cut in with an amused wave of her cigarette. 'We were just comparing notes on our Coorg stallions, that's all.' She placed a hand on Appu's chest, lightly stroking the lapel of his jacket. 'And judging from the roses in her cheeks, I would wager your bride has a real stud to contend with.'

Appu grinned, and taking Daisy's hand in his, had kissed the tips of her fingers. While Baby had watched impotently, painfully aware of just how removed she was from this circle with its throwaway banter and sexual repartee.

'Appu!' Devi cried now, making Baby jump. 'Appu!!'

'All right, all right, all right. Avvaiah, you are worse than that blasted cockerel outside. I am going to wring its neck one of these days, I swear. Barely did I fall asleep when . . .' Appu gingerly made his way down the stairs.

'When are you going to be done with all this merrymaking?' Devi asked, frustrated. 'It would be nice to have you home with us for dinner now and again.'

'Merrymaking with a cause, Avvaiah. The elections . . .'

'Why do you not take Baby with you?' Devi forced a reasonableness into her voice. 'Come Appu, you have a wife now. Look at her, the poor thing has hardly eaten a morsel, all she's done is wait for you.'

Appu said nothing. He reached for the coffee pot but Baby was quicker, refilling his cup in a single fluid movement.

'Baby . . .' Mildly irritated, but unsure why, Appu decided to let it go.

It felt like being swaddled in cloth. Like the time when, as a child, he had tottered into one of Avvaiah's bloody trunks filled with all those saris she never wore. Layer after layer of fabric, and as he had struggled to get out of the trunk, they had seemed to shift, to wrap themselves around his arms and legs, pulling him into their folds, until he had yelled out in panic. He had been very young of course. Appu frowned as he remembered.

Sometimes, this felt like that. When Baby pleaded with him not to visit their friends, to stay home, 'just us, just the two of us.'

Their marriage had, for a while, quelled the restlessness within him. The first few months, he had still suffered from the nightmares that had begun after . . . after that bastard Stassler . . . Appu would jerk awake, drenched in his own sweat, too drained to address the questions in Baby's eyes. She would take him in her arms then, crooning songs in his ears as if he were a child. Slowly, the awful images would subside, the room righting itself once more.

And when he woke the next morning, Appu would lie still and marvel at her, his lovely rose of a wife. Her lips slightly parted, the lashes lying long and thick against a porcelain-skinned cheek. He would lie there, as the damned cockerel crowed loud enough to wake the dead, revelling in the stillness in his heart.

'It doesn't last, you know,' his cronies at the Club had said to him. 'They change after marriage. Everything changes. The sex is the first to go. There's nothing new about it after a while, just go at it and get on with it, and oh, be quick darling, because we have guests for supper. And after the sex dulls, the nagging starts. Must you comb your hair quite so flat? Must you laugh so loud? Must you do this, go do that instead.'

Appu had laughed disbelievingly. He knew they were jealous, the lot of them, he'd seen their faces whenever they looked at Baby.

Still, their words had picked away at him that evening like ants might a downed partridge. Would they really tire of each other as his friends had predicted? Surely not? He had practically torn the blouse from her shoulders that night, trailing bruises with his mouth as he nipped and sucked in a frenzy at that creamy skin. She had responded in kind, clawing at his back, biting his ear, pulling at his lower lip until they had finally cried out in unison, collapsing together in a shuddering, sweat-soaked jumble. And Appu's heart had gladdened.

It used to be a treat, to have parties at home in the formal dining room and watch her from the corner of his eye, turned out in one of the dresses he had ordered for her, the green and gold beetle-wing earrings from Berlin swinging from her ears.

Of all the jewellery he had given her, it was these earrings that she seemed to love the most. She had stared at them in wonder when he first presented them to her. 'From *wings*? Really?' She traced their edges with a finger. 'So fragile . . .' She had raised them to the light, watching as they were shot through with green and gold sparks. 'Fairy wings, for a fairy princess.'

'What's that?' Appu had asked, startled, certain that he must have misheard. Hadn't the proprietress of the shop said exactly that when he'd bought them? 'What did you say?'

'Fairy . . .' She raised puzzled eyes to his. 'I don't know – the words just popped into my head. They are *so* beautiful Appu. From actual wings, imagine!'

She wore them every chance she got, despite the far more expensive pieces he bought her. The earrings sparkled against her hair as she moved among the guests, catching the firelight as she spoke, as if keeping time with Baby's halting, lilting English that he found so irresistible.

Where had those days disappeared? Now she refused to come with him to the Club. 'I don't understand what they say, the other women. All these dirty jokes they keep cracking, all this man-woman talk. It isn't decent. And that Daisy . . .'

At first, he had been amused, thinking she was in one of her moods, it was that time of the month perhaps. 'Come, what did Daisy say now? The trick is not to take her too seriously. And she is really quite fond of you, did she not send over that basket from Hans' shop when you were ill?'

Baby said nothing. The basket had been filled to the brim with canned sardines. Just the other day in the Club, the women had been discussing the prices at Hans' – ridiculous how even a tiny can of sardines cost a full rupee. 'I go to the fish market every Sunday,' Baby had interjected helpfully. 'Fresh fish – mathi, katla, all kinds. You should talk with my fish-seller, he always gives me a good price.'

The women had stared incredulously at her and then burst out laughing. 'The fish market? The *fish market!*' Daisy had spluttered, wiping the tears from her eyes. 'Oh, Baby, precious rosebud, whatever will you say next? Do you really expect us to go there? Invite your fish-seller home for tea afterwards perhaps?'

The next week, Baby had feigned a fever and not gone to the Club; Daisy had sent the get well basket, filled with can upon can of tinned sardines.

She had not even attempted to explain the insult implicit in the gesture to Appu; it would have been hopelessly lost on him.

'Monae,' Devi tried again, placatingly. 'What are all these late nights? When are you going to learn about the estate, there is so much to be done . . .'

'Later. Please Avvaiah, we can discuss all of this and more, but when my head stops ringing.'

'If it were *Nanju* . . . ' Devi began, and then thinking the better of it, stopped mid sentence.

'Yes?' Appu asked, his voice cold. 'Do continue Avvaiah, what were you saying?'

'That's enough Appu,' Devanna said quietly.

Appu shrugged and began to butter his toast. Still Devi refused to give up, fiddling with the tablecloth as she waited for Appu to finish his eggs. 'The weekly wages. Sit with me this morning, we'll do the disbursals together.'

'*God* Avvaiah. Are you deliberately trying to worsen this headache? Later. Maybe.'

Devi's face fell. 'Nanju was always so good about . . .'

'Yes, yes, we know,' Appu said sardonically. 'Nanju this, Nanju that, perfect Nanju, prince of a son. If he were still here, he would not dream of staying out so late. If he were here, he would have taken over the running of the estate long ago. He isn't here, though, is he?'

'I said that's *enough* Appu,' Devanna snapped, and so uncharacteristic was the anger in his voice that they all froze.

Appu looked shamefaced for an instant. He opened his mouth as if to apologise and then his expression hardened. Throwing his serviette bitterly onto the table, he got up and left.

Devi bit her lip, precariously close to tears. She shouldn't have praised Nanju so, she knew, but it was as if she couldn't help herself. With each passing year, she seemed to talk more and more about him; he had become larger in memory than he had ever been in life. More loving, more conscientious, crafted by sorrow into an impossibly flawless child. Appu was hurt when Devi talked of Nanju in this way, mistaking her eulogies for an unspoken disappointment in him.

He was unable to see behind the words, did not recognise the guilt coating her tongue. The guilt of a mother who has outlived her child, the soul-crushing weight of it strapped to her back. And even worse than the guilt, an awful truth. A truth so appalling that Devi would not admit it even to herself – the knowledge that no matter what, she loved the remaining son more than the one who was gone.

Loss seemed to till her memory, uncovering incidents from years ago. 'Perfect prince of a son ...' Wasn't that what Appu had just said? The fancy dress competition organised by the mission school. They had still been in Mercara; it had been before Appu, before Tiger Hills even. She had been bent over a piece of lace, racing against the clock to get it done by the next morning. Nanju had kept asking her about the competition, 'But Avvaiah, what will I wear? It's a fancy dress competition, I need a costume.'

'How about going as a prince?' she had said distractedly.

'What do they wear? And when will it be ready?'

'Later,' she had promised him, 'Avvaiah is busy, she will make your costume later.' He had come to her time and time again that evening. Her back hurt, her eyes stung, and still the lace was far from finished. 'Later.'

'I said, not now.'

Until he had burst into tears, startling her into pricking the needle yet again into her thumb. She had risen from the stool then, in a fury, snatching up a pair of scissors.

'You want a costume?' She had taken the scissors to her bridal sari, ripping through the red silk, tearing out its gold spangles. 'Here!'

'Devi!' Tayi had said, shocked. 'Your *wedding* sari!'

The child of course had entirely missed the significance of what she had done. He stood there, so *little*, gazing in wonder at the ruined sari. 'My prince costume.'

'Nanju won second prize you know,' Devi said now to Baby. 'At the fancy dress competition in his school. Such a prince he looked . . .' Her words trailed into silence.

The 1936 Olympics came and went. 'What about organising a trip to Berlin, Dags?' the chaps at the Club had suggested. 'Let's go cheer Dhyan and his boys, show a bit of support?'

They missed the brief flicker of panic that the mention of the city brought to Appu's face, even after all these years. 'I don't think Dhyan Chand needs our cheering for him to work his magic,' Appu said, then changed the subject.

Once again the Indian team, captained now by Chand, had coasted to an 8–1 victory in the finals against the Germans. So impressed was Hitler by this performance that at the dinner held afterwards, he offered to elevate Chand, then a humble Lance Naik in the Indian Army, to the rank of Colonel if he migrated to Germany. Dhyan had politely turned him down.

Appu's marriage continued to derail, a gradual misalignment that he neither understood nor knew how to correct. With each passing month, and each failed attempt to become pregnant, Baby seemed to cling more desperately to him, 'Stay, Appu.' The more she did, the further he pulled away, repulsed by her need of him and secretly despairing of the sorrow he saw every month on her face, the questions it cast upon his own potency. Restlessness stirred within him once more, a sharp clawed mistress who would not be denied. 'Don't go,' Baby would plead as he dressed for the Club. 'Please, stay with me.'

'Come with me,' he said helplessly to her. 'It's a dinner to welcome the new head of the Mission – you should come.'

'I can't. It's beyond me.'

She was still crying when, exasperated, he left the room and bounded lightly down the stairs.

'Why the long face handsome?' Daisy asked that evening.

'Nothing . . . it's nothing.'

She studied him for a moment, then leaned closer. The new Reverend was speaking, thanking the Club members for the generosity of their welcome and extolling the virtues of Christianity. 'So . . .' she said softly, 'do you know why Jesus could never have been born in Coorg?'

He shook his head.

'Well, wherever are you going to find three wise men and a virgin here?'

He started to laugh and she leaned in further, whispering in his ear. A brief pause, a guilty glance in Timmy's direction and then Appu, eyes dancing, whispered back.

After Daisy, there were others, now and again. It relieved the monotony.

The Indian Independence movement continued to swell, was debated in Persian carpeted drawing rooms and *Whites Only, No Dogs or Indians Allowed* clubs across the country. 'Surely,' the British asked uneasily of one another, 'nothing is going to come of all this nonsense?'

His earlier reservations forgotten, Appu had embraced the political cause wholeheartedly. 'Chief Minister!' Timmy said. 'With your family background and money, Dags, you could be Chief Minister of independent Coorg.'

Suddenly, it had seemed an entirely reasonable notion. '*I am the son of the tiger killer.*'

He began to travel extensively with his political coterie, to the government offices that lay along the Mysore–Bangalore–Madras corridor as they promoted the cause for independent Coorg. 'An acceptable compromise,' they offered, 'we can work something out between us, as gentlemen.'

He did not take Baby with him, indeed, he no longer even expected Baby to accompany him to the Club. Baby, for her part, stubbornly refused to go anywhere at all; even at the galas Appu hosted at Tiger Hills, she stopped mingling with the guests. She would make the arrangements for the party and then, despite Devi's worried advice, she remained upstairs, watching as the headlights of the cars threw patterns across the lawn.

*

'A child,' Devi said distressed to herself, 'what we need is the sound of little voices to lighten our hearts.' A baby would set things right between Appu and Baby, she thought, touching her fingers to the tiger brooch as if to reassure herself.

'One must *fight* for happiness,' she urged Baby. 'When Appu becomes a father . . . try kunyi, you must try harder.'

Baby was trying, how she was trying. It was not as frequent as before, but still, every time they lay together, Baby tightened her muscles, trying to hold on to the juices that dribbled into her. 'A baby, please, let there be a baby,' but without fail, in a few weeks, the cramps would begin.

Devi hung an old calendar behind the door to her room. 'See this,' she told Baby. 'Here, we need to track your monthly blood better. Whenever it comes, make a mark on the date.'

Month after month, Baby stood silently in front of the calendar. She would read the prayer printed on its pages. 'May the *wind* be in your face, the *sun* always at your back.' Month after month, sometimes a week late, once nearly three, but eventually, Baby would make the slow, unhappy journey to Devi's room, and circle yet another date.

When nothing else seemed to work, Devi consulted a tantric from Kerala. He measured a white powder into a screw of newspaper. 'Make the husband eat this on the twentieth day after the full moon. I promise you the child that follows will be a boy.'

Baby and she surreptitiously mixed the powder into Appu's rice and that night, Baby got precious little sleep.

The next morning, she awoke, her body languid and ever so slightly sore. It had been like the old times, the previous night. She rubbed a hand over her stomach, watching Appu sleep, and smiled.

That entire day proved magical. Appu too was in a languid mood, coming out of the bathroom to place his arms around her. 'Wife.'

'Things will be different Appu,' she said softly, smoothing the hair back from his face. 'Just you watch.' Even the light seemed different, the dust particles in its shafts alchemised into shards of broken, dancing gold.

The family had a leisurely breakfast with the gramophone playing in the background. Later, Baby plucked armfuls of roses, lilies and lotuses, filling porcelain and crystal alike, all through the house. Now and again, she touched her belly, smiling to herself. *Their child*.

They lay together again after lunch; a slow, relaxed coupling, Appu gazing into her eyes until she thought her heart would explode. They fell asleep like that, him on top of her, and when she awoke, it was past five in the evening. She smiled at the tuneless whistling coming from the bathroom.

He came out, and she looked at him, the smile dashed in an instant from her face. 'You're going out *tonight*?'

'Billiards evening, remember?' Appu grinned. 'You're not going to make a fuss now I hope? Or,' he bowed and took her hand, 'perhaps you will surprise me and give me the pleasure of your company?'

'Appu,' she began. 'Appu . . . please don't go.'

They started fighting again, the magic of the day vanished into a cold hardness. 'Stay with me. Just today, don't go.'

He had almost given in but then something snapped. 'No,' he said to her. 'No. I can't go through this again. I'm going. You're welcome to come, but . . .' He walked down the stairs.

She threw on her petticoat, her body still unwashed from the afternoon, still smelling of him, a clean, earthy smell, like moss after the rains. She fastened her blouse, one of the fitted variety that she had finally capitulated to, and draped a sari, a thin red silk he had always liked on her. 'The very shade of your lips,' he used to say. 'My Snow White lovely.'

'Snow White, Snow White,' Baby muttered to herself, as she pulled her hair away from her face, tears smarting in her eyes.

She rushed to the window as she heard the engine of the car. 'Appu,' she called, 'Appu!'

'Appu!' she called again, running to the library where the windows lined the wall.

The engine of the Austin revved up and the car began to move down the drive. 'Appu!' Baby screamed, suddenly furious. 'You *cannot* leave, stay with me.'

The Austin continued to pull forward and then it hesitated, stalled.

He stepped from the car, shading his eyes with his palm as he stared up at Baby framed in the library windows. 'If it's so very important to her . . .' he thought tiredly.

'You can't leave,' she shouted, not caring who might hear. She pummelled a fist against the window frame. 'Stay with me, you must stay with me.'

He stood in the drive, not saying a word, just staring up at her. The sun was beginning to set, casting its burnished glow. How lovely she looked, standing there. A rose, his blushing rose. And yet . . .

Appu was gripped suddenly by a deep sadness. He stood looking at her, completely immobile. She fell silent too. And in that stillness, something ineffable passed between them, husband and wife. A realisation; not yet the resigned acceptance, for that would still take time, but the awareness, inescapable, that things had changed.

The sun sank further. The knife grinder beetles began to drum their feet on the trees, heralding the dusk. A buzzing, a sawing, hundreds upon hundreds of them, in the plantation, from the surrounding jungles. Baby's lips moved silently, but he knew, even without hearing, the words. '*Stay*.' Her eyes pooled with tears.

'I cannot,' Appu thought wearily. 'It's not in me, even if I wanted to.'

He turned around and slowly got into the car. The engine revved, kicked into motion, and the Austin set off down the drive. Baby stood watching, tears running down her face. She stood there alone in the darkening library, cradling her stomach in her arms, craning her head from the window until the last flash of the headlights vanished down the road.

Chapter 36

There never came a child. Tiger Hills seemed to sink into a prolonged period of drought. Oh, the rains came every year, sometimes early, sometimes late, but always unfailingly ferocious in that first, initial onslaught. The lychee seeds that Devanna had planted on the periphery of the estate germinated lavishly, proliferating into small shrubs that shot higher with each passing year. They began to bear fruit, tart and wizened in the early years, maturing into sweet-fleshed juiciness after a few more summers.

Baby, though, seemed permanently caught in the grip of some still, lifeless afternoon. Gradually, the light seeped from her. Almost imperceptibly, until she no longer remembered what it felt like to float a few inches off the ground, moored by disappointment, into shadow. Finally, Devi took down the old calendar that had hung behind her door. She did not replace it.

The deliverance that Devi felt whenever she looked at Appu and Baby had long since disappeared, the delight she used to take in their togetherness forgotten. Appu and Baby seemed to drift along like two parallel currents, coming occasionally together and then, inevitably, Appu would pull away once more. Devi tried, occasionally. 'Appu, enough,' she would plead. 'Enough billiards for the week, stay home with us tonight.' More often than not, she remained silent. There was a newfound frailty about her, a shrunkenness almost. As if this final disappointment, this dismantling of Appu and Baby's once perfect union – 'such a beautiful couple' – had at last managed to stoop her shoulders.

Devanna was filled with sadness to see the fire so quenched within her, to see her sitting still, hands folded in her lap, staring into space. He would look at that perfect face, rendered all the more lovely by the lines etched into it over the years, like the rings on a deep-rooted jungle tree.

There was so much left to say.

'*Bambusea Indica Devi*,' he wanted to tell her, as the first light began to gild the trees, and the garden, *her* garden emerged from the dark. 'That was what I once planned to name the bamboo flower.'

He would look at her, the words remaining locked inside him, as bees droned over the flower beds and the lotus pond murmured in the sun.

The workers on the estate came to see him in great excitement one year. The flower that he had so wanted? The bamboo flower? Word had come through the Korama tribals that the groves were in bud! How many of the plants did he want? Devanna had hesitated and then slowly shaken his head. 'No,' he said quietly, 'leave them be.' Some things were better left unspoiled. Like jungle flowers, growing wild. The groves flowered en masse that summer of 1939. Unfettered, untamed. Now and again a whiff of their perfume was borne honeyed upon the wind, velveting all of Coorg.

War began to foment once more in Europe, sending the prices of even the most basic goods – cotton, salt and oil – skyrocketing. Appu's biggest grouse against World War II, however, was the cancellation of the 1940 Olympics that had been scheduled for Sapporo. Boosted by wartime demand, coffee prices rose once more. The planters who had stuck out the Thirties did handsomely for themselves. They were loath to talk of their fortunes, reaped in wartime, it would hardly be in good form. Nonetheless, traces of this shiny new wealth became apparent in Coorg. Gordon Braithwaite bought his wife a thick choker of diamonds – it suited the bitch, Daisy said spitefully at the Club, gaudy dog collar that it was.

Devanna's health began to falter. Some days were better than others: sometimes he felt strong enough to work on his beloved gardens; on others, he was listless, weakened by a persistent, low grade fever. Tukra once more devoted himself to caring for Devanna, but the years had taken a toll on him too – he was no longer able to lift Devanna into the

442

planter chair without assistance. The doctor was summoned again and again to Tiger Hills. Devi would hover at the entrance to Devanna's room, waiting for the doctor to complete his examination. Each time, his diagnosis was the same. 'PUO,' he would conclude, 'Pyrexia of Unknown Origin.'

'There is no real remedy,' he explained. 'Just make sure he is comfortable, get him some hot soup.' Devi would nod, her eyes fixed on Devanna, tracing the lines of exhaustion on his face.

In the evenings after the doctor had been, Devi would light the prayer lamp and then stay a while in the prayer room, her hands clasped together. 'Let him . . .' she would begin. 'Please Swami Iguthappa, let him . . .' and then she would falter.

The Indian independence movement gained even more momentum, seeping into the smallest towns and villages. Vandals desecrated a number of the tombstones in the Mercara cemetery one clammy, moonless night. The watchman swore he had not heard a thing, but given that he was known to be sozzled on arrack more often than not, his account did not carry much weight. The vandals had attacked the tombstones willy nilly, hacking the wings off an angel on one and drawing a luxuriant moustache and sideburns on the cherub carved into another. They did not even spare the Reverend, hanging a ratty pair of slippers from his tombstone and depositing a generous scoop of turd on his grave.

When a brick was launched through the windows of the Mission Church, right in the middle of the Sunday sermon, the message was unmistakable. The white planters began to talk of the imminent independence of the country. At first they thought they might stay on in India, even post-handover – this was their home, dash it. They still had a good fifteen years or so before they needed to think of retiring, and even then, who was to say England was the only option? What about Bangalore, or Madras? They milled around together in the Club, working their way through their options over scotch and gin and tonics. Appu and the other Coorgs listened without comment.

At a hockey match held in the grounds of the Mission, nationalists in khadi kurtas and cotton topis stormed the field shouting British, Quit India, Quit India. They were dutifully rounded up and taken to the two cells at the Mercara court, but not quite sure what else he ought to do, the local superintendent let them off with only a reprimand.

The emboldened nationalists next targeted old Hans' store. They smashed the porcelain dolls and china tea pots, tore the leaves from books and crushed dozens of tins of sweets underfoot. Hans came rushing out from his living quarters wild-eyed, night cap askew. The leader of the gang held him off effortlessly with just one hand, laughing all the while. He let his guard slip, however, and Hans picked up a chair and hit the boy on the head with it, cracking open his skull. The mob pounced on Hans then, changing in an instant from a gaggle of rowdy students into a thing of snarling, bestial fury. The police found the old man the next morning lying in a pool of his own blood and vomit, his body already stiffened amidst the shards of broken porcelain.

Devi burst into tears when she heard the news. 'They killed him,' she sobbed, 'they *killed* him. Such a harmless old man, what did he ever do to anyone? The sweets he used to have in that store ...' On and on she sobbed, as if Hans' murder had jolted the last remaining fortitude from her, her outpouring of grief almost grotesquely out of proportion to the event at hand. She insisted Appu attend the wake.

One then another of the planters began to sell their properties and prepare to leave Coorg. There were rounds of farewell cocktails and luncheon parties, proclamations of undying friendship – sisters forever! – and teary eyed promises to write. The departing planters held jumble sales on their lawns; pianos, gilded chairs and carved picture frames sitting forlornly on their verandahs amidst piles of sawdust and wooden packing crates. The slow trickle of departures notwithstanding, the Club was collectively shocked when Gordon Braithwaite announced one evening that he and his family were moving back to England.

'This is what it comes down to in the end,' he said sadly to his wife, fingering the piles of hessian. 'Our lives, all these years spent here, packed off in a few crates back to England. The officials, they come and go through the colonies, but we planters ... we're the ones who have always stayed. Through wartime and peace, we have always stayed.'

He looked out at his manicured lawns, his eyes clouded with melancholy. 'Coorg ... My grandfather came here with the first ... 1843. Ceylon was too crowded for him, he said, so he took off for India instead. Absolutely certain he was, apparently, from the very first time he laid eyes on these hills, that this was going to be home.' Braithwaite absent-mindedly repeated the story for the thousandth time; his wife pursed her lips but seeing the expression in his eyes, she decided to let it go. 'He was buried here,' he continued slowly, 'as were both my parents, God rest their souls. That hedge of hibiscus over there, my dear mother planted it herself. Coffee King, they used to call me, the Coffee King of Coorg!'

He sighed, gazing at the greenhouse and its birdcages. 'Remind the gardener,' he said heavily to his wife, 'to let the birds go free.'

Timmy suggested that he and Appu affiliate themselves with the national political party operating out of Bangalore. 'It will cost us a goodly sum, old chap, but it makes sense – strength in numbers and all that.' Devi, despite her misgivings, came up with the money.

When, despite several messages, he had not heard from him, Appu drove to Timmy Bopanna's home to talk about their next step; they should leave for Bangalore soon, shouldn't they, to talk to the party about their vision for Coorg?

'Not now, Dags. Patience, old chap, the situation isn't quite right, we need more time before we press our cause—'

Appu finally erupted. 'Not now? Then when Timmy? Bloody nonsense. I'm fed up of these delays. We leave for Bangalore tomorrow. And if you're not coming, then I'll go without you.'

Timmy looked down at his hands. 'I hoped it wouldn't come to this,' he said. 'Dags,' he continued, playing with his watch, 'there's something you ought to know.'

'Can you believe the man? Can you believe the temerity of the man?' When Appu later told Devi what had happened, he was so livid with rage, the veins stood out in the side of his neck.

'Appu, calm down. Politics is a dirty game, didn't I always tell you that?'

'Behind my back! All these years of campaigning together, "Chief Minister, Dags, you could be Chief Minister one day," he used to say to me, and here he's sewn up the seat and the campaign behind my back.'

'Kunyi . . .'

'I'm going to Bangalore.' Appu came to an abrupt decision. 'Tomorrow, first thing in the morning.'

'Bangalore? Whatever for?'

'The party officials. I need to meet them. Maybe I can still change their minds.'

'Go with him,' Devanna urged Devi that evening when she brought him his dinner. He lay back against his pillow, and tiredly shut his eyes. 'He has worked himself into such a temper, it's better he doesn't go alone.'

They left for Bangalore the next morning, and Appu drove straight to the home of the leader of the party. 'No entry without appointment, saar,' the guards said.

Appu threatened and shouted, but it was only when Devi intervened that they relented. 'He is my son,' she said to them, 'my good child. He means no harm, all he wants is to meet with your master. I will wait at the gates with you until he returns. Now which child will knowingly put his mother in harm's way? And for your trouble, here' – she took out a roll of rupees from her purse – 'ten rupees for each of you.'

She waited in the car for what seemed an indeterminable time. Bangalore was sweltering, the sun beating down on the black car, turning it into an oven. She mopped at the sweat running down her forehead, staring anxiously at the gates. As soon as he came out, she knew. She opened the car door and stepped outside. 'Kunyi, it doesn't matter.'

Appu shook his head, so defeated he couldn't even look at her. 'He would not listen Avvaiah. The deal is done, he tells me. Timmy . . .'

'It doesn't matter,' Devi tried to say again, but the heat, the lack of water, had turned her tongue fuzzy. The sky was pale blue, cloudless. The sun, so brilliant in her eyes . . .

'Watch out,' she heard Appu say sharply as her knees buckled beneath her. Devi fainted.

When she came to, she found herself lying in the crisp white bed of a clinic, its sheets cool against her skin. 'Where . . .?' She tried to sit up and felt a throbbing pain in her knee.

'Easy now,' the voice was gentle. 'That was quite a fall you took. I am Dr Ramaswamy. Your son brought you in. Nothing to worry about, a spot of low blood pressure, that is all.'

He waved a hand in the air, brushing aside her thanks. 'Now tell me madam, and I apologise for my forwardness, but I could not help noticing on the form ...' He tapped a finger to the file in his hand. 'Is yours not a Coorg name?'

'Yes,' Devi said simply, 'I'm from Coorg.' She tried to flex her knee.

'Easy now. Gently, gently ... I knew someone from Coorg also,' he continued. 'A classmate of mine, Devanna. Many moons ago, while I was still at medical college.'

Devi looked at him sharply. 'Where? Here, in Bangalore?'

'Yes.' He shook his head. 'Committed suicide, I heard, poor chap. Took a gun to himself. Though really, who could blame him after all he had been through.'

Devi was just about to correct him, telling him it had been an *accident*, and that Devanna had survived, when the latter half of his sentence caught her attention.

'What do you mean?' she asked puzzled. 'What had he been through?'

Dr Ramaswamy took off his glasses and blew on the lenses. He pursed his lips, the action making his buck teeth even more prominent. 'Ragging. In those days, it could get quite rough. There was one senior who had it in for this poor chap. Day in, day out – it was utterly relentless. Beatings, thrashings, possibly worse ...' He sighed. 'There are times when I wonder if we should not have done more, brought it to the attention of the authorities perhaps. Nice sort of chap he was too, Devanna, and really quite exceptionally gifted. Madly in love with some girl back home, he used to talk about her sometimes. I remember he brought a pet squirrel to the hostel. It was against the rules, but it was a gift from her, you see. A Malabar squirrel.' He squinted as he tried to remember. 'Nancy, I believe we had named her. Such a charming pet, and Devanna, he absolutely doted on the little thing. All of us did, actually, but Devanna most of all.'

The baby squirrel. Devi had forgotten about the pet she had given Devanna. He had never mentioned Nancy again, and she had never thought to ask; too much had happened, too many lives twisted out of shape.

The doctor was continuing. 'Thomas – the senior – he butchered the squirrel. While it was still *alive*. Poor Devanna, he went up against Thomas, but he was no match for him. A gold medallist in boxing in the Army ... none of us was a match for Martin Thomas.' He was staring into the distance, lost in the past. 'Devanna left college that same day. He was in no shape to travel – he had a very nasty concussion and was terribly distraught. We tried to stop him, but he kept mumbling something about this girl. Said he had to find her ...'

Devi was very still. 'And what happened to him?'

Dr Ramaswamy shook his head. 'A suicide, we heard.'

'Not Devanna. Him. The Thomas fellow, what happened to him?'

He grimaced. 'Nothing really. It was never reported, the fight with Devanna. Keeping the squirrel in the hostel was against the rules, and telling the authorities would have got everyone into trouble. Besides, technically, it was Devanna who started that last fight with Thomas, he was the one who threw the first blow. Thomas graduated, joined the Army. Got into a few more scrapes after that. One, I heard, was particularly horrendous.' He looked apologetically at Devi. 'Sodomy, it was rumoured.'

'Sodo ...?' Devi began and then, understanding the meaning of his words, she flushed. 'Oh.'

'Yes. He was headed for a court martial, I am certain of it, but then the war happened. 1916 ... any and all medics were welcome in those days, I suppose. Thomas did quite well in the war apparently, managed to receive a commendation of some sort.'

He glanced at Devi who was sitting ramrod straight, completely absorbed in his tale. 'He is retired now, right here in Bangalore. Quite the drinker too, I hear. Never did settle down, raise a family, that sort of thing. Tried coming to the College reunions once or twice, but he was ostracised so completely by our class and the other students who had known him, that he stopped.'

He grimaced again, exposing those unfortunate teeth. 'Even now, all I associate with those years is Martin Thomas and the hell, the absolute living hell he put us through. And Devanna, he fared much worse than any of us. Those later rumours of Thomas' penchant for sodomy. I have often wondered ...' He shook his head.

'Why?' Devi asked, her voice bitter. 'Why Devanna?'

Ramaswamy sighed, absently rubbing the end of his stethoscope against his sleeve. 'Who can say, madam? Sometimes, it would seem, we are simply cast in the path of misfortune.'

Night had fallen by the time they got back to Tiger Hills. Devi alighted gingerly from the car, her knee still sore from the fall. 'I'm fine,' she said wanly to an anxious Appu. She reached up and patted his cheek. 'Go on, Baby must be waiting.'

She stood looking up at the façade of the house, lights glimmering here and there from its silent interiors. 'Hot water akka?' Tukra shuffled on to the portico. 'Shall I run your bath?'

Devi nodded. 'And lay out dinner. Devanna anna,' she asked haltingly, 'how is he?'

'Not well. He is in his room. He has not eaten as yet, said he would wait for you.'

She stopped by the old photograph in the foyer, touching her fingers to it. '*Loving you is like having wings.*' Slowly she walked on. The door to Nanju's room, the old nursery, stood ajar; she paused in the hallway and looked inside. There they used to sleep, her boys, brothers both. Nanju-Appu, her pride, her heart, her sun-and-moon. The stars began to wink in the inkiness outside, the scudding clouds now shadowing, now revealing the tiger that proudly strode across the wall. In the half light, his eyes seemed to bore into her. '*For you, I would have given up my God.*' Tawny eyes, so fierce, forever beloved. Golden, dancing eyes, such tenderness in their gaze.

At last she turned away and continued upstairs, past the silent library, towards Devanna's room. She hesitated an instant and then knocked on his door. 'I'm back.'

He looked sombrely up from his book. 'Appu?'

'No.' She walked over to the bed. 'No, of *course* it did not work.'

She placed a hand on his forehead, and he started with surprise at the unaccustomed touch. 'You still have a fever.'

'It's nothing.'

She sat on the edge of bed, looking at him. So much to talk about. So much of the past, their past, left unacknowledged. So many questions unasked. 'I met . . .' Devi began, a catch in her throat. 'The doctor . . .' she started again, then stopped. A wave of tiredness swept over her.

Devi lay down on the bed and rested her head on Devanna's chest.

She could hear the beat of his heart, quickened now by surprise. He hesitated and then moving slowly, very slowly, as if not to scare his wife away, he set his book down on the table and put his arm about her.

Inseparable they had been, as children. Close as two seeds in a cardamom pod, that's what people said about them. He was the one she unfailingly depended upon, to remove the thorns from her soles, to set the world right again.

'He is in love with you,' Machu had said to her, and she had thrown her head back and laughed out loud.

She had known though, hadn't she? She *must* have.

Devi lay there, feeling the comforting rise and fall of his chest beneath her cheek, his arm tight about her, holding her close.

Tayi's voice in her ears. 'Forgive him kunyi, he has suffered too.'

She was tired, so very tired. Shackled to loss and to grief for so many years. A stone about her neck, growing heavier with the years, with nowhere to set it down.

So many years gone, so much time lost in regret. 'Do not be so brittle,' Tayi had said to her, 'that you shatter at the first lightning. Do not be the tree that can bear no fruit.'

Hurt accumulates. Unless consciously cast aside, it accumulates, building on itself. Hardening, thickening, gouging our hearts apart. We try at first to pick at the scabs, to render ourselves as untainted and innocent as we once were. Over time, though, it becomes too difficult. This forced unbandaging, this revisiting of painful memory. Easier to lock it away, unseen, unspoken. To haul it about like an invisible stone about our necks. We leave our wounds alone. Layer by layer our scars thicken, until one day we awaken and find ourselves irrevocably hardened. Rooted in a keloidal past while the world has passed on by.

'*Be the jungle orchid that perfumes the wind.*'

To let go of hurt, to cast bitterness aside. This is the only way forward. To cast aside the pain and allow hope a chance once more. We drift through time, sometimes in shadow, sometimes blistering under the sun, laying ourselves open to the skies. Until, inevitably, we begin to heal, the lips of our wounds coming slowly together. We fill with light, with grace, capable once more of opening our hearts, of letting someone in.

The breeze catching our wings once more.

'It was for you.' Devanna's voice was barely audible.

'When I awoke, still alive, and found the bullet had missed ... that at this too, I had failed, I was so ashamed. Had I been able, I would have lifted a gun to myself once more. It was only later that I grasped how slim the odds had been of my survival. Nanju, I had thought, then, that he was the reason. That I had been left alive for the sake of our son. I was wrong.' He swallowed. 'When Machu died, that was when I understood. To look after you. That was why I was spared, to look after you.'

He stopped, trying to gather himself. 'What I did to you Devi,' he said shakily. 'If I could take it back, what I did, I ...'

'Enough,' Devi whispered. She moved her hand, finding his fingers, and clasped them in her own. She shook her head, and her hair at once sprung free of its bun, even with so small a movement. 'Enough,' she whispered again.

Devi shut her eyes, letting go. Sinking softly into the past, floating towards that innocent time when both their lives lay unsullied ahead of them, shining with promise. A clear summer sky, two children running laughing through the fields. The sun glittering upon the crab stream, the water, like molten silver against their legs. A length of chicken gut, cast it in, draw it out, the water, so bright, *look*, a cluster of fat black crabs, glistening like gems.

'So many crabs we caught that day.'

'Thirty-three.'

'Tayi made crab chutney. And you ... you ate so much you were sick in the bushes after that.'

Devanna lay very still. Then lifting his hand, he gently pushed the hair back from her face.

Epilogue

Dawn hung suspended over Tiger Hills. Devi watched, as gradually, like a curtain being lifted, the night began to part. A fulgent mist rolled in from the mountains. The light seemed phosphorescent, glimmering over the flower beds and the pale green scum of the pond. Silently she called their names, one by one, all those who were gone, as colour streaked the velvet skies and a cockerel began to crow.

Miles away, a car climbed steadily along the winding roads. It had motored all through the night, the light from its lamps thrown back from the grey banks of fog, now flaring briefly inside the car, then casting it once more into shadow. The driver had pressed on, undeterred by the poor visibility, navigating as much from memory as by sight. He glanced to his right, not really seeing the rising sun, or the valley emerging blue-gold into sight. *Not long now, not long at all.* His foot pushed unconsciously down on the accelerator, lifted again. The car surged forward, sunshine probing its bumper and diffusing in a morning haze.

Deep within the estate, something stirred in anticipation, the beginnings of a breeze, shivering through the coffee. Tentative at first, questing, and then, like a coil unsprung, it whirled outward, erupting through the mist, banging unfastened windows to and fro down the length of the house, raising puffs of red dust from the gravel as it sped down the drive. It bowled past the gates, shaking loose a burst of carmine from the flame trees lining the road. The flowers spun in the air, this way and that, one blowing in through the open window of the car. The driver picked it absently from his lap, pressing its petals between his fingers,

452

then cast it aside, flexing his palms against the wheel. The sun caught the gleam of metal at his wrists: a watch on one hand; on the other, an old silver amulet, fastened with cord. The flower oscillated mid-air for an instant until the wind scooped it up once more. The car flew on towards Tiger Hills, a flash of colour beneath the trees.

He did not remember the accident, only the aftermath; finding himself awake and disoriented in a grimy hospital bed. He had moved tentatively, and pain had shot through his leg. It had come back in a rush then, everything that had led up to this, the events of the past months, his self-imposed exile, amplified by his physical vulnerability. He had lain there, grief swimming up his body, as the words, his mother's terrible words, repeated themselves in his ears.

'A curse, a punishment, that is what you are to me.'

One by one, they had seemed to loom at him from the shadows. Avvaiah. Appaiah. Appu. Baby. In his pain-addled state, each had then seemed to turn their backs upon him and disappear. He had shut his eyes, so much weight, such pressure in his chest that for an instant he was certain it must fall apart. And then something did give way within him. He had sat up and, ignoring the stab of pain in his side, he had set his feet on the floor. It hadn't taken much to bribe the attendant. The collusion that had followed at the hospital morgue, a death certificate, faked to perfection.

'This is the way, the only way,' he had repeated to himself. Where he would go, he did not know. Down this road and that he had turned, his mind blank, tamping down the past, his chest so tight it was as if the breath were being choked from his lungs.

In the end, however, it came to nothing – not the distance, nor the years. For it never left him, the shape of these hills, the lay of this land. This dark fragrance of mulch and jungle earth that pooled within his heart. He used to imagine, as a child, how a marble might roll, mapping in his mind its route. Starting at the back stoop, rolling past the kitchen, beyond the pig sty, past the garden, dipping south and past the first coffee bushes, now gaining speed as it clipped towards the birdhouses, now slowing as it climbed uphill. In the end, we are each drawn to what we love most. And for him, it had always been this. Through evening fogs. In noon-time shadows and the first moonlight. Through rustling leaf, in water and stone, in the glowing charcoal wings in the trees. It never stopped, not once through all that time, this clarion call of home. Rising to such a crescendo that, one day, there was nothing to do but return.

The car hesitated at the open gates, as if unsure how best to herald its arrival. The wind swept through the windows, katabatic, untamed, the promise of rain in its spores. Nanju drew a deep breath and floored the accelerator, sweeping up the gravel drive.

Far off in the distance, down by the paddy fields and a stream that shone with silver, a flock of herons took wing. Silently they climbed, an arrow of purest white, silhouetted against the skies. Past the rows of gleaming coffee they soared, through the trees, and over the waiting house.

Acknowledgements

My deepest thanks to:

My lovely mother for reading draft after draft with such enthusiasm and insight.

My husband for his infinite patience and support. My father for his staunch belief in this book; my sister, for her objective and unfailingly honest eye.

Jeff Willner, Sukanya Dasgupta and Biswarup Chatterjee. Critics extraordinaire and friends indeed.

Pussy Tayi for painting such vivid pictures of a Mercara before my time. My uncle Mani for sharing with me his seemingly inexhaustible knowledge of all things Coorg. To uncle Bobjee and aunty Titi for their invaluable compilation, the *Pattole Palame*, and for answering my questions in such generous detail. My in-laws, and all the aunts and uncles who took me to old ancestral homes, gave freely from their libraries and thought up still more people I could speak with.

The wonderful ladies at DGA: Heather Godwin, Charlotte Knight and Sophie Hoult – efficient, extraordinary.

Kirsty Dunseath, early champion of *Tiger Hills*, and the most thorough, insightful and constructive editor a person could hope for; Sara Weiss, for believing so fully in *Tiger Hills*, and for her acutely intelligent editorial counsel. You made this story better. Diya Kar Hazra and Nicole Winstanley for their unwavering advocacy.

Rebecca Gray, Sophie Buchan, Lisa Milton, Susan Lamb, Claire Brett, Dallas Manderson, Meirion Todd and the rest of the team at W&N for all their support and assistance. Every author should be so lucky.

Finally, the two people I owe so much to: David Davidar, without whom this book might never have been. And David Godwin, but for whom it might never have been seen.